TONGUES OF FIRE

TONGUES OF FIRE

A NOVEL BY

PETER
ABRAHAMS

M. EVANS AND COMPANY, INC.
NEW YORK

Library of Congress Cataloging in Publication Data

Abrahams, Peter.
  Tongues of fire.

  I. Title.
PR9199.3.A17T6   1982   813′.54   82-1390

ISBN 0-87131-374-X   AACR2

M. Evans and Company
216 East 49 Street
New York, New York 10017

Design by Diane Gedymin

Manufactured in the United States of America

9 8 7 6 5 4 3 2 1

for Enid, in memory

many thanks to Ron Tysick

To depart from evil is understanding.
—Job, Chapter 28

PROLOGUE

It was the night Israel died.

It was night as bright as day.

It could have been day, on another planet where the sky was red and purple and green; where the clouds were balls of orange and yellow fire; where the ground never stopped trembling; where there was no air to breathe, only smoke and dust, cordite and oil, shrapnel and blood.

It could have been a colossal experiment to drive rats crazy; but people, not rats, went mad. The rats would go on as they always did.

It was the night Isaac Rehv crouched behind a gutted school bus on the southern slopes of Mount Carmel: Isaac Rehv, lieutenant in the Israeli army reserve, lecturer in Arab history and literature at the Hebrew University in Jerusalem, husband of Naomi, father of Lena, aged ten. He still carried his weapon, he still wore his grimy fatigues, but his part in the organization of the war was finished. Syrian and Iraqi tanks had wiped out his unit a few hours before outside the village of Hamra three kilometers to the east. They had wiped out the village too. It was hard to imagine the whole country ruined like that—Tel Aviv, Jerusalem, Haifa. But Isaac Rehv knew it was happening.

He listened to Israeli artillery near the summit shelling Egyptian positions somewhere on the plain. He listened to Egyptian rockets answer back, and Syrian ones from the north. They burst against the mountain in hot fury. He felt their power in the soles of his feet.

Rehv had not eaten for two days or slept for three. He had stopped thinking about the war or the enemy or defeat. He had even stopped hating the Americans. He thought only of Naomi and Lena. Was it only a week before he had sent them to his mother's in Haifa? "Until they settle this West Bank situation," he had said. But you can't arrest a million rioters. That was the beginning.

Rehv peered through the twisted body of the bus, scanning the lower slopes for the streets and shops and houses he had known since boyhood. He was looking for a little white house in a small square about a third of the way up the mountain. It took him a long time to picture what had been from what he saw. The buildings were rubble, the bombed streets were buried in debris. He wanted badly to rise and start running up the mountain to that little white house, but he forced himself to stay where he was until he was sure of his bearings.

At last he crept into the open. Even before he could take a first running step across the road a steely insect hissed by his ear, and another whined against the body of the bus. He dropped to the ground and rolled under the bus. Two more bullets bit into the road in front of his face. The stranger who was trying to kill him was hidden somewhere to his right, not far away. In the past week Rehv had grown knowledgeable about the sounds different weapons make, the way he had once learned to identify the instruments in an orchestra; he knew that the stranger was trying to kill him with a Russian-made AK-S. It was not much different from the standard AK-47, but to his ear it had a more authoritative crack. It also fired fragmentation bullets, which dug holes the size of soccer balls and carried legs away instead of wounding them. He made himself very small. That didn't stop the sniper from firing a few more rounds. One shattered glass; one tore up a lump of pavement; the third didn't appear to hit anything at all, shot somehow into the void.

But the third bullet drew a brief staccato reply—the familiar voice of the Uzi submachine gun. It was so near it made Rehv's tired body jump. To his right, where the man with the fragmentation gun was hidden, he heard a muffled cry, then nothing.

Rehv looked around. There was another man under the bus. With some difficulty he was pulling himself out into the road. For a moment Rehv thought he must be wounded, but then the man stood up and the reason was clear: He was enormous, the kind of man called a giant in former times. He carried one Uzi in his hands and another across his back. They both seemed like toys. With surprising lightness of foot he advanced on Rehv, reached down, and took him by the elbow. Rehv glimpsed the sergeant's stripes on the sleeve as he was whisked to his feet. Rehv was six feet tall. That brought his eyes to chest level with the sergeant, where he read the name tag sewn on his shirt: "Levy."

The big man smiled down at him. "You're lucky he couldn't hit anything, Lieutenant," he said. "You'd be dead."

Rehv didn't need to be told. And in no way did he feel lucky. The big man seemed to notice how his words had been understood. He patted Rehv lightly on the shoulder. "Take care of yourself," he said, and turned to leave.

"Wait. Where are you going?"

Sergeant Levy pointed his gun barrel at the summit. Rehv looked up. Fans of flame erupted from its surface like storms on the sun. He heard the pounding of the enemy guns, so incessant now that he couldn't separate one explosion from the next. They merged into one roar like a ghastly drumroll. He could no longer hear the Israeli artillery fighting back.

"Don't be ridiculous," he said to Sergeant Levy. But the big man had already disappeared quietly into the shadows.

Carefully Rehv picked his way up the mountain, half bent over, edging along from crumpled house to splintered tree. He recognized a butcher's shop. Mr. Kardish's, he remembered, where his mother bought her meat. One wall remained, and on its meat hooks in a tidy row hung sides of beef.

Rehv turned into the next street, a narrow street which opened into a small square. In the center of the square stood a stone fountain. Rehv saw that it was still working: The big green fish spouted a steady stream of water into a scalloped seashell below, as it had done for years. He couldn't hear the fountain's gurgle because of the bombardment, but he could see that it was undamaged. So were all the houses around the square, including the little white one at the end. He began to hope.

He ran to the familiar blue door and turned the handle. The door opened and he stepped inside.

"Naomi? Lena? Mother?" He listened to his voice call their names through the dark house. "Naomi? Naomi?"

He tried the light switch by the door but there was no electricity. Automatically, without bumping into anything, Rehv went to the dining room and felt along the dining room table until he found the candleholder. His mother liked to dine by candlelight. He took a wooden match from his chest pocket and lit a candle.

"Naomi? Lena? Mother?"

He went from room to room. Everything seemed completely normal. A bottle of sherry stood on the drink tray, and American magazines were scattered on the coffee table. Rehv walked quickly through the living room, the study, the kitchen. He opened the broom closet. It was full of brooms.

He climbed the stairs. His mother's bed was made. So was the one in the guest bedroom where Naomi would sleep. An open box of tampons lay on the bedside table. In his old bedroom Lena had left the bed unmade. On the pillow was a book of stories by Edgar Allan Poe, in English. Lena liked scary stories.

Rehv returned to the study. Perhaps, he thought, they've gone somewhere safe and left me a note? He began opening the drawers of the desk. He found bills, receipts, letters, stationery, keys, and 6,420 shekels in Israeli currency, far too much money to be left lying around the house. But no note.

And far too much money to be left behind.

Suddenly Rehv thought of the toolshed in the back garden. He had often hidden inside as a boy, playing hide-and-seek. There was plenty of room for three people, especially three small ones. He ran to the kitchen and threw open the back door.

In the wild light he saw the shed door dangling at an angle, torn off its hinges. Naomi, Lena, and his mother lay in the rock garden. Rehv felt his insides turn to ice. Almost against his will he went closer, as if drawn by magnets.

They were naked, bloody, raped, battered, and dead. He could see a streak of semen on Lena's cheek. It was not quite dry.

Rehv began to scream; but all the screaming stayed within his head. His screams pounded from one side to the other of his skull, crashing back and forth in overwhelming waves. He did not utter a sound.

Isaac Rehv was not a religious man; he did not believe in heaven or hell, or any sort of life after death. Prayers for the dead, funerals, burials were meaningless. That was the kind of man he was.

Rehv went into the house, found a large washbasin under the

14

kitchen sink, and turned on the tap. There was no water. He carried the washbasin out into the square and filled it at the fountain. He returned to the backyard with water, soap, towels. Then he knelt in front of Lena and washed her face. He washed her body, and his mother's, and Naomi's. Clutched in Naomi's hand he found a torn scrap of cloth—the black-and-white check of the Palestinian Army keffiyeh.

Gently he dried them with the towels. In the toolshed he found a small garden spade. He began to dig a hole in the middle of the lawn. He wanted to dig a very deep hole. He took off his shirt so he could move more freely. Sweat ran down his arms, soaked the wooden shaft, dripped off the blade. He dug for hours, not conscious of the bombardment or the small-arms fire coming closer. He heard two sounds: the shovel slicing into the earth and the screaming in his head.

When he thought he had dug deeply enough he reentered the house and gathered some clothing—sleeping gowns for Naomi and his mother, flannel pajamas for Lena. He dressed them and lowered them carefully into the hole, side by side. For a long time he stood at the edge, watching them. Down in the shadows they might have been sleeping. Then whiteness flared around him and showed how they really were. He threw in the first shovelful.

Later, when he had filled in the hole and made the ground smooth, he went looking in the garden for flowers. He wanted roses, but his mother was a poor gardener; he could find only morning glories, closed for the night. He plucked a few and scattered them over the grave. There was nothing more to do. He had buried them in Israel.

Isaac Rehv walked into the square. The fountain was gone. Broken stone lay scattered on the ground, and water gushed from the broken pipe. A large dark form was crawling slowly away.

Rehv didn't reach for his rifle; he didn't have it anymore. Or his helmet. Or his shirt. He was content to let the dark form crawl away when something about it made him think.

"Wait," he called. He felt he had to shout to be heard above the screaming.

The form stopped. Rehv, crossing the square, stumbled. He looked down: a leg, a human leg with an enormous black army boot at one end and horror at the other. He hurried over to the form. It moved, and a scratched and blackened face looked up at him, smiling faintly.

"This time I will," Sergeant Levy said.

Rehv stripped off his trousers—all the clothing he had—and tore them into strips. He tied a tourniquet around the massive upper thigh and tried to fashion a bandage over the wound. But it was a difficult fit because the femur hung down several inches lower than the rest of the leg.

"I've always like this fountain," Sergeant Levy said. "Fighting makes me thirsty."

"Can you sit up?"

"Sure."

But he couldn't for a while.

Finally Rehv helped him rise up on his one leg.

"Not too much touching of the old stump," Sergeant Levy said very quietly.

"Sorry."

"No need to shout. It's all right."

Rehv tried not to hear the screaming. He lifted Sergeant Levy's arm and braced himself beneath it. "Ready?"

"Where's your weapon?" Sergeant Levy asked.

"I don't know."

"You're not much of a soldier, are you, Lieutenant?" Sergeant Levy said. He still had a Uzi strapped on his back.

Before Rehv could think of anything to say, the sky turned white and exploded in their faces, knocking them down. He and Sergeant Levy huddled together on the shaking earth. When it stopped shaking, Rehv looked up. There was nothing left of the little white house; only the toolshed remained, its door dangling from broken hinges.

They started walking down the mountain, making their way around the broken buildings, craters, and fires of Haifa toward the beach. They walked very slowly. It gave them time to look at the famous view. On the beach black figures were massed by the edge of the sea. From time to time they moved about frantically like nervous ants. Their long shadows ran after them in the red glow.

"Dunkirk," Sergeant Levy said.

"No. At Dunkirk the boats came right up to the beach."

Rehv was right. Beyond the beach stretched the sea, empty

16

and black for a long way out; three miles, Rehv guessed. And beyond that, like a phosphorescent tide, shone the lights of boats and ships, dozens, hundreds, thousands of them. Some were huge—American warships, they could tell that from the shore. They waited out there like the promised land.

"I always thought the Americans would step in if it came to this," Sergeant Levy said softly. "They say there was a secret agreement."

"That's the trouble with secret agreements. Who do you complain to if they're broken?" What's the value of a secret agreement, Rehv thought, when regular gasoline was selling for six dollars a gallon at the pumps in Cleveland, Ohio?

They kept walking.

When they came to the beach Rehv felt the cool wind blowing in off the sea. He saw that only a few of the thousands watching the ships offshore realized that they would come no closer. They were the naked, pale figures swimming off in ones and twos. He lowered Sergeant Levy onto the sand while he removed his boots, the only clothing he still wore. Sergeant Levy took off his boot and his shirt.

"I'd better leave the pants on, don't you think, Lieutenant?"

His stump was turning the sand red.

"Yes," Isaac Rehv replied.

He knelt down to get his shoulders under Sergeant Levy's arm. It occurred to him how much he admired Sergeant Levy for making no false offer to be left behind.

Someone else said it for him. "Surely you don't propose to take this poor man into the water?" Rehv looked up into the angry eyes of a tall, middle-aged woman. She was wrapped in a sable coat against the cold.

Rehv didn't answer.

"It's one thing if you want to drown yourself, quite another to drown this poor man."

"I'm not a poor man," Sergeant Levy said.

She ignored him. "I insist that you leave him where he is." He knew from her tone she had done a lot of succesful insisting in her life. "The landing craft will be here any moment."

Rehv tried to laugh a bitter laugh, but it was swallowed up by the screaming. He lurched to his feet, bringing Sergeant Levy upright.

17

"I insist," the woman began again, but her words were drowned out by noise from above. Everyone on the beach looked up. A helicopter passed overhead.

"You see!" the woman shouted.

But all Rehv saw was a cameraman leaning out of the cabin and the letters CBS on the fuselage.

Isaac Rehv and Sergeant Levy stumbled into the cold sea. "Don't worry," Rehv told him, "I was on the swimming team at university."

"Really? I can't swim a stroke."

Rehv began by swimming on his back, holding Sergeant Levy's head on his chest with one arm and paddling with the other. At first he tried a frog kick, but he kept bumping Sergeant Levy's bad leg, so he gave it up. Above the night sky shone in many unnatural colors. Isaac Rehv never forgot the way the sky looked that night.

After a while he had to stop.

"Can you tread water?"

"Sure."

But Sergeant Levy couldn't, and Rehv had to bring him up, the two of them sputtering and splashing. He knew he had kicked Sergeant Levy again. The big man didn't say anything, but his face turned to tallow.

Rehv looked at the lights of the waiting ships. They were no closer than before.

They began again. Sergeant Levy was very heavy. Rehv tried a modified sidestroke. They seemed to move faster.

"Now we're doing it," Sergeant Levy said.

Rehv could hardly hear him. He heard only his own grunting, the screaming, and from time to time odd sounds like a hand smacking the water with force.

They stopped again, and turned to the lights. They were no closer.

"I think we'll do better if I try some swimming on my own," Sergeant Levy said.

"You told me you can't swim."

"I was exaggerating."

"I don't believe you."

"It's true." Sergeant Levy pushed himself free. He made some movements in the water. He didn't sink.

18

"All right," Rehv said.

He swam beside Sergeant Levy. He felt the cold sucking all the strength out of his body. He felt his heart beating faster to keep him warm. He didn't even know why he was exerting all this effort. Then he remembered: Sergeant Levy.

He heard more of those odd splashes around him. He tried the breaststroke. Something bumped him in the back. What? Something.

"Sergeant Levy," he called. "Still swimming?"

"Right," came Levy's voice. It sounded far away. Perhaps it was the screaming.

He swam and screamed, swam and screamed, swam and screamed. "Sergeant Levy. Still swimming?"

"Way ahead of you," came the big man's reply, from very far away.

So he swam and screamed some more.

He felt a hand touch his shoulder. "Sergeant Levy?" he said.

"Here's a live one for a change." An American voice.

"Have you got Levy?" Rehv asked in English.

Two sailors in white pulled him into a lifeboat. He glanced around. "You haven't got Levy."

"Look how blue the bastard is," one of them said. "Better get some blankets."

"There's no time. Levy's still out there."

"Sure, pal."

Isaac Rehv looked back at the coast. Mount Carmel burned like a funeral pyre. High above its summit tongues of fire blazed in the night. Their reflections licked toward him across the dark sea, touched him, held him, baptized his body in cold fire. In the mirrored glare he could see that Sergeant Levy was gone. Even at that moment he knew that Sergeant Levy was one of the lucky ones.

PART ONE
BABYLON

CHAPTER ONE

Slowly the sleeping pill released its grip. "Try these," Quentin Katz had said. "You'll sleep like the dead." And he did every night. No nightmares, no dreams, no renewal. "You look like hell," Katz told him one day. "Are you taking those pills?"

"Yes."

"Better double the dosage."

He lay with his eyes closed, watching green spots jump across the salmon-colored insides of his eyelids. He heard heavy traffic grumbling in the street below. Gasoline was a dollar a gallon.

He didn't want to get up, fold the camp cot, and put it in the storage room. He didn't want to turn on the coffee machine and sweep the polished pine floor. He didn't want to see the latest exhibit: four clapboard cabins the size and shape of telephone booths, standing in a row in the center of the high-ceilinged room.

"You like?" Quentin Katz had asked after they had carried the booths up the stairs.

He hadn't known what to say.

"You go in, sit on the little bench, drop a quarter into the slot, and a projector beams a two-minute film of nothing but close-up violence. Close-up. If that's not a real tour de force I don't know what is."

"Why?"

"Why? It's obvious why. There are hundreds of booths like these around Times Square, but all they show is porn. The artist is making a statement."

"What?"

Katz had sighed. "It's hard to put into words, exactly. It's conceptual art."

"Are they for sale?"

"Not really. I suppose if there was an offer . . . Why? Do you know someone who might be interested?"

"No."

"Well, don't worry about it. We've got a grant from the National Arts Council to show them for six weeks."

Katz and his wife, Sheila Finkle, were his sponsors in America. He slept in The Loft, a gallery they owned in SoHo. To Rehv the word had always meant London.

"They've got one too," Katz had agreed. "But ours is better." They had one child, a little boy named Joshua Katz-Finkle.

He didn't want to open his eyes, but after a while his back began to hurt, so he did. The room was just the way he had seen it in his mind—the high tin ceiling, the four booths, the polished floor—everything the same, except for the man in the dark suit standing by the window. He was a slight, small-boned man with white hair, pale skin, and bright blue eyes: a Jesuit scholar with a burn scar on his left cheek the size of a rose in full bloom.

"Good morning," he said gently. "I envy you such deep sleep." He spoke English but a faint Hebrew rhythm moved behind the words. "You are Isaac Rehv?"

Rehv sat up quickly. "How did you get in here?"

"The door was open."

"No it wasn't."

The little man softly rubbed the raw flower on the side of his face, perhaps making sure it was still there. "Does it matter?" Rehv heard fatigue slip in round the edges of his voice. "I'm in now. I'm sorry if I've startled you."

"Who are you?"

"You can call me Harry," he said with a shy smile.

Rehv stood up. He noticed the man who wanted to be called Harry looking at his body in a curious professional way, like a judge at a dog show. He supposed it was recorded under early middle-aged, muscular, slightly heavy. As he rummaged through the small pile of clothing on the floor he said, "Go away, Harry." He put on a pair of Quentin Katz's trousers, too big around the waist and half an inch too short, a shirt of Calvin Klein's that Quentin Katz could no longer get into, and stuffed a worn and

24

shapeless leather wallet bearing a faded gold Q.K. into the back pocket. He remembered a wallet with I.R. printed on one corner. Inside were a few photographs that he wished he had sometimes when he was alone.

"Go away, Harry." He wanted nothing to do with Harry, or spray painting the Statue of Liberty, or kidnapping men in white robes, or throwing Molotov cocktails across embassy lawns. "You seem like a nice man, but please go away."

"I'm with the Haganah," Harry said, as if that settled everything.

Rehv folded the camp cot and carried it to the storage room. "That's why I want you to go."

Harry followed him through the door, perhaps because he didn't want to raise his voice, perhaps because he didn't like the bare white room filled with dirty white light that came in through the tall windows. Rehv felt Harry touch his arm. "I just want to talk to you. Would a cup of coffee be too much trouble?"

Coffee was easy. Quentin Katz believed in offering visitors coffee the moment they walked through the door: "It's good business." In the storage room were a stove, a small espresso machine, a coffee grinder, a percolator, and tins of coffee beans from Colombia, Brazil, Kenya, and Java. Rehv kept a jar of instant on the top shelf.

They sat on the polished pine floor drinking black coffee from ivory-colored Rosenthal cups. The dirty white light turned the bad side of Harry's face into lunar crust. Rehv saw his hand tremble slightly as he raised the cup to his lips, and wondered how old he was.

"It's very good coffee, thank you," Harry said after one sip. He placed the cup carefully on the floor and didn't touch it again. Little concentric waves of coffee pulsed across the surface of the cup, back and forth, colliding, diminishing, dying. Rehv looked up to find bright blue eyes gazing at him thoughtfully.

"So," Harry said. "You've decided to assimilate, is that it?"

"Oh shit." Rehv waved the back of his hand at the four booths in the center of the room to show Harry how wrong he was.

"What are those?"

"Art."

"I see." The blue eyes ran their gaze over the exhibit. Then suddenly a glitter broke through their surface, as if Harry were

25

about to smile. He didn't smile, but he said, "I do see. They're the portable toilets Americans use at construction sites. What a funny idea."

"You should get yourself a grant."

"I beg your pardon."

"Nothing."

Harry shifted slightly. He wasn't comfortable on the floor. "I'm afraid we don't know much about you, Mr. Rehv."

But you knew where to find me, Rehv thought. He said, "Why don't you tell me what you want? It won't be long before the owners come to open the gallery."

Harry inched closer on the floor. His breath smelled of mint toothpaste. "We want you to do one little job. It will be very simple, but a very big help."

"To what end?"

The gentleness dropped away from Harry's voice like a button from a fencing sword. "For the cause," he said angrily. The good side of his face went scarlet. The bad stayed the way it was. The word *Israel* hung in the air unsaid. It always did.

"I've had enough of hopeless causes." Rehv was surprised to feel himself becoming angry too. "Blowing up buildings won't turn back time."

"It worked for them."

"There's no comparison and you know it."

"And it worked for us before that," Harry added more quietly.

"I know. I was there."

"In the forties?" He didn't look as old as that.

"This is the second Haganah for me," Harry said.

Rehv wanted to tell him that it was Hitler who had given Israel to them, that they had bought it with six million lives; that the Americans hated them, the American Jews hated them, the Russians hated them, the oil companies hated them, the Arabs for some reason still hated them; that the reason Harry and his friends kept fighting was not because there was hope but because if they stopped there would be nothing to do but blow their brains out, the way a few refugees did every day—you could read about them in the back pages of the newspaper. Instead he stood up and said: "I'm sorry, Harry. The answer is no."

Harry didn't look at him. "Very well," he said. Rehv held out his hand to help him rise, but Harry ignored it. Rehv heard his bones crack as he slowly got to his feet. "I'm sorry too," he said, slightly short of breath. He walked to the door and paused with his hand on the knob. "It was about a man named Fahoum."

"I've never heard of him."

Harry spoke without turning. "Abu Fahoum. He led the Palestinian commandos during the attack on Mount Carmel."

Rehv did not speak. Harry still stood facing the door. Someone knocked lightly on it. Harry turned the knob. A man's head, no, a boy's, with pimples and a yarmulke, poked into the room.

"Mr. Nissim. Are you all right? I thought I heard you at the door."

"I'm fine. Wait outside." Harry closed the door and turned around.

"What do you want me to do?" Rehv said. He had trouble forcing the words through the narrowness of his throat.

"You work at a restaurant called La Basquaise?" Rehv nodded. "Abu Fahoum will dine there tonight. We want him to sit at a certain table."

"I don't seat people. I'm only a waiter, not the maître d'."

Harry smiled, this time with his mouth as well as his eyes. "That's a problem I think we can solve." The smile made him seem even younger. It lent a little life to the side of his face that was crust.

From the tall windows high above, Issac Rehv watched Harry and the boy cross the street. The boy helped Harry into the passenger seat of a low-priced Honda–General Motors product. Then he took the wheel and pulled into traffic without looking. A taxi honked and swerved. The car headed uptown.

"A certain table," Harry had said. Long after the car was out of sight Rehv stood at the window, seeing nothing; hearing the soft Israeli voice repeat the number of the table: "Twenty-three."

CHAPTER TWO

Sixty blocks. Isaac Rehv walked to work as he always did. A cold winter drizzle settled over the city like a punishment, shutting out the sky, color, and sun. Men hurried by scowling, women hugging themselves, their made-up faces garish in the gray light. Rehv kept his eye on the store windows, watching their evolution from jumbles of crude crafts and mass-produced junk to reverently lit shrines for suede suitcases. He left Fifth Avenue for the quiet side street where La Basquaise offered its old-world hospitality every night except Monday to anyone who could afford to shop within a ten block radius.

Rehv passed under the soft pink awning that hung over the sidewalk like a lure and went in by the staff entrance. Pascal, co-owner and chef, was waiting for him in the small waiters' changing room. He wore *le gros bonnet* as he did every second he was in the restaurant, and since he was always first to arrive and last to leave no one ever saw him without it. It was to him what De Gaulle's nose had been to De Gaulle: not a symbol to others but the true source of all his power. On New Year's Eve the year before one of the waiters had jokingly knocked it off. He was fired on the spot.

Pascal was agitated. "Finally! Where have you been?"

"I'm not late," Rehv said. He shook off his nylon jacket and hung it in a locker.

"No no no non non. I know how to tell time. Don't be so touchy." He darted across the cramped room like an angry hen, turned, darted back, and sat heavily on a stool. "Quel catas-

28

trophe!" he cried, then buried his hands and said it again, sepulchrally.

Rehv pulled his woollen sweater over his head, folded it, and laid it on the shelf in the locker. He hung his shirt on a hanger and his pants on a hook. He heard Pascal's barely audible groan. The next one would be only slightly louder.

Rehv sighed. "What's wrong?"

Pascal was on his feet. "What's wrong? Just like that. So . . . so tranquille. So John Wayne. Well my friend, I'll tell you." He closed in. Rehv smelled garlic, red wine, vinegar, thyme, and basil. "It's Armande." Armande was Pascal's partner and maître d'. "He isn't coming in tonight. He has never missed a night. In six years. Jamais. And tonight he isn't coming in. Is not, cannot, come—he called me from the hospital."

Rehv bent down to unlace his shoes. He didn't want Pascal to see his face. "Is he sick?"

Pascal bent down with him. "Sick? It's worse than that. He has to stay overnight for observation. He's puking in the toilet!"

"Was it something he ate?"

"Idiot." Pascal pronounced it the French way. "What do you think? Something went in the other way?" Pascal's eyes widened. "Merde." He sat on the stool. "You're probably right. What a whore he is, that fucking Armande." He buried his face in his hands. Rehv waited for him to say "Quel catastrophe." Instead he suddenly looked up in alarm and said, "Tonight, of all nights."

"What's special about tonight?"

Pascal's thin lips curled contemptuously. "Ha." He rose to his feet, strode from the room, and slammed the door. He reopened it with a crash, stood in the doorway like a gunslinger, and pointed his finger at Rehv. "Tonight you're the maître d'. That's what's special about tonight."

There was really no one else. Rehv was the only waiter who spoke French, and although most of the waiters were Italian, the only one Pascal thought of as European.

"Do I get a raise?" Rehv asked.

Pascal laughed like Lady Macbeth. "No one gets a raise. Not as long as I'm wearing this." He tapped *le gros bonnet,* reached for the door to slam it again, missed, and spun off toward the kitchen.

Isaac Rehv dressed for his night's work in black pants, white shirt, black bow tie, and short green jacket: the kind of outfit a minor performer in a bullfight might wear. He checked himself in the mirror. He was always surprised at how young he appeared. No gray hair, a solid chin, a strong brow. Only when he looked closely, especially into the dark brown eyes that didn't quite come to life, did he see a man as old as he felt.

Rehv walked along the shabby corridor, as rich in smells as a bloodhound's world, and into the kitchen. Behind clouds of steam that rose from copper pots, men with knives worked urgently, turning dead animals and uprooted vegetables into mousses and braises, fricassees and daubes.

"Mais non." Pascal, half hidden by hanging black frying pans, was looking at him in horror. "Dressed like this? What can you be thinking?" He parted the frying pans and burst across the room. "Armande wears a dinner suit. What are you trying to do to me?"

"Don't worry. No one will notice."

Pascal went rigid. "Souche! Those assholes notice everything."

"That's too bad. I don't own a dinner suit."

"Ha. I see your game. You're still trying to squeeze a raise out of me." Pascal's tone jumped an octave. "Never. Go out there stark raving naked. I don't care." He caught sight of a yellow sauce warming on the stove, jabbed his finger into it, tasted. A death cry rose from his throat. Rehv walked off: He wanted to read the evening's guest list. As he opened the door that led to the dining room he heard Pascal scream: "I want hollandaise, not lemonade." Something heavy crashed in the sink. No one took any notice.

Backstage, the kitchen, was Pascal's territory. The stage itself, the dining room, was all Armande's. The idea had been his: the blue shutters on the walls, the suggestion of leaded windows, the pastel mountain scenery in the distance. It was a clever trompe l'oeil that made the customers feel they were sitting in a lodge in the Pyrenees. They loved it. They paid for it.

By six o'clock everything was ready. Thick lavender table-cloths were laid on the forty tables, white china, Scandinavian cutlery, and long-stemmed wineglasses were in place. At six-fifteen Rehv heard the front door open and a few muffled words from the coat checkroom.

Smiling, he went forward, the words *Bon soir* on his lips. They remained unspoken. Standing self-consciously in the hall was the pimply boy who had blurted Harry's real name.

Rehv felt relief spread through his body. Something had gone wrong. They had sent the boy to tell him it was all off.

The boy cleared his throat. "Reservations for Jones," he said in a high voice, without looking Rehv in the eye. For the first time Rehv noticed the young woman at the boy's side. She was pale and very thin. She wore a baggy sweater and an unfashionably short skirt and carried a large purse. "For dinner," the boy explained, perhaps sensing Rehv's hesitation. He was wearing a cheap dark suit and a white shirt with a frayed collar. At least he had left his yarmulke behind.

"Please follow me," Rehv said, and led them into the dining room. He gestured toward the tables. "Where would you like to sit?"

The boy glanced around quickly. Rehv guessed he was trying to match the actual room to a diagram he had been shown. The young woman pointed. "There," she said. "That looks nice." Her voice sounded confident, deeper than the boy's, but her Israeli accent was unmistakable.

"Certainly, madam," Rehv said. He took them to the table she had indicated, a small corner banquette that commanded a good view of the whole room. Number sixteen. It was one of the most popular tables. It had a particularly good view of table twenty-three, a round table set about twelve feet away in the slightly sunken area Armande had filled with plants and called Le Jardin.

When they were seated, Rehv handed them the large elegantly printed cartes. "Something from the bar?"

"No thank you," the woman replied.

"Water please," the boy said.

"Any special kind, sir?"

The boy flushed, as though Rehv had insulted him.

"From the tap, please," the woman said.

Rehv nodded. "Bon appétit." He left them to study the menu. He hoped they could understand it. Much more than that, he hoped they had come in a very minor supporting role. He looked back at them as he went to greet some more customers. Instead of the menus they were studying table twenty-three.

The restaurant filled with people. They came in out of the rain, had a stiff drink, lit cigarettes, and read the menu care-

fully and with relish, as though it were a will and they the bene-
ficiaries. As the food arrived they made happy sounds, clanked
their knives and forks, dropped them on the floor, spilled wine,
got *cassoulets d'écrevisses* stuck between their teeth. Rehv was
very busy, acting as maître d' and also taking orders in his own
section. Once or twice he glanced at table sixteen. They had
ordered the saddle of lamb Provençale, the cheapest entree on the
menu. They picked at it and pushed it around their plates, but
they didn't eat it. They kept watching table twenty-three. So did
Rehv. It was in his section.

As he poured white Châteauneuf-du-Pape for a man who had
said to his wife, as they always did before they asked for it, "Look
at this, dear: a white Châteauneuf-du-Pape," Manolo, the Filipino busboy, drew up to his side.

"The boss wants to see you," Manolo whispered. Rehv heard
the mischief in his tone and turned to look down at the boy. He
was showing all his big white teeth. He really was a boy; legally
he should have been in school. But La Basquaise was his life. He
thought it was the most beautiful place on earth. Everyone liked
him.

Rehv waited for the Châteauneuf-du-Pape lover to stick his
nose in the glass, sniff, sip, squirt it through his molars, and pronounce it "merveilleuse," getting the gender wrong, before he
went into the kitchen. It was bad, but not as bad as he had seen.
The *saucier,* red-faced, was pulling on his raincoat in a manner
that said clearly he would never return, pots were boiling over
on the stove, and the *rôtisseur*'s assistant was sobbing in the
corner. A large *croquembouche* lay upside down on the floor.
Pascal was pacing around it in a tight frenzied circle.

"Cretin!" he screamed at Rehv. "You're crucifying me."

"Don't be silly. Everything's fine."

"Fine! Fine! Who are those peasants you've put at sixteen,
Mr. Fine? What are they doing in my restaurant? What are they
doing at my best table?"

"They were the first ones here. They asked for it. I couldn't
very well put them in Siberia."

"Of course you could. Armande does it every night. They're
drinking tap water." Pascal closed his eyes very tightly, so tightly
that his face wrinkled like a dried fig. "Nothing but tap water,"
the fig repeated through clenched teeth. Rehv slipped out while

32

Pascal's eyes were still shut. In the main entrance to the dining room three Arabs stood waiting.

Silvio, one of the older waiters, was approaching them with welcome on his face. Rehv wanted to shout, "Silvio!," but it wasn't that kind of restaurant. Instead he hurried across the room. Silvio was taking them to number four, in the corner of the room opposite sixteen.

"Good evening, gentlemen," Rehv said. They turned to face him. Two wore white robes; the third, a big man missing his left earlobe, wore a dark suit. Rehv knew that Abu Fahoum must be the younger of the two robed men, not so much from his proud military bearing, but from the black-and-white checked keffiyeh he wore on his head. "I'm afraid this table is already taken. We have another one for you in the Jardin." He held out his hand to show them where it was.

The older man and the man in the suit looked in the direction he had indicated; Abu Fahoum did not. "We prefer this table," he said. He spoke with an Oxford accent.

"I'm terribly sorry." Rehv allowed his eyes for a split second to glance beyond them. Even from across the room he could see the anxiety on the faces at table sixteen: The woman's lips were parted.

"Are you really?" Abu Fahoum had drawn back his head and was regarding Rehv's face very closely.

"Yes, sir, I am. But it is already spoken for."

Abu Fahoun turned to his older companion and said in Arabic: "You see why he's making trouble, don't you? He's a dirty Jew."

Rehv almost grabbed him by the throat. He felt his rigid body churning out waves of rage, waves that swept across the room, unseen.

The older man said, also in Arabic: "It's nothing like that. He's just doing his job. Besides, it is a better table." He tugged at the sleeve of Abu Fahoum's robe. Without looking at Rehv again, Abu Fahoum turned and walked with enormous dignity to table twenty-three. He sat with his back to sixteen. The big man in the suit sat facing him, the older man in between.

"Where the hell were you?" Silvio said in a low voice. "I didn't know four was taken."

"It's all right."

33

Rehv hurried over to twenty-three to hand out the cartes. The man in the suit kept his hands at his sides and shook his head.

"He isn't here to eat," Abu Fahoum said with amusement, as if Rehv had just offered a menu to a dog.

"Very well. Would anyone like something from the bar?"

Again Abu Fahoum lifted back his head, almost the way a cobra rears above its coils. "It is forbidden."

"In America the expression *something from the bar* does not necessarily mean alcohol. We have bottled water and soft drinks as well," Rehv said. He tried to remember what politeness sounded like.

Just beneath the skin of Abu Fahoum's forehead a thick vein began to throb. He placed his hands on the table, as if to get up. The man who had not come to eat pushed his chair back from the table, very quickly.

"Stop it," the older man said in Arabic. "Relax. He's right." In English he said to Rehv: "Water will be fine. Vichy for me. Abu?"

Abu Fahoum said, "Perrier." He made it sound like a threat. The man in the suit pulled his chair back to the table. Rehv saw him glance at the young couple sitting twelve feet away. They were no longer making any pretense of eating, or even being at a restaurant: They sat with their hands in their laps, heads bowed over the table as if in silent prayer. The man in the suit didn't seem to notice anything unusual. He turned in his chair and ran his eyes methodically over the other diners.

Rehv brought the drinks on a silver tray. It was the drink waiter's job, but Rehv wanted to do it himself. As he began to pour, he wished he had stayed in the kitchen. He felt Abu Fahoum's eyes on him, and it made his hands shake, not much, but enough to spill Perrier on the lavender tablecloth. Manolo noticed and hurried over with a napkin.

"Are you ready to order?" Rehv asked as Manolo leaned across the table to mop up the little pool of sparkling water.

"I will start with the salmon mousse in two sauces," Abu Fahoum said. Rehv was about to tell him that one of the sauces contained champagne when the man in the suit made a little frightened noise in his throat and reached inside his jacket. Rehv whirled around to see the pimply boy on his feet, pointing a

34

small black gun at Abu Fahoum's back. His face was white and waxy like the face of a corpse.

"Now," the woman said in Hebrew.

The gun went off. Manolo arched back and slumped to the floor. The pimply boy stood very still, pointing the gun. Comprehension was just surfacing in his eyes when the man in the suit shot him in the middle of the forehead. His gun was more powerful. It made a much louder noise, and knocked the boy against the wall. He fell under the table. The woman drew a small metal cylinder from her purse and threw it at the man in the suit. It shot out a pinwheel of stinging smoke as it flew through the air. The woman dove to the floor, rolled, and ran for the front entrance. The canister bounced off the chest of the man in the suit and onto the table. He grabbed it, hurled it across the room, jumped from his chair, and fired at the woman just as she went out the door. She seemed to stumble, but kept going.

"Let her go," Abu Fahoum shouted in Arabic before the man in the suit could take another step. Pink patches had appeared on his dark face: He was exhilarated.

Rehv knelt on the floor and took Manolo in his arms. He was only dimly aware of screaming, running, and tear gas. He wanted to say, "Don't worry, Manolo, you're going to be all right." But the words wouldn't come. Manolo looked up at him, watching, waiting, his big black eyes filled with pain and fear. Then they were filled with nothing at all.

After a long time Rehv raised his head. Pascal stood silently before him. Tears ran down his cheeks. In his hand he held *le gros bonnet* and he was twisting it, over and over.

CHAPTER THREE

Abu Fahoum and his two friends went away in a limousine. The police had wanted to take the gun from the man in the suit because he had no permit, but they couldn't because of his diplomatic immunity. Pascal went away in a taxi, Silvio took the subway. Manolo went in an ambulance, although he didn't need one.

Isaac Rehv walked. The rain came down hard and cold but he didn't feel it. He walked quickly, hoping to tire himself, to trick his body into sleepiness. It would be futile, he knew; his body was not the problem. The problem was the wave that undulated inside his brain, sometimes softly, subtly licking at the edges of his thoughts, sometimes rolling over him with a smothering tidal force. Then he would hear Lena saying, "Daddy, read me a story." She said it again and again but from so far away he could barely make out the words.

The rain fell in cold hard balls. They bounced off the cement, became ovals, and hung in the air. In the dirty yellow light they looked like his sleeping pills. He imagined them in the palm of his hand—one, three, a dozen.

He climbed the stairs to The Loft, his feet sloshing in his shoes. As he slid the key in the lock he heard a sound from the other side of the door. He didn't make another movement, not even to take his hand from the key. He thought of the thin, pale woman bleeding on the polished pine floor beside the four wooden booths. He thought of Abu Fahoum and the man in the suit, waiting in the dark. Leaving the key where it was, he very slowly

36

stepped backwards toward the top of the stairs. A woman laughed, a loud aggressive laugh that ran through several registers but didn't find mirth. Sheila Finkle. He opened the door.

No bleeding woman. No man with a gun. Instead Sheila Finkle, tall and thin, except for the heavy breasts she couldn't diet away; and Quentin Katz, shorter, rounder, with a bald spot on the top of his head where a horseshoe would neatly fit; and others, talking and smoking and drinking white wine and kirs and champagne that didn't come from Champagne. He noticed that the violence exhibit was gone. No one noticed him.

He turned to go. Sheila Finkle screamed. "Oh. You scared me. I didn't hear you come in."

"Isaac. You're just in time," Quentin Katz said. "We've got a new showing to put up tonight." Katz came forward to greet him. "My God! Did you swim here?"

"I'm not very wet."

"Not very wet? Here, try some champagne."

"No thanks."

"Of course. You need something to warm you up. How about cognac?"

"No."

"Armagnac."

"All right."

Katz raised an eyebrow. "Armagnac, huh? Have we discovered your secret vice at last?"

In fact he didn't like any kind of brandy. He just didn't want to hear everything Katz had to offer. He tried to smile like a person who has been found out about some foible.

Katz turned to the group. "Hey, everybody," he said loudly. "Isaac Rehv." As he went to the storage room to fetch the armagnac he added, "Sheila, why don't you introduce him around?"

Before she did she said: "Isaac is our very nice night watchman. I sleep so much better knowing he's here." Then she told him everyone's name.

Katz returned with the armagnac. "And not just any night watchman: the smartest in Manhattan. In real life he's a professor of Arabic literature." He finished on a note that seemed to invite applause, like a game show host.

A woman of about his own age with long red fingernails said, "Really? That must be a very good field these days."

"It must be," Rehv replied. "Now if you will excuse me, I'll change into something dry." He went into the storage room, shut the door, and stayed there until all the guests had left.

"Good-bye, good-bye," Katz and his wife called down the stairs after the last one. There was a pause. Then Sheila spoke in a hoarse, angry whisper: "I don't care what you think. He was appallingly rude." Rehv could not distinguish the words of Katz's reply, only the soothing tone. This time Sheila made no effort at all to lower her voice: "Do what you like. I'm going home." The door closed sharply.

Footsteps. A light knock. Once. Twice.

"Isaac? You in there?"

Rehv picked up the camp cot and opened the door. Quentin Katz stood there, trying to look genial. "One more armagnac before beddy-bye?" He stuck a partly full glass into the space between them. His hand was pink and plump and ill defined.

"I'm very tired, Quentin," he said. It wasn't true.

"Oh come on. Live a little."

He took the glass. They went into the gallery and sat on folding chairs. Six or seven sculptures, Rehv supposed they were sculptures, had been placed around the room. One was composed entirely of escargot shells: He recognized Napoleon, hand hidden inside his coat, overlooking some battle. And a waxy, smiling Dwight Eisenhower, done in Madame Tussaud style, except he was naked and had a corncob for a penis. There was Genghis Khan brandishing an egg roll, and a sausage Rommel with sauerkraut hair.

"Well?" Katz was looking at him closely.

"I'm not sure I understand it."

"What's to understand? This is going to be the best show we've ever had." Katz downed half his armagnac and leaned forward conspiratorially. "Guess what we're calling it?"

"An Army Marches on Its Belly."

Katz blinked and sat back. "I don't get it." He waved his hand in the air, as though knocking Rehv's words to the side. "We're calling it 'Hungry Warriors.' Sheila came up with that." He gazed happily at Genghis Khan. "We're going to get a lot of publicity. I know it."

"Who is that?" Rehv asked, pointing.

"Gordon. Falling at Khartoum." Gordon was made of crumpets with wounds of jam.

Rehv sipped at the armagnac. He waited for Katz to leave. Katz took the bottle and poured himself another glass. "A lot of publicity," he repeated dreamily. They sat in silence. After a while Katz turned to him and opened his mouth as if to speak; but he changed his mind and said nothing, although his mouth remained open for a few moments.

"Who is the artist?" Rehv said, to say something.

It was the kind of opening Katz had been waiting for. "You met her tonight, Isaac. She wanted to know about your Arabic studies. You gave her the cold shoulder."

Rehv stood up. "I'm really very tired."

"Please, Isaac. I'm worried about you." He corrected himself. "Sheila and I are worried about you. You look very, very depressed. Now, if it's coming home tired and finding this party going on, I'm sorry, but you've got to realize this is a business. A growing business."

"It's nothing like that." He sat down.

"What then? You're still taking those pills I gave you, I hope."

"Yes."

"If you run out, just say the word. I'll get another prescription. It's a matter of picking up the phone."

"Thank you."

Katz set his glass on the floor, then slowly, almost ceremoniously extended his pink hand and placed it gently on Rehv's knee. "Isaac, I don't want you to take offense, but in the long run those pills are not the answer."

"What is the answer, Quentin?" He wanted Katz to remove his hand, but he seemed in no hurry to do so. It rested on his knee like a little lobster claw, one more piece of edible sculpture.

"It's obvious," Katz answered. "You just have to face it, that's all. What you have to do is start building a new life. Step one: Find a real job. You're a trained professor, for Christ's sake. Anything to do with the Arabs is booming these days. Start sending out resumes. Make a few phone calls. You're not a waiter."

"The restaurant's all right," Rehv said. As he spoke, he felt a sudden and strong desire to tell Katz what had happened. Perhaps it was the armagnac. Or guilt. "There was a shooting there tonight."

"Oh?"

"A boy shot at some Palestinians."

39

Katz took his hand from Rehv's knee. "What kind of boy?"

A dead boy, Rhev thought. "What do you mean?" he asked.

"What nationality, that's what I mean," Katz said with annoyance. "Do I have to spell it out?"

"Israeli, I suppose."

"Goddamn it." One pink hand made a fist. The other wrapped around it and squeezed hard. "Was anyone hurt?"

"The boy died."

"Stop calling him a boy. Boys don't shoot guns at people. Anyone else?"

"Manolo."

"Who's Manolo?"

"He was the busboy."

"Dead?"

"Yes."

Katz nodded as if he had known it all the time. "An innocent victim." It was one of those redundancies Rehv heard Americans use quite often, like eternal damnation.

Katz stopped nodding. His face began to go the color of his hands. Rehv was surprised that he could look so angry. "Something has to be done about this terrorism. It's turning this town into a hellhole. You people —" Katz stopped himself, and resumed in a quieter voice: "Some of your people, Isaac, I'm not saying you, but some of the other refugees, are being very unrealistic. There is no Israel. There is Palestine. Israel is ancient history, like Bosnia and Herzegovina and the Apache nation."

"But there are still Apaches, aren't there?"

Katz grunted. "Look at them." He paused to let that sink in. One of his hands twitched slightly, as though about to set off for Rehv's knee, but it stayed where it was. "It's what I've been trying to tell you, Isaac. There's no going back, so the longer you stay marginal, the harder it will be to get into the game."

But Rehv didn't feel like getting into the game. Maybe it was because of the waves in his head, maybe because of the hurt in his back.

Katz saw something on his face that he must have decided was discouragement. "But don't get me wrong," he said. "It's not as tough as all that. My grandfather came from Russia without a dime, and in five years he owned his own house and was renting out the top floor." He smiled brightly, hoping to kindle some enthusiasm. Quite suddenly, in mid-smile, he had a thought that made him start visibly. The teeth still showed, but the smile was gone.

"You weren't involved in it, were you?"

"Of course not," Rehv said.

"Good. I'm glad to hear that, I can tell you." He picked up his glass, drained it, and smiled again at Rehv. He did look very glad. He licked his lips and pulled his chair a little closer to Rehv's. His tone softened, became confidential. "You see, Isaac, I'm Jewish. That's the truth and I'm proud of it. But first and foremost I'm an American. And America is a Christian country. Step off this island, Isaac, and you'll find that it's a very Christian country, and getting more Christian every day. Do you see my point, Isaac? I'm just saying that terrorism is wrong, under any circumstances."

Katz stood up and looked at his watch. Rehv saw that he had fumbled the usual leave-taking sequence: The polite way is to first show surprise at the time and then get ready to go. He felt a laugh begin to build uncomfortably, painfully inside him.

"My God!" Katz said. "Look at this. And with an opening tomorrow." He walked quickly to the door. "You'll come, I hope?"

Rehv nodded and murmured something. Katz went out and down the stairs. Rehv held his breath as long as he could, and then let the laugh out like an embolism. He heard himself laugh and laugh. It was a raucous laugh with no humor in it at all. He and Sheila Finkle laughing together would be bedlam.

When the laugh finally died away, he swallowed two sleeping pills with the rest of the armagnac. Then he set the camp cot beside General Gordon, shut off the lights, and lay down. For a long time he looked at Gordon, yellow brown in the dingy light of the streetlamps, as if he had been toasted. He wanted to roll over and say to Naomi: "If we get hungry we can always have him for breakfast."

Later the drug wrapped its arms around him and he stopped thinking.

Too soon something punched a hole in the sleep that held him. It kept punching, insistent and mechanical, until he opened his eyes. It was still dark. The phone was ringing in the storage room.

He pushed himself off the cot in the darkness and carefully crossed the room, finding a path between the hungry warriors. He lifted the receiver.

"Hello."

"Mr. Rehv," said a voice. It was the man who preferred to be known as Harry.

"I don't want to talk to you."

"Please listen to me, Mr. Rehv." He spoke very calmly, very quietly. "I'm very sorry about what happened tonight. I accept full responsibility. At least we have the girl. She is going to be fine."

"I don't give a shit about the girl."

"I do. She is my granddaughter," Harry said. "She tells me you were extremely able, Mr. Rehv. I very much want to talk to you at greater length. Perhaps —"

Rehv cut him off. "I'm hanging up now. Don't ever call me again."

'Wait, Mr. Rehv, please. A man like you can't spend a lifetime sitting on the fence."

Rehv paused, not because Harry's words changed his mind in any way, but because they recalled Quentin Katz talking about staying marginal. In this brief silence Rehv thought he heard a faint metallic sound.

"Mr. Rehv?"

"Quiet," he hissed into the phone. He listened very hard, and after a few seconds again heard a muffled scraping. It seemed to come from the hall outside the front door of the gallery. "Don't go away," he whispered through the wires to Harry.

He laid the receiver softly on the counter and opened one of the drawers. Inside, his hand found the knife Quentin Katz used to cut the cakes he sometimes gave visitors with their coffee. He walked slowly into the gallery, his bare feet noiseless on the pine floor.

The front door was opening. A large dark figure moved out of the blackness in the hall and into the room. Rehv stood behind the sculpture of Genghis Khan. The pencil beam of a small flashlight shot through the darkness. It ran in a short arc, then fastened on the falling Gordon. The dark figure dropped quickly into a crouch. In the slight diffusion of the beam's light Rehv could make out an extended arm, a hand holding an object.

42

Nothing happened. The beam swept around the room, prodding the other sculptures. Rehv knelt behind Genghis Khan and made himself small. The beam passed over the camp cot, stopped, returned. The dark figure rose and began moving very slowly toward the cot, arm still extended.

The figure bent forward. Light shone on the empty cot. Quickly the figure turned; the beam glanced off the object in its hand—a gun with a long silencer attached to the barrel. Carefully, methodically, the beam began probing the shadows in the room. Eisenhower. Rommel. Genghis Khan. It rested on Genghis Khan.

The figure came closer. Slowly the beam examined Genghis Khan from head to toe. Then it touched Rehv's knee. He dove across the floor. There was a noise like dry spitting. Something crashed. Rehv rolled at the dark figure, hitting it at knee level. It did not fall; it did not even budge. The beam shone on him. The long barrel pointed down, gleaming.

Rehv drove up from the floor and sank the knife into the middle of the dark mass. He heard a grunt, which softened to a sound like leaking air. The figure slumped away, pulling the knife from his hand. The flashlight was pointing its narrow finger at the ceiling. Rehv picked it up and shone it on the figure at his feet: a dark suit, a dark face, an earlobe missing. A sticky wetness flowed around his bare feet.

Rehv stood there for some time. Suddenly he turned and ran to the window. In the street below he saw only parked cars, and wet black pavement, like a river of oil.

He walked back across the room. The sticky wetness had spread. He went into the storage room and picked up the phone.

"Harry?"

"Yes."

"Come here."

Night was slowly going gray when Harry arrived. The black mass on the floor was turning into a dead and bloody man. Rommel's sausage head lay nearby. Harry glanced quickly around the room.

"They've changed exhibits," he murmured, almost to himself. For a moment Rehv wondered whether he had made some sophisticated joke about modern art; but Harry had given no sign that he had even noticed the man on the floor. Harry smiled at him. "You speak Arabic, don't you, Mr. Rehv?" he asked encouragingly, like an interviewer trying to coax a lively answer from his guest.

"Yes."

"Good." He was so brisk Rehv thought he might rub his hands together; brisk the way a man is when things are going his way. Perhaps in his mind this body canceled the two at La Basquaise.

"We'd better do something, Harry." He was suddenly very tired. He felt the drug pulling down his eyelids.

"Don't worry," Harry said. "I'll handle everything. There's just one little detail I'd like you to take care of. It's really quite simple."

"That's what you said this morning." He looked out the window. "Yesterday morning."

"Don't be so suspicious." Harry sounded almost jovial. "Where is your telephone?" Rehv showed him. Harry lifted the receiver, took a clean handkerchief from his pocket, and stretched it over the mouthpiece.

"I am going to dial a number and hand you the phone. In a very low voice, as if you are afraid of being overheard, say in Arabic: 'It is done. There was difficulty. I will be gone for two days.' Then hang up immediately. Do you understand?"

Rehv was tired, and tired of Harry, too: "No. I don't want to play these games."

Harry's briskness sank into his depths, out of sight. "It's too late," he said quietly. He dialed the telephone and gave the receiver to Rehv. It was answered in the middle of the first ring. "Yes?" said a man in Arabic.

He spoke the words he had been told to speak, thinking at the same time that he had heard the voice before. He hung up.

"Who is he?" he asked Harry.

"Abu Fahoum. Did you think your visitor came without orders from him?" Rehv remembered the long black car disappearing in the rain. They must have dropped the bodyguard near the restaurant, to follow him on foot.

"Now do you understand, Mr. Rehv? Abu Fahoum will wait two days before he sends someone else, or comes himself, or talks to the police. He won't know that anything is wrong. We have given ourselves two days of grace."

44

Rehv shook his head. "I'm very tired."

Harry looked at him thoughtfully. Night had now withdrawn, revealing the shapeless brand on his face. And his bright, cold blue eyes.

"I am saying, Mr. Rehv, that we have two days to kill Abu Fahoum. But don't worry: I'm going to help you." He bent and picked up Rommel's head.

CHAPTER FOUR

Krebs sat in his office, watching the rain try to break through the glass of his little window. He didn't like the weather in New York. He didn't like anything about New York. He didn't like Armbrister, his boss, or Bunting, Armbrister's boss. He didn't like Alice, his wife.

Krebs liked the weather better in Kuala Lumpur, Rio, Lisbon, or Kinshasa. He liked the girl who brought him coffee. He liked her hard little ass and her hard little smile. He daydreamed of being rough with her, but he never did anything about that: It would have meant risking his job.

His job meant a lot to him. He wanted to keep it, to become better at it, to rise. He ran five miles a day and did one hundred push-ups the moment he got out of bed. He knew two quick ways of killing a man with his bare hands and had employed one of them successfully. In Rio. He had just spent a long lonely year in Kinshasa, finally turning a Chinese engineer who had worked on the nuclear project at Lop Nor and was supposed to know something important. Krebs never found out what it was. He always worked hard, did what he was told, and tried to keep his mouth shut unless he was sure what he had to say was what they wanted to hear. He didn't drink, didn't smoke, took no drugs, wasn't queer.

Because of all that Krebs didn't understand why they had brought him to New York to ride herd on a ragged little mob of Israelis who sometimes threw Molotov cocktails into the offices of airlines they didn't like. They had no money, no support, foreign or domestic, no safe base. It was a step backwards, and it worried him. He had thought they might send him to Islamabad, or even Warsaw. What had he done wrong? He had been over the past year fifty times, and he couldn't think of a single mistake. He sometimes thought of asking Armbrister—"Look, Armbrister, just tell me what it is, I'll make up for it"—but would never give Armbrister that pleasure. He would make up for it without knowing what it was. He would work harder, do more push-ups, learn another quick way of killing a man with his bare hands. He turned to the square green face of the computer screen on his desk.

He was trying to match suspected terrorists with their previous lives in Israel. It was very difficult. Immigration had been very sloppy—they had just let them roll in wave after unsorted wave. Names were wrong, ages were wrong, they weren't arranged by family or profession or even military rank, which should have been easy, since by the end almost the whole population was in uniform.

Hunched over his desk, Krebs tapped questions on the plastic keys. After a short pause the screen flickered and gave its usual answer in square white letters: "Negative." Krebs tapped more questions. Sometimes the screen fed him a scrap or two of information. He made short notes on a writing pad. Outside, the rain softened into snow. Krebs didn't notice.

The telephone rang. "Mr. Armbrister would like to see you in his office," a woman said. It was Armbrister's secretary. She had trouble with her *r*'s. The way she pronounced Armbrister always reminded him of Elmer Fudd. Krebs thought Elmer Fudd was very funny; he still sometimes watched the cartoons on Saturday morning for half an hour or so, while he cooled down from his run, and Alice fixed his breakfast. Or didn't.

"Right now?" Krebs asked, but she had hung up.

Krebs shut off the computer terminal. He made a symmetrical arrangement of his pens, pencils, and writing pads. From the bottom drawer of his desk he took out a small round mirror. He studied his reflection closely: to be sure that his short sandy hair was neatly parted, that his eyebrows, much thicker and darker, were straight, that the aviator-style glasses really did make his square face seem longer and thinner, that there were no bits of food between his teeth or blackheads on his nose. He was about to put the mirror away when he noticed one tiny hair poking out his right nostril. He gripped it between thumb and index finger and yanked, immediately feeling a sharp pain surprisingly deep in his nose. He examined the hair: It was easily an inch and a quarter in length, perhaps an inch and a half. There was no time to measure. He blew it into his paper shredder.

Krebs locked his door and walked quickly to the end of the corridor. He ignored the elevator and took the stairs, climbing them two at a time—better for his legs and usually faster as well. He always used the stairs, except when he was with other people.

In the outer office Armbrister's secretary sat bent over a typewriter. Her limp black hair hung forward like blinders. "Go right in," she said without looking up. Krebs paused for a moment to catch his breath, and entered Armbrister's office.

Armbrister was on the phone. He was listening carefully and writing notes on a piece of paper. With exaggerated fishlike movements of his face Armbrister mouthed something at him, probably "Hello. Sit down." Krebs sat. Armbrister resembled a fish in any case, with his thick red lips and slightly bulging eyes, always bloodshot because the central heating dried his contact lenses. He made a very poor physical impression, Krebs thought. It was one of the reasons he disliked Armbrister—he preferred his superiors to look more distinguished.

"Of course I won't forget," Armbrister was saying. He picked up the sheet of paper and read from it. "Four salmon steaks, butter, eggs, parsley, and a bottle of Aligoté." He listened, nodded, kissed the mouthpiece, and hung up.

He turned to Krebs. "It's a new code," he said with a laugh. He laughed a little more in case Krebs wanted to join him. Krebs tried to smile.

Armbrister stopped laughing and began pushing papers around his desk. "I've got something here that should be right up your alley." He opened a drawer and rummaged inside. "If I can ever find it." He loathed Armbrister. They had been in the same class at MIT.

"Here we go." Armbrister held up a yellow file. "There was a bit of contact last night."

"Serious?"

"Probably not. But there might be some interesting angles. It seems they were after a man named Fahoum." Armbrister turned his red fish eyes on Krebs. He was waiting for Krebs to say something.

"I've never heard of him."

Armbrister smiled. "Abu Fahoum," he said. "He was a commando leader. British educated. Also a cultured and witty man. Right now he's attached to the Palestinian legation at the UN."

"But he's in the business?"

The fish eyes opened wide in puzzlement. "The business?"

"Our business," Krebs said.

"Oh, very much so." If Armbrister had heard the impatience in his tone he chose to ignore it. He handed Krebs the file. "Give him a call. I'm sure he'll have a few ideas."

"How much can I tell him?"

"As much as you like. We're allies, after all. Just make sure he gets the impression that this job is very high priority."

Krebs stood up.

"One more thing," Armbrister said. "It might make things smoother if you mention my name."

Krebs spent the rest of the day working on the yellow file. It was a thin file: no identification of the body, no autopsy results, no suggestion of who the young woman was, or where she had gone. There was a police report that included a diagram of the restaurant showing two Xs, almost touching, and a statement of the blood types of the young woman and the busboy. They were both O positive.

Krebs began making telephone calls. He tapped the keys of the computer terminal, wrote on the note pad. He didn't go to lunch. Once the girl brought him sandwiches, later a pot of coffee. Both times he watched her closely as she turned and walked away, but he recovered his concentration quickly and returned to work.

Snow turned to rain and back to snow. Deep shades of pink and orange blended into the gray light, meaning night had fallen on the city. Krebs had made the file much thicker, but he hadn't learned anything he wanted to know. The dull ache from cheap sandwiches and too much coffee descended slowly through his intestines. He stared for a while at the diagram of the restaurant. Then he sat back, stretched, cracked his knuckles one at a time, and telephoned Abu Fahoum.

The man who answered spoke a few harsh sounds in a language Krebs didn't know.

"Mr. Fahoum, please," Krebs said.

"This is he," said the man. In English the voice sounded smooth and fancy, like the voices of British actors on educational television.

Krebs introduced himself, and asked if they could meet.

"I'm very busy," Abu Fahoum said. "I've told everything I know to the police. Why don't you talk to them?"

"I have," Krebs said. He wanted to add: "Do you think I'm a goddamned amateur? We taught you everything you know." But he remembered that Abu Fahoum had probably learned from a Russian teacher. He mentioned Armbrister.

"The name means nothing to me. Now if you don't mind —"

"Just answer one question, Mr. Fahoum," Krebs said quickly. "It may be important: Did any of the staff behave strangely, or do anything unusual?"

There was a brief pause. Krebs felt a powerful mind on the other end of the line. It seemed to intensify the electronic connection between them. "Staff?" Abu Fahoum said.

"The maître d'. The waiters."

Krebs heard a spitting sound in his ear. "I am not in the habit of noticing waiters," Abu Fahoum said very coldly. "Now I really must say good-bye."

Krebs leaned forward, squeezing the phone tightly. "I wish you would think a little more about this, Mr. Fahoum. Don't you want us to find the people who tried to kill you?"

Abu Fahoum laughed. "For that, Mr. Kreb —"

"Krebs."

"— I am happy to rely entirely on your expertise." The line went dead.

Krebs banged the receiver into its cradle. He glared at the telephone, picked the receiver up, and banged it again. He stood up and paced around the office. Krebs was an easy name to get right.

After a while he approached the desk and gazed again at the diagram. The two tables were so close together. Sixteen was on a slightly higher level than twenty-three. That allowed someone sitting at sixteen who wanted to shoot someone sitting at twenty-three to fire down on him. It was very convenient. He decided he needed the names of everyone who worked at La Basquaise. He filled a Styrofoam cup with cold coffee and reached for the telephone.

CHAPTER FIVE

It was a city of wind and stone. No one roasted chestnuts on the corner, or stepped out for a quick cigarette, or walked his dog. No one made a sound. There was nothing to hear but the wind cutting its way through the stone canyons. And no one to hear it except Isaac Rehv, huddled in the little car, waiting for the night to be over. The wind had long ago found him hiding there, and worked through the cheap body of the car to blow its cold breath in his ears and up his pant legs.

"Don't worry," Harry had said. "I'll help you." He had helped: He had lent Rehv his car; he had shown him the apartment hotel on the Upper East Side where Abu Fahoum lived; he had given him a gun. "Wait for nighttime," Harry had told him: "He likes to go for walks at night."

"How do you know?" Rehv had asked.

"Joel," Harry had explained. "He watched him for a month." That didn't make Rehv feel more confident. Joel was the boy with the deep red hole in his forehead.

On the first night of grace Abu Fahoum did not appear. Perhaps it had been the snow. Perhaps he didn't like going for walks after all. Rehv had waited. From time to time he had stepped out of the car to clear snow off the windows. Once he had made a snowball and thrown it at a tree. It had stuck to the bark of the trunk like a round white birthmark.

Now, on the second night of grace, he waited again. He kept his eyes on the gray stone building on the other side of the street. Warm lights glowed through heavy curtains in the windows. Behind the thick glass doors walked the doorman, back and forth, back and forth, in his chocolate brown uniform. He had nothing to do. No one came in. No went went out.

Rehv rehearsed all the reasons he had to kill Abu Fahoum. Abu Fahoum had tried to kill him. He would try again. At the very least he would send the police after him. Tomorrow. And there was Haifa. He had reasons. They were sound and logical, but his heart wasn't in it. Rehv wasn't sure he could bring himself to kill Abu Fahoum without his heart being in it. He hadn't told any of this to Harry, but the little man had sensed it all the same.

"You wouldn't have had any trouble killing him during the war, would you?" Harry had asked.

"Probably not."

"Good. This is the war. We're still fighting."

But so far from the front. Rehv wore gloves, but his hands were still cold; he squeezed them between his thighs. The front. Where was it? A year ago in time, and gone forever in space, unless you counted the space inside Harry's mind, and the minds of a few others. The cold sank its teeth through his thin nylon jacket. It made his back ache. He waited. He wasn't waiting for Abu Fahoum; no one went for walks in weather like this. He was waiting for the night to be over.

Rehv stamped his feet a couple of times and wriggled his toes. He wanted to start the car and turn on the heater, but he remembered the silvery billows that cars exhale on cold nights, and thought the doorman might notice. Parked silently in the shadows it was just another empty car. He tried singing: "When the Saints Go Marching In," "La Cucaracha," "Hava Nagila." His voice sounded harsh and brittle and somehow frightening in the confined space. The notes shriveled into tuneless muttering.

In the distance Rehv saw a patch of yellow light run across the faces of the stone buildings. A taxi turned off one of the broad avenues and onto the deserted street, pointing its headlights at Rehv. He slid lower in the seat, watching from behind the steering wheel. The taxi approached slowly, almost haltingly. Rehv could sense the driver scanning the brass or wrought-iron numbers on the doorposts. The taxi stopped in front of the thick glass doors.

The doorman in the chocolate uniform came forward and

looked outside. He turned his face back toward the lobby; his lips moved. He pushed hard against one of the doors and held it open. The wind must have been pushing the other way, Rehv thought. A man walked through. He was tall and dark, and wore a thick black leather coat that almost touched the ground. He seemed to shrink inside it as he felt the wind. It made him hurry toward the taxi. The doorman was quicker: He got there first to open the door. To reach into the pocket of his trousers the dark man had to undo most of the buttons of his coat. The doorman waited patiently. Money changed hands. The dark man sat down inside the taxi. He wasn't wearing a white robe or a black-and-white checked keffiyeh, but he was still Abu Fahoum. The doorman closed the door.

The taxi pulled away. Rehv started the motor of Harry's car, made a sharp U-turn, and followed. He felt the cold and heavy gun tucked inside his shirt: a Smith & Wesson .38 with a silencer attached. The silencer reminded him of condoms, although there was no analogy at all.

The taxi headed downtown. There was very little traffic. Rehv followed closely. He had seen that New York taxi drivers were often unpredictable, and he expected this one at any moment to run a red light or push the accelerator to the floor. Instead he drove almost sedately through the empty midtown streets. When he reached the middle forties he turned west, onto a street of garish signs and gaudy lights. After he had gone a block or two the driver drew over to the curb. Rehv slowed but kept going, careful to keep his face hidden as he passed. In the rearview mirror he saw Abu Fahoum pay the driver and enter a seedy cinema. Sheba said the sign in red neon.

Rehv parked and got out of the car.

"My friend," someone called to him from the shadows of a doorway. Rehv said nothing and turned toward the cinema. A black man stepped out of the doorway. He was very tall, at least a head taller than Rehv, and very thin. "My friend," he said again, blocking Rehv's path. "How about some nice soft pussy?" The black man had a voice like a honey-coated knife. He wore a pink suit and red shoes, but no coat. He was tall and strange and dangerous, but his lips were blue and his teeth were chattering. Rehv pushed past.

"Soft pussy, you motherfucker," the black man shouted at his back, but Rehv heard little anger in his voice. "Soft," he repeated more quietly, urgently, as if it had been on that point that negotiations had broken down.

Rehv walked quickly to the cinema and pulled at the door handle. A dark-colored van went slowly by, distracting him for a moment. The wind caught the door and blew it wide open with an angry scraping of metal on metal.

"Shut the fuckin' door," someone yelled from inside. Rehv jerked it closed and entered the lobby.

It was cramped, ill lit, and dirty, but he noticed none of that at first. He noticed the smells: armpit sweat, foot sweat, crotch sweat, urine. And other smells that he couldn't identify precisely, but were all bodily. At the end of the lobby a stained and shabby curtain hung across a narrow doorway. In front of the doorway was a small booth, enclosed completely by clear plastic walls. In the booth sat a fat, bald man with mustard on his cheek and a thick salami in his hand.

"You think it's summertime or something?" the fat man asked. He bit angrily on the salami. Rehv could not remember having seen a fatter man. Fat hung in pouches under his shirt and under his chin; its invasion of his face was almost complete: Only two pinprick eyes remained to show that there had once been defined features.

Rehv approached the booth. "One admission please," he said.

"One admission please," the fat man mimicked in the voice of a cabaret homosexual. Rehv felt himself becoming angry, not because he cared what the fat man said, but because he was drawing attention to himself. "Five bucks," the fat man said, forcing the words around the meat in his mouth.

Rehv slipped a bill into the slot and walked toward the dirty curtain. As he drew it aside he realized that the tiny eyes had never once focused on his face. Maybe the man had grown tired of looking at the kind of people who came into his lobby; maybe he couldn't see past the salami.

Rehv stepped inside the theater. It was very dark. He waited for a minute or two until his pupils dilated. The theater was much bigger than he would have guessed, as large as those that showed the latest expensive features from Hollywood. Nothing like that was playing at the Sheba. On the screen a black man was sitting on a sprung and tattered couch. An overweight white woman sat on his lap with her back to him. His penis appeared to be partway inside her rectum. In a tinny voice she told the black man, or perhaps no one in particular, that it made her feel nice. But she sounded quite bored, and the words weren't synchronized with the movements of her mouth. The actress bounced up and down a couple of times. The actor was looking off to the side. After a few moments another man appeared from that direction. He wore a cowboy outfit. Soon he didn't. He tried to push his penis into the actress's vagina. She said it felt nice, and attempted to bounce up and down again, but couldn't. None of the principals seemed able to move at all. The camera went to a close-up of the two penises, vagina and anus, but the lens was very much out of focus: It showed a close-up of a large and indeterminate shape, something that might wash up on a beach after a gale, and that might have once been alive.

Rehv swept his eyes over the rows of seats. In very tight ranks they descended right to the foot of the screen, as though every inch of space saved meant more money for the owner. But there were few customers: Here and there a solitary figure slouched in the shadows.

Rehv moved slowly down the aisle, careful to make no noise. In a row near the front he saw a lone silhouette that seemed to sit taller than the others. Rehv went nearer. The silhouette moved slightly, catching a gleam of light in the wrinkle of a leather coat. It glistened like the skin of a black snake. Quietly Rehv walked down the aisle. He turned into an empty row and moved along it in a crouch. In the middle of the row he stopped and very gently sat down, directly behind Abu Fahoum.

Abu Fahoum did not sense his presence. His eyes were on the screen. Another actress had entered. She was skinny, and looked very young. She pulled the black man's penis out of the over-weight women's anus and took it in her mouth. The camera moved in for a close-up. The girl raised the corners of her mouth in a grin. Abu Fahoum moaned softly.

Rehv took out the gun. "Just be sure you are too close to miss and pull the trigger," Harry had told him. "When you are finished drop the gun and walk away. It is untraceable." The army had taught him guns. He was no marksman, but more than good enough for this.

Abu Fahoum's seat squeaked. Rehv felt him straining against it. The metallic back touched his knees, and he drew away.

"Now," came a voice from the screen. Rehv looked up. The

girl pulled the black penis from her mouth. It dribbled weakly. Semen fell on her cheek. She grinned again. Abu Fahoum moaned. Rehv stood up and held the gun two inches from the back of Abu Fahoum's head.

A little movement made him glance down, over Abu Fahoum's shoulder. The thick leather coat was unbuttoned. Abu Fahoum's zipper was open and his legs were spread wide. A girl knelt on the floor between them. She was licking the tip of his penis with her pointed tongue.

Rehv felt the gun in his hand, felt the trigger against his finger, but he could not squeeze it. Even the thought of Lena could not make him do it. He stood motionless. Deep within his consciousness he heard the screaming start. Only very dimly did he sense a slight form slipping toward him along the row. He dropped the gun. Abu Fahoum turned, startled. The little form moved quickly in front of Rehv. Steel flashed. A blade bit into Abu Fahoum's neck. He rose turning from his seat, eyes huge and white, and toppled onto the girl. She screamed a scream that everyone could hear.

The killer took his arm. "Come," he said. By the grainy light of the screen Rehv saw the face that was half dead.

"Come," Harry said again, and led him up the aisle. None of the slouching figures moved at all. Whatever had happened in the dark was no business of theirs. In the lobby the fat man was counting money. He did not look up as they left.

They sat silently in the dark green van. Harry drove. Rehv listened to the screaming slowly die away. The wind blew trash cans across the streets. Harry guided the van through SoHo. He stopped in front of the building where the gallery was and turned to Rehv.

"Good-bye," he said. "I have no use for you."

Rehv set the camp cot down beside the falling Gordon and lay down. He pulled the covers up to his neck and curled into a ball. Gordon loomed above him in the darkness. Crumpet Gordon with his eyes of jam, forever falling. The jam eyes gazed down fiercely, refusing to admit vulnerability even then, refusing to acknowledge doom. Harry's eyes were like that. But they were blue, and Gordon's were strawberry. Blue for Israel and red for England. There was still an England, Rehv thought, no matter what it had come to.

In his mind he saw a little patch of land where he would like to lie down. A little patch of land where they were buried. He would never see it again. Like Gordon they were all doomed, but they had no Kitchener to avenge them, no Kitchener to come and make everything the way it was. Harry thought it was 1948 all over again, but it was not. There was no Jewish Agency, no American money, no Zionism, no men, no arms. There would only be an Israel if the Arabs gave it back to them.

For a long time Rehv lay in the fetal position beneath the strawberry gaze. The wind rattled the windows. He closed his eyes and began to dream of the desert and General Gordon and the warrior hordes of the Mahdi who had killed him. He sank deeper into sleep. The desert grew broader, the hordes vaster. He rode with them on a huge black horse. Faster and faster he rode. He led them. The hooves of the great black horse scarcely touched the ground. The warriors followed him, filling the whole desert. Invincible. Nothing could stand before him. He was the wind.

When Isaac Rehv awoke, he was not the same man.

CHAPTER SIX

Krebs spent part of the night in bed and part of it on the couch in the den. This was not unusual: A blanket waited for him there, folded on the bottom shelf of the liquor cabinet, a mute and commonplace symbol of the difficulties of his marriage.

He had come home late from the office, eaten a ham sandwich, and gone to bed, thinking of Armbrister and his salmon steaks. Alice arrived much later. Krebs listened to her turn the car into the drive. He heard a new squeak. She made no effort at all to maintain the car, but he never said anything. It was her car, bought with money her father had given her.

Krebs heard her footsteps on the stairs, slightly too heavy, slightly unsteady, and heard her go into the bathroom. He heard her urinate and flush the toilet. He didn't hear her wash her hands or her face or brush her teeth. He knew her too well to attribute this to the sound of the toilet flushing.

She came to the bed. He kept his eyes closed.

"Robert?" she said in a stage whisper. He said nothing. First he smelled a little puff of whisky breath, then he felt the mattress undulate beneath him as she got into bed. Krebs was about to fall asleep when he felt the light touch of her hand on his thigh. It was very light. He knew it was meant to be flirtatious and sexy. Without looking he knew exactly the expression on her face: eyes big and coy, lips slightly parted in anxiety and expectation. He hated that expression.

They made love, or had intercourse, or performed the sex act: He didn't know what to call these infrequent attempts. Krebs kept his eyes closed the whole time, and tried to imagine he was inside the hard girl who brought him coffee. But Alice wasn't hard. She was soft and plump.

"That's too rough, Robert," she said. But it was over anyway. The whole time hadn't lasted long enough. Her body went very still, waiting rigidly for him to move off her. Then she rolled to her side of the bed and pulled the blankets over her like armor plate. He was wide awake. He sensed her tense body across the sheets, full of complicated emotion. After a while he got out of bed and went down to the den. As he left he heard her make a soft sound between her teeth.

Much later he slept. He dreamed of cows under the sea. He had not finished dreaming of them when the telephone rang. Krebs was always very quick to shake off sleep. The telephone sat on a little desk on the far side of the room, but he answered it before the second ring.

"Krebs?" It was Armbrister.

"I've got it, Alice," Krebs said. He waited. "I've got it, thank you," he said again. He heard a muffled click, and the connection with Armbrister became less diffuse.

"Separate bedrooms?" Armbrister said, sounding pleasantly surprised.

"I was just up doing some paperwork."

"Good for you. Since you're up anyway a drive to Manhattan won't be such an annoyance. Your friend from the East has run into some difficulty. Forty-third and Seventh. The Sheba."

"We'll meet there?"

"No. It's a one-man job."

Krebs hung up. It was too much of an annoyance for Armbrister to go, although he lived in Manhattan. Krebs lived in New Jersey.

He went to the window and looked out between the curtains. It was still very dark, but there would be no point in coming home after he looked in at the Sheba. He would go right to the office. Since he was up for the day, he lay prone on the floor, dug his toes into the broadloom, spread his hands, and pushed his body up until his arms were fully extended. He did this ninety-nine more times, counting in a grunting whisper. The last dozen grunts grew louder and further apart. Krebs put it down to lack of sleep.

Upstairs he quickly shaved and showered. He went into the bedroom and found what clothing he could in the dark. He carried it into the hall, closing the door behind him. He knew Alice was awake because he heard the little sound she made between her teeth.

As he drove into Manhattan the sky became lighter: a gritty colorless budget-priced dawn with no extra-cost options. As morning seeped through the clouds the wind began to die, as if there was a fixed supply of energy to power the atmosphere, and all the elements had to share it.

A city patrolman stood in front of the Sheba cinema. His face was oily and needed a shave. He looked at Krebs suspiciously the way policemen do after a crime has been committed. Krebs identified himself and went inside.

Yellow overhead lights had been switched on in the theater. They exposed it mercilessly, like a cop's flashlight on the face of an old whore. Three men stood near the front, two wearing uniforms, one a duffle coat. Krebs joined them.

"You Krebs?" the one in the duffle coat said. He had a bad cold. Krebs nodded. "Christ, you took your time getting here. They said we couldn't move anything until you showed up."

"I live in New Jersey," Krebs said.

"Christ," the man in the duffle coat said again.

Krebs looked down at what was wedged between the seats. The three men watched him look. "Had his throat cut from ear to ear. First time I've really seen it," one of the uniformed men said. "Course I've seen plenty of throats cut," he added quickly. "Plenty. But not like this. Ear to ear."

But Krebs saw it wasn't like that at all. The point of a sharp and narrow knife had been stuck deeply into the side of the neck, then the edge of the blade had sliced forward through the front. The throat had been cut from the inside out by someone who knew how.

They waited for him to say something.

"Any witnesses?"

"Not so far," the man in the duffle coat replied. He pulled a dirty Kleenex from his pocket and blew his nose, making a little explosion that the big empty room blew back at them. "The manager didn't see this until the show was over. He says he always checks that no one's passed out on the floor or something like that."

"How many customers were there?"

"Don't know."

60

"Where's the manager?"

"Got him in the car."

"I'd like to talk to him. First get him to count the take."

"Ferguson," the man in the duffle coat said to the cop who was seeing his first ear-to-ear. Ferguson started walking up the aisle. "And bring me some Kleenex," he called after him. "There's a box under the seat." They watched Ferguson go through a soiled red curtain. "One other thing," the plainclothesman said to Krebs. "There was a girl. Sucking him off. She was kind of trapped under the body." Mention of the word drew their eyes back down to the fact on the floor. "She wasn't hurt or anything. Shock, maybe."

"She's in the car too?"

"Yes."

Ferguson returned with the Kleenex and a fat man. "Nine tickets sold," he said to Krebs. He handed the Kleenex to the plainclothesman.

"I'm tired. I want to go home," the fat man said in a self-pitying tone.

"Shut your mouth," the plainclothesman said. He blew his nose.

"What's your name?" Krebs asked the fat man.

"Melvin."

"I just want to ask you a few questions, Mr. Melvin. Then you can go."

"Melvin's my first name."

"Shut your mouth," the plainclothesman repeated. The rims of his nostrils were red and sore. "Fatso," he added.

"Nine customers, Melvin," Krebs said. "Is that right?"

"Yeah."

"That means just nine faces to remember. That's not too many, is it?"

"I don't remember nothin'."

"Do you remember when the dead man came in?"

"No."

"Was he with the girl?"

"I don't know."

Krebs turned to the plainclothesman. "How old is the girl?"

"Thirteen, fourteen."

"Did you hear that, Melvin? If she's not a very young-looking eighteen it may not be so good for you."

"I don't look at faces, mister," the fat man whined. "I just take the money, that's all. Why should I look at faces? They's just jerks that come in here. They come, I take the money, they beat off. That's all."

"Christ," the plainclothesman said.

"I don't need him anymore," Krebs told him. He went to talk to the girl. He heard the fat man say:

"You're not going to charge me or nothin'?"

"Shut up, fatso," the plainclothesman replied. "If you can't shut up on your own, Baker'll help you. He likes that when he's tired. Tired, Baker?"

"Beat," said the cop who had not spoken.

The girl sat in the back seat of an unmarked car. There was another uniformed cop behind the wheel. He was working on a crossword puzzle.

Krebs sat beside the girl. She was small and fair. She wore a lot of makeup, but it didn't hide her freckles. Her hair was long and blond and curly, like the hair of Irish girls in soap commercials; except hers was matted with blood. There was more on her jeans. And her sweatshirt with the picture on the front—Porky Pig, Krebs noticed.

"What's your name?" he asked in the gentlest voice he could manage.

"Neon."

"That's a nice name. How old are you?"

"Nineteen."

"Really? I'd have said twenty."

She looked up at him, squinting. "What do you mean?" Her voice was light and high.

"I meant it as a compliment," Krebs said.

"Thank you." She brushed a lock of hair out of her eyes, leaving a trail of blood across her forehead.

"I know you're upset," Krebs said, "but I need to ask you a couple of questions."

"I'm not upset."

"Good. Then maybe you'll tell me how long you knew the dead man."

"He's not dead."

"Yes, he is," Krebs said, dropping some of the gentleness from his tone. "When all the blood pours out of people that way, they're dead."

She looked up at him again, and stared for a few moments. Krebs didn't think she was seeing anything in particular.

"So?" she said at last.

"Would you like to help me find whoever killed him?" Krebs remembered saying something like that to someone else quite recently.

"I don't know."

"You can help me a lot," Krebs said. "What was his name?"

"Who? My date?"

"Yes."

"Ab."

"Ab what?"

"Just Ab."

"Was it your first date?"

"No."

"Second?"

She closed her eyes tightly, like someone recalling something from long ago. After a little while she nodded. Her eyes stayed closed.

"Did he call for you tonight?"

"What?"

"Did he come to get you in his car? Or a taxi?"

"No."

"You met him here?"

She nodded.

"How did you know to do that?"

"He told me to."

"When?"

"The other time." She tugged the lock of hair back over her eyes, as if the eyelids weren't cover enough.

"How did you meet him the first time?"

"On the street. I'm good at meeting people." The eyes opened; they were a golden brown and might have been pretty once, when they still had some life. Six weeks ago, or a month.

"How much did Ab pay you?"

The eyes closed. "He gave me a present."

"How much?"

"It was a present. I don't have to tell about a present."

"Twenty bucks? Ten?" From her eyes he could see it was more like ten.

"Did he give you a present tonight?"

"Not yet."

"What do you mean, not yet? Don't be stupid." She shrank into the door. He lowered his voice. "Now, I want you to tell me what happened in there tonight. Did you see anybody sneak up behind Ab?"

"No."

"Or hear any strange noises?"

"No."

"Tell me what you remember."

"Ab stood up. Then he fell down. On top of me." She opened her eyes; maybe she didn't want to be alone with the memory.

"Okay," Krebs said to her. "That's all for now. We're going to take you home. Where do you live?"

"Nowhere."

Krebs got out of the car. The cop behind the wheel turned and said over his shoulder: "What's a five-letter word for upright?" Krebs closed the door.

He drove to the office in heavy traffic. For some reason he didn't feel very tired. Cars coughed dirt into the dirty sky.

Krebs sat at his desk. The hard girl brought him coffee. "You're in early," he said.

"I'm always here at this hour." He noticed for the first time how educated her voice sounded.

He took the pot of coffee from her. "Smells good today," he said. She didn't reply, and moved toward the door. Instead of fastening his eyes to her buttocks Krebs opened his mouth and said, "What's a five-letter word for upright?"

"Erect," the coffee girl said as she closed the door behind her.

Krebs turned to his in-basket. On top he found a list of names with a note attached. The note said: "Names not easy to find. Restaurant closed for a week. Hope this is accurate enough." He didn't recognize the scrawled initials at the bottom.

He looked at the list, and began dividing the names by ethnic group: two French, six Spanish or Portuguese, nine Italian, three Greek, four Anglo-Saxon. And a man named Isaac Rehv. Krebs circled Isaac Rehv in black ink.

CHAPTER SEVEN

Snow fell in lumpy overnourished shapes that had lost the light parachuting grace of normal snowflakes. They were modern result-oriented snowflakes, dropping in plumb lines and covering the hills and fields as fast as possible in cold meringue. Although the snow had been coming down like that for hours, the clouds were no lighter or higher or thinner. The meringue slowly rose to meet them.

Through this dense white air the silver bus moved far too quickly, wrapped in a cocoon of salted frost and frozen mud. Beneath his feet Isaac Rehv could sense nothing at all of rubber treads clinging to the asphalt: The bus seemed to float like a dirigible. He saw that the driver was unaware of any danger. All her concentration appeared to be focused on the toothpick stuck in the side of her mouth. She was oblivious to the weather and, he noticed, to her own personal snowfall as well—a sparse crescent that had settled on the gray shoulders of her uniform.

Rehv didn't mind how fast she drove. He was in a hurry. It seemed a long time since he had felt hurried about anything, but that morning, under the red eyes of General Gordon, he had dressed quickly and been halfway out the door when he had met Quentin Katz coming the other way.

"Good morning, Quentin," he had said, trying to squeeze by.

But Katz had taken him by the arm. "Big news," Katz had said. "I've got a lead on a good job."

"I didn't know you were looking for a good job."

Katz had laughed. He had seemed unusually full of physical

energy. His flesh wasn't used to it, and jiggled from the internal vibration. "Not for me. For you." He had turned Rehv around and marched him back into the gallery.

"I was just on my way out, Quentin."

"So? What's more important than this?" Some of the energy had been diverted into annoyance, and the jiggling stopped. "I'm talking about a good job, a twenty-five-grand-a-year job, and that's just for starters."

Rehv had sighed deeply, trying to exhale some of his impatience. "What is it?"

"That's better. Actually you've got Sheila to thank, not me. She met the head of modern languages at NYU last night. He said they're looking for someone in the Arabic department." Katz had looked up at him brightly, as though he had just performed a clever trick. Rehv had said nothing. The brightness in Katz's eyes had faded a little, and he had brushed his hand tentatively across the top of his head, perhaps to confirm that his hair was really gone. "Naturally she mentioned you. He wants you to send him your CV."

"I'll think about it, Quentin." Rehv had moved toward the door.

"What's to think? They're desperate and you've got the goods. Stop going out the door every second. Sit down and have a cup of coffee. I'll tell you the details."

"I haven't got time."

"How about Brazilian? We've got Santos and Paraná."

Rehv had shut the door and gone down the stairs. He had heard Katz muttering to himself as he went away: He had probably wanted a more definite commitment to report to Sheila.

The bus swept through a small quiet town. It rolled by Rehv's window like a film going too fast: old oaks and elms bearing snow instead of leaves, tidy white houses with black shutters and snow piled high and round on the roofs, a simple white church with a narrow steeple. He understood where Christmas cards came from.

A woman leaned across the aisle. "That's the Congregational church," she told him, quite loudly. She was a middle-aged woman with well-cut gray hair, clear skin, and clear gray eyes. She wore a heavy gold cross around her neck, and seemed too rich to be riding the bus. "Some of the churches around here are really beautiful, aren't they?"

66

"I don't know this area very well," Rehv replied.

"I thought so," the woman said happily, leaning a little farther. "The Lord made me notice the way you were looking out the window, praise Him."

She paused, and tilted her handsome face up to his, expectantly. Rehv suddenly felt he was in the midst of a liturgy and the next line was his. He remembered Quentin Katz talking of the Christian country that lay beyond Manhattan. It was an odd place for the prime minister of Israel to be living.

"I'm very interested in churches." The woman was still leaning across the aisle. She spoke loudly and clearly, as one whose life is open to all, without fear or shame or secrets. The few passengers scattered through the bus seemed unaware of her. "Not just the church, but churches, if you see what I mean," she continued. "I've photographed thousands of them. They're all in albums at home. It's a big job, but I never get tired when I'm doing the Lord's work." She lowered her voice very slightly: "I've been to the Seven Churches of Asia." She wasn't telling him a secret, he realized: She was just being modest.

"You've done some traveling, then?" Rehv said.

She resumed her normal tone. "Oh, yes. Ever since Baron passed on I've done nothing but. The Lord has seen fit to give me all the money I could ever need."

Rehv noticed that she felt no need to be modest about that, and supposed she had been guarded about the visit to the Seven Churches because it was a spiritual, not material accomplishment. Rehv thought she should be guarded about the money too: He saw that one or two people had turned to look at her as soon as she had mentioned it.

The bus entered another town, much like the last except the church was bigger and made of stone.

"Episcopal," the woman said, as they drove past. "This was very religious country once," she went on, keeping her eyes on it. "Jonathan Edwards. Winthrop. The City on a Hill."

"And the Salem witches," Rehv said, before he could stop himself.

Slowly the woman turned toward him. She had a serene smile on her face. "And it's going to be a very religious country again," she said. "Praise the Lord."

The bus stopped in front of a small cafe in the center of the town, and Rehv got off. He wondered whether Baron was a title, the name of her husband, or the name of her dog. He went inside the cafe. Two big men wearing bulky coats sat at the counter, their backs to him. One was handing a cylindrical sugar dispenser to the other. The old woman behind the counter looked up. The glare from the light striking the greasy lenses of her glasses hid her eyes.

"I'm looking for the Tehiyyah Kibbutz," Rehv said to her.

The sugar dispenser stopped in midair, two thick hands wrapped around it. "That would be the old Cutler farm," the woman said in a high, brittle voice. "First right after the Mobil station."

"Is it far?"

"Two miles."

"Thank you." He turned to go. The sugar dispenser resumed its journey.

Two miles was far enough when the roads weren't plowed and the snow lay knee-high. Ice wedged inside Rehv's shoes and up his pant legs, soaking his feet, ankles, and calves. The snow fell silently. Once he left the town he saw no people, no buildings. He heard only the muffled tramp of his feet, and his own excited breathing.

He reached the top of a small hill and paused to brush the snow from his hair. In the distance he saw a large isolated farmhouse, surrounded on every side by empty rolling fields; he saw a barn, several smaller outbuildings, and three long trailers parked by the side of the house; he saw a wooden flagpole, not very high, flying the Star of David. He saw the headquarters of the Israeli government-in-exile, a government recognized by no one. The capital of Israel.

He began running to it, slipping and sliding in the snow. He was breathless when he reached the wooden gate. Inside the gate was a car with an official crest on the side. The door opened and a Vermont state trooper got out. He wore sunglasses.

"Training for the marathon, pal?" he said. He opened his coat to show the gun on his hip, but he didn't bother drawing it.

"I'm an Israeli," Rehv said. "I want to go inside."

"Oh yeah?" A snowflake landed on the left lens of his sunglasses and clung there like a white spider. "No one told me about any visitors." He tried to dislodge the snowflake by twitching his cheek, but it stayed where it was. Perhaps he had a tic.

"I'm sure they'll see me," Rehv said. They stood watching each other over the top of the gate. The white spider melted and dribbled off the trooper's lens and onto his cheek. It twitched again. After a while he decided he didn't want to stand outside anymore.

"You wait here," he said to Rehv, and walked toward the house.

"Tell them I was a lieutenant in the army and an assistant professor at the Hebrew University," Rehv called to him.

The trooper showed no sign of having heard. He knocked at the door. It opened. Rehv saw a dark-haired woman in a red plaid shirt. The trooper said something to her. She looked over his shoulder at Rehv. He realized what she must see, his wet hair over his forehead, his cheap nylon jacket, his trousers wet to the thigh. The woman nodded. The trooper turned and came back to the gate.

"Okay," he said, pulling it open. "But first I need ID." Rehv handed him the plastic card he had been given at Immigration. The trooper copied from it into his notebook. Rehv turned to go. "Not so fast. I've got to search you." Rehv raised his arms to shoulder level. The trooper took off his leather gloves, stuck them between his teeth, and patted his hands up and down Rehv's limbs and over his body. "Looking to catch pneumonia, pal?" he asked, his words muffled by the gloves. "You're turning blue."

Rehv walked to the front door. "My name's Isaac Rehv," he said to the woman in Hebrew. "I want to see the prime minister, please."

"What about?" she replied in English.

Chinese Gordon, Rehv thought. "It's confidential," he said. "I wouldn't feel right telling anyone else. That's for him to decide."

For a moment she looked at him without saying anything. She had large brown eyes and thick hair of the same shade. It needed washing. Wrinkled indigo depressions were stamped under both eyes, like brands of fatigue or worry. She motioned him inside. "You should get out of those clothes, Mr. Rehv."

"I'm all right."

Inside the front hall it was cold and dark and quiet. A long corridor stretched away into the shadows. He saw several doors, all closed. He thought of kibbutzim as noisy and busy, but there

69

were no sounds of children playing or work being done. Maybe it was because of the winter.

Somewhere nearby a man was talking on the telephone: "In that case put me on to his assistant," he said with irritation in his voice. There was a pause. Then he spoke again, more angrily: "But I've been leaving messages for a week." Another pause, slightly longer. "No, I have not been out when he calls. I'm never out." Rehv heard plastic strike plastic. On one side a door opened. A man stood in the doorway. His face seemed familiar. Rehv remembered seeing it from time to time in Israeli newspapers.

"I can't even get through to the assistant to the assistant undersecretary," he said to the woman. His tone was very bitter. Rehv thought he heard a certain pleasure in it too, the pleasure of self-hatred being fed. The woman opened her mouth to say something and then closed it. "I can't even get past the goddamned secretary," the man said, his voice rising with every syllable. He banged the palm of his hand hard against the doorjamb. Rehv felt a light vibration in the walls.

"Don't," the woman said gently, and with some fear.

He rounded on her. "Don't. Sure. Don't." He was gritting his teeth so hard Rehv thought they would crack.

"Excuse me," he said.

The man noticed him for the first time. "Who are you?"

"My name is Isaac Rehv. I hope I haven't come at a bad time. I want to see the prime minister."

"It's a splendid time," the man said sarcastically. "What makes you think we have bad times around here?"

"Mr. Rehv was a professor at the Hebrew University," the woman said quickly.

"Mazel tov." The man and the woman exchanged a look. Something in it made him inhale deeply and try to assert some control over himself. He turned to Rhev. "What do you want to see him about?"

"I'm sorry," Rehv said quietly, afraid he might knock the man's temper loose again. "I don't want to tell anyone but him. After, if he permits, I'll be happy to tell you."

The man smiled a cold smile. Rehv did not understand its meaning at all. "I'm not sure you see the situation," the man said. "I am his chief assistant. The deputy prime minister. The cabinet. The Knesset. Everything goes through me."

70

"I'm sorry," Rehv said.

"Then I'm sorry."

Rehv felt confusion begin to undermine his resolve. He looked at the woman for some kind of help. She was looking at the floor. He turned again to the man: "But what about the government-in-exile? There must be some sort of procedure."

"I am the government-in-exile," the man said. Something in the way he said it made Rehv remember who he was: a right-wing politician who had pushed for the annexation of the Golan Heights.

"In that case," Rehv said, "the prime minister will certainly let you know whatever I tell him."

The man laughed. "Do you really think so?" He turned to the woman and spoke to her in a voice that was suddenly crisp and unemotional, as if he had tired of sport and was impatient to return to business: "Very well. Let him see the prime minister."

"How is he feeling?" the woman asked worriedly.

"Tip-top. The prime minister is always feeling tip-top." The man withdrew into the room he had come from and closed the door.

The woman sighed. "I hope this is important," she said to Rehv as she led him down the long corridor.

"It could be very important." She sighed once more, as though nothing could ever be important again.

At the end of the corridor she paused before a closed door, and knocked softly.

"Come in," a man answered immediately in Hebrew. Rehv had heard that voice many times.

"Don't keep him too long," the woman said to Rehv. "He tires very easily." She opened the door.

Rehv walked into a room lined with books. A small fire burned in the grate. There was a faded couch along one wall and a worn easy chair by the fire. The old general was sitting in it with a wool blanket drawn over his knees. He seemed to be asleep: His chest rose and fell in slow even rhythm; his face, fleshy in the days when he was planting Jewish settlements on the West Bank, was now thin. And very old. There was no one else in the room.

Rehv walked quietly to the couch and sat down. He waited as patiently as he could, his idea struggling to burst up through his throat. In the grate a log cracked loudly, shooting a fan of sparks up the chimney. With a little start the old general awoke, and stared directly at Rehv.

"Don't talk to me about the British," he said in Hebrew. "I'm finished with the British. The British are a tricky people. Look at the Balfour Report: 'a home *in* Palestine for the Jewish people.' Only tricky people know how to make such trouble with prepositions." He glared at Rehv.

"I haven't come to talk about the British, General," Rehv said. "I've had some thoughts about what our course of action might be."

The general looked annoyed. "Thoughts. We don't need thoughts. We need tanks. If we had more tanks we could be on the canal in three days. Tanks are the answer. Nasser is helpless against tanks. Why doesn't anyone understand that? It's so simple."

Rehv looked out the window at the falling snow.

"Why?" the general repeated. He had not been putting a rhetorical question.

"I don't know, General."

"Of course you don't. Throw another log on the fire. I'm cold."

Rehv went to the wood basket by the fireplace, selected a split birch log and dropped it into the grate. "Is one enough?" There was no answer. Rehv looked at the general. His eyes were closed.

Softly Rehv approached him. The old man's chest rose and fell slowly; the thin face was at rest. Rehv pulled the blanket a little higher and left the room.

There was no one in the corridor, no one in the hall. Outside, the snow still fell heavily, covering the trooper's car in thick white pile. The trooper sat on the front seat with his head thrown back and his mouth open. Rehv could not be sure if his eyes were shut because of the sunglasses. Anyone could easily rush the farm and wipe out the government of Israel. Who would want to?

Rehv walked back along the road.

CHAPTER EIGHT

"Why are people so afraid of violence these days?" the little gray-haired woman on the television was asking. The camera tightened on her face, projecting into homes from coast to coast her cunning brown eyes: a Jewish grandmother on the make. "It's become a fad. Whenever you tell someone about a new movie, it's the first question they ask: 'Is it violent? I don't go to violent movies.' Why is this happening?"

The director cut to the interviewer, a middle-aged man dressed, made-up, and lit to look like a Princeton senior. Kick her in the shins, Rehv thought. Then she'll know. But instead the interviewer smiled and said very drily, "I have a feeling you're going to tell us." This was just what the laugh track wanted to hear. It also seemed to please the interviewer, who managed to keep himself from laughing aloud, although he permitted his eyes to twinkle mischievously, and the sly woman, who opened her mouth and emitted sounds to show she knew something amusing had just taken place. But Rehv could see from her eyes that she was impatient for the fun to be over so she could squeeze in a few more cutting phrases before the closing theme. She was a violent woman.

"I want to watch something else," Joshua Katz-Finkle said. Rehv hadn't heard him come into the room. He was standing at the door with his hair in his eyes and two trails of mucus running from his nostrils.

"Have you finished your homework?"

"Yes," Joshua said defiantly. He was a very poor liar, even for a seven-year-old.

"All right."

The boy came into the room, took the remote-control box from the arm of the couch, and lay prone on the rug in front of the television. He watched everything the television had to offer at once, never staying with one channel for more than fifteen or twenty seconds.

Rehv removed his shoes and socks. They were still damp. He wriggled his toes and arched his feet. He never thought they were really his, those feet: long and narrow and weak, like the feet of an El Greco saint. They didn't match the rest of him.

"P.U.," Joshua said. He was looking at Rehv's feet with disgust, his nose drawn slightly down as if the nostrils were trying to close themselves.

"Don't be rude," Rehv said.

"You're the one who's being rude. Stinking up the place like that. It's disgusting."

"Watch TV."

The boy jabbed rapidly at the remote-control box, threatening to watch with a vengeance. On the screen images appeared and vanished as fast as they could be identified: a smiling housewife, a man wearing a diaper, a box of detergent looming over a crowd of people, Marlon Brando trying to mount a horse.

Rehv stood up and went to the window. It was a very large window, shaped like a half-moon, and overlooked the northern half of SoHo and Greenwich Village. The apartment was at the top of one of the tallest cast-iron buildings in SoHo—an official historical landmark, Quentin Katz had told him the first time he had come to baby-sit. It was owned by Sheila Finkle's father and his brothers. A small sign by the front door said: "Another Finkle Property."

The snow had stopped falling. The sky had cleared. He could see a few stars that were strong enough to penetrate the umbrella of pink light over the city. One of them was Betelgeuse, much redder than usual. Bayt al-jawza', of course. It was Arabic. He watched it glowing red in the pink sky, and thought for some reason of the Star of David on its little pole. It made the screaming start, far away.

He turned to the boy. He was propped up on his elbows

watching a man wrestle a calf to the ground. "Come here for a minute, Josh. I want to show you something."

"What?"

"Come. You'll like it."

The boy slowly rose and backed to the window, his eyes locked on the screen. Rehv turned him around and pointed to the sky. "Do you know what star that is?"

"What do you mean, what star?"

"The name of it. Don't they teach you the stars in school?"

"Sure. The Big Dipper."

"What else?"

"The Little Dipper."

"Any others?"

"I don't know."

"Here's another one, then. Do you see that star? The red one?"

"It's white."

"Look carefully."

"It's white."

The screaming came a little closer. He bent over the boy. "It's called Betelgeuse. That's an Arab word. It forms the shoulder of Orion, the hunter."

"I don't see any hunter."

"That's because the sky's too light."

"What do you mean, light? It's nighttime." The boy wiped his nose on his sleeve, looked at it, and wiped the sleeve on the leg of his jeans. He glanced curiously at Rehv, wondering if there would be a reprimand.

Rehv pointed again to the sky. "What's the name of the star?"

"I don't remember."

"Try."

"I don't want to," the boy said. "I'm tired of looking out the window. I want to watch TV."

"Try," Rehv said again. Something in his voice seemed to frighten the boy. He took a step back, and his lower lip quivered very slightly, as though a tiny electric current had run through it.

"Beetle something."

"Good, Josh." He tried to speak in a quiet even tone. "Betelgeuse. Say it."

"Beetle juice." Another current ran through the thin lip.

75

"Close enough. Do you know any other Arab words?"

"No."

"Yes you do. Zero is an Arab word. Except in Arabic it's *sifr*. Sifr. Say it."

"No. I'm going to watch TV." The boy turned. Rehv grabbed his arm.

"Sifr. Say it."

The current ran stronger now, and didn't stop. Neither did the screaming. "See fur."

"Sifr. Try again."

"I don't want to."

"Sifr."

"Hey. What's going on?" Rehv and the boy turned. The boy's parents were standing in the doorway, wearing their coats. "What's going on?" Katz said again. Rehv took his hand from Josh's arm. The boy began to cry. Sheila ran across the room and lifted him in her arms.

"What's he done to you, my precious boy?" He was crying too hard to tell her.

"I didn't mean Josh any harm," Rehv said. The screaming withdrew into the distance. His voice seemed to be someone else's, high and strained. He had to fight to make it his own.

Sheila looked at him with hatred. "His name is Joshua," she said. "If we had wanted people to call him Josh we would have named him Josh, wouldn't we?"

Rehv had no answer. He looked down, and saw his bare, pale feet, with black hairs curling on the toes. He tried to remember how hard he had been gripping the boy's arm.

"He wouldn't let me watch TV," the boy wailed between two sobs.

Katz came toward him, his broad forehead wrinkled in puzzlement from eyebrows to bald spot. "Why not, Isaac? You know he's allowed to watch TV after his homework's done. Was his homework done?"

"Yes."

"He hurt my arm."

"He did?" Shiela pulled up the boy's sleeve.

"The other one."

She pulled up the other one. They all looked at it. On the biceps was a faint flush of pink, no bigger than a penny.

"Jesus Christ," Katz said. "You'd better have some explanation for this, Isaac."

He couldn't think of anything to say. The boy stopped crying, sniffed, and pointed a finger at him: "He tried to make me say bad words."

"What kind of bad words, honey?" Sheila Finkle asked in a tone that had two distinct strata: sweetness above and menace below.

"Not English." His cheeks and upper lip glistened with mucus and tears.

Sheila raised her voice. The sweetness broke off and fell away. "Have you been teaching him Hebrew? Joshua's religious education is none of your goddamned business. Quentin and I are atheists. We don't want any of your stupid mumbo jumbo."

"I'm an atheist too," Rehv said.

She ignored him. "You people have been here for a year now. When are you going to learn to stop dragging everyone into your petty little problems?"

Rehv found himself staring into her angry brown eyes. He saw the anger change to something else. She was scared. "Don't you touch me," she said, withdrawing from him. Joshua began to cry again.

"Don't be silly," Rehv said. "I was only trying to teach him a few Arabic words, that's all. I didn't mean to upset him." He turned to the boy. "I'm sorry, Joshua," he said. "I hope we can still be friends."

The boy sniffled and wiped his nose on his sleeve. "Joshua," Sheila said. "How many times have I told you not to do that? It's disgusting." Rehv noticed that mother and son pronounced the word with identical cadence.

Katz said: "If you want to teach so badly why don't you send in that goddamned CV?"

"I'm going to," Rehv said, realizing that he meant it.

"I don't care what you do," Sheila said. "From now on you'll have to make it on your own. You have until the end of the week to find somewhere to live."

"Wait a minute, dear," Katz said. "Maybe we shouldn't be so drastic."

Sheila glared at him. "Very well, Quentin. You and I will go into the kitchen and discuss it. Joshua, it's bedtime. Go change and I'll come in five minutes to tuck you in." To Rehv she said: "Stay here."

She and Katz moved around the tall benjamina that hid the open doorway to the kitchen. "I don't want to go to bed," the boy said.

His parents turned. "But it's bedtime, angel," Sheila said.

"I'm not tired. I want to watch TV."

"Just for fifteen minutes."

Joshua returned to the television. Rehv stayed where he was by the window. Sheila and Quentin went into the kitchen. Rehv could hear them talking in low voices. They talked for a long time. The television screen showed gunfights, car crashes, and roll-on deodorant. Joshua seemed unaware of him standing there a few feet away. Clouds rolled across the night sky. Betelgeuse was gone.

Far below Rehv saw two men carrying a large chest across the street. They both seemed to be bearded, perhaps because of the way the streetlamp shone down on their faces. On the far side of the street they had difficulty with the wall of dirty snow the plow had made: The chest balanced on top, the men struggled on either side. After a few moments one man let go of the chest and walked away. The other man stood straight, and watched him go. Then he too let go of the chest, and ran after him. The chest remained perched on the snowbank. The second man reached the first and put an arm around his shoulders. The first man shrugged it off. The second man put his arm around the first man's shoulders again. This time it was not shrugged off. They walked back to the chest like that. They turned to each other, kissed, lifted the chest, and carried it off.

Rehv heard footsteps approaching behind him. He turned around. Sheila and Quentin stood side by side like jurors who have reached a verdict.

Katz said: "We've decided to allow the present situation to continue on one condition." He paused, and looked at his wife.

"That you see a psychiatrist," she said.

"A psychiatrist?"

"Yes," Katz said quickly. "There's no stigma attached to it here, not at all. I don't know what it was like in Israel, but here everyone does it. It's nothing."

"Do you do it?"

"No. But I would."

He and Sheila were watching him carefully. To his surprise he realized he felt no strong opposition to the idea. He thought of the pink imprint on Joshua's arm.

"We think you have some problems, Isaac," Katz said quite gently. "It's very understandable after all you've been through."

"I can't afford a psychiatrist."

Katz smiled. "There is a free psychiatric service for the refugees. We'll make all the arrangements."

"All right."

Isaac Rehv walked through the snow to his borrowed home. He thought of the boy: not strong enough, not smart enough. And far too literal minded. He was glad he had said nothing to the sarcastic man at the farmhouse in Vermont. "Where are you going to find the boy who can do all that?" he would have said immediately.

Nowhere. He thought of the pink mark darkening into a bruise. As he turned into his street he realized that he had forgotten his shoes and socks.

CHAPTER NINE

"Rehv," the psychiatrist said. "What a nice name. It means dream in French, doesn't it?"

He looked at her for a moment, wondering if she would base her whole treatment on this fact. He saw no answer in her narrow eyes, which changed from blue to green as the gap grew between her question and his reply. She was short and dark, with a soft round body, heavy in the hips and thighs; a body that reminded him of Naomi's when she was careless about her diet. This slight resemblance of body, not at all of face, sent a brief pulse of uneasiness through his chest.

"And I think your name means spear in German, Dr. Lanze."

"Does it?" The eyes stayed green. "I'm afraid I don't know any German. One of my great-grandfathers came from Austria, I believe." While she spoke she watched him very carefully, whether looking for obvious signs of madness or to see if he believed her about the great-grandfather, he didn't know. "In any case last names don't matter here. There are enough barriers already when it comes to human communication. In this room it's first names only. Call me Madeleine."

She raised her eyebrows, shaped by tweezers into two Roman arches, to show she wanted some sign of agreement. He nodded.

"And I'll call you Isaac."

He nodded again, without being prodded, and waited for her to say what a nice name Isaac was, or to make some reference to the biblical Isaac.

"Take off your shoes," she said instead, "and sit down."

Rehv guessed that shoes were another barrier to human communication. He looked for a place to sit. There were no chairs on the thick brown broadloom, only a few large pillows of Indian design. He sat on one and pulled off his shoes, thinking of Joshua Katz-Finkle. He smelled no unpleasant smells, but saw that his socks were embroidered with hundreds of tiny golf balls. He could not remember wearing them before. He had a lot of socks: The refugees had been given large amounts of used clothing.

Dr. Lanze drew up a pillow and sat down facing him, closer than he would have liked. Her suede jeans bunched in tight wrinkles that looked very constricting. She pulled one of her high-heeled leather boots onto her opposite knee and tugged at it. She grunted. The boot didn't budge. She tried again, straining against the handicaps of tight clothing, short arms, round stomach. He heard a louder grunt. She looked up at him and said, a little out of breath, "God, I hate winter." She straightened her leg, holding the boot over his lap. "Would you mind?"

Rehv pulled it off. Underneath, her foot was bare; it was short and broad and strong, the toenails painted bright red. He took in slightly more air than usual through his nostrils, and smelled leather mixed with something medicinal. He pulled off the other boot.

"Thank you, Isaac," she said, setting the boots beside her on the floor. "I hope you like this room. Most people find it very relaxing."

Rehv looked around. Three of the walls were painted white and had no windows. The fourth was brown to match the broadloom and had two large rectangular windows. The ceiling was brown too, like a low and dirty cloud. On a mushroom-shaped stand in one corner sat a small aquarium, full of algae. A single goldfish looked out at them, its transparent fins waving gently in the water. Two paintings hung on the walls: a Renaissance print of Adam and Eve on their way out of the garden, seething at each other—Eve quite hefty, like Dr. Lanze; and a modern oil that made him think of a Helmholtz contraction. He didn't find the room relaxing.

"What do you think of when you look at that painting?" Dr. Lanze asked.

"Is it part of the examination?"

"No." She laughed, but not very hard. "And don't call this an examination. We're having a little talk."

Then why do I have to sit on a pillow without my shoes,

Rehv thought. He said: "It reminds me of a Helmholtz contraction."

The round arches of Dr. Lanze's eyebrows narrowed to points. "Excuse me for a minute," she said, rising heavily to her feet. "I've got to use the bathroom." She crossed the room and went out the door, closing it behind her.

Rehv waited. He watched the goldfish. In the aquarium were plants to nibble at, a stream of bubbles to swim through, and a small conch shell to hide in, but the goldfish did not want to do any of these things. It watched Rehv.

Dr. Lanze returned and sat on her pillow. "Sorry," she said. Her eyebrows had resumed their roundness. He realized he had not heard any sound of plumbing. "Now," she went on, "where were we?"

"Helmholtz contraction."

"Ah yes: It's interesting you should say that," she said, and he knew she had gone to look it up. "The artist called it *Starburst.*"

As long as they were having a little talk he thought of saying, "That would fetch a higher price than Helmholtz Contraction," but then he remembered the four wooden booths and decided it might not be true.

"I think you're the first person who has guessed right," Dr. Lanze said. "Not that it has to be about any specific subject, of course," she added quickly. "Do you know what most people think it's about?"

"Death," Rehv said, because he thought any abstract painting made most people think of death.

The eyebrows rose again to points. "You're right," she said slowly. The green eyes regarded his face, then slipped down his body and back up again.

"Now then," Dr. Lanze said more briskly. "We've had a chance to get to know each other a little." She twisted around on the pillow to get more comfortable; the suede wrinkles loosened their bonds. "I should start by saying that Sheila has told me something about you. And I think I've found out quite a bit more during our chat. You're intelligent, well-educated, you know something about the stars, you know languages, you've been a university professor." She looked at him to see if he was with her so far. He said nothing. "The question I think we should ask is this: Can a man like that be happy working as a waiter and a night watchman?"

Rehv gazed at her feet and his feet pointing at each other across the rug: two square naked feet with ten red faces and two long narrow ones in golf ball socks. There was something unhappy about both pairs.

"Are you happy?" Dr. Lanze asked.

"Happy?"

"Do you know how it feels to be happy?"

"Yes."

"You've been happy before?"

"Yes." Something rose from his chest and filled his throat; he had trouble getting the word out.

"That's good. Many of the people I see have never been happy, not since they were babies." That made sense to him. Happy was a silly word: It had a nonsense sound like syllables babbled by a baby; like baby talk it was soon outgrown. He knew enduring words for it in other languages.

"What were you thinking, just then?" Dr. Lanze asked quickly.

"Nothing."

"Something."

"I was thinking you should clean the aquarium. The fish will die with all that algae in there."

"You're avoiding me, Isaac." She wriggled forward on the pillow. "It's hard to talk about, but you have to talk. I know you lost your wife and child."

"I didn't lose them." He looked at her angrily. The green eyes looked back with an expression he didn't understand: patient, knowing, professional, and something else. Fear? He wasn't sure. His anger died away.

"Do you want to talk about it?"

"No."

"Why not?"

"There's nothing to tell. It happened to lots of people. You must have read it in the papers."

"I'd like to hear you talk about it."

"I don't think you would." He was growing more uncomfortable sitting on the pillow. His back hurt.

"How do you expect to adjust to it if you won't talk?"

"I will never adjust to it." He heard the fierceness in his own

83

voice, and saw again the odd look in her eyes. It was not fear, but some other kind of excitement, partly suppressed.

"I can understand why you say that," Dr. Lanze said. "But there are many other refugees —"

"I'm not a refugee. I am an Israeli." Again he saw the look.

"There are many other Israelis who are beginning to adjust," she continued in a quiet, almost husky voice. "Why not Isaac?"

Rehv thought of the prime minister, Harry, and the young woman with the tear gas. "Is shooting Arabs in the streets adjusting?"

"Everyone knows that the terrorists are a tiny minority, and they're being rounded up very quickly," she said patiently. "The majority is learning to accept the world as it is. Why not Isaac?"

"I don't know." He really didn't know. He decided he would tell her about the screaming.

"I'll be frank with you, Isaac," Dr. Lanze said before he had a chance. "I've been working with a number of other Israelis in the past few months, and most of them were much worse off than you are. You're young, you're highly trained, you're smart, you're even good-looking. And you were happy before. All your problems come from one traumatic incident. So there is no need for us to ferret about in your childhood or early sexual escapades." Dr. Lanze smiled. She had sharp, even white teeth. "All we have to do is find ways to deal with that trauma. But first you must accept the world as it is."

He thought he would like very much to deal with the trauma, but never under that condition. "Maybe there is another way."

"No," Dr. Lanze said. "There isn't." Her lips were still slightly parted, lips the color of her toenails, the tips of the white teeth showing behind. "Let me tell you about a study that was made after the war, the Second World War. It's about this same subject, coping with trauma, adjusting. It was done on German housewives, women who had lost their husbands, children, everything. The study found that many of them almost immediately began having sex with the occupying troops." Dr. Lanze wriggled farther forward until her plump buttocks rested on the edge of the pillow. Her voice became huskier. "But more interesting, of these women a very large percentage, quite spontaneously and voluntarily, had a strong desire to perform analingus on the men of the occupying army. The study found that the women who gave in to this desire were generally the quickest to adjust and start building new lives. It was a symbolic acceptance of things as they were."

The green eyes moved very close to his, narrowed like slits in a pillbox. Now Rehv understood those eyes. He knew that one word from him, a look, and the suede trousers would be off, and he would be on his back on the floor, her heavy buttocks spread across his face: on his back, building a new life.

Rehv stood up. He saw Dr. Lanze's hand go to her waistband. He thought the screaming would start, but it did not. Instead he felt very tall, very controlled, very strong, stronger than he had felt in a long time. He looked down at her and quietly said: "I will never adjust." She shrank back on the pillow.

Rehv slipped on his shoes and walked out of the room, down the stairs, and outside into Greenwich Village. An old African trader shuffled slowly by in floppy yellow sandals, carrying an ivory camel that seemed very white in his blue black hands.

Rehv crossed the street. He did not need the prime minister, the deputy prime minister, the government-in-exile, or men like Harry. He could do it all by himself. It might take a long time, even a lifetime, but it would be the life that was Isaac Rehv. He walked quickly down the street, thinking about the boy who could do what had to be done.

In a parked car sat a sandy-haired man with dark eyebrows. He was reading the comic page of the newspaper.

CHAPTER TEN

Armbrister packed the perforated silver ball with tea. "Keemun," he said. Carefully he lowered the ball by its thin silver chain into a white china mug, and filled the mug with boiling water from the kettle. Steam rose. Armbrister inhaled some of it and closed his bloodshot fish eyes with pleasure. Krebs waited while he removed the silver ball, said, "I really shouldn't," and stirred in two spoonfuls of clover honey. While Krebs waited he drank instant coffee from a Styrofoam cup.

Armbrister sat back in his padded chair and sipped the tea. Krebs saw that he was putting on weight: The roll that strained the lower buttons of his Tattersall shirt had grown in diameter from a French stick to a double rye. He rested the mug on it, and glanced over his untidy desk; probably in search of a tidbit, Krebs thought. Their eyes met.

"Let's hear it," Armbrister said, in the weary tone he used to indicate that being badgered was his lot in life.

Krebs opened the yellow file on his knees. "I want to go after a man named Rehv," he said. "Isaac Rehv. First you'll need some background." He opened his mouth to begin, but Armbrister interrupted.

"Let's see what you've got," he said. He put the mug on the desk and reached across for the file. He didn't like being told what he didn't know; he preferred to see it on paper, like a teacher grading essays.

Krebs watched him read. Armbrister read slowly, moistening the pad of his index finger on the tip of his tongue before turning each page. Nothing he read changed the expression on his face, which was that of an old city editor who knew there was no such thing as a new story. Armbrister closed the file. He set it on the desk and gave it a little push, like a child bored with his dinner.

"Why?" he asked, reaching for his tea.

"Why what?"

Armbrister sighed. "Why do you want to go after this man Rehv?" He put "go after" in quotes. "He's a waiter. Someone paid him some money to see that Abu Fahoum sat at a certain table. Maybe he did it for nothing. Maybe he didn't even do it at all. But, accepting for the sake of discussion that he did, that's all you've got." He looked at the file with something like pity. "Small beer." Armbrister was fond of British expressions.

"What about the maître d'?"

Armbrister began rubbing his eyes very hard, as though in a frenzy of disbelief. Krebs knew that his contact lenses were bothering him. "Maybe someone poisoned him as you say," Armbrister replied, mauling his eyes. "Nothing here says your man was involved."

"He's not my man."

Armbrister stopped rubbing and lowered his hands. His eyes had swollen to red bulbs: Looking at them made Krebs's own eyes start to water. "Let's not argue, Krebs," Armbrister said. He made it sound like a threat. "Whether or not he had anything to do with the poisoning, the fact remains he is a very little fish. A minnow. You know we don't want minnows."

"I don't think he's a minnow."

Armbrister blinked at the file. "Why not?"

Krebs leaned forward. "First of all, he faced down Abu Fahoum at the restaurant."

Armbrister laughed the laugh of a man-about-town. "They learn that from day one at waiter's school."

Krebs hated that laugh. He gulped his anger back down. "He's smart—a professor of Arabic."

"Assistant."

"And he has military experience."

"In the reserve."

Krebs rose and walked across the room. On the wall hung a photograph of Armbrister playing croquet with his family. He walked back and stood in front of the desk. He felt better looking down at Armbrister. "This is what I think happened," he said, trying to keep his voice down. "Rehv is a high-ranking terrorist. He works in a fancy restaurant, not a bad cover and a useful place to be. He looks at the reservation list and sees Abu Fahoum's name. He knows who he is. He sets him up. It fails only because he didn't have time to round up better people. Abu Fahoum is smart—he knows what Rehv is. He sends his goon to kill him. Abu Fahoum waits. He doesn't know what's going on. When I talk to him he's very evasive. Why? Why shouldn't he be helpful?"

"Did you mention my name?" Armbrister asked.

Krebs ignored him. "The reason he's not helpful is that he's waiting to hear from his goon. But the goon disappears. Rehv doesn't. Before Abu Fahoum can decide what to do next, Rehv gets him too."

Armbrister pulled the top off the silver ball and dumped the damp tea leaves on a sheet of paper. "You haven't got any evidence," he said, poking about in the tea leaves as if he might find some there.

Krebs leaned over him. "What would you say if I told you Rehv paid a little visit to Vermont last week?"

Armbrister looked up, his eyes very red. "Are you telling me?"

"Yes."

"Why wasn't it in the report?"

"Because I just got the information this morning." They looked at each other for a moment: Both men knew it wasn't the whole truth.

Armbrister poked at the tea leaves with his index finger. "It still doesn't mean anything," he said. "We have nothing at all to connect Vermont with any of the terrorists."

"Not yet."

Armbrister pushed the tea leaves into a little pile. Then, taking, care not to spill, he rolled the paper into a ball and dropped it in a wastebasket. "What do you want?"

"Twenty-four-hour surveillance, three-man team."

"For five days. No more."

"And something else."

"What?"

"He sees a psychiatrist. I'd like a look at her files."

"No."

"Very discreet."

Armbrister made an odd, puckering face, as though he had just tasted sour milk. "No," he said again.

It was a dark, moonless night. Krebs had dressed discreetly in a heavy black sweater, blue jeans, worn tennis shoes dyed black, and black leather gloves. He walked silently along the quiet street, the kind of street in Greenwich Village where the three- and four-story town houses are renovated every ten years. In a few windows he saw the cold flickering blue light of the last late movie; but the windows of the house he wanted were dark.

Krebs mounted the steps of the cement stoop and stood before the door. He had three keys in his pocket. The first one fit the lock. He turned it, heard the tumblers shift, and pushed. The door remained firmly closed, bolted from the inside. Krebs put the key back in his pocket and went down to the sidewalk. He knelt in front of the basement window: It was small, with four dirty panes, and seemed to be hinged at the top. He pressed it gently with his fingertips to discover whether the latch was closed. It was. He sat down on the sidewalk and put his heels against the lower part of the frame. He pushed hard. There was a sharp splitting sound, almost a squeak, as screws were torn from wood. It sent little waves of adrenaline down his arms and legs. He looked around. No lights went on in any of the windows; nobody screamed. Krebs placed his hands on the edge of the frame, twisted around, and lowered himself into the basement.

He crouched on the cold cement floor and listened. Two machines were humming: a refrigerator somewhere above and a hot water heater nearby. A car honked far away. Krebs took a small flashlight from his pocket and examined the remains of the latch. He saw a narrow bolt that would fit into a curved piece of metal attached to the wall. He found this piece on the floor, and the two screws that had held it. Using his multibladed Swiss Army knife, he screwed it back into the wall, changing its position slightly to hide the cracks in the wood. He closed the window and shut off the flashlight.

He stood in the basement waiting for his eyes to adjust to the darkness. In a few moments he could see the washer and the dryer, and a row of five or six old toilets against one wall. Then he made out a little bicycle with fat tires, a hula hoop in the corner, and the stairs along the side wall. He had excellent night vision: It had been noted during his training. He started toward the stairs very quietly. Something soft fell across his nose and mouth. He jumped back, switching on the flashlight. Three pairs of silk panties hung on a line in front of his face. He turned off the flashlight and went up the stairs.

At the top of the stairs Krebs came to a closed door. He could hear the refrigerator on the other side. He put his hand on the knob and pulled and twisted at the same time, to prevent the catch from scraping. The door opened silently.

Krebs looked into the kitchen. It was brighter than he had expected: A weak white light spread through the center of the room, leaving the edges in shadow. The light came from the refrigerator on the far side of the room. It was open. A heavy naked woman stood in front of it, her back to him. She was bending forward to get something from one of the lower shelves.

Very slowly Krebs pulled the door toward him, not quite closing it. He kept his hand on the knob and did not move.

He heard the refrigerator door close. The woman's bare feet moved across the tile floor. A plate clicked on a ceramic counter. A drawer opened, rattling its metallic contents. The drawer closed. Silence. The feet approached, very close, and stopped. He heard a sound he didn't recognize immediately: rhythmic, moist, sucking. He realized she was chewing. The chewing stopped. He heard a faint wet rubbing that might have been her tongue licking her lips. The feet went away. They climbed the stairs. They pressed on a floor above. A bedspring squeaked.

Krebs stood still. He looked down at the green numbers on his wristwatch. Three-thirty. He didn't move again until four o'clock.

When the green point of the hand covered the green dot of twelve he gently opened the door and entered the kitchen. He walked quietly through an arched doorway and into the front hall. Faint street light penetrated the windows and pushed the darkness into the corners. Off one side of the hall was the living room; he could see the low soft shadows of couches and chairs. On the other side was the dining room, most of its space taken by a long table. Behind him the stairs led to the second floor. He climbed them one at a time, keeping his feet to the outside edge.

At the top Krebs found himself in another hall, smaller than the first, and darker. He looked around, trying to make his eyes absorb every particle of light. He saw three doors, one open and two shut.

He took slow even steps toward the open door, his tennis shoes silent on the thick carpet. He peered inside and saw nothing. The curtains must be closed, he thought. He raised the flashlight and flicked the switch on and off, very fast. In the moment that the beam shot across the room he glimpsed the large bed, and the single lump rising in the middle. He stared into blackness where the lump had been. Nothing moved. He listened very hard but heard nothing, not even the sound of breathing. For some reason he suddenly thought of Alice. He didn't know why.

He backed into the hall and turned to the first closed door. He opened it very carefully, the way he had opened the door at the top of the basement stairs. He didn't need the flashlight. He felt the cool air against his face and quietly closed the door. Bathroom.

Krebs went to the third door, opened it, and looked in. Something bubbled in a dark corner. He flashed his beam: an aquarium. A goldfish faced him, pressing its lips against the glass.

He closed the switch. A little light came through two rectangular windows and advanced partway across the room. At first he thought it was empty; then he saw large dark shapes on the floor. He touched one with his toe: a pillow. The office must be on the third floor, he thought. He turned to go, but he didn't take a step. He looked again at the dark shapes on the floor. Something about them made him think that the room was set aside for work, what sort of work he didn't know. He shone his light around the walls. There was a closet in one corner.

He crossed the floor and opened it. Inside stood a tall wooden filing cabinet. Krebs went to the door that led to the hall, closed it softly, and returned to the filing cabinet. He ran the little circle of light over the labels on the drawers, and pulled out the one marked "Q to S." His fingers hurried through the files. Rafferty, Rainey, Rapaport, Rather, Reed, Rehv.

He opened Rehv's file. Inside was a single sheet of paper, covered in handwriting. He knelt, laid it carefully on the floor, and took the little camera from his pocket. He held it twelve inches from the sheet of paper and pressed the button. There was a flash that seemed very bright. Krebs listened, and heard nothing but the refrigerator, very faint. He put the paper in the file, put the file in the drawer, and closed it. He closed the door, put the camera and the flashlight in his pockets, and left the room.

Softly, trying to slow down, he walked past the dark bedroom, down the stairs, and into the hall. He thought of leaving by the front door but remembered the bolt he would have to leave open. Neither could he close the latch of the basement window, but that might never be noticed. He went down the basement stairs and across the hard cement floor to the window. He pulled it open, placed his hands on the sidewalk, and lifted himself through.

Hot white light bored into his wide-open pupils.

"Freeze," said a voice.

Krebs froze.

"Hands up high. Turn around real slow. Against the wall."

Hard hands ran quickly over his body. They took his Swiss Army knife, flashlight, camera, and wallet. While they were doing that he realized what it was about Alice that he had tried to remember while he stared in the darkness at the lump in the big bed: It was the tension in her body when she pretended to be asleep.

He heard the front door open. "Police?" said a woman. She sounded very frightened.

"That's right, lady," said the voice behind him. "It's all over."

"Is that him?"

"Yup."

"I don't want to see him." The door closed.

There were two of them. They handcuffed him and pushed him into the back seat of the patrol car. One went into the house to talk to the woman. The other sat in the front seat.

"Better look at the wallet," Krebs said to him through the steel screen.

"Better shut your fuckin' mouth," the cop said without turning his head.

They sat there waiting, Krebs looking at the back of the cop's head, the cop at nothing in particular. After a while the cop took Krebs's wallet off the dashboard and opened it. He saw what Krebs wanted him to see.

"You could call McCulloch at Midtown South," Krebs said. "He knows me."

"I'll bet a lot of cops know you," the cop said, but he didn't sound sure.

The other cop returned. The first one opened the wallet and showed him the yellow card inside. They called McCulloch.

Darkness had begun to give up the eastern part of the sky by the time McCulloch arrived. His cold was worse. His nose was red, and he had a wad of Kleenex tucked into the sleeve of his duffle coat, like a maiden aunt. He looked at Krebs and said nothing.

McCulloch went to his own car and talked on the radio for a few minutes. He got out of the car and returned. "Suspect escaped custody on the way to the station," he said to the cop behind the wheel. He turned, got into his car, and drove away, without looking at Krebs again.

The other cop opened the back door and unlocked the handcuffs. Krebs got out rubbing his wrists. They gave him his wallet, but they kept the Swiss Army knife, the flashlight, and the camera. Krebs walked away. He felt their eyes on his back.

CHAPTER ELEVEN

Everyone was rich. They broke around Isaac Rehv in waves of fur and high-priced scent. They carried packages wrapped in thick paper of red and green and gold, and tied with ribbons and bows: a luxurious caravan bearing away the riches of the West. The wealth they shared did not seem to make them any friendlier toward each other. They still walked as fast as they could, eyes straight ahead, mouths shut. The only mingling went on over their heads where their breath condensed in the cold air and came together in silver vapor that hovered above. Rehv supposed that must be the Christmas spirit.

He stepped out of the flow of people and stopped in the lee of a phone booth. He took out his wallet, the wallet with the faded Q.K. stamped on one corner, and counted his money. He had three twenty-dollar bills, four tens, a five, and nine ones. In his front pockets he found a quarter, a nickel, and three pennies. One hundred and fourteen dollars and thirty-three cents. That was it. No bank account, no stocks, no bonds, no real estate: the man who would do it all himself. He thought of Quentin Katz's twenty-five-grand-a-year job. He needed more. Sooner.

Rehv looked up and saw a tall thin Santa Claus watching him across the sidewalk. His hard little eyes were locked on Rehv's wallet. He folded it, put it away, and continued walking to work. Santa Claus shook his bell at him.

La Basquaise had been closed for a week. When Rehv arrived he found that all the tables had been moved and their numbers changed.

"Pascal is very superstitious," Armande explained. He picked up a dessert knife, examined his reflection, and shook his head. "It's so ridiculous," he said: "People shoot each other in Italian restaurants." He allowed a pained expression to cross his handsome face, as though some horrifying gaffe had been committed. He held up the dessert knife and looked into it again. The pain went away.

"Stomach all better?" Rehv asked.

Armande gripped the back of a chair, his knuckles white. "It was ghastly," he said in a voice that was suddenly hoarse. "I vomited. I defecated. Sometimes both at once, if you understand what I mean. It is better left unsaid. Both at once." He sighed deeply, then looked at Rehv and narrowed his eyes. "I will never eat *pieds et paquets* again in my life."

"But you're better now?"

"Physically, yes," Armande replied. "We went to Walt Disney World for a few days. Pascal likes to go on the rides."

The first customers appeared in the doorway. "Okay," Armande said, "let's make some money." He went off to greet them like an amiable wine baron welcoming old friends for dinner. He looked fine. His tan was deeper, his yellow hair yellower, his blue eyes bluer. He hadn't said anything about Manolo.

It was a good night for making money. People were hungrier and thirstier than usual: Hours of frenetic shopping and lugging heavy presents in the cold made them that way. They wanted steamed lobster and *quenelles des crevettes* and *galantine de volaille à la gelée*. They wanted Burgundy, and lots of it.

Two men in Rehv's section ordered steak tartare. Women never seemed to order it: It was a dish for men who were men. For Rehv it meant a performance at their tables with egg yolks and capers and Worcestershire sauce. At the first table conversation ceased and everyone watched him as if he were about to do some magical trick; at the second table the man who was a man wanted to direct preparations: "More capers. Another egg yolk. Haven't you got HP?" While Rehv was ruining the dish according to these specifications he felt a brief hush fall over the dining room. He looked up and saw Armande leading a famous screen actress and two companions to a table in his section. The hush was very brief, and no one stared, except out of the corner of the eye; not because they valued her privacy, but because they were important too. La Basquaise was that kind of place.

The actress had eaten there before, but never at one of Rehv's tables. Armande gave her a banquette in a shallow alcove designed like a balcony overlooking rolling meadows. She was wearing a pearl-colored coat that almost touched the floor, made from the earthly remains of numerous chinchillas, and a matching hat which served as a monument to two or three more. She would have been warm on the retreat from Moscow, Rehv thought, although she probably had not come from far away: Armande had said once that she always stayed at the hotel across the street when she came to New York.

Rehv scooped the last of the steak tartare onto a plate and set it before the man who knew how he liked it. "Bon appétit," he said. The man picked up his fork and jabbed it into the midst of the raw meat. Rehv turned and moved toward the banquette. He heard a woman say, "How can you eat that?" The man answered, "It's perfect," with his mouth full.

The actress and her friends were sitting with their backs to the pastel meadows. She sat in the center, listening to something Armande was saying. Whatever it was made her smile. She had big teeth, white as piano keys, and glossy hair as black as the sharps and flats. Her eyes were huge and dark, surrounded by huge and dark frameworks of makeup; there were no lines on her face, but Rehv saw a slight tautness around her eyes and mouth, where lines should have been appearing by now: She had been a movie star for a long time.

On one side sat a man who looked a lot like Armande, except he was younger, had longer hair, a deeper tan, and less intelligence on his face; and at that moment his smile was not quite as broad as Armande's, although his mouth seemed capable of reaching such extremes. On the other side sat a thin dark woman who may have had an Oriental ancestor two or three generations before. Her face was much more intelligent than the man's, but right now her mind was somewhere else.

Still smiling with every muscle in his face, Armande turned to Rehv and said: "I think these people would like champagne."

"Good evening," Rehv said to them. "What kind do you prefer?"

"Laurent Perrier," the actress said, rolling her *r*'s. She rolled them very nicely. The thought that she had chosen as she had for that reason crossed Rehv's mind; but he remembered that

96

there were good *r*'s for rolling in Krug, Dom Pérignon, and Pol Roger as well.

"Do they make a pink champagne?" the young man asked. He had a light voice that made him sound even younger than he looked.

"Yes," Rehv said.

The young man turned to the actress. "Do you feel like some of that?"

"Oh, you silly boy." She laughed, a laugh that began high and thin but was quickly pushed into a lower, warmer register.

"The pink, then?" Rehv asked her.

She looked up at him, revealing diamond seashells on each earlobe and a narrow middle-aged wrinkle at the base of her neck. "No," she said coldly.

For a moment no one spoke. Rehv heard a glass shatter on the other side of the room. Impatiently the thin dark woman said: "Let him have the pink if that's what he wants, and we'll have the other."

"Tania, you clever girl," the actress said without looking at her. "That's just what we'll do. Magnums," she told Rehv.

He nodded and went away. He heard the girl hiss, "Don't call me a clever girl."

He and the sommelier and Armande brought the ice buckets and the champagne. Armande's smile grew more sincere as the corks popped. Each pop meant one hundred and ninety dollars. Armande poured some for the actress to taste. She raised the flute, touched it to her lips, tilted it, flared her nostrils, and allowed a little trickle of pale gold into her mouth.

"Very nice, Armande. Thank you."

"Je vous en prie." Armande's lips were drawn so far back his molars showed.

Rehv poured pink champagne for the young man. He gulped it down. "Delicious," he said defiantly. No one contradicted him. Rehv filled his glass.

The actress ordered fois gras and lobster; the young man *bouchée de ris de veau* and shrimp wrapped in sole; the woman called Tania *assiette de charcuterie* and steak tartare.

"A woman just ordered steak tartare," Rehv said to Armande as he went into the kitchen.

"What woman?"

"The dark one at number nine."

Armande grunted and gave him a little wink he didn't understand. Something about it made him look back at number nine and think of the three of them in bed together.

By the time Rehv brought the main course, two-thirds of the champagne was gone. He refilled their glasses and began making the steak tartare. The woman named Tania stared into the wooden bowl, watching his hands.

"Christ, I hate New York," she said suddenly. "Let's go back to LA."

"But we only just got here, Tania darling," the actress said. She placed her hand on Tania's. Rehv noticed she had rather short, stubby fingers, but they were well hidden by rubies and emeralds.

Tania pulled her hand away. "Or Paris. Or somewhere."

"You're just tired," the actress said in a soothing tone. "Have some more champagne."

"I hate that piss." Tania leaned forward and looked past her. "Have you got any coke, Jamie?"

The young man put down his glass. His cheeks had gone the color of his drink. "On me, you mean?"

"Of course 'on you,' jerk."

His cheeks went a little pinker. "Not on me," he said through clenched teeth. "There's some in the room."

"I know that. Christ Almighty."

"That's enough," the actress said, quite calmly, as if she were dealing with unruly toddlers. She drained her glass. "Let's go dancing tonight."

"Great," the young man said.

"Where?" Tania asked without enthusiasm.

"The Pink Flush," the young man suggested.

"Shit."

"We'll go to Giorgio's," the actress said.

Rehv set a plate of steak tartare in front of the dark woman. She glanced at it, then pushed the table out three or four inches and stood up.

"Where are you going?" the actress said.

"To smoke a joint in the can," the dark woman replied, pushing past Rehv. The chinchilla coat, which had been on the seat beside her, slid to the floor.

98

Rehv bent down to pick it up. He saw that a key had slipped out of the pocket and was lying in the folds of the soft fur. It was a long brass key held by a chain to a thick brass disc. On the disc was the number 916. Rehv stuck the key in the side of his shoe, laid the coat on the seat, stood up, and poured more champagne.

"We'll need some more," the actress said.

"A magnum?"

"Yes."

"And of the rosé as well?"

"Go ahead if you want, darling," the actress said. "You should have what you like."

"No. I'll share yours."

"What a nice thing to say."

Rehv walked toward the kitchen. "Another magnum at number nine," he told the sommelier.

"That pink shit?"

"No."

Rehv went through the kitchen door, but turned right and continued quickly down the hall to the waiter's changing room. He opened the closet in the corner where Armande kept his spare suit. He removed his green jacket and put on Armande's black dinner jacket. He took the key from his shoe, slipped it into his pocket, and went to the door. He looked both ways along the hall. He saw no one. He ran down the hall, through the staff door, and into the street.

The hotel stood on the other side. Eight or nine broad stairs led to the well-lit entrance. Rehv crossed the street and mounted them, trying to look like a man on his way to a party. He stepped into the revolving doorway.

"Good evening, sir," said a doorman, touching the rim of his red top hat. He gave the door a little push to help Rehv through.

He walked across the marble floor of the lobby toward the elevators at the other side. A white poodle ran past him, dragging its leash. A woman called: "Mignon! Mignon!" The poodle ignored her and ran into a waiting empty elevator. Rehv followed it inside. It looked up at him and growled. He pushed it out the door with his foot and pressed the button marked nine. As the leather-padded doors slid closed he heard the woman say, "Bad, bad doggie."

The elevator stopped at the mezzanine. Two men entered. One was dressed just like Rehv. The other wore a burnous. The man who was dressed like him pressed number eight. The man in the burnous pressed no number at all. Perhaps they're together, Rehv thought.

On the eighth floor the man who was dressed like him got out. The doors closed. Rehv and the man in the burnous glanced at each other. Their eyes met. They looked away. The doors opened. Rehv walked through them, the man in the burnous after him.

A plaque on the wall read: "901–948." Rehv followed it. He heard the man in the burnous behind him, moving quietly on the thick blue carpet. At the end of the broad hall he came to a longer intersecting corridor. Another plaque indicated that rooms 901 to 921 were to the left, rooms 922 to 948 to the right. Rehv turned left. The Arab's footsteps faded away.

Rehv walked along the corridor, listening carefully. He passed room 916. He was almost at the end before he heard the muffled click of a door closing, far away. He turned and looked down the length of the corridor. There was no one to see.

Rehv hurried back to room 916. He inserted the key in the lock, turned it, and pushed the door open. He was in a sitting room. It was very bright. There were three floor lamps, two table lamps, a desk lamp, and a chandelier, all turned on. In the middle of the room a dozen mauve leather suitcases of different sizes stood in a row. That's that, he thought. It would take someone an hour to go through those, even if he knew what he was doing, and Rehv didn't. He glanced into the bedroom and saw no sign that anyone had been in there. He was about to leave when he remembered the bathroom. He hurried to it through a door that led from the bedroom.

On the counter by the sink he saw a mauve leather case, the size and shape of a workman's toolbox. It was open. Inside were jumbled tubes of lipstick and eye shadow, jars of face creams and body lotions, bottles of rubbing alcohol and contact lens solution, mascara, hair brushes, combs, birth control pills. He reached in, feeling an unpleasant sensation in his stomach, one that somehow reminded him of boyhood masturbation. It didn't stop him.

Near the bottom his fingertips touched something large and metallic. He pulled it out: a rectangular cookie tin. After prying off the top he found a clear plastic bag full of white powder, a small velvet-covered box, and five thick stacks, each held together by elastic bands, of one-hundred-dollar bills. He opened the velvet box. Diamonds, gold, silver shone inside.

Rehv took off Armande's dinner jacket. He forced the plastic bag into one sleeve, and filled the pockets with the bundles of currency. He closed the velvet box, replaced it in the cookie tin, and pressed the top on. He wiped the cookie tin with a damp piece of toilet paper and put it back in the bottom of the case. He left the room.

Rehv opened the front door very slightly and listened. He heard no voices, no footsteps. With Armande's jacket over his arm he walked quickly to the elevators, and beyond, to the door marked exit. He ran down the stairs very fast, taking them two at a time and leaping the last three or four to each landing. When he reached the ground floor he paused to catch his breath.

Rehv opened the door and stepped into the lobby. He saw no one except the clerk behind the desk. The clerk did not see him; he was bent over an adding machine, pushing buttons. He crossed the lobby without hurrying, trying to move with even, deliberate strides. His heels sounded very loud on the marble. He reached the revolving door and stepped into one of the wedge-shaped quadrants. From the street someone walked into the quadrant opposite his. For a moment they looked directly at each other. Rehv saw the dark young woman with a trace of Oriental blood: Tania. She didn't seem to notice him at all. She was too angry for that. They pushed each other around.

The doorman touched the brim of his red top hat. "Good evening, sir," he said again, although there was nothing in his tone to indicate he recognized the same sir who had entered a few minutes earlier. "Taxi?"

"No thank you." The doorman looked slightly disappointed. Perhaps he expected a tip.

Rehv crossed the street with the same deliberate pace, wondering if the doorman was watching him, noticing how lightly dressed he was for winter. He reached the staff door and went inside.

Now he ran down the hall to the staff changing room. He tore the money and the plastic bag from Armande's jacket, rolled the bundles inside his nylon windbreaker, and locked them in his locker. He hung Armande's jacket in the closet, pulled on his green waiter's jacket, and hurried into the hall. Armande was walking quickly toward him.

"Where the hell have you been?"

"The toilet."

"What were you doing in there for so long?"

"What are you talking about?"

"Okay, okay. Eleven is waiting for their profiteroles. Hurry."

He brought profiteroles to number eleven. Out of the corner of his eye he saw the new busboy clearing the main-course dishes from number nine. The actress was allowing another golden trickle to pass between her lips. The young man wasn't watching her, he was lighting a cigarette; but the busboy was. Rehv's hands shook as he poured the chocolate sauce.

He turned to number nine. "Dessert, madame?"

"What have you got?" She had drunk a lot of champagne, but her speech was not at all slurred, nor did she speak too clearly, the way drunks sometimes do when they think they are fooling people. Only the large dark eyes seemed a little changed: vague, blurred. Rehv watched them while he recited the litany of desserts.

She smiled at him in a conspiratorial way. "Just coffee, please."

"Mocha mousse for me," the young man said, blowing smoke across the table.

"And for the young lady?" Rehv asked, glancing at the empty chair.

"Nothing," the actress said. Suddenly she sounded very tired. "My children still have trouble sitting still for an entire meal."

"Christ, Mother," the young man said.

Their bill was $773. The actress left nine one-hundred-dollar bills on the silver plate and reached for her coat. Like waiters everywhere Rehv got to it first and helped her put it on. While her back was turned to him he slipped the key to room 916 into her coat pocket. Then he went to get the change.

When he returned they had gone.

CHAPTER TWELVE

" 'Pimps needed for sociological study,' " read the young woman, squinting slightly at the text through wire-rimmed glasses. " 'Involves one fifteen-minute personal interview. Strictest anonymity and confidentiality assured. No names will be used in the study. Fee will be paid. Call Dr. Vere at 462-8315 between 11:30 P.M. and midnight, Tuesday and Wednesday only.' " The young woman looked up, still squinting. Fingerprints and dust coated the lenses of her glasses. "Is that it?" she asked.

"That's it," Isaac Rehv replied.

"How many issues? The more you do the cheaper it gets."

"One."

"One," she repeated, and with a pencil made a tick in a box at the bottom of the form. She counted the number of words aloud, touching each one with the dull point of the pencil. She counted them again. Rehv felt an urge to clean her glasses. "Forty-two," she said. She punched a few buttons on an adding machine. "Nineteen dollars and forty cents."

Rehv paid her and left the offices of the weekly. He hoped that Sheila and Quentin didn't read the classified announcements in the *Voice*. They would want to know why the telephone number of The Loft was there. "Any publicity is good publicity," he had heard Quentin say. He could remind Quentin of this, or he could say it must be a misprint and he knew nothing about it.

Rehv knew it wasn't perfect, but he could think of nothing better.

CHAPTER THIRTEEN

Armbrister had a look on his face that Krebs had seen before. It said: I am about to do something that is thought to be unpleasant, but I don't really mind. It was a solemn face, but pleasure glowed in the convex windows of his eyes.

Armbrister opened a drawer in his desk and groped about inside. For a moment Krebs thought he might be searching for tea, but only for a moment. One at a time, his hand hooked like a mechanical pincer used for moving contaminated objects, Armbrister lifted out the camera, the flashlight, the Swiss Army knife. He swept some papers aside with his forearm and set them on his green blotting pad in a little row, exhibits A, B, and C. They faced him like newly invented chess pieces whose moves he didn't know.

"I'm told these belong to you," Armbrister said.

Krebs said nothing. He felt his neck muscles tighten, pushing his head forward in the dogged way that Alice didn't like. "Toro. Olé," she would say. Once it had made him hit her.

"Do they?" Armbrister asked.

The muscles bunched a little more. "You know they do."

A shadow moved behind the convex windows. Armbrister opened his mouth to say something, but before he could the telephone rang.

"Hello," Armbrister said. Krebs always answered the phone by saying, "Krebs." Armbrister listened. His right hand picked up a red pencil and began drawing on the blotting paper. A sombrero. Two sombreros. A guitar. A cactus with spines. After a while he frowned and said, "Beaujolais? You think that's good enough?" He listened some more, added spines to the cactus. "What did they bring us?" He began another sombrero. "Better make it a Bordeaux," Armbrister said. "Bye-bye." He put his lips to the mouthpiece, looked up at Krebs, and stopped himself from kissing it.

Armbrister massaged the corners of his eyes with the tips of his index fingers, and blinked once or twice. Krebs remembered the goldfish in the dirty tank. "I'm going to be writing reports about you for the next month," Armbrister said.

They watched each other for what seemed like a long time. Finally Krebs spoke: "What are you going to say?" He couldn't help himself.

Armbrister did not reply. He sat back in his swivel chair, keeping his eyes on Krebs.

"What are you going to say, goddamn it?" Krebs stood up, knocked the camera, flashlight, and Swiss Army knife onto the floor, and leaned across the desk. Armbrister's eyes bulged even more than usual, showing their pink rims. He pushed his chair back a foot or two from the desk. "Tell me," Krebs shouted. Behind him a door opened. He whirled and saw Armbrister's lank-haired secretary standing in the doorway.

"Did you want something, Mr. Armbrister?" she asked. But she wasn't looking at Armbrister, she was looking at Krebs, and she sounded frightened.

"No thank you, Jenny. We're fine," Armbrister replied. She closed the door. Krebs sat down. Silently Armbrister watched him for a minute or two. "What would you like me to say in the report?" he asked at last.

"Explain how it really was. Overzealousness in the performance of duty."

"I don't see it that way."

"I do." His neck muscles clenched again. "And they will too if they read it in your report."

Armbrister shook his head. "You don't learn very well, do you, Krebs?"

"I finished ahead of you at MIT." Krebs began biting the inside of his cheek as soon as he had said it. Armbrister raised his eyebrows in a puzzled way. Then he smiled.

"And you live in the past as well, perhaps."

"The hell I do."

Armbrister's facial muscles twitched, and the smile was gone.

"The fact that we were classmates doesn't give you the right to be rude to me in this office," Armbrister said. His tone was threatening, although he did not raise his voice. Krebs saw the little glow of pleasure in his eyes. "Did you ever wonder why they assigned you to this job, Krebs? Why they brought you to New York?"

It was not a rhetorical question. Armbrister sat silently in his chair until Krebs said, "Why?"

"They liked your work. They wanted a closer look at you." Armbrister smiled. "Of course there was some talk about impulsiveness. Temper. Insubordination. They wanted to see for themselves. They were interested in you, Krebs."

The past tense stuck in his mind like a fishhook. He was barely aware of the secretary entering the room and handing Armbrister a large manila envelope.

"Thank you, Jenny." Armbrister tore it open. He took out a black-and-white photograph, the size of a sheet of letter-writing paper. He studied it. "A very nice job," he said. "The focus and the lighting couldn't be better." He held it up for Krebs to see: the photograph he had taken of the psychiatrist's report. "Too bad the woman woke up. It was the flashlight that did it, apparently. She's a very light sleeper."

Armbrister began reading it to himself. "What awful handwriting," he said, holding it closer. He was in no hurry. Krebs watched his eyes move slowly from left to right, line by line. He saw the rounded edge of a contact lens, sitting on the cornea like an eyelash. Finally he looked up. "This was all there was?" he asked. Krebs nodded. Armbrister grunted and offered it across the desk, not quite far enough across to allow Krebs to take it without leaving his chair. He stood up and took it.

Krebs read:

Rehv Isaac. 35. Is. ref. ex-prof Ar. H&L.
S. survivor fam. Waiter & watchmn—Sheila F. Ref.—Sheila.
Trd. force Heb. less. J. (Q. says Ar.)
Repr. uncommuntve. host. phys—OK. Attr. Jogg therap.?
Trm. depr. Susp. masoch. Poss. anal tend., sex dysf.?
Release nec. Tried—unsucc. Try again?
Group?—disruptv.?
Time?
Bill—Isr. Ref. Fund—$175

Sir/Madame

    This is to notify you of fee schedule change re refugees, effective as of this date. Due to increased costs and in keeping with accepted practice note new rate of $175 per hour for private consultation. Please observe that this is still twenty percent less than the rate charged regular clients.

        Yours truly,

$190?

    Krebs kept his eyes on the photograph for a while after he finished reading. He knew Armbrister would be watching him when he raised his head. He was.

    "Scandalous, isn't it?" Armbrister said. "The fees they charge. It's an outrage."

    "None of this means he couldn't have cut Abu Fahoum's throat."

    Armbrister did not appear to have heard him. "What do you make of sex dysf.?" he asked.

    "None of it means anything one way or another," Krebs said more loudly. "It doesn't change a thing."

    Armbrister placed the palms of his hands on the desk and leaned forward. "It does for you," he said softly. They stared at each other. "I'm giving you two weeks off, Krebs. I want you to take a holiday. Go somewhere with your wife. Relax. Think about something else."

    "I don't want a holiday."

    "You're a very stupid man sometimes, Krebs. Don't you understand I'm trying to save your job? Now go away and let me do it."

    Again he felt the fishhook pulling inside him. "Is it that bad?"

    "Go."

    Krebs stood up and turned toward the door. "And take your toys with you," Armbrister said. Krebs picked up the camera, flashlight, and Swiss Army knife and left the room. As he walked through the outer office the secretary glanced up from her typing and gave him a cold look. But Krebs did not notice: He was looking into the future, a future full of Armbristers, junior positions, and dead-end assignments. If it was that bad, he had nothing to lose. He would spend his vacation watching Isaac Rehv.

CHAPTER FOURTEEN

Midnight, and very cold. Isaac Rehv stood beside a lamppost, not far from the entrance to a bar. Neon signs hung in the window of the bar, advertising different brands of beer. The cold condensed a skin of moisture on the window; in the center it gathered into trembling droplets that sometimes ran erratically toward the bottom; at the edges it was turning to frost. The cold condensed the vapor in his breath as well, twelve silvery puffs a minute, each slightly different from the one before. They rose, changed shape, and vanished. Across the street and half a block away the cold was doing the same thing to someone else's breath: another person standing on a sidewalk in the middle of a winter night.

From time to time people went into the bar, or came out. Some of them were dressed like cowboys, movie cowboys. When the door swung open and shut he heard snatches of songs from within. They were songs about being lonesome, sad, drunk, divorced, and stupid. They all seemed to be in four-four time.

A long silver car drove slowly by. It came to a stop, reversed, and stopped again beside Rehv. Noiselessly a rear window descended, and a voice said, "Dr. Vere?"

"Yes," Rehv answered.

The door opened and he got in.

There were two men in the car: the driver, a lean black man with a shaved head, who did not turn to look at Rehv, and a well-dressed lighter man in the back who at first did not look at him either. His eyes were on the small television mounted beside a polished wooden liquor cabinet. Tiny flickering figures were playing a silent game of basketball. Then they faded away and were replaced by an anxious-looking woman holding a garbage bag that was about to split. The well-dressed man switched off the television.

"The best game in the world," he said, turning to Rehv. By the light of the streetlamp Rehv could see his large dark curious eyes, his neatly trimmed glossy mustache, and his smooth immaculate skin, the color of café crème. He wore a dark three-piece suit of some heavy cloth like tweed, and a shirt so white it seemed to have a luster of its own. Rehv was conscious of his shabbiness. He had expected someone like the shivering man in the red shoes.

A potbellied man in a fringed shirt was standing outside, looking at the car. "Move, Leon," the well-dressed man said. The car shot forward with enough acceleration to push Rehv back into the soft suede seat. After a block or two it slowed and continued at a gentle pace.

The well-dressed man shifted in his seat so he could see Rehv more clearly. "Tell me something about your study, Dr. Vere. You said on the phone you were at NYU."

"I'm afraid I've arranged this meeting under false pretenses," Rehv said. His words made the tendons in the driver's neck stand out in sharp ridges.

"Oh, I already know that," the well-dressed man said. "There is no Dr. Vere at NYU."

Rehv felt suddenly very silly and slightly annoyed to have to explain his credentials to a pimp. "I'm prepared to pay for your time," he said, reaching inside his windbreaker. The driver braked violently, throwing Rehv against the back of the front seat. Almost before the car had stopped completely, he sprang around and tightened a forearm of twisted steel cables around Rehv's neck, pinning him to the headrest. Rehv struggled against the pressure, but that only made it worse, like a dog fighting a choke chain. He stopped struggling. Casually the well-dressed man leaned toward him and ran his hand quickly over his trunk and limbs. A diamond caught what light there was and gave it back in little pulses as the hand moved. Fingers closed on the envelope in his shirt pocket.

"Okay, Leon, he's clean," the well-dressed man said.

"You sure, Mr. Cohee?"

"Okay, Leon," the well-dressed man said again, in a tone that indicated he did not like to be asked if he was sure. The steel cables relaxed, turned to flesh and sinew, and withdrew.

Rehv wanted to rub his neck, but he didn't. "Was that really necessary?" he said, and heard the rasping in his voice. He turned his head to look at the man with the steel arm, but he had resumed his place behind the wheel and all Rehv could see was a high prominent cheekbone and a valley of shadow below.

"When Leon's driving I always fasten my seat belt," Mr. Cohee said, patting the buckle. "Leon has very quick reflexes." He opened the unsealed envelope and took out the one-hundred-dollar bill that was inside. "Why thank you," he said. "This will buy half a tank of gas." In the front seat Leon laughed, a high little laugh that seemed to come from his nose. "Don't laugh," Mr. Cohee said. Leon stopped laughing. "It's not funny. Gas is going to a dollar thirty next week. Maybe more. That wasn't supposed to happen." He shook his well-groomed head at Rehv. "Inflation is killing me."

"How do you know what will happen to the price of gas?" Rehv asked.

Mr. Cohee smiled. He had square white teeth with a narrow dark gap between the cuspids. Leon laughed his tinny laugh. Mr. Cohee didn't stop him. Leon laughed for quite a long time. After a while Mr. Cohee said, "Better pull over to the side, Leon." The big car was sitting in the middle of Madison Avenue. "We don't want to get a ticket." This set Leon off again, fueling his laugh like lighter fluid on hot coals. He barely had enough strength to put the car in gear and double-park.

Mr. Cohee pulled back a white cuff and looked at his watch. "Fifteen minutes are almost up, Dr. Vere. What is it you want for your hundred dollars?"

"A woman." This was too much for Leon.

"That's enough, Leon," Mr. Cohee said. The laugh subsided. Mr. Cohee's curious dark eyes studied Rehv's face. "You've gone to a lot of unnecessary trouble, Dr. Vere."

"You don't understand," Rehv said. "I'm looking for a very special woman. You'll get much more than a hundred dollars if you help me find her."

"Who is she?"

There was a pause while Rehv thought. "I'll know her when I see her," he said.

The tendons at the back of Leon's neck twitched very slightly, like sensitive antennae. "Are you playing some kind of game with me?" Mr. Cohee asked quietly.

"I'm very serious," Rehv said just as quietly. Behind them a car honked. Leon glanced in the rearview mirror. The car honked again. Leon watched it. It backed up and drove around them, honking as it went by.

"Go on, Dr. Vere," Mr. Cohee said.

Rehv looked right into the curious brown eyes. "The woman I want is intelligent. Very intelligent. So smart she always seems to know just what you're thinking. I mean you personally, Mr. Cohee." He half expected to hear Leon's laugh, but no sound came from the front seat. "She's strong, physically strong. And tall. Five feet ten or more. With skin the same color as yours."

"Anything else?"

Rehv considered. "No defects, of course," he said. "Diabetes, bad heart, shortsightedness. Or mental illness."

"Is that all?"

"All I can put into words."

Mr. Cohee gazed at him for a moment in silence. "What do you want, Dr. Vere? A fuck or a wife?" The first notes of Leon's laugh squeaked in his sinuses. "Shut up, Leon," Mr. Cohee said, cutting the sound off before it could properly begin.

"Something in between," Rehv said.

"It's going to cost money."

"I'll pay her going rate."

"That's understood. You'll have to pay me, too."

"How much?"

"That depends how much work I have to do."

"All right."

"How do I know you can afford to pay?"

"You'll have to trust me."

Curiosity vanished from the dark eyes, leaving emptiness in its place. "I don't trust anybody, Dr. Vere."

"Then trust that hundred-dollar bill. I gave it to you to show I wanted everything done in a businesslike way."

Mr. Cohee began to laugh, a soft rumbling, pleasant laugh from deep in his chest. Leon joined him in a nasal descant. When the laughter had gone, Mr. Cohee said, "I'm all for the businesslike way. That's why I have Leon." The three men thought their different thoughts about that.

Rehv broke the silence. "Can you help me?" he asked.

"Can we help him, Leon?" Mr. Cohee said.

"Angel," Leon replied.

"Maybe," Mr. Cohee said slowly. "Let's go."

Leon pressed the accelerator, and Rehv again felt himself being pushed deep into the soft seat. Mr. Cohee switched on the television and opened the liquor cabinet. He took out two glasses and set them on a sliding shelf that pulled out from the side of the cabinet. "Scotch? Gin? Vodka? Rum?"

"Scotch." He suddenly wanted a drink very badly: Something at the edge of his mind was waiting for his attention. Naomi.

"On the rocks?"

"Please."

Mr. Cohee poured two drinks. "To businesslike ways," he said, raising his glass.

Mr. Cohee watched the miniature men playing basketball. Rehv tried to drink the scotch slowly and keep the ice from rattling against the sides of the glass. He could do neither. "Just help yourself," Mr. Cohee said. Rehv did.

The miniature men ran back and forth, jumping, twisting, falling. "Poor white boy," Mr. Cohee said sadly. He glanced at Rehv: "This is the only time I ever feel sorry for white people— when I see them playing basketball."

"Say it," Leon said.

Leon parked the silver car as close as he could to the entrance of a famous disco. It was not very close. The best parking places had all been taken. So had the best double- and triple-parking places: by cars from Rolls-Royce, Mercedes-Benz, Ferrari. They were all expensive and they all had parking tickets on the windshield.

Mr. Cohee reached into an inside pocket and handed Leon a card. "Go get her," he said. Leon got out of the car and started walking toward the door. For a moment Rehv saw his face— hard, fleshless, with eyes sunk deep and safe in bony nests. It didn't seem to go with his body, a lean, strong body that moved lightly, gracefully, economically. His feet barely appeared to graze the sidewalk as he walked along. Mr. Cohee noticed him watching. "Leon was a Golden Gloves champion," he said. "Could have gone further than that, much further."

"Why didn't he?"

"He got mixed up with the wrong crowd," Mr. Cohee answered with a little smile. "Ended up doing most of his fighting in prison. It took all the purity out of his style."

Leon spent a long time in the disco. It was owned by a woman whose face appeared in a certain kind of magazine almost every week. It was a greedy petit bourgeois face, not at all softened or disguised by her thick red hair, cut in the latest style. Rehv had seen her on television: The cameras had revealed that her hair was dyed, she couldn't dance, and her face was the way he had thought.

Leon came out of the disco. Beside him walked a woman as tall as he, which Rehv guessed to be a little under six feet. She hadn't put on a coat. She wore a short dress and long leather boots that disappeared beneath its hem. She was slender and might have walked as gracefully as Leon if the high heels of her boots had not lifted up her small, firm buttocks and pushed her pelvis forward.

Leon said something to the woman, walked around the car, and leaned his body against the long hood. He didn't bother to open the rear door for her. She opened it herself. Rehv shifted to give her room. She sat down and closed the door. Her long legs took a lot of room. Despite the size of the car Rehv felt closer to both of them than he wanted to be.

Without switching off the television Mr. Cohee leaned forward and turned to her. "Hello, Angel," he said. "This is Dr. Vere."

"Uh-huh." She was gazing at a ring on her long middle finger: a large dark polished stone.

"He wants to have a look at you." Mr. Cohee pressed a button on his armrest and a bright yellow light glowed from the back of the seat in front of her. "Look at him, Angel. He can't see you that way."

The woman turned her head and faced him. In his mind Rehv felt a sharp prick of self-disgust that made him want to shake his head, or close his eyes, or say, "Oh, God." But he forced himself to look at her.

The color of her skin was perfect, perhaps a shade lighter than Mr. Cohee's. It was smooth and unmarked, except for a tiny curved scar under her lip. That would not matter. Her face was thin, angular, Cubist, he thought, suddenly realizing that the twentieth-century ideal of female beauty somehow had its roots

113

in twentieth-century art. She wore green makeup above and below her eyes, eyes the color of dull brass. They didn't appear to be seeing him at all.

"Satisfied?" Mr. Cohee asked.

Again he felt a pang of self-disgust. He wanted to squirm away from himself. Instead he nodded. "But I'll have to talk to her." To the woman he said: "I'd like to talk to you for a few minutes."

"He wants you to talk, Angel," Mr. Cohee said. "Talk."

"Talk?"

Rehv looked at her. Her eyes still were not seeing him, but the tiny plucked lines that were the remains of her eyebrows had lifted in puzzlement. "Just for a few minutes," Rehv said gently. "Tell me a little about yourself," he suggested, feeling so stupid he almost blushed.

"I'm a whore," Angel said. "I charge one hundred dollars an hour. Five hundred a night."

There was a long silence while Rehv tried to think of something else to say. Mr. Cohee watched television. Angel gazed at her ring, which in the light he could see was an amethyst.

Finally he said: "Have you ever thought of modeling? I think there's a lot of money in that, too."

The woman laughed bitterly, but did not reply. Mr. Cohee laughed as well. She jerked her head toward him, the brass eyes suddenly hooded and seeing very clearly. "What are you laughing about, you bastard?"

Mr. Cohee leaned across Rehv and slapped Angel across the face, very hard. "You fucker," she said. Rehv felt her saliva spray on his face.

"The other cheek, Angel?" Mr. Cohee said very calmly.

"Stop it," Rehv said. He must have said it very loudly, because Leon sprinted to the door where Mr. Cohee sat and yanked it open.

"Something wrong, Mr. Cohee?" Leon's little eyes peered at them from their deep craters.

"Nothing at all, Leon. Close the door. It's freezing."

"Keep that fucking murderer away from me," Angel said, raising her voice.

Leon leaned far into the car, tilting up his chin, and held his face very close to hers. "Touch me," he whispered. "Go on. Just touch me."

She glared at him, but she didn't move a muscle.

"It's cold in here, Leon," Mr. Cohee said. And colder after he said it. Leon withdrew and closed the door. He left behind an odor that made Rehv think of iron filings.

He looked at Mr. Cohee. "I've got nothing more to say."

"And? She'll do? Or not?"

"I don't think we should discuss that in her presence."

"Why not, Dr. Vere? She's not applying for a seat on the stock exchange."

"Then it's no." He wanted to say something polite to her, like "I'm sorry," but he could not think of anything that wouldn't sound ridiculous.

"Split, Angel," Mr. Cohee said.

"I want some money."

"You're lucky you still have a face."

Angel got out of the car, slammed the door, and walked quickly away. Leon called after her, words that Rehv could not quite distinguish, but she didn't turn.

Mr. Cohee turned to him; the curious eyes searched his face. "Why not?" he asked.

"She just wasn't right. I can't really explain it," Rehv said. But he could very easily: If she wasn't smart enough to handle Mr. Cohee, she wasn't nearly smart enough.

Leon got into the car. Mr. Cohee looked thoughtfully at the back of his shaved head. "Where to, Mr. Cohee?"

Mr. Cohee didn't answer him. Instead he looked at Rehv and said: "Have you got another one of those envelopes?"

"No."

"What about what was in the envelope? Any more of those?"

"Yes."

Mr. Cohee smiled. "Better give me one. With a car like this it's nice if everyone chips in on the gas." Leon didn't laugh: He was no longer in a laughing mood, Rehv thought. He gave Mr. Cohee another one-hundred-dollar bill. Mr. Cohee slipped it inside his jacket pocket and tapped Leon very lightly on the shoulder. "Paulette."

"Paulette?" Leon said, with a little whine in his voice. "She's too dark."

"I don't think so."

"She's got no class."

"I don't think Dr. Vere cares very much about that. Do you, Dr. Vere?"

"No."

"Paulette," Mr. Cohee said again. Leon started the motor and pulled away.

Outside the night went by. Taxis took over the streets, their drivers hunched forward, watching for shadows waiting on the curb. Rehv began to feel tired. He knew from the whine in Leon's voice that he was tired too. Mr. Cohee did not seem tired at all. He refilled their glasses and gazed into the flickering light of the little television.

Leon stopped the car in front of an old brick apartment building on the East Side. It was the kind of building where doctors and lawyers had lived long ago, and might still if they were very old. Mr. Cohee opened the door. "Wait here," he said to Leon. To Rehv he said, "Come with me."

They opened the outer door to the building and went inside. Mr. Cohee ran his index finger over the row of black buttons and pressed one. After a few moments he pressed it again.

"She's probably asleep," Rehv said.

Mr. Cohee didn't reply. He pressed the buzzer once more and kept his finger on it for what seemed like a full minute. From the square mesh of the speaker came a female voice that sounded deep and harsh and angry: "What is it?"

"It's me," Mr. Cohee said. The inner door buzzed. Mr. Cohee pulled it open before the buzzing stopped.

He led Rehv to an old elevator with two doors—the outer solid and the inner a folding brass grille. They rode to the sixth floor and got out.

Rehv and Mr. Cohee followed a worn brown carpet to the end of a hall. They stopped in front of number 606. Mr. Cohee knocked. Immediately the door opened wide. A very tall woman stood in the doorway, an inch, perhaps two inches taller than Rehv. She wore blue plastic curlers in her hair and a blue flannel nightgown, which was slightly too tight and revealed the strength of her body. She was much broader than Angel, and darker, too dark, Rehv thought. She had large eyes, larger and darker than Mr. Cohee's, and they weren't friendly.

"What do you want?" she said. Her voice sounded the same as it had through the speaker, only bigger.

116

Mr. Cohee nodded toward Rehv. "What do you think?"

The woman looked down at him over Mr. Cohee's shoulder. "He can't afford me," she said. "All those Jewish refugees are stone cold broke."

Rehv stepped closer to her, pushing Mr. Cohee slightly to the side. "What makes you think I'm an Israeli refugee?"

"I got eyes, man," she said, tapping the crest of her cheekbone.

He knew she was the one.

CHAPTER FIFTEEN

"I want a baby," Isaac Rehv said.

They sat in Paulette's living room: Paulette on an orange corduroy couch that looked new, Mr. Cohee in a patched and faded stuffed chair that had once been either brown or yellow but now had a shiny surface of no particular color, and Rehv on a folding card table chair he had pulled to the center of the gray unpolished hardwood floor. Beneath the window on the far side of the room a tiny old woman was sitting in a wheelchair, a blanket over her knees. Her skin was very dark and deeply creased; her hair the color of old ivory. Her watery eyes were fixed on a very large television screen, where some pirates were fighting with cutlasses. There were no books in the room, no magazines, no newspapers, and nothing hung on the walls except a big oil painting of John Kennedy, Robert Kennedy, and Martin Luther King, Jr., wearing dark suits and standing on clouds.

Mr. Cohee looked at Rehv, frowning. "A baby?" he said. "That would take me two or three days. More than that if you want a white one."

"Don't be a fool," Paulette told him. "He's talking about a nine-months baby."

"That's right," Rehv said.

"Sure," Paulette said, leaning forward a little to look at Rehv more closely; her strong shoulders strained the fabric of her nightgown—it was split slightly along the seam, revealing an oval of chestnut-colored skin. "You want me to have a baby. Your baby."

"Yes."

"You see?" she said to Mr. Cohee.

"He's crazy," Mr. Cohee said with annoyance. He turned to Rehv: "You're crazy." Annoyance grew into anger, and Rehv caught some of it.

"I'll pay. Business. Remember?" He heard a little chuckle in the back of Paulette's throat.

"Leon outside?" she asked Mr. Cohee. He nodded. She chuckled again.

"Talk," Mr. Cohee said.

"First I want to ask Paulette a few questions." She narrowed her eyes, assuming the problem-solving face of a schoolgirl called on by the teacher even though she has not raised her hand. Rehv was surprised to see an expression like that on such an intelligent face. He tried to imagine her as a schoolgirl, sitting at a desk in an orderly row, and couldn't.

"How did you do in school?" he heard himself say. It was not one of the questions he had meant to ask.

Paulette laughed. She threw back her head and laughed some more. Her breasts jumped up and down. Her nostrils flared like tiny laughing mouths. The plastic curlers clicked together.

"Hush," said the old woman in the wheelchair in a thin irritated voice. "I can't hear a word they're saying." She spoke without looking at them. She did not take her eyes off the screen for a second.

Gradually Paulette's laughter subsided, flaring up once or twice the way a badly tuned motor does after the ignition has been turned off. "Men have asked me a lot of funny things," she said, in a tone that was much less harsh; perhaps laughing cleansed her voice, Rehv thought.

"It doesn't matter anyway," Rehv said. "But I do need to know if you've ever been pregnant."

"Yes."

"How many times?"

"Five," she answered immediately.

"Any children?"

"I don't have children. I have abortions."

"That's not true, child," the old woman called from the other side of the room.

"Shut up," Paulette said. Harshness reentered her voice like a cactus that thrives in a desert of bad feeling.

"What does she mean?" Rehv asked.

Paulette lowered her eyelids, whether to shut him out or to threaten him he didn't know. "Nothing. She's a stupid old meddler."

Rehv glanced at the woman in the wheelchair. She hunched forward, narrowing the gap between her eyes and the television. "She had a baby, sir," the old woman said. "A little baby girl."

"Don't call him sir," Mr. Cohee said suddenly, very angry.

"Why not?" Her weak tired voice sounded angry too. "She should have another baby. Be the best thing in the world."

Mr. Cohee glared at her but said nothing.

"When did you have the baby?" Rehv asked Paulette. She folded her arms across her chest and kept her mouth shut.

"June the fourth nineteen hundred and seventy-two," the old woman answered.

"I'd like to see her," Rehv said, fearing as he did that the child might have been taken to live somewhere else by its father.

"Then you'll have to be able to see through six foot of solid ground," the old woman said. "She got run over, right here on this street."

"I'm very sorry." The room grew quiet, except for a man on television who was threatening to burn every settlement on the Spanish Main unless he got his way. Rehv thought about Lena. He was vaguely aware of the two dark faces watching him, and tried to push her away, but she would not go. Her presence made it much harder to say what he had to say; he came very close to not saying it at all. But finally, as if to keep them inside was as impossible as holding one's breath forever, the words came out: "Was she a healthy child?"

The color seemed to drain from Paulette's face, like chocolate ice on a stick when someone sucks it. "Jesus." She spoke the word so softly he could barely hear it.

"She was a perfect baby in every way," the old woman said.

"Shut your fucking mouth," Paulette shouted.

"Perfect," the old woman muttered defiantly, hunching closer to the screen.

Rehv looked at Paulette, trying to will a little friendliness into her angry eyes. "I have nothing more to ask," he said gently. "I'm sorry, but I had to know." Her eyes stayed the same.

"I have a question," Mr. Cohee said. "A money question."

"I'm offering Paulette fifteen thousand dollars, payable the day

120

the child is born. It must be a boy." He felt a little surge of nausea inside himself and took a deep breath to force it back down. "Because of that Paulette will have to be tested as soon as possible after she becomes pregnant. If it's a girl it will have to be aborted and we'll try again."

None of that bothered Paulette or Mr. Cohee. "I want more than that," she said.

"You forgot to mention how much you were paying me," Mr. Cohee said. "If we go ahead with this Paulette will probably miss a month of work. Sometimes they miss two."

"Paulette won't be working at all. We can't risk having the baby infected with a venereal disease."

"You're a dreamer," Mr. Cohee said. "Tell him how much you give me every week, Paulette."

"Five hundred dollars."

"Can you multiply, Dr. Vere?"

Rehv ignored him. "On the day the baby is born I will give you one pound of cocaine."

Mr. Cohee pulled himself closer to the edge of his chair. "What kind of cocaine?"

He had no idea. "Colombian," he said, remembering an article in the newspaper. "Very pure."

"How pure?"

"Ninety percent," he said, trying to recall the text of the article.

"Have you got a sample?"

Rehv took a small plastic bag from his pocket and unrolled it. In one corner was a teaspoonful of white powder. He rose, walked over to Mr. Cohee, and handed him the bag.

"Wait here," Mr. Cohee said. He stood up and went out of the room by the front door. Rehv sat down and looked at John Kennedy, Robert Kennedy, and Martin Luther King, Jr. Paulette twisted the curlers in her hair and flexed her long, muscular feet. The pirates hauled their cannon through the jungle.

After a while Mr. Cohee returned. "Leon says it's not ninety percent. But it's good enough."

"Then we have a deal?" Rehv asked, wondering whether it was one hundred percent pure.

"If you give me coke now, yes, we have a deal."

"No. One-third tomorrow. The rest when I said."

Mr. Cohee stared at him for a moment, looking for something he didn't find. He sighed. "I'll have to trust you."

"That won't be hard for you," Rehv said. "You've got Leon."

Mr. Cohee laughed and offered his hand. Rehv shook it, thinking of the way it had cracked across Angel's cheek. It was a very hard hand. "Leave the coke here with Paulette," he said. "I'll pick it up tomorrow night." He turned to go.

"What about me?" Paulette said to him. "I can't stop working for nine months. Who's going to pay the rent?"

"I'll take care of your expenses," Rehv said.

Paulette and Mr. Cohee exchanged a glance. She shrugged. "Have a nice holiday," he said to her as he went out.

"Holiday," Paulette repeated, as though it was a word from a foreign language. She rose and walked toward Rehv, with a look in her eye that made his chest feel tight. She stood very close to him and asked, "Why me?"

Rehv tried to think of something that would make sense. "We'll go well together," he said.

Paulette laughed her big laugh. He was very conscious of her size and strength: They seemed to give her an invisible power, like gravity. She stepped forward and put her arms around him.

The Spanish Main went up in flames.

But only for a moment: And in that moment he felt a flooding of desire in his penis that was so strong, so quick, that it sucked in all his energy and made his mind a haze; and he knew without thinking that he had reached the shore of a dangerous land, more dangerous than the Battle of Haifa, more dangerous than Abu Fahoum's bodyguard in the night. And danger found him right away: In the haze he saw Naomi's face as it was in orgasm. His penis, not quite fully hard, fell like a bird shot at the instant of takeoff.

"Come on," Paulette said, pulling him toward a dark corridor.

"Not now," he said, drawing back, feeling light-headed, almost faint.

"Don't worry about her," Paulette said. "She's used to it."

"It's not that." Rehv bit the inside of his cheek, hoping it would clear his head. "There's no point until you're off the pill."

"No?" He heard mockery in her tone. "But I don't use the pill. I have a diaphragm." She drew him into the corridor.

122

"It's not that simple. We're trying to produce a baby. We have to know where you are in your fertility cycle, for example."

"What?"

"When was your last period?"

"About a week ago."

"Then you're probably not ovulating yet."

Paulette stopped tugging at him. "So you want to get me pregnant with just one fuck? You think that's going to happen?"

Rehv said nothing. He had really not thought about it. While he was thinking he felt her tongue touch his ear. She ran it all around the edges and then stuck it inside. "Come on," she whispered.

She led him to a bedroom at the end of the hall. In the bedroom were an unpainted plywood chest of drawers, all of them opened, a scattering of clothing on the floor, a lamp made from a bottle of gin, and an unmade double bed. Paulette went to the window and lowered the venetian blinds. "No free shows," she said. She turned to Rehv: "Take off your clothes."

"Maybe we should turn off the light."

He heard the low chuckle, deep in her throat. "Why? Don't you want to see what I got?" She pulled her flannel nightgown over her head, and Rehv saw: the long heavy muscles of her legs, the thick curly black pubic hair reaching almost to the round, deep navel, the long hard nipples of her breasts, the little circles of hair under her arms, her smile, her eyes, amused, and the blue curlers in her hair. Paulette lay on the bed. "Take off your clothes," she said again.

Rehv took off his clothes, feeling her dark eyes on him. "You have a very nice body," she said. She spread her legs a little. Rehv approached the bed. Paulette reached out and took his penis and testicles in her big hand and tested the weight, like a shopper at a fruit stall. "This will be nice too, when it gets hard."

But it wouldn't get hard.

Rehv lay on his back. Paulette knelt over him. She licked his penis. She took it in her mouth. She took his testicles in her mouth, one at a time, together, with his penis. She licked her middle finger and forced it into his anus. She removed it, licked it again, and put it in farther. Rehv was aware of all this, but he felt nothing, as though his nerve endings no longer reached his brain. He watched her work. She was an experienced mechanic in a country where spare parts were scarce and only clever improvisation kept the faulty, damaged cars on the road. She did not seem surprised, upset, or disappointed.

Rehv felt something gathering force in his body, not where he wanted it, but higher. It was a kind of laughter, building in his chest. An insane laughter that once begun would never stop, could never be stopped by him. His heart began to pound with it. His penis, his sexuality, his manhood as people used to say, were betraying him, were destroying the last hope for his own salvation and the salvation of his people. He had thought of everything but that: to be beaten by himself.

The laughter pushed up his throat like a fist. He opened his mouth; and felt Paulette swing her body over his, and lower her huge, strong buttocks onto his face. "Lick," he heard her say. And then: "Come on, man. I want that big Jewish cock inside me."

Suddenly, as his tongue touched her and he heard those words, he felt again the wild rush of blood to his groin, and he turned her over—she seemed to weigh nothing at all—and sank his penis deep inside her. He began to pound her body, and pound and pound. He heard her gasps and her cries. Their pores opened and cloaked their bodies in a common wetness, like giant twins in an amniotic sac. Her cries changed to soft whistling sounds in the back of her throat. He felt her great body slowly tire. He did not tire at all.

And when he finally came it was so long and so painful he felt he was losing his insides. Like childbirth.

Later he awoke. He heard Paulette snoring quietly beside him. Carefully he got out of bed and looked out through the slats of the venetian blinds. The night was completely still, except for the little wisps of vapor someone was exhaling across the street.

CHAPTER SIXTEEN

"I'm sorry," Armbrister said. "I did all I could."

"Like hell you did."

"I did, Krebs. I really did." Armbrister wore a solemn face that strove for compassion but did not quite achieve it, and so seemed ambivalent instead: the kind of face usually seen by unpleasant relatives on their deathbeds. "Confidentially, it was Bunting. Right from the beginning I could see his mind was made up. 'The asshole got caught.' That's what he said whenever anyone spoke in your favor." Armbrister looked down and began poking through the piles of paper on his desk.

"What if I told you they're trying to raise money by moving into drugs and prostitution?"

Armbrister lifted a stack of files and peered underneath. "Why do you say that?"

"I've been watching him."

"Who?"

"Rehv."

Armbrister stopped shifting papers and raised his head. There was no longer the slightest ambivalence in the expression on his face. "You make everything very difficult, Krebs." He had more to say, but he kept it to himself, staring coldly at Krebs while the thought unfolded in his mind. Then he sighed and again began pushing papers around his desk. "Ah. Here it is," he said, holding up a white envelope. He handed it to Krebs.

Krebs opened it. Inside was a check for $5,722.33.

"Severance," Armbrister said.

Krebs took the check, his pen and pencil set, and his round mirror and left the building. On the way to the garage where he kept the car he went into a bar and ordered a scotch on the rocks. There was no one in the bar except the bartender, cutting his nails, and a middle-aged waitress dressed like an Eastern European folk dancer. Krebs drank his scotch and thought about Armbrister. He drank another and thought about Bunting. He had several more and thought about Isaac Rehv. People came in. They were hungry and thirsty. They smoked and laughed. They talked shop. Lunchtime. Krebs paid his bill and left.

At the garage he asked for a rebate on his monthly payment.

"We don't give rebates," the attendant said.

"I'm not going to pay for twenty days of parking that I'm not using."

The attendant shrugged. "Sorry, bud."

Krebs got into the car and slammed the door shut. Something rattled in its innards, and the window slid down crookedly. He tried to roll it back up, but it was stuck. "Shit," he yelled, alone inside the car. "Shit."

Krebs drove across town, over the bridge, toward home. Cold air rushed in through the crooked opening and swirled around him. He turned the heater to maximum and pressed on the accelerator. Alice. He could say it was a budget cut. Office politics. Personal jealousy. Maybe she wouldn't bitch. There hadn't been much bitching lately. She'd been cooking his dinner every night. They were sleeping in the same bed. They'd even had sex. When? Last week? She'd had an orgasm. She said.

Siren. Stop. Police. Krebs pulled over. Automatically he reached for his wallet, had his hand on it before he remembered the little yellow card was no longer inside: Armbrister had it.

"Do you know how fast you were going?"

Krebs shook his head. He didn't want to play quiz games. He didn't want the trooper to smell his breath.

"You should always know your exact speed when driving a vehicle." There was a silence while the trooper waited for Krebs to say something.

"If you're going to give me a ticket, then do it," Krebs said at last.

"You just made up my mind," the trooper said.

Krebs left the turnpike and entered the town where he and

Alice had lived since their marriage. He stopped at the bank, deposited the check, and drove toward the suburb they shared with other members of their income group, although they did not know any of them except to say hello. Many of the streets were crescents; in his neighborhood they had been named after trees— Maple Crescent, Elm Crescent, Beech Crescent. Krebs lived on Willow Crescent, a short street that curved very slightly at one end and had no willows. A spruce tree grew on the front lawn at number thirty-nine. At the top its needles were turning orange and brittle, and falling whenever the wind blew. Krebs raked them up on Sundays.

He saw that Alice had not left him enough space in the driveway, and parked on the street. He went into the house. Mail lay scattered on the floor in the front hall—five or six letters, all written by computers. In the living room the pillows had not yet been plumped up; last night's dishes were where they had been last night. She probably sleeps all morning, he thought as he climbed the stairs, and starts neatening the house ten minutes before I come home.

The bedroom door was closed. Krebs stood outside, testing phrases in his mind. "I've resigned." "I couldn't work there anymore." "We came to a parting of the ways." "I've been let go." "I've been fired." "Wake up, lazy bitch, this is going to make your day." He heard laughter in the bedroom: surprised, happy laughter. At first he did not realize it was hers. He threw the door open.

Alice was in bed with a man. On the bed. The covers had fallen to the floor. The noise of the door startled them. They turned. Krebs had never seen the man before. He was young, with long blond hair and a blond beard. "Oh, my God," Alice said, and lifted her leg awkwardly to climb off the blond man. Krebs moved in and started hitting.

Alice twice with the back of his hand. Face. Breast.

The blond boy moved between them. He was bigger than Krebs. Maybe that gave him the courage to ball his hands into fists. "Don't," Alice screamed. "He'll hurt you." Belly. Belly. Belly. The blond boy tried to defend himself. Chin. He felt Alice behind him, tugging at his arms. He turned and punched very hard at the middle of her face. Her eyes rolled up as she fell across the bed. She bled on the sheets. The blond boy backed into a corner, hunched. His penis had gone very small and pale. Krebs wanted badly to hit him again; it was a deep physical need, as though his fist was the source of desire. But he knew that once started he would not stop, and he fought to control his passion while the boy trembled in the corner and Alice lay still on the bed. He turned and walked out of the house.

He drove. Willow Crescent to Poplar Crescent. Poplar Crescent to Spring Drive. Spring Drive to Mariposa Road. Mariposa Road to the turnpike. The turnpike to Trenton. In Trenton he stopped and bought a bottle. He drank and drove. Philadelphia. Baltimore. He thought of driving to California. He turned back. He switched on the radio. He tried to sing along with the songs it played, but he didn't know the words, and his voice sounded hoarse and ugly. He went into a bar in Philadelphia. It was full of black people. He drank. No one talked to him. He went into another bar, full of white people. He drank. No one talked to him. He said something to the waitress because she had a hard little mouth and a hard little ass like the girl who brought him coffee. The manager asked him to leave. He sat in the car and tried to remember the name of the girl who brought him coffee, and where she lived. She was smart, and hard. She'd been waiting for him to make the first move, but he never had because they didn't go for hanky-panky at the office. He'd been a good little boy, so good he'd lost the chance to dig his fingers into that hard little ass. He passed out.

A dog howled. A cat screamed. He woke up and vomited on the seat, his clothes, his hands. He lay in it, too weak to move. The dog howled. The cat screamed. He sat up, started the car, and drove home. The sun rose, small, cold, and far away in the east, but the light it cast was very bright. It hurt his eyes. He felt the vomit congealing in his hair and under his collar. He smelled his smell.

When he reached thirty-nine Willow Crescent it was midmorning. Sunny and cold, with an ice blue sky. Alice's car was gone. He parked in the driveway and walked past the dying spruce tree, into the house. No Alice. No blond boy. He lay across the bloodstained sheets and fell asleep.

He dreamed of Alice. She was driving on the turnpike, singing a song. There was a man lying in the back seat, but she didn't know it. He sat up. Isaac Rehv. He touched the side of her neck.

Alice turned and smiled at him, smiling and smiling. She twisted around to kiss him. The car veered toward the guardrail. Alice laughed.

Krebs awoke the next morning. He showered and shaved and put on clean clothes. He noticed that most of Alice's clothing was gone. He went outside, cleaned the inside of the car with hot soapy water and a sponge, and drove to the bank. Alice had withdrawn every cent.

CHAPTER SEVENTEEN

On a Monday, his day off, Isaac Rehv woke up early and went to the library. At the foot of the stone steps a short bow-legged man was roasting chestnuts and rocking rapidly from side to side, either to fight the cold or because his bladder was full. Rehv bought a bag of chestnuts for his breakfast. Automatically the little man's hands, turning blue at the fingertips, filled the bag and gave Rehv his change; the man himself was absorbed in his rocking, his dark eyes far away, as far away as the Mediterranean, Rehv thought. He climbed the stone steps, his mind on what he and the chestnut man had in common.

Inside he found an empty table and gathered a pile of books. He read about nutrition during pregnancy, fetal growth, birth, babies, childhood development. For Lena he had known very little about these things. He had relied on Naomi. Now he would rely on himself.

He read quickly, bent over the black formations arranged in endless rows on the white pages. He felt hurried, pressed, as though another pair of eyes was chasing his across the paragraphs. He had thought of leaving La Basquaise to give himself more time, but Paulette's expenses were very high. Even with the money he earned there he would barely have enough. He had years, he knew, but so little time. His back hurt. He ignored it and kept reading. After a while he became aware of a rhythmic creaking noise, close by, and suddenly realized that he was rocking back and forth, like the little man outside.

Later the words began lining up in phrases, theories, counterarguments that he had seen before. Rehv made a list of vitamins Paulette should be taking and foods she should be eating. He rose, stretched, and went off for more books: books on cattle and water, Kordofan and Darfur, guns and ammunition. He read.

"You deaf, or something?"

Rehv looked up and saw a slight, angry old man who wore a brown uniform several sizes too big. "What?"

"Closing time, that's what."

Outside it was night. The chestnut man had gone. Rehv felt the stone steps through the soles of his shoes, cold, as though cut from huge blocks of ice. As he started down, his eye caught a movement in the shadows behind a marble column. He was turning to look when something hard poked him in the middle of his back, where the pain was worst. A voice whispered: "Don't move." Male. American. Tense. He didn't move.

"Down the stairs," the voice said. "Slowly. Be smart." Poke.

He walked down the stairs, feeling the man behind him, although they were not touching. "Right." Poke. They walked north, in single file but too close for strangers. A young couple approached, arm in arm and gazing into each other's eyes, about to kiss. He could cry for help, spin, dive, tackle. Poke. The young couple kissed, went by.

"Right." They turned onto a street. Forty-sixth. How was it done? A thrust of the elbow, a quick pivot, the edge of the hand. He had seen it hundreds of times in the movies. "Don't even think about it," the voice said. Poke.

They came to a car parked by the curb. "Stop." He stopped. "Get in. The driver's seat." It was an American car, not big, not new. He did not know the make. He tried to read the license plate but the car had been parked in the dark margin between two streetlamps, where their cones of yellow light did not quite meet. He could read none of the numbers; he was unsure even of the state; it did not appear to be New York.

He opened the door and sat behind the wheel. The man got in the back seat. "You're going to drive." Rehv glanced down and saw there were no keys in the ignition. He waited for the man to give them to him. He did not hear the sound of fingers searching in a pocket, or clinking metal. He felt a little breeze touch the back of his head. And then nothing.

He was in the hospital. Paulette lay naked on a bare table,

her legs spread, her stomach huge. "It's coming," she screamed. The doctors and the nurses left the room. He called after them and ran to the door. It was locked. "It's coming." Paulette pushed. The ball inside her quivered and moved slowly toward the opening between her legs. "Help me." He reached inside her, felt a hard roundness. "Gently." He pulled on it gently. It stuck. He twisted it carefully and pulled some more. Suddenly it began to slide, wet and slippery, out of her body and into his hands. Abu Fahoum's head. He dropped it and ran to the door, and beat on it with his fists. Paulette began to laugh. "Come back," she called. "There's more. I've got another one for you." He beat harder on the door.

He had a headache, a strange headache at the back of his head. It was digging tunnels of pain down his neck as if trying to join forces with the ache in his back. He didn't want to be alone with the pain, so he opened his eyes.

He was in the gallery. Home. The Hungry Warriors—Napoleon, Genghis Khan, Eisenhower, Rommel, and General Gordon —were gone. In their place stood a small platform, crudely built of unfinished plywood. It supported a tall wooden beam that almost reached the ceiling. At the top was another beam, much shorter, which stuck out over the platform at a right angle. From it hung a noose.

A man sat on the platform, watching him. He was a sandy-haired man, with thick eyebrows that were much darker and not at all hidden by the aviator-style glasses he wore. Rehv thought he had seen him before, and was about to ransack his brain for the memory when he felt something biting into his wrists and realized that his hands were behind his back. He tried to move them but could not. He looked down and saw that his legs were tied with electrical wire to the legs of a card table chair, and that he was naked. Sweat began to pool in his armpits: He felt a little drop of it trickle down his ribs. He ran his eyes quickly over the gallows, searching for some sign that it was art. Screwed to one side of the platform was a small plastic sign: "Olé."

"Totally useless," the sandy-haired man said. "No trapdoor, no diagonal support, rope's too thin. You couldn't hang a pygmy with it." Standing up, he approached Rehv and spoke to him in a tone that indicated the preliminaries were over. "My name is Major Kay," he said. "I'm conducting an investigation for the

U.S. government. I have some questions to ask you. If you co-operate there will be no unpleasantness, and it will be over very quickly. I don't want to hurt you, but I will if I have to."

But from the excitement that crept into his voice and the look in his eyes Rehv knew that he did want to hurt him. "I don't believe the U.S. government conducts its affairs like this."

Major Kay raised the back of his hand. It trembled close to Rehv's face for a few moments before he lowered it in jerky stages. "Then you're very naive," Major Kay said, a little thickly. Something in his tone made Rehv think that he had stopped his hand only because he did not want to take the edge off his antici-pation so soon: He wanted it to build. Rehv felt another drop of sweat trickle across his ribs, but he tried to keep his voice calm and even.

"You don't look very military to me," he said. Major Kay wore a heavy black sweater, blue jeans, and tennis shoes smeared with black shoe polish; he needed a shave. "Have you got some identification?"

Major Kay smiled down at him, a smile Rehv did not like at all. He reached into his back pocket and drew out a snub-nosed revolver. He pointed it at Rehv's face, and very slowly brought it closer and closer until it touched the tip of his nose. Looking into Rehv's eyes, he held it there, and then pushed the barrel into his right nostril. "This is my ID," he said softly. "Do you understand? Nod if you understand, Isaac."

Rehv nodded, tilting his head slightly up, slightly down. Major Kay took advantage of the descending motion to drive the bar-rel a little farther into his nostril. "Now you're starting to co-operate." He withdrew the barrel and replaced the gun in his pocket.

Rehv felt warm liquid dribble from his nose and onto his upper lip; and he felt the chill in his torso from the cold sheet of sweat that was slowly covering him. He looked at Major Kay: A rosy flush had risen in patches to the surface of his cheeks. What was being drained from Rehv's body was somehow nourish-ing the other man.

"You're enjoying this, aren't you?"

Major Kay smiled at him, the calm, cruel smile a big brother sometimes turns loose on a little one when the parents are out of the house. "I'm doing my job."

Rehv knew there was much more to it than that. He stared again at those dark eyebrows, and searched his brain for a memory he knew was there. He could not find it.

Major Kay drew up another card table chair and sat opposite Rehv, so close that their knees were almost touching. "Where is Nuri Said's body?"

"I don't know what you're talking about."

"Nuri Said was Abu Fahoum's bodyguard," Major Kay said patiently. "Before you killed Abu Fahoum you killed Nuri Said. What did you do with his body?"

"I've never killed anyone. Those names mean nothing to me." Major Kay continued to smile. "And you're not working for the U.S. government," Rehv added.

The smile vanished. "What do you mean?" For the first time Rehv heard uncertainty in his voice.

"If I was suspected of a crime I would be formally charged," Rehv said, hoping his words would keep Major Kay off-balance. "It wouldn't be like this."

The smile returned. "It would be just like this."

He had failed to find whatever it was that Major Kay feared. Major Kay pulled his chair a little closer. Their knees touched: Rehv felt the rough fabric of the denim.

"Was it your idea to raise money selling drugs? Is that why you went to Vermont?"

"I've never sold drugs in my life," Rehv replied. "Is that what this is all about? Are you a narcotics agent?"

"Stop trying to outthink me, Isaac. I'm not interested in drugs. I'm interested in what your people in Vermont are planning to do with the money."

"I don't have people in Vermont."

"You're going to have to lie much better than that," Major Kay said. "I'm talking about the farmhouse in Vermont that calls itself the capital of Israel. You went there on the twenty-seventh of November."

He gave Rehv another big-brother smile. It was not the smile itself that was frightening—lips, gums, teeth—but the eyes that did not smile at all. They were pale brown eyes, closer in color to his hair than his eyebrows, and they were full of hurt and the wish to hurt at the same time. Major Kay was right. He had to lie much better; he had to keep him talking all night, like a clever little brother who plays for time. He glanced up at the skylight: It was very dark. He had no idea of the hour.

"It's early yet," Major Kay said, pulling back the edge of his sleeve to look at his watch. He kept its face out of Rehv's sight. "You weren't out very long at all."

He had to keep him talking. It was all he could think of to do. "I went to the kibbutz in Vermont. There's nothing unusual about that. I'm an Israeli. It's the same as you visiting Washington. It didn't have anything to do with drugs."

But there was nothing in that little forest of words that interested Major Kay. He ignored it and said: "And the prostitution. Is that a money raiser too? Or just a freebie on the side?"

At last his memory released an image: puffs of vapor in the cold night, across the street from Paulette's window; and somewhere else. And another image: sandy hair, dark eyebrows, the comic page of a newspaper—Major Kay sitting in a car outside Dr. Lanze's office. Rehv felt his heart beat faster. The fresh blood seemed to wash some half-formed ideas from his mind, and leave in their place one clear thought: He must keep this man away from Paulette.

"I sleep with prostitutes sometimes. Is that unusual?"

"No," Major Kay answered. Again he seemed uninterested in what Rehv was saying. Rehv began to think he was behaving like a man going through the motions; he began to hope.

Major Kay reached into his pocket and took out a piece of paper. "I almost forgot," he said. "What's this: 'Vitamins A, B-complex, C, and E. Balanced diet, slightly more intake. Milk, greens, fruit, cereals. No coffee, tea, chocolate, alcohol.'"

Rehv laughed, the laugh of an innocent man caught in an absurd situation. "I've been feeling run-down lately. That's my new regimen."

Major Kay smiled. Were his eyes smiling too? He stood up, and Rehv let himself think that he was about to go. But Major Kay shook his head. "I don't believe you, Isaac. You haven't been very smart at all. Maybe you're a masochist."

"I'm not a masochist."

"We'll see." Major Kay turned and went to the far side of the plywood platform. He bent down and reemerged holding a brown paper bag. From it he took out a long black extension cord. He plugged one end into an outlet and returned to Rehv, unrolling the cord as he walked. "Just long enough," he said, dropping the free end at Rehv's feet. He sat down facing Rehv, and placed the paper bag on his lap. "These things follow a pattern, Isaac. First you deny everything. Then, when the pain starts you make up a long and clever story that often resembles the truth quite closely, but never really says anything. Finally, you tell the truth. Everyone does. So think about it, Isaac. We can skip all that." His smile said he didn't want to skip a thing.

"I've told you the truth. You're making a big mistake." He could not take his eyes off the paper bag.

"Not me, Isaac," Major Kay said. "You. I lost my goddamned job because of you."

"But we're complete strangers."

"Not at all. I know you very well." Major Kay opened the paper bag and pulled out another electrical cord, only a few feet long. At one end was an ordinary plug. At the other the plastic insulation had been removed, revealing a single copper wire five or six inches long. It was pointed and of nearly the same thickness as the cartridge of a ball-point pen.

Major Kay pulled his chair forward. Their knees touched again. "I'm going to ask you some questions, Isaac." His voice was almost sugary. "Questions you know the answers to. If you respond with a false answer I am going to insert this wire into your urethra. I will then repeat the question, although it might mean waiting until you regain consciousness. If you again answer falsely I will plug this cord into the extension, which will send a current as far inside you as the point of the wire happens to be. Is that clear?"

Rehv jerked backwards with all his strength. The chair overturned. As it toppled he twisted his head to keep it from being struck again at the back. The chair fell sideways. He took most of the impact on his shoulder. He rolled over, straining every muscle against the electrical cords that bound him to the chair. He couldn't loosen them at all.

Major Kay watched him struggle without getting up. "I see you're beginning to take me seriously." He rose, grabbed the back of the chair, and righted it with an ease that made Rehv aware of a physical strength he had not suspected from the man's appearance. Major Kay pulled the chair back to its former position and sat down. He grasped the copper wire in his hand.

"Where is Nuri Said's body?"

Rehv felt himself losing control of his body—his heart, his lungs, his sweat glands, his sphincters. They all began behaving wildly, as if they were cut off from his brain. He thought: If this had happened a few months ago, I would have told. Jail, death would not have mattered much. But now it was different. He had to live. He had to be free. "I don't know what you're talking about." His voice sounded high and faint, barely audible beyond the tumult in his ears.

Major Kay leaned forward. His pale brown eyes had gone soft and dreamy. With his free hand he gripped Rehv's penis. Rehv contracted his muscles to rock backwards again, but before he could, Major Kay stamped on his bare foot and pressed hard, pinning him motionless. With his other hand he took the copper wire and did what he said he would do.

Rehv fell into a sea of screams. He swam. Was he still swimming? He had been swimming in that sea for a long time. He would swim there forever.

"You're a tough boy, Isaac. Most men pass out on the spot." He heard Major Kay, far away, but he saw nothing more than a round shiny blur. "Where is Nuri Said's body?"

Rehv tried to say, "Fuck you." The shiny blur moved in front of his face. He sank to the bottom of the cold blackness.

A noose dangled over his head. Two big fish eyes looked down at him. They were red and sore. "You're going to be fine, just fine," a worried voice said. "The doctor says there's no permanent damage, none to speak of. Rest, that's all you need." He felt a little pinprick in his biceps, and something soft and warm being drawn over his body. "Here's some money in case you miss any work." Paper rustled. "Just take it easy."

"Major Kay?" He heard the voice of an old man.

"Major Kay? Oh yes. Major Kay. Don't you worry about him. He's had it. You can take it from me."

Rehv sank back down to the bottom.

CHAPTER EIGHTEEN

Isaac Rehv rested his hand lightly on Paulette's bulging stomach. A seismic tension was building beneath the surface. "Here comes another one," he told her, checking his watch.

"Christ," Paulette said. She waited for it, her eyes wide and unfocused, like someone who has heard a faint sound in the night and strains to hear another. He felt a trembling in her flesh. Deeper inside something tightened and kept tightening. A tiny drop of sweat squeezed through the skin of her forehead, just below the hairline. It grew. Two more appeared. Paulette gritted her teeth. "Christ," she said again, more loudly.

The trembling diminished, and died away. The muscle within relaxed. Rehv glanced at his watch. "Thirty-seven seconds," he said. How many more of these tremors would there be before the pressure was strong enough to finally shift the two beings along the fault line, and begin the separation of baby from mother? Somewhere nearby a woman yelled in pain.

Paulette looked at him. For a moment he thought she was going to ask him to take his hand off her stomach. Instead she said, "I'm thirsty."

He should have thought of it himself. He went to the sink in the corner of the small labor room and filled a paper cup with cold water. He handed it to her and helped her lift her head to drink, feeling for a moment an intimacy with her he had never felt before: not in bed with her the few times it had taken until she became pregnant; not on his visits to bring her vitamins, oranges, coffee substitutes, and money, and take her for walks;

certainly not the night, long after the confirmation of her pregnancy and the amniocentesis, when she had asked him to go to bed with her again, and he had gone, and been unable, not because of Naomi, but something else. No physical damage to speak of.

Rehv became aware that she had stopped drinking, although the cup was still between her lips. Her eyes again had that inward, unseeing look. Rehv withdrew the cup, returned to the side of the long table, and laid his hand on her stomach. Another hand appeared, small, pale, freckled, and rested beside his. He looked up and saw a woman who needed sleep. Her eyelids were puffy, her eyes sunk deep in dark pockets. Her frizzy hair was the color of newly minted pennies. The rest of her had no color at all. She wore a white robe with her name stitched in black thread over the pocket: F. Pope, M.D.

"She's in good labor," the doctor mumured, taking her hand away.

"Christ, Christ."

"Thirty-nine seconds."

The doctor pulled on a rubber glove and dipped it into a jar of lubricating jelly. "What's your name?" she asked Paulette in a friendly way.

"Paulette," Paulette answered warily.

"This might hurt a little, Paulette," the doctor said, bending over her groin.

"Then don't do it."

The doctor smiled a smile she didn't mean and probed inside Paulette's vagina. Paulette grunted. "Sorry," the doctor said, but she continued to probe. Rehv looked into her eyes and saw a thought go by, just under the surface. She kept it to herself.

"Christ Almighty."

The doctor withdrew her hand. The glove was smeared with thick liquids—clear, yellow, red. "Is everything all right?" Rehv asked.

"Fine." The doctor turned to Paulette. "We'll be able to give you an epidural in a little while."

"We'd rather not," Rehv said. "We've agreed to try to do without one. For the baby."

"That's up to you." From the look on her face Rehv had expected her to say a lot more than that. She left the room. Rehv followed her, remembering the thought he had seen in her eyes.

"Is everything all right?"

"I told you," the doctor said, walking away. "Fine." She stopped and turned. "Are you planning to watch the delivery?"

"Yes." She nodded slowly and went off.

He reentered the room. "What did she tell you?" Paulette asked.

"Nothing. I went out for a breath of air, that's all."

"There's air in here." She opened her mouth to add something, but another contraction began, and she grunted instead. It became very quiet. He heard the distant rumbling of an elevator.

"Thirty-five seconds."

"Stop looking at your goddamned watch."

He gave her more water. The woman nearby yelled again. Paulette flinched. "Don't worry," Rehv said. He wiped her forehead with a damp cloth. "You're in good labor. That means it won't be long."

But two hours later Paulette was still in good labor, and she was yelling too. "Goddamn you. This is worth a lot more than fifteen grand."

He moved to wipe her forehead. She jerked her head away. You've had a baby before, he thought. You knew what it was like. Her mind must have been moving in the same direction. "It wasn't like this the other time."

The doctor returned. "She says it wasn't like this with her first baby," Rehv told her, trying to say it in a conversational way.

The doctor ignored him. She probed again with the greasy rubber glove. Paulette yelled. For some reason he had thought she wouldn't do that in front of the doctor. The doctor stripped off the glove and went to the sink to wash her hands. "The baby's in breech," she said.

Rehv remembered a few paragraphs from his reading at the library. "Does that mean a Caesarean?"

"No," Paulette said. "No scars." To Rehv she said: "I've still got to earn my living after this is over."

The doctor looked at her and parted her lips as if to say something, but whatever it was stayed inside. She was very tired.

"Does it?" Rehv repeated.

"I always avoid it if I can. I'll try to turn the baby around with forceps."

"No forceps," Rehv said.

Wearily the doctor turned to him. "What's your name?"

140

"Isaac Rehv."

"Listen, Isaac —"

"Mr. Rehv."

She sighed. "Mr. Rehv. We like having fathers here during delivery. We really do. But you're here to watch, that's all. If you interfere we can send you out of the hospital."

"But it's too big a risk."

The colorless, almost lifeless skin of the doctor's forehead wrinkled. "I don't understand."

"Forceps."

The doctor managed a thin smile she meant to be reassuring. "Don't worry, Mr. Rehv. I've done hundreds of perfect forceps deliveries. This one won't be any different."

"But I don't want him marked. Or damaged in any way. His brain."

"I'm not going to argue," the doctor said. Her lower lip began to quiver. "I'm not."

"Oh, Christ."

They looked at Paulette, lying on the table. Her head was thrown back. The tendons in her neck stood out like flying buttresses under her skin. "And she's having an epidural," the doctor said. Paulette yelled. The woman nearby yelled. Someone dropped a tray of metal instruments.

"All right," Rehv said, but the doctor had already gone. He found the damp cloth and pressed it gently on Paulette's forehead.

A nurse entered. She was slight and dark, with large black eyes and straight black hair. She looked like Manolo. She handed Rehv a little pile of white hospital clothing and wheeled Paulette out of the room.

Rehv dressed himself in the clothing: cloth boots that went over his shoes, a starched gown that tied at the back, a cotton headdress that looked like a shower cap, a mask that covered his nose and mouth, gloves. He waited. He paced. He removed the face mask and drank a cup of water. He put it back on. He heard footsteps cracking the air pockets under old linoleum, quarters drop into a vending machine, two men arguing in Spanish, a woman's laugh, a baby's cry. The nurse who reminded him of Manolo opened the door. She had changed into an outfit much like his, except that it was green. She beckoned.

He followed her along a broad corridor and into a large room. Under a harsh white light he saw Paulette lying on another table, shorter than the one in the labor room. There was no more sweat on her brow, no more pain in her eyes. She was partly covered by a coarse green cloth. Her legs were drawn up, her pelvis close to the edge of the table. Two black nurses stood on either side of the table. The doctor was crouching between Paulette's legs. The Filipino nurse pointed to an empty stool drawn up to the end of the table nearer Paulette's head. Rehv sat down.

One of the black nurses glanced at him. "You have to look in the mirror if you want to see anything," she said. "We used to let the daddies sit at the side but they got in the way there when they fainted." The nurses laughed under their masks. Rehv raised his head, and in the small round mirror that hung from a horizontal light support at the far end of the table he saw Paulette's gaping vagina, its lips pried wide apart by two steel forceps. He looked at her face, upside down. She looked back. They had nothing to say to each other.

"Push, honey," said the nurse who liked to see men faint. "Push. Push." Paulette pushed. The force of her body shook the table. "That's it, honey. That's it. Okay."

Paulette stopped pushing and waited panting for the next contraction. In the mirror Rehv watched the forceps slide deep inside her body. One moved up, the other down, in a twisting motion. He thought of the baby with its head dented, its face torn open, or its brain bruised where no one could ever see. And what if something was wrong already? A bent spine. Mild retardation. An extra toe. Even an extra toe would mean the end of everything.

"Push, honey." Paulette pushed. The doctor pulled on the forceps, very hard. "Push. Push. Push." Paulette grunted. "Okay, honey." In the mirror Rehv saw, deep inside her body, a narrow pale crescent that had not been there before. He couldn't take his eyes off it.

"Push." The pale crescent came closer. The doctor did something with a scalpel at the base of Paulette's vagina. Blood spurted. Rehv barely noticed. He watched the crescent coming closer and closer. It was no longer a crescent at all, but a sphere, round and hard and matted with wet dark hair.

"Last time, honey." Paulette pushed. He heard a baby cry, somewhere far away. The baby cried again, and he knew suddenly

142

that it was his baby, crying inside Paulette. The doctor took the hard sphere gently in her hands and turned it very slightly. Slowly the sphere squeezed through the opening, inch by inch. Then, crying and bloody, his boy slid out into the doctor's hands. She held it up for Paulette to see.

"A perfect baby," the Filipino nurse said. She laid it, him, on Paulette's heaving breast. He stopped crying. He lay quietly, his head turned toward Rehv. Rehv wanted to touch the side of his face, but he was afraid. The baby opened his eyes. He seemed to look directly at him. His eyes were big and dark and alert. He was looking at him. He was everything Rehv had wanted. But for the first time Rehv understood he was his son as well.

"Here," the Filipino nurse said. She was handing him a piece of paper tissue. He realized that tears were rolling down his face, and he wiped them away.

"Thank you," he said. She had gone. They had all gone: the nurses, the doctor. He had wanted to thank her too.

"Are you all right?" he asked Paulette. She nodded. He saw that she was crying. "What's wrong?" But he knew what was wrong.

Paulette held the baby on her breast. Very still, he lay there, watching his father. After a while he turned his head a little and moved his lips against Paulette's breast. She helped him. He suckled.

"He's a beautiful boy," Paulette said.

"Yes."

"We could stay together." It was a question. They both knew the answer. He shook his head.

The door opened. A nurse stood there, one they had not seen before. "Time to go up to the ward."

Paulette reached out for him, gripped his arm. "I want to give him a name," she said.

"What name?"

"Paul."

"All right." The boy would need an American name, he thought. For now.

The nurse began to wheel them away. The baby felt the movement and stopped suckling. His eyes were still opened wide. He kept them on his father as he disappeared out the door.

CHAPTER NINETEEN

Krebs heard a quiet metallic click followed by a very soft thud. The mail. Sliding through the slot. Falling on the carpet in the hall. Yesterday, bills for water and electricity, notice from the credit card company that he had exceeded his maximum. The day before, the phone bill, with an enclosed threat to cut off service if payment was not received by some date or other.

He looked at the clock. The hour hand pointed into the gap between four and five. The minute hand was right behind it, a tiny sliver of white clockface away. Four-twenty-two. But as he watched the sliver did not become tinier, disappear; the minute hand did not gain ground, pass over the hour hand, turn on the speed toward the far turn at six and up the other side, in the daily race to noon and midnight that always ended in a dead heat, the hour hand coming from nowhere to tie. They were not racing today. Time had stopped.

Four-twenty-two. He had probably gone to bed by then, perhaps he had fallen asleep. Or had he still been sitting in front of the television, watching unfamiliar actors relive the Oklahoma land grab in black and white? And eating: three hamburgers with everything—he had forgotten to say, "No pickles"—and two orders of fries. With ketchup.

Krebs pushed back the covers and got out of bed. The curtains, not quite closed, admitted a shaft of late September sunlight that bisected the dark room like a wall of golden glass. He drew them completely together. The wall vanished. He began picking through the shadowy pile of clothing by the foot of the bed. He didn't bother going to the chest of drawers or the closet: They were empty. All his clothing was in the pile, waiting to go to the cleaner's. It had been waiting there for a month or two.

Krebs pulled on a pair of gray flannels. He left the button unfastened and the zipper halfway down because he had to. His flesh bulged over his waistband like a scoop of ice cream too big for the cone. In the bathroom he urinated but neglected to give his penis a shake after he had finished, or perhaps he hadn't quite finished, and when he started down the stairs he felt a warm dribble seep into the flannel and spread across his thigh.

The mail lay fanned on the floor. He bent down to pick it up: a letter from the bank, no doubt to remind him that his mortgage payment was overdue, something from a record club, something else from a skiing magazine, a letter from France that should have been delivered next door, and a bill from a florist in Raleigh, North Carolina, addressed to Alice. He would write on it, "Not at this address," and leave it in the slot for the postman, as he always did. Nothing but bills ever came for her.

Krebs stood up, thinking about Raleigh, North Carolina. He was aware of movement outside, and glanced through the small round window in the top of the door. Bunting was walking up the path. A long black car was parked at the curb. Quickly Krebs stepped to the side, away from the door.

The doorbell rang. It rang again. Knuckles knocked against the glass. Then something scraped inside the lock, and Krebs knew Bunting was coming in whether he opened the door or not. He opened it and, conscious of his unshaven face, his new fat, and his stained trousers, said: "What do you want?"

Bunting responded to his words, not his tone. "No time to explain now," he said, brushing past Krebs and into the hall. "I'll tell you in the car. Throw some clothes on. You've got two minutes."

"I don't have to take orders from you anymore."

"Of course you do, Krebs. You're back on the team. Unless you've found some better work, that is."

A daydream was coming true, like finding a sack of money on the sidewalk or a beautiful girl in your bed. Krebs knew that daydreams didn't come true in life, not in his life. "Why?"

"Don't be so suspicious, Krebs," Bunting replied. "You were right. We were wrong."

"I was right?"

"Yes. About Isaac Rehv."

Bunting waited in the living room. Bunting in his hand-tailored charcoal gray suit, with his pink skin, his prematurely gray hair, and reading glasses hung around his neck, waited in a little clearing in the refuse: fast-food cartons, moldy spareribs, beer cans, empty bottles, comic boks—Porky Pig, Archie, Superman. Upstairs Krebs splashed cold water on his face and wished he had time to shave. He noticed a hair growing out of his nostril—so long, how could he have missed it?—and yanked it out on his way to the bedroom. He put on a shirt and jacket less wrinkled than the rest, and hurried down the stairs, breathing hard.

"You look like hell, Krebs," Bunting said as they went out the door.

Krebs and Bunting sat in the back seat. "The city," Bunting told the driver, who started down Willow Crescent at a speed that made a small boy look up as he pedaled his tricycle along the sidewalk.

Bunting reached down to the floor and picked up a small reel-to-reel tape recorder. He pressed a button, listened to himself say, "That's not dill," and pressed the fast forward. "I won't bore you with the whole thing," he told Krebs. Bunting found the part of the tape he wanted, and sat back, the recorder on his knee.

A man said: "Believe me, I'd like to help you." He had a soft Israeli accent and sounded tired and old.

Bunting said: "Then tell us about the Haganah."

The old man laughed, but he didn't put much into it: "There is no secret about that. I was with the Haganah in the forties. I know nothing of this new Haganah, if it exists at all."

Bunting said: "Okay, Dennis."

The old man screamed in pain.

"Hell," Bunting said, stopping the tape. "That's not it." He ran it forward. Krebs found a striped necktie in one of the pockets of his jacket and put it on. "Maybe here," Bunting said. He pressed the play button and turned to Krebs, a worried look in his eyes. "Checks and stripes, Krebs?"

The old man was crying. He made a high nasal sound, but with plenty of volume, Krebs noticed, like a small child.

146

Bunting said: "Take this away." There was a rattling sound Krebs could not identify. Bunting said: "I can't eat cafeteria swill one more day. From now on we'll order from that deli across the street."

Someone said: "The Belly Deli?"

Bunting said: "Right."

The other man said: "I think they close early."

Bunting said: "Find out." Footsteps. A door opened and closed.

The old man cried.

Bunting said: "Have you got a cigarette, Dennis?" A match was struck. The sound was very good: Krebs could hear it scrape against the sandpaper strip. He glanced at Bunting and saw him dipping into his pocket for cigarettes. He lit one with a gold lighter and began filling the car with blue smoke.

The old man's crying turned to sniffles, shivers, nothing.

Bunting said: "Feeling better?"

So quietly Krebs could barely hear him, the old man said: "Yes."

Bunting said: "Good. Where is the girl?"

The old man said: "My granddaughter?"

Bunting said: "Yes, yes."

The old man said: "She died that night. She was badly wounded. We couldn't stop the bleeding."

Bunting said: "Where's the body?"

The old man said: "In the ocean. I rented a little boat at Montauk."

Bunting said: "We'll want to see this boat."

The old man said: "I can show you."

Bunting said: "You're telling me you drove to Montauk, carried the body onto the boat, rode out to sea, and dumped it over the side. How old are you, Uri?"

The old man said: "Sixty-eight."

Bunting said: "I don't believe you did all that yourself." There was a long pause. Krebs looked down and watched the shiny brown tape spin silently around the spools. After a while Bunting said: "Dennis."

The old man said: "No. No."

Bunting said: "Wait, Dennis."

The old man said: "Rehv helped me."

147

Bunting said: "Rehv? The waiter?" Krebs bent closer to the machine.

The old man said: "Yes. But he's not just a waiter. It was his idea in the first place. He took the bodies to Montauk and waited for me on a beach. I brought the boat along the coast until I found him. Then we took them out to sea."

Bunting said: "Bodies." There was another pause, not as long as the first.

The old man said: "Abu Fahoum's bodyguard. Rehv killed him later that night. In self-defense."

Bunting said: "And Abu Fahoum?"

The old man said: "I know nothing about Abu Fahoum, except what I read in the newspapers." The tape sped on. Another match was struck. Krebs heard it fall with a very slight ring into a glass ashtray. In a low voice the old man added: "But the bodyguard was killed with a knife as well." Then, for no apparent reason, the old man began to cry again.

Bunting pressed the stop button. "There's a lot more, but nothing to concern you immediately." He placed the tape recorder carefully on the floor, glancing at Krebs. "You look a bit better," he said.

"I'd like to question him," Krebs said.

Bunting shook his head. "Too late. He's already transferred."

"Transferred?"

"The usual way."

"When did this happen?"

"Last night. Early this morning, in fact."

"You've got Rehv then?"

"Not yet. We tried that gallery in SoHo, but he had already gone. We're watching it though, and the restaurant. We'll get him when he comes in to work." Bunting spoke a little faster than he normally did, and Krebs knew that there had been a mistake. Perhaps they had not moved fast enough.

"There's one place we could look while we're waiting," Krebs said. He told Bunting. Bunting told the driver.

Traffic grew denser as they neared the city. They crossed the bridge at less than walking pace. The sun turned the dirty air to smoky gold. Inside the car it was smoky blue. Looking out, Krebs realized that he had hardly been aware of spring and summer. If you watched enough television it was always winter. "Does Armbrister know about this?" he asked.

148

"Armbrister? No." His eyes straight ahead, Bunting inhaled smoke and let it out with a little sigh. "I'm not sure what to do with old Armbrister. Now that you've taken over his job." Thoughts, too many to examine individually, burst in Krebs's mind like a meteor shower: Sell the house, run, do push-ups, shave, fire Armbrister's secretary. The hard-assed girl. And others he would dwell on later.

The driver parked in front of a brick apartment building that was slowly sinking through the class structure, working its way down generation by generation while its occupants were trying to go the other way. A black man in a pearl gray suit came out of the building, carrying a small package wrapped in brown paper. He was dressed better than Bunting.

Krebs stared up at the facade. "I don't know the apartment number, but it was that window—two from the end and six up." He led Bunting into the building. The inner door was held open by a pail of brown water. They rode the old elevator to the sixth floor and followed the worn carpet to the end of the hall. Number 606. "It has to be here," Krebs said softly. He knocked twice.

The door opened as his knuckles tapped it the second time. A tiny old black woman in a wheelchair faced them across the threshold. "What has to be here?" she said. Even though the apartment was warm she wore a wool blanket over her knees.

"We're very sorry to bother you, madam," Bunting said. "We're looking for a man named Isaac Rehv."

"Name means nothing to me." She pulled the blanket a little higher.

"We're looking anyway," Krebs said. He grabbed the arms of the wheelchair and pushed the old woman into the living room.

"Go on," she said. "Kill me. Do you think I care?"

Krebs and Bunting left her there to search the apartment. They found nothing. When they returned to the living room she was in the corner watching television, sitting less than three feet from the screen. Without looking at them she said, "Take all I got. Kill me. I'm ready."

"You're making a mistake," Bunting said gently. "We don't want to hurt you. We're just looking for Isaac Rehv. We don't want to hurt him either."

"Just do it," the old woman said, rolling a little closer to the television. "I'm ready."

Krebs took a step in her direction, but Bunting took him by the arm and turned him toward the door. They went outside and sat in the car. "Do you want me to stay here?" Krebs asked. "Or will you send someone else?"

Bunting lit another cigarette and examined its burning tip. "Are you sure about the apartment?" he said at last.

"Two over and six up. Of course I'm sure. I saw him look through the blinds."

"But it was night," Bunting said mildly. "It would have been easy to make a mistake."

"I haven't made any on this one so far."

"All right," Bunting said, and he asked the driver to give him the telephone.

"Goddamn it," Krebs said suddenly. He jerked the door open. "We should have cut her phone cables."

"Krebs. She's senile."

"Maybe." Krebs ran into the building and up the stairs, taking them two at a time at first, then singly, finally walking. He had not realized how badly out of condition he was. When he reached number 606 he was panting. He knocked. This time the door did not open immediately. He knocked again. And again. It was not going to open at all. He turned the handle. It was unlocked. He went inside. She was gone.

Early morning. Isaac Rehv, carrying two small packages wrapped in brown paper, unlocked the door to number 606 and walked in. The old woman was watching television. He stood beside the wheelchair for a few minutes, watching with her. It was the movie critic again. "The liberal middle class has a very weak stomach these days, and it's getting weaker. It can't digest anything raw—everything has to be sugarcoated. And this applies especially to any sort of violence. I'm talking about the kind of liberals who —" The interviewer smiled and held up his hand like a traffic cop: "We'll find out all about it after this short break." The movie critic smiled a thin smile. It was just as false as the interviewer's, but at least it meant something. Talking intestinal bacteria appeared on the screen.

"I've brought these packages," Rehv said.

"Shh."

He waited until the intestinal bacteria were dead. "One is for

Paulette. It's her money. The other is for Cohee. He'll come for it soon." He laid the packages on the old woman's lap. Without looking she took them one at a time in her bent, arthritic hands and tucked them under her blanket.

"When's she coming home?"

"Tomorrow."

"Then she's going away."

"Just for a few days. To the Bahamas. She's tired."

"Me too."

The movie critic reappeared and began talking about movies she didn't like. Her mouth moved very fast. Rehv looked down at the old woman and saw that her eyes were closed. He turned to go.

The old woman's hand reached up and caught his. "I want to see that baby," she said. Her hand was cold. "Please. I've got a right. He's my great-grandson." She opened her eyes and twisted her body around in the wheelchair so she could see him: eyes staring up at him, blurred and wet.

"I'll bring him by at the end of the week."

"Thank you. Thank you, Mr. Rehv." She turned back to the screen.

He spent most of the day in the library, reading about Islamic prayer rugs and studying photographs of them. When he had learned about them he telephoned a few dealers from the booth outside and asked about prices. Then he started walking to work.

The sidewalk was very crowded. He stepped on someone's heels; someone else stepped on his. He passed a blind man holding a box of orange pencils who had very little money in the upturned hat at his feet, and a man who was playing Beethoven's Fifth Symphony with a saxophone. He wasn't playing it very well, but his hat was almost full. Two blocks from La Basquaise he slowed down to watch a supple man in whiteface who seemed to be miming the story of Adam and Eve: He was curled around an imaginary tree and flicking his pointed tongue wickedly; then he was a buffoon biting an apple.

"Mr. Rehv?" A woman's voice, almost a whisper. He looked around and saw her, pale and thin, her back to a window display. She stepped forward and touched his arm. "It is you?" He heard the soft Israeli accent. He had seen her somewhere before. "You work at a restaurant called La Basquaise?"

He nodded.

151

"Don't go there." Her voice rose. She pulled him toward the window, out of the flow of people. "I've been waiting here all afternoon to warn you. They've got my grandfather."

He remembered. Tear gas. "Harry?"

"That's not his real name. His real name is Uri Nissim."

"Who has him?"

"The Americans." Panic circled the edges of her voice, threatening to engulf it. One of her eyelids was twitching uncontrollably.

"I'm sorry." He couldn't think of anything else to say.

She looked at him for a moment, puzzled. "You don't understand. He's had enough pain. He won't be able to take any more. He's going to tell them everything."

He understood. Quickly he crossed the sidewalk and raised his hand for a taxi. She followed him. "Where are you going?" She pressed her fingers against her eye, but it didn't stop the twitching. A taxi pulled up in front of him. As he opened the door he felt her hand clinging to his arm. "Where are you going?"

He looked into her frightened eyes. She wanted to come with him. He looked away. "Don't worry about your grandfather," he said, as gently as he could. "They won't send someone his age to prison."

"Prison? They don't send any of us to prison. They hand us over to the Arabs."

"What do you mean?"

"It's a deal the Americans made. They try to keep it a secret, but everyone knows. If they catch you they send you back to . . ." The word stuck in her throat. "To Palestine."

Someone honked. "In or out, bud," the taxi driver said.

Rehv got in and closed the door. Through the window he saw her bury her face in her hands. "Roosevelt Hospital," he said. He left her standing hunched on the edge of the sidewalk.

The taxi moved forward, stopping frequently in the heavy traffic. "I'm in a hurry."

"Then fly."

One block. Two. Rehv looked down the second street. In front of La Basquaise a few workmen in yellow hard hats were standing around an open manhole. The one using the walkie-talkie was Major Kay. Rehv slid down out of sight.

At the hospital he paid the driver and started running. Inside. Into the elevator. Twentieth floor. Down the hall. The nursery.

Behind the glass were babies, rows of them, lying in bassinets, the girls wrapped in pink blankets, the boys in blue. Most of them were crying with their mouths wide open, but the glass kept all the sound inside.

Rehv went to the nearest door and knocked. A nurse opened it. "Yes?"

"I want to see my baby."

She pointed to the clock at the end of the hall. "Forty-five minutes until visiting time."

"Please. I have to go to work in half an hour."

"Oh, all right, all right. Don't look so desperate. Boy or girl?"

"Boy."

"Surname?"

"Rehv."

"Go to the window. I'll wheel him up to the front."

"I'd like to hold him. I haven't held him yet."

"For God's sake."

"It's not against the rules, is it?"

She sighed. "No, no." She took a folded white coat from a counter beside her and handed it to him. "You have to wear this."

She went inside the nursery. He put on the coat and waited. In a few minutes she returned carrying a baby wrapped in blue. He could have picked him out among a thousand babies. He was not sleeping or fussing or crying. He was just watching, with his big dark eyes. She handed him to Rehv.

"I'm going to take him for a walk. He likes walks."

"Five minutes."

He nodded. He started walking down the hall. He went past the nurses' station and smiled at the nurses. They smiled back. He kept going, around the corner, past the elevators, to the stairs. He walked down twenty flights, through a service entrance, and into the street. The baby did not make a sound.

"That's a good boy," Isaac Rehv said to him quietly. "That's a good boy."

Krebs stood at the foot of the bed, riffling through the green bundles: three bundles of one-hundred-dollar bills, held together by elastic bands; fifty bills in each one.

"That money belongs to me," the black woman said, propping herself up on her elbows. Her body seemed to fill the bed. "I haven't broken any law."

"Shut up." When he had said that to the nurse a little while before she had burst into tears and run from the room. But the black woman just said: "I'm right and you know it."

Krebs walked to the window. Outside the sky was changing from black to gray. "It belongs to me." The old woman had said the same thing, when he went back to the apartment building and finally found her in the corridor on the seventh floor, sitting in her wheelchair, waiting through the night for her granddaughter to come home from the hospital.

He went to the bed and dropped the green bundles on the thin beige blanket. "You can keep the money. We're not interested in you. We're interested in Isaac Rehv."

"I've told you everything I know."

They went through it again. Once. Twice. Once more. The same questions, the same answers; each time a little nastier than the time before. At last he gave up, and turned toward the door. "You're making a mistake," she called after him. "He's not a criminal."

He sat in the back seat of the car. Bunting lit cigarettes and breathed them until they were gone. "He kidnapped his own baby. Why would he do that?"

"He must have known we were coming," Krebs replied.

"How?"

"I don't know how."

Bunting rolled down the window and tossed a cigarette butt into the stream of traffic. "Maybe he's crazy."

"No," Krebs said. "He's not crazy."

CHAPTER TWENTY

Slowly, as slow as the weakest calf, the nomads moved south into the Goz. The women and children rode on the backs of oxen, wedged between straw mats, rolled hides, and cooking pots. Rich men rode horses; poor men rode donkeys. The cattle plodded on, heads down, dewlaps hanging limp; some of them switched their tails hopelessly at the mosquitoes and horseflies, most did not bother. Above them hovered a red brown cloud of dust, visible miles away, that followed them from first step to last. The dust found its way into their nostrils, under their eyelids; mixed with sweat it ran in muddy tracks on their faces, light lines against dark skin. Above the red brown cloud were other clouds, the dense gray rain clouds of late autumn, clouds that never rained, or if they did, rained somewhere else, a thousand miles away. What rain there would be had already fallen, the rain the nomads would live on for the year. It had been very little. That was why they were moving south so early, to the feeble river; to more mosquitoes, more flies, and other cattlemen, black man who had once been their slaves.

Late in the afternoon the nomads halted on the savannah, near a large shallow pool of rain trapped in a red clay depression. They looked at the level of water and saw how low it was, lower than even the oldest could remember ever seeing it at that time of year. The cattle smelled the water, made restless sounds, and funneled toward it. The children went to gather thorns from the bushes that grew here and there in the midst of the coarse grasses; they piled the thorns into a circular *zariba* to pen the cattle in for the night. The women began building the tents, straw mats arranged on a frame of branches to form hemispheres. Later they would collect bits of wood and cattle dung for the cooking fires. The men started walking over a small rise toward the men's tree, an old deep-chested baobab that gave them shade while they waited for their food. As they walked they brushed the dust from their *jubbas* and talked of the water in the pool, and how it had been the year before, the year before that, ten years before, twenty.

When they reached the top of the rise they saw that someone was already there, under the tree. It was a man, wearing a white turban and a white robe. He was bent prostrate on a prayer rug, in silent prayer. They saw no horse, no donkey, or any other sign of how he had come. Quietly they drew closer, watching.

The man prayed for a long time, unaware of their presence. Then he slowly lifted his head and rose to his feet. His skin was very light, much lighter than the skin of the lightest Baggara, lighter even than the skin of an Egyptian. One or two hands moved a little closer to the long knives worn under the jubba.

"Call the women and children," he said to them. He spoke Arabic, but Arabic different from theirs, classical and not easy to understand.

No one moved.

"I bring you no harm," the man said. "I want nothing from you. Call the women and the children."

They turned to Bokur, the *omda*. He looked closely at the light-skinned man. He nodded. A man went off. No one spoke. They watched the light-skinned man. His eyes showed nothing. A drum beat. The women and the children came. They crowded around the baobab tree.

"I bring you no harm," the man said again. "I want nothing from you. I have come to tell you something. Then I will leave you in peace." He paused and looked at them. They were very quiet.

"Once men thought it was the end of the age. A man came to your ancestors, a divinely guided man. They rode with him. He drove the outsiders from Khartoum."

"The Mahdi," some of the nomads murmured.

The man's voice rose. "But it was not the end of the age. The end of the age is still to come. It is not far away. And another

156

divinely guided one will come to you. But he will not be from another people, like the man your ancestors knew. He will be one of you. Dark like you. He will show you the way. He will find water when the pools are dry."

A man spoke, a rich man. He had eight hundred cattle and four wives. "Why should we believe you?" he asked.

The light-skinned man looked for him in the crowd, and when he found him his eyes turned hard. "You will believe what you are destined to believe," he told him.

He said no more, but prostrated himself again on the prayer rug and began to pray in silence. Later they offered him food to eat and a tent to sleep in, but he refused both, saying that he was fasting and liked to watch the stars.

In the morning when they awoke he was gone. The prayer rug lay beneath the baobab tree. It was a dark red prayer rug, very old and very fine. Bokur took possession of it in the name of the tribe.

The sun was already hot enough to bring sweat to their foreheads. The nomads broke camp and moved on. The red brown dust rose above their heads. As they rode on the backs of the oxen, the women began to make up songs about the light-skinned man and what he had said.

PART TWO
THE PROMISED LAND

CHAPTER TWENTY-ONE

The boy paddled little whirlpools at him. Kneeling in the stern of the wooden canoe, Isaac Rehv watched them twist by, a chain of holes across the smooth surface of the lake. Each whirlpool looked the same as the one before—just as round, as deep, as swift in its rotation; his eyes went to the whirlpools he himself was making, and he saw they were all slightly different.

Under the summer sun the boy's back had grown browner, like coffee with one plastic container of cream instead of two. It was a straight, lean back that rippled in an easy rhythm as he paddled. In those ripples Rehv saw the cores of the man's muscles that were soon to come. Very soon, he thought, trying to remember his own puberty and remembering only pimples and awkwardness and fatigue, nothing at all of the grace and beauty he saw in that back.

"Paul," he said, speaking Arabic. "What is the Kaaba?"

The boy said nothing. His back went on moving with the same steadiness, but the whirlpools he was pushing back were deeper and wider, and spun much faster, with thick white tails that bored into the green water.

"Paul, I'm talking to you."

"I heard you," the boy said in English. He had begun to speak English more and more.

"When we're alone we speak Arabic. Why do I have to keep telling you?"

"Because you're compulsive."

161

"Don't talk to me that way," Rehv said, raising his voice. His words echoed around the lake, ringing them in the ugliness of his temper. Was that his voice? When had it become like that? Thinking of it he forgot the lake, the canoe, his paddle. The paddle turned, caught in the water, and tipped the canoe to one side. Instantly the boy stuck out his paddle and made a feathering stroke with the blade on the surface of the water. The canoe regained its balance.

The boy twisted around and looked at him with an expression in his large dark eyes that he often had and that Rehv had never been able to understand. The boy's face was thin and spare, like a modern sculpture—clear brown skin stretched over fine, prominent bones; but it was also the face of an aristocrat, the kind of aristocrat who comes from somewhere in the East. "Let's not spend the night in wet sleeping bags," the boy said. He kept his eyes on Rehv for a moment more, then reached into the top of one of the packs and took out the canteen. Delicately he held it to the edge of his lips and allowed a very small amount of water to flow into his mouth. The way he drank reminded Rehv of something important.

"The men can never see the women eating," he said.

The boy screwed the top on the canteen and replaced it in the pack. "That makes three," he said, turning away and lifting his paddle. He plunged it into the water. "Three times you've told me that."

"I'm sorry, but it's the kind of thing that will have to be second nature."

"When?"

"When we go."

"When's that?"

"When we're ready."

The boy's back began rippling its even ripples. The canoe glided across the lake. Pale green water. Dark green islands. Blue sky that always seemed a little cold, even in the middle of summer. Insects ran in zigzags on the water. Fish darted up from below to catch them. Birds dove down for the fish. Sometimes the water made sucking sounds at the paddles. Otherwise there was nothing to hear. The boy's back rippled.

Rehv's own back started to hurt, as it always did on their canoe trips. If it wasn't for that he thought he felt as young and strong as ever. But as they paddled he found himself wishing they were back at the cabin, five lakes, almost six now, to the south. There he could lie down with his back to the fire and his knees drawn up in the way that made the pain almost disappear.

"What's the next lake?" Rehv asked. "I've forgotten." It had been three years, maybe four, since they had come this way.

"Crutch."

"Any good spots to make camp?"

"It's early."

"I'm sorry. I'm getting tired." How often he seemed to be telling the boy he was sorry. What did he have to be sorry about? Nothing. There was something about the boy that drew the words from him anyway.

The boy sighed. "There's a little V-shaped island with a nice spot, about a third of the way across. Three big spruce trees."

"How can you remember all that?"

Without breaking the motion of his paddling the boy shrugged his broad shoulders. "First there's a two-mile portage," he said. Rehv tried to decide whether there was any malice in his words. "The last part's uphill," the boy added. And Rehv knew. He thought about adolescents and how they sometimes turned against their parents.

"I didn't mean to lose my temper," Rehv said. "I'm trying to be a perfectionist, that's all."

They paddled. After a while the boy spoke quietly, in Arabic. "The Kaaba," he said. "A big cube-shaped shrine in the mosque at Mecca, said to have been built by Abraham."

"There, that wasn't so hard, was it?" Rehv said, thinking at the same time that maybe he had given in because he felt sorry for him.

"Speak Arabic," the boy said.

They came to the far shore of the lake. The mosquitoes and the blackflies flew out to greet them. They pulled on sweatshirts, sprayed themselves with insecticide, and smacked at the bugs whenever they landed. None of that stopped the mosquitoes and blackflies from trying to eat them alive. It just made it more sporting.

The portage was an old dirt track used long ago by lumbermen and now overgrown. The nearest road was two hundred miles to the south. Rehv carried the canoe. The boy carried one of the packs. In the past Rehv had taken the second pack at the same time; this summer he had started making two trips.

They walked along the path. The insects moved with them, the way an atmosphere clings to a planet. On both sides trees grew thick and tall, shutting out the sun. It was cool and dark and silent, except for the sounds of their feet and the insects whining in their ears. Once or twice Rehv stopped to rest his back. The boy went ahead, out of sight.

When Rehv reached the end of the portage he saw the pack and Paul's jeans, sneakers, and sweatshirt lying on a rock. The boy was swimming in the lake. It was a small, round, slate-colored lake, with a V-shaped island where the boy had said it would be.

"Don't go out too far," Rehv called to him. His voice scared a large brown bird out of a treetop, but Paul didn't seem to hear it. He went on swimming with fluid strokes out into the lake. "Don't go out too far." The brown bird circled high above. Rehv lowered the canoe, letting the bow rest on the water, and started for the other pack.

By the time he returned, the sun was low in the sky. The lake had darkened to the color of charcoal; a long thin cone of reddish gold stretched across the water, narrowing to a point at the far side. The canoe, pack, jeans, sneakers, sweatshirt were where they had been, but he didn't see the boy.

"Paul. Paul." He shouted the boy's name. The lake shouted it back. "Paul." Rehv dropped the pack, stripped off his clothes, and ran into the water.

He swam. He swam as fast as he could until he thought he had reached the area where he had last seen the boy. He took a deep breath and dove toward the bottom.

The lake was much deeper than he had expected. It grew colder and darker as he went down. Tall slimy plants that he could barely see rose up from the bottom, cutting off the re-maining light and winding around his body. He fought past them, swimming with jerky, breath-wasting movements, until his hands touched the bed of the lake.

Opening his eyes wide he strained to see: He saw nothing but swaying shadows. He pulled himself along the bottom, reaching out with his free hand to feel. He felt smooth rocks and oily weeds and rotting tree trunks. He stayed there, running his hands over the lake bed until he could hold his breath no longer. Then, his breath growing inside him like a balloon, he swam up frantically; not to save his life, but to draw another breath and dive again. The balloon burst, up from his lungs, through his throat, out of his mouth. He broke through, into the air. Gasping, he sucked it inside. He felt faint and far away; he saw only blackness, with flashes of red gold.

Slowly the faintness left him, his breathing became more even, his normal vision returned. He was taking a few deep breaths for another dive when he noticed the plume of blue smoke rising from the V-shaped island across the water.

Rehv swam back toward the shore, his body numb from the cold, numb everywhere except the lower back. As he swam he heard a distant screaming. He listened. It wasn't distant at all. He remembered it from long ago. He swam. How much farther? "Sergeant Levy. Still swimming?" His head struck the bow of the canoe.

Rehv dressed, set the packs in the canoe, and paddled out to the V-shaped island. As he approached he saw a few canoes drawn up on a pebbly beach. Some people were sitting around a campfire. One of them was darker than the others.

He made a few sweeping strokes to bring the stern around and glided up to the beach sideways. A tall silver-haired man came forward to help him out of the canoe.

"Quite a swimmer, your lad," he said, grasping Rehv's hand to steady him. "Still, no matter how good, no one should go swimming alone. Eh?" He gave Rehv's hand a little squeeze for emphasis.

Rehv looked across the beach at the campfire. Sitting around it eating hot dogs and potato chips were five or six boys and another silver-haired man, shorter and rounder than the first. And Paul, wrapped in a sleeping bag and drinking something steaming from a cup. Rehv walked over to the fire and stood in front of him.

"Did you bring my clothes?" the boy said.

For the first time Rehv wanted to hit him. He stood there, waiting for the desire to pass through him. He tried to think of the right thing to say to the boy. All he could think of was "Shit."

The boys stopped eating hot dogs and potato chips and looked up. The tall silver-haired man said, "Pardon my French."

"I'm a good swimmer."

"That's not the point."

"Of course it is," the boy said. And, lowering his voice, he added in Arabic, "You're the one who says I'm special. If I'm special you have to trust me."

"Don't," Rehv said in English, but it was too late: All eyes were on them.

"How about a hot dog, Mr. —"

"Reeve."

"Mr. Reeve. Glad to know you." Their right hands grasped each other again. "Starling. Scoutmaster. First troop of Kitchener-Waterloo. My brother, Cromwell. Everyone calls him Crommie. And Davey, Bobby, Wally, Billy, the other Bobby, and Ned. Here. Take a load off your feet. Mustard or ketchup?"

"Thank you, but —"

"Go on. You'll be doing us a favor. We've got three boxes of food left, and the plane's coming to get us in the morning."

They sat around the campfire eating hot dogs, potato chips, peanut butter, roasted marshmallows, chocolate bars, canned ham, and slices of cheese that looked and tasted like yellow wax. Very slowly light faded from the sky, trailing dusk westward over the lakes, the prairies, the mountains, the sea. They moved closer to the fire. So did the mosquitoes.

"Your son tells me you've got a place over on Lac du Loup," Starling said.

"Yes."

"I've never been down that way. You like it?"

"Very much."

"What's it mean, anyway, Lac du Loup?" Crommie said.

"Lake something or other," his brother replied.

"I know that."

"Lake of the Wolf," Rehv said.

"Are there any wolves?" one of the boys asked.

"Big ones," Paul said.

"How big?"

"Wolves won't bother you if you don't bother them, Bobby," Starling said. He jabbed a marshmallow with a pointed stick and held it close to a tongue of flame. "Any other folks around your way?" he said to Rehv.

"No."

"You just come up for the summers?"

166

"That kind of thing."

The tongue of flame reached out for the marshmallow and set it on fire. "Yikes," Starling said. He blew the fire out, waved the marshmallow in the air to cool it, and popped it in his mouth. "Where do you live the rest of the time?" he said around it. "If I'm not being nosy."

"Toronto."

"Really? I taught high school there, many years ago."

"Not that long ago, Ralph," Crommie said.

"What grade's your son in?" Starling asked.

"Going into tenth."

A mosquito landed on the end of Starling's nose. The firelight threw its long-legged shadow across one side of his face. "What school does he go to?"

"We haven't decided yet. He's changing schools this year."

Starling jabbed another marshmallow. "Where was he last year?"

Without looking, Rehv knew that Paul's dark eyes were watching him. "Prince of Wales."

Starling smacked his palm against his nose. "The little devil." He held his palm in front of the fire and looked at the squashed brown body lying in a drop of blood. "He got me right on the nose."

After dinner they sang. Starling beat time with the pointed stick. Rehv knew none of the songs. He got up and walked along the beach. Betelgeuse was redder than he had ever seen it.

My paddle's keen and bright
Flashing with silver
Follow the wild goose flight
Dip dip and swing.
Dip dip and swing, my boys
Dip dip and swing.

Paul had not known any of the songs either. Still, Rehv heard him singing the words along with the others. He noticed how well Paul sang, and tried to recall hearing him sing in the past. He couldn't.

Dip dip and swing, my boys
Dip dip and swing.

167

Later the singing died away. Rehv returned to the fire and saw that they were all watching a large portable television set. Rehv thought of them carrying it over the portages. On the screen were four men in business suits, sitting around a horseshoe-shaped table. In the background, to prove that it wasn't radio, were winking lights in the shape of a maple leaf. Rehv sat down.

"The boys need their TV," Starling said, shaking his head. "Even up here."

The four men in business suits were trying to define Canadian culture. It was hard work, and they never smiled.

"Can't you get any American stations?" one of the boys asked.

"We're not on the cable, Davey," Starling said. "This is all there is."

The boys got up and went to their tent. "You too, Paul," Rehv said. Paul walked off down the beach toward the two-man tent they shared. The four men in business suits ran out of time before they found an answer, but the program was part of a series, so they would have another chance the next week; and if not them, four other men in different suits. Rehv rose. "Good night."

"Sleep tight," said Starling, turning away from the television for a moment. "We never miss the news."

Rehv entered the tent and zipped himself into his sleeping bag. "Paul?" he said quietly. He heard the boy's deep regular breathing. Rehv lay beside him, trying to fall asleep, his mind full of thought about the boy he had made special. An owl hooted in the darkness.

During the night Rehv awoke, needing to urinate. He went outside. The moon had risen. He saw the two tents on the beach, the big one for the boys, the small one for Starling and his brother. He thought he heard people talking, and very softly walked closer. He heard Starling say, "It sounded like German to me. And his father still has an accent. Not much, but it's there."

Crommie said, "I'm trying to sleep." One of them sighed. Then the other. Rehv went back to his sleeping bag.

Just after dawn a red seaplane flew in low and skimmed onto the lake. It came across the water to the V-shaped island, sending little waves onto the pebbly shore. The scouts and their leaders paddled over to it and lashed their canoes to the tops of the pontoons. Rehv and Paul stood on the beach, beside their tent.

They watched the seaplane roar over the surface of the water, rise, clear the trees on the far side of the lake, and disappear to the south. Rehv turned to his son, remembering the way he had sung with the others around the fire.

"They were so boring," the boy said.

CHAPTER TWENTY-TWO

"What does the Koran say about interest?"

"What did Ibn Khaldun think about nomads and civilization?"

"Who milks Baggara cattle, men or women?"

"How did Gordon die?"

After a few more days of this, and little whirlpools, and loons calling their sad unanswered calls across the water, Rehv and the boy paddled back to Lac du Loup, entering by a narrow stream at the northern end. The cabin, sheltered from the wind by dense spruce trees, stood on the southern side of a long point that almost cut the lake in two. When they came around the point they saw the red seaplane moored to the dock.

On the dock sat a man and a woman. The man was chewing gum and reading a magazine. The woman was pulling files out of a big briefcase and sorting them into two piles, one on each knee. Neither of them heard the canoe. When they were quite close Rehv let his paddle shaft scrape the gunwale. The man and the woman looked up.

"Oh good," the woman said. "We'd almost given up." The man went back to his magazine. Rehv could see the name: *Aviation Now!* On the cover was a photograph of a man beaming in a cockpit.

They tied up, unloaded the packs, and climbed onto the dock. The woman rose, putting the files back into her briefcase. She was stocky, with thick dark hair stretched tightly to her head by an elastic at the back; the huge round lenses of her glasses gave her the telepathic look that beings from outer space have in the movies.

"I'm Mrs. Hume," the woman said. "From Social Services, northern section. This is Wes. He's the pilot." Wes nodded and cracked his gum. Rehv moved a little closer to the boy.

"Yes?"

"You're Mr. Reeve, is that right?"

"Yes."

"And this is your son, Paul?"

"Yes."

"Good. Is there somewhere we can talk?"

"Here."

"It's not the kind of thing we like to discuss in front of the children."

"What kind of thing is it?"

She looked at him carefully. Behind the lenses the sockets of her eyes were small and very shallow, almost flat with her face; the eyes inside them were small too. Ice floated to the surface of those little eyes; her voice turned cold.

"It's against policy to have these discussions in front of the children. Ministry policy."

"Go up to the cabin, Paul," Rehv said. He didn't want the woman in there, where the walls were covered with pictures of Kordofan and Darfur and most of the books were in Arabic. Paul slung one of the packs over his shoulder and walked off the dock.

"A fine-looking boy," Mrs. Hume said.

"What is it you want?"

"First of all, Mr. Reeve, we like to get to know all the permanent residents. We stopped at the general store on Frog Lake and they said you'd been here for years. We'd had no idea."

"It's not a secret."

"Maybe not, Mr. Reeve, but the fact is there's no Prince of Wales High School in Toronto." The great lenses loomed at him. Wes glanced up from his magazine.

"Meaning what?" Rehv asked quietly.

"Meaning I've come to find out what arrangements are being made for your son's education."

"I'm teaching him myself."

Wes spat his gum into the water. It sank slowly in little arcs, the way a feather falls. Mrs. Hume took a notebook from her briefcase and wrote a few words on a blank page.

"What qualifications do you have?" she said.

"I'm qualified."

Mrs. Hume snapped the notebook shut. "We need your precise qualifications, Mr. Reeve. I don't think you understand the situation very well. Occasionally, very occasionally, we allow people in your situation to educate their children at home. But first they must meet our standards." She reopened the notebook and wrote "standards." "That usually involves taking a teaching course from the Department of Education. Second, they must follow a course of instruction set out by the department." She wrote "course" underneath "standards." "Third, they must satisfy the requirements of a teaching inspector who spends a day or two watching them in action." She wrote "inspector" in the notebook.

"And otherwise?"

Mrs. Hume drew a little box around the three words. "Otherwise you will probably have to board the boy with a family at Frog Lake. Unless you move to another school district."

Wes pulled a package of gum from his shirt pocket and held it out. "It's the kind that explodes in your mouth." Neither of them wanted any. Wes unwrapped a piece and put it in his mouth. He chewed it once or twice; then his eyes went blank as though he was listening to something far away. The wrapper drifted across the water.

"All right," Rehv said. "What do you need to know?"

"Thank you, Mr. Reeve." She turned to a new page. "First we need your social insurance number, and the boy's mother's."

"His mother doesn't live with us. They must have mentioned that at the general store."

It made her blush: a pinkness that began around her mouth and rose like a thermometer to her cheeks and her forehead. She hid behind her glasses until she was white again. "Your social insurance number, then," she said, writing "#" and holding the pen poised over the page.

"I don't know it."

She looked up at him. Clouds were passing overhead, and he saw them reflected in her lenses. "Have you got your card?"

"I haven't seen it for years."

"Maybe the number's written somewhere else. In your passport? Health insurance card?"

"Don't have either."

"What about an old income tax form. It's printed on those automatically."

Rehv shook his head.

Mrs. Hume wrote "?" beside "#." "Have you got a driver's license?"

"Where would I drive, Mrs. Hume?"

The pink thermometer rose, but not as high as the last time. "You are a Canadian citizen, Mr. Reeve?"

"Yes."

"Naturalized or born?"

"Born," he said. He heard no Israeli accent in his voice.

"Where?"

"Toronto."

Mrs. Hume wrote it down, and added a number of other lies he told her. Finally she closed the notebook. "There's not much time before the fall term to get all this done," she said.

"Please try."

"That's what we're here for."

Mrs. Hume and Wes got into the red plane. Again Rehv watched it roar across the lake and begin rising off the water, foot by foot. "Crash," he said aloud, but it cleared the trees as it had cleared them before, and Rehv knew it was the last summer on Lac du Loup. He lifted the canoe out of the water and laid it overturned by a tree. Then he picked up the pack that remained on the dock and walked up the path to the cabin, to tell Paul that they would be moving to another school district, and to lie with his back to the fire.

Rehv lay on the couch with his eyes closed. He heard Paul close by, poking the fire. He heard sparks crackle in the air. He heard Paul, walking softly in his sneakers, go outside onto the porch, down the steps to the side of the house. Metal struck metal. Liquid gurgled out of a can. The pump motor started. The old pine floorboards vibrated, and so did the couch, very gently; it made his back feel better. Lake water ran up the pipe under the cabin, making a hollow little echo: In the morning he would wade out and clean the filter. The dock creaked. Once. Twice. He heard the high whistling sound of a fishing fly cast through the air. It fell on the water with a tiny splash. The wind began to rise in the north.

"Wake up." The dark eyes were watching him.

"I was just dozing."

"They're back."

Quickly Rehv got up and went to the window. Clouds were blowing in from the north in long dark rolls. The lake was tinged with gray, like cold skin. Across the water came the red seaplane, fighting the chop.

Slowly it approached the dock, propeller whirling: first a translucent disc, then a dozen flashing blades, finally three that didn't move. A cabin door opened and Wes climbed down onto one of the pontoons. He had a line in his hand and a pink bubble in front of his face. The plane glided up to the dock and stopped dead. Wes reached forward about a foot and hooked the line around a wooden cleat. He stepped onto the dock and turned to the plane, waiting.

The other door opened. A big black shoe appeared, feeling around for something solid. It found the pontoon. Another big black shoe. Two long and heavy blue legs. Wes held out his hand. A tall, heavy man in blue clambered onto the dock.

"We should have taken the pictures down," Paul said.

Wes knelt on the dock, hanging bumper pads on the pontoons. The big man came up the path.

"It wouldn't have made any difference."

A knock at the door. Rehv opened it. "Derlago, Provincial Police," the big man said. He had a mouth full of crooked yellow teeth. "Got a few minutes?"

What if I didn't, Rehv thought. "Come in."

Derlago took off his hat and came in, ducking his head as he walked through the doorway. He looked at the stone chimney that stood in the middle of the big room, open on both sides. The fire was almost out. "Very nice. You keep warm in the winter?"

"Warm enough."

"Insulation behind those pine boards?"

"Lots of it."

"Very nice." Derlago walked around the chimney to the other side, where the kitchen was. He put his hat on the heavy wooden table and sat down. "Oak?" he asked, running his hand along the grain.

"I think so."

"They sure knew how to make them." He stuck a thick finger into one of the holes gouged in its surface and trapped an apple seed under his fingernail. He flicked it at the fireplace. "Been on the phone to Immigration," he said. "They told me to get up here and see some ID. So I'm here. Let's see some."

"I don't have ID."

Derlago looked at Paul. "The boy neither?" he asked, keeping his eyes on him.

"No."

Derlago stuck his finger into another hole and felt around inside. "You anarchists or something like that?"

"No. I had ID, but it's all been lost over the years. We've just never had any use for that kind of thing up here."

Derlago sighed. "Then I've got to take you back."

"What for?"

"Questioning. Fingerprinting. Whatever else they want."

"I meant, what have we done wrong?"

"That's what we'll have to find out," Derlago said. He turned and looked again at Paul. "See, they think maybe you're not citizens. There's lots come in these days from the West Indies on visits. Visits that last forever."

Rehv took two steps across the room and stood over Derlago. "Are you telling me you're doing all this because of the color of my son's skin?"

He felt Paul suddenly behind him, tugging at his arm. "Control yourself," the boy said quietly.

Derlago looked up at Rehv, but otherwise he didn't move. "I'm doing this because they told me to do it." Paul pulled him away. "So let's not make a fuss. If you're citizens you're citizens, and if you're not you can go to court. That can take years. So why waste all your energy now?"

Rehv looked out the window. The wind was stronger. It made the dark trees on the far side of the lake look like a crowd applauding wildly. On the dock Wes had put on a leather jacket and was staring into the northern sky. "Do we both have to go for questioning?" Rehv asked.

"Not for questioning, no. There was no talk of questioning the boy. But they want his prints too."

"Can't you do that here? I don't see why he has to be involved."

Derlago found another apple seed and rolled it beneath his thumb and forefinger. "Can he stay here by himself for a day or two?"

"Of course."

"Okay," Derlago said, standing up. "I don't see why not." He went to the door, opened it, and called to Wes. "Bring up my kit, will you? It's under the seat."

Rehv heard Wes say: "Weather's coming up." He glanced at Paul. The boy was watching him thoughtfully.

"That's all right," Derlago said. "Just bring the kit."

Wes came in with a small black case. "You're not going to be long?" he said, handing it to Derlago.

"Not long. Sit down and take it easy for a few minutes."

Wes shook his head. "I'll put another bumper on." He went away.

Derlago opened the case and took out a black ink pad and a few sheets of stiff paper. On the sheets were printed a few rows of boxes, the size of fingertips. "Who's first?"

"I thought you were going to take mine at Frog Lake," Rehv said.

"Might as well do them both while I'm at it."

"I don't mind waiting."

Derlago pried the tin cover off the ink pad. "Let's not make a fuss."

"Do I still have to go with you?"

"Yup," Derlago said. "Who's first?"

Paul sat down beside him at the table. "Right hand." Derlago took the boy's long brown hand in his big square white one. One by one he rolled the well-shaped fingers on the ink pad and then inside the boxes on the form, as though the fingers were in-animate parts that had come down the assembly line. "Left to right, left to right," he said as he rolled them. His mouth opened a little. Rehv watched his tongue, thick, white, and dry, rubbing back and forth around the inner rims of his crooked teeth; they did not look like teeth at all, but chips of hard yellow bone stuck into his puffy gums by a dentist in a hurry.

"Next."

Derlago took Rehv's thumb in his hand and rolled it on the ink pad. He wasn't one of those big men with a surprisingly light touch. "Left to right, left to right." Rehv looked over Derlago's shoulder and saw the trees on the far side of the lake in frenzy. The wind was driving whitecaps across the water and tearing their heads off if they were slow.

"No, no. Left to right. Christ. Now I have to start over." Derlago reached for another form. He squeezed Rehv's fingers a little tighter, pressed them a little harder, but something went wrong anyway when there were only two fingers to go. "Shit. Don't you know left from right?" Derlago said, starting again. The northern sky was one huge black cloud, closing in. Lightning cracked across it like a battle standard. The sky ripped its bloated belly on the treetops and roared.

Wes came running into the cabin. "Let's go, for Christ's sake."

"We would have been gone long ago if this son of a bitch would cooperate," Derlago said, mashing Rehv's thumb into the ink pad. Rain moved in from the northern end of the lake like a curtain of steel pellets.

"Come on," Wes said, rocking on his feet the way a child does when it has to go to the bathroom badly.

Derlago threw the ink pad and the forms into his case. "Move it," he said to Rehv.

"Just give me a second to get my overnight bag."

"Hurry," Wes said. He opened the door and started running toward the dock.

Rehv crossed the big room and went through the doorway that led to the bedrooms at the back of the cabin. In his room he took a small canvas bag from the closet and put in it two pairs of socks, two pairs of undershorts, a pair of corduroy jeans, and his shaving kit. He was folding a shirt when Derlago burst inside, grabbed his arm and yanked him out of the room. "Goddamn it. Move."

They hurried down to the dock, leaving Paul in the cabin. Wes had both hands on one of the pontoon struts and was leaning on it hard to keep the plane from banging into the dock. The wind ripped Derlago's hat off his head and blew it way. "Get in, get in," Wes yelled. Then the rain hit, drenching them in seconds. A bolt of lightning struck very near, behind the cabin. They heard something crash in the forest, just before the thunder boomed.

"No way," Derlago shouted.

"Get in. I've taken off in worse than this."

Lightning flashed in front of their eyes like a hacksaw blade of fire. Thunder shook them at the same moment. "Not with me." Derlago ran heavily toward the cabin. Rehv turned to follow.

"Wait. Help me get another line around her."

"What?" Rehv shouted at the top of his voice, although they were close enough to shake hands.

"Another line. Or we'll lose her." A wave broke over the dock.

They struggled with the line. The wind tried to wrench it out of their hands. It tried to blow them into the water. Cold steel pellets stung their skin. Lightning dove at them like lines on a graph in 1929.

When the line was secure they ran up the muddy path. Inside the cabin Derlago was sitting on the couch, wrapped in a blanket, and Paul was adding logs to the fire. Derlago's outfit was spread across the stone hearth: gun and holster, blue uniform, black socks, black shoes, frayed white jockey shorts, stained blue. "We'll just have to wait it out," he said.

"It'll be dark soon," Wes said.

Rehv looked outside. It was dark already. "Anyone for a drink?" he asked.

"I never drink when I'm in uniform," Derlago replied. "But I'm not in uniform."

Rehv poured Canadian whiskey into thick plastic tumblers. The tumblers had fishing flies embedded in their bases. "Very nice," Derlago said, holding his up for a better look. He drank. "Very nice."

"None for me," Wes said. "It might blow over."

When it didn't, he drank too.

They finished the bottle. Paul made sandwiches. Ham. Cheese. Tuna. Peanut butter. Derlago had one of each. Wes kept putting on Rehv's oilskins and going outside to look at the plane. "Better radio in," Derlago told him. "Say we'll be back tomorrow." Paul went to bed. Rehv opened another bottle. They played three-handed cribbage for a penny a point. Rehv won two dollars and fourteen cents. Then they played hearts. "Have you got Monopoly?" Derlago asked.

"No."

They played crazy eights. Wes chewed gum and drank whiskey

at the same time. The fire roared inside. The storm roared outside. They finished the bottle. And started another.

"Bedtime for me," Rehv said.

"I guess we should too," Derlago said. He rose, swaying slightly, and pulled the blanket around himself like a toga. He picked up his gun and his black case.

Wes stood up too. "Have you got anything to read?" he asked. "Like flying magazines?"

"No."

"Doesn't matter. I'm seeing double anyway."

Rehv led them to the door that opened into the hall at the back of the cabin where the bedrooms were. Derlago paused in front of a photograph of the savannah hanging on the wall. "Where's this?"

"Arizona," Rehv said.

"Yeah? My wife's brother goes there every winter." He gazed at the photograph. "Doesn't look so great to me."

There were three bedrooms off the hall: Rehv's at the lake end, Paul's in the middle, and the spare one at the other end, where Rehv took Wes and Derlago. It had an old bunk bed, left behind by the lumbermen who had once lived there. "Dibs the bottom," Derlago said. He put the gun and the black case on the bedside table and lay down. Rehv went out and closed the door. He walked down the hall to his own bedroom. Inside, Paul was kneeling on the floor, refilling the two packs by candlelight.

They put out the candle and waited. Rehv had drunk very little, but it was enough to make him sleepy. He put his mouth close to Paul's ear. "Don't let me fall asleep."

But he fell asleep anyway. He dreamed he was swimming on a cold black sea. "Wake up," said a voice, very calm, very close. Paul. He sat up with a start.

"How long have I been asleep?" he whispered.

"Half an hour."

He listened. The house was very quiet. The storm was dying down. They picked up the packs and walked slowly and quietly out of the room and down the hall. Rehv thought of his fingerprints in the black case on Derlago's bedside table, but without the noise of the storm he could not risk it. They went into the big room. Rehv closed the hall door very softly behind them.

179

Cinders glowed in the fireplace, casting a faint orange light on Derlago's uniform. Paul gathered it up—shirt, trousers, socks, shoes, underwear—as they crossed the room.

Outside, a light drizzle drifted down, wafted over the water by the last exhausted panting of the wind. A few stars showed in the north. Rehv carried the canoe from its place by the tree to the shore. He avoided the dock because of the chance it might creak. Gently he lowered the canoe into the water. They set the packs inside. Paul knelt in the bow. Rehv pushed off and knelt in the stern. They glided to the end of the dock. Paul untied the two lines from the cleat and passed them to Rehv. He retied them to the seat and looked back at the cabin. It was quiet and dark.

They paddled away, towing the seaplane behind them. In the middle of the lake Paul stopped paddling for a moment and fumbled for something in the pocket under the bow. Rehv heard a faint splash. Derlago's clothes sank to the bottom. Rehv looked back again and in the darkness saw the shadows of the spruce trees that protected the cabin. He tried to distinguish the outline of the cabin itself, but he couldn't. He didn't look back again.

They crossed the lake. The wind breathed its last few breaths and died. The water was as smooth as black jelly. The sky cleared and the moon appeared, a new moon like jaws wide open to devour the dark part that didn't show.

When they reached the far side they paddled along the shore until they came to a rocky point that rose steeply out of the water. They pulled the canoe onto the shore and then gripped the struts of the seaplane and began dragging it up the steepest part of the rocks, tail first. The seaplane was much heavier than Rehv had expected, and it took a long time. "One, two, pull," he whispered. "One, two, pull." When it would go no higher they each stood by a pontoon and rocked the plane forward toward its nose. Rehv held it like that while Paul found two large round boulders and rolled them under the raised parts of the pontoons. Then, with the round boulders as a pivot they began rocking the plane tail to nose, tail to nose, until at last it tipped up on its nose and stayed there. They leaned against the pontoons and pushed it over into the water. It landed on its back with a splash that threw silver drops high into the moonlight.

They put the canoe back in the water, retied the lines, and

began towing the plane out into the lake. It was much harder with the plane upside down. When Rehv thought the water was deep enough he dropped the lines and guided the canoe around to one of the doors of the cabin. The water reached a third of the way up the door. Rehv pulled on the handle, but it would not open. Carefully he lifted himself out of the canoe and stood on the underside of the wing with water up to his knees. He pulled on the handle. And pulled again with all his strength. The door opened. The lake began to pour inside. Rehv climbed back into the canoe and pushed off.

·They watched the seaplane settling lower in the water. First the cabin disappeared, then the tail, then the struts, leaving only the pontoons. There was plenty of room in the plane, room for four people and some baggage. When the water had taken all of it, the pontoons too sank out of sight. A big silver bubble rose up and broke on the surface of the black jelly.

Paul turned to his father and grinned, his teeth as hard and white as the moon. Rehv wanted to grin too, but he was too busy thinking about the other times his fingerprints had been taken: once for the army, the other time when he had arrived in America. And thinking about the black case on the bedside table.

They paddled south. The night was quiet and still and very long. They were quiet too, except once when Paul said, "Where are we citizens, Dad?" He hadn't called him that in a long time.

CHAPTER TWENTY-THREE

The big helicopter droned on and on. A thousand feet below lakes and forest were gliding by. "Beautiful, isn't it?" said the young RCMP man looking down. "That's the real Canada."

Green and blue. Green and blue. Krebs was bored with it right away. He had never flown in such a slow helicopter. For something to do, he opened his briefcase and looked at two photostats he had already looked at a lot. One showed a set of fingerprints, incomplete and of a quality so poor he found it difficult to believe they had been taken by a professional; but there was the provincial police seal at the bottom. The other was a copy of a special immigration permit, almost sixteen years old. It was the kind of permit issued for a short time by the U.S. government, after the fall of Israel. This one had a thumb print in the lower right-hand corner and the name Isaac Rehv written on the top line. The Interpol computer said that the print in box B-1 of the provincial police form and the print on the immigration permit had been made by the same thumb. The Interpol computer had said this without being asked, the way it did nowadays. Information on a man named Reeve had been fed into it; it had thought for a second or two and then told Krebs's computer the whole story. The system had worked perfectly. But for some reason no one had given the Interpol computer a look at the prints until two weeks after the disappearance of Mr. Reeve.

Krebs felt the body of the RCMP man suddenly go tense. "Bring her down, bring her down," the RCMP man said to the pilot. He had binoculars in his hand, and he was training them on the narrow end of a pear-shaped lake below. "Look, sir," he said. "A moose." He gave the binoculars to Krebs. The helicopter went down to about a hundred feet. Krebs saw something brown and stupid standing in the water.

They saw two more moose on the way, and one tree stump that looked like a moose. "That's the real Canada, sir," the RCMP man told him a few more times. A tree stump that looks like a moose? Krebs wanted to say; and once, even a few years ago, he would have. But not now.

Now he kept all that inside. Now he was a man who knew how to get along with other men. He had to be, after five years at headquarters. Two thousand four hundred and sixty-three meetings. He numbered them in his desk diaries. It proved how busy he was. But no one doubted that: They kept adding people to his staff.

Krebs was the number-two man in the Middle Eastern section. When the computer in Virginia had dredged Isaac Rehv up from the past he decided to assign himself to the case. "You don't have time for that stuff," everyone had said. And besides, it wasn't important anymore. Most of the Israeli refugees were quiet now. They were working, raising families, in jail, or dead. Sometimes there was trouble—a bombing or a hijacking or someone shot on the streets—but it was nothing like the trouble they had with the Filipinos. There were some people who thought that a mistake had been made. Oil prices had fallen, but they soon started rising again; and the Palestinians had never stopped shooting: Now they shot at each other. But Americans were importing so little oil that it hardly mattered anymore what the price was; and they had much more leverage in the Middle East than before. They had lost nothing. And gained a little.

Krebs knew that Isaac Rehv was no longer important. But at the same time he knew that he was doing the right thing. It was right for his reputation as a man who never quit. Isaac Rehv had beaten them long ago. Krebs wanted to see the look on his face when he finally caught up with him.

He looked out the window and saw green and blue. He focused on the faint reflection of his face in the glass. Then he slipped one hand under his jacket and pinched himself around the middle. He didn't like what he felt. A few more pinches didn't make it any better.

"This is it," the RCMP man said. They flew in low toward a lake that at first was blue like others but grew grayer as they approached. Krebs saw a Zodiac rubber boat at the southern end of the lake. There were three men in it. They looked up. Ahead he saw a long narrow point that almost divided the lake in two. Near its tip a wooden dock stuck out into the water. There was a cabin almost hidden in some spruce trees. The helicopter hovered for a few moments over the cabin and then settled slowly down on the narrow pebble beach. The pilot shut off the motor and the electrical systems. It was very quiet.

"This is it," the RCMP man said again. "Lac du Loup. That's Wolf Lake in French." He opened the cabin door and held it for Krebs. Krebs took his briefcase and stepped onto the ground. Something bit him hard on the top of his head, where there hadn't been any hair for a few years.

"Jesus Christ." He smacked it. It bit him on the hand.

"Blackfly," the RCMP man said. "They're hungry this year." He gave Krebs a piece of tissue to wipe away the blood.

They walked up a dirt path that led to the cabin. A big man in a blue uniform was standing in front of the door, picking his teeth. "This is Corporal Derlago," the RCMP man said, trying to maintain a pleasant tone of voice, and failing.

The big man took his hand out of his mouth and offered it to Krebs. "You're the one who took those prints," Krebs said, shaking it.

"What there were of them," the RCMP man said.

Derlago looked down at his big black shoes. "It's a good thing you got them," Krebs said. "They were all we needed." Derlago showed a mouth full of ugly teeth and gave the RCMP man a defiant look. Krebs realized he had gone too far. "Of course it would have been nice to have the man too," he added. It didn't make the big man look at his shoes again, but at least he stopped smiling.

"You can say that again," the RCMP man said.

They went inside. "It's just the way it was," Derlago said. "No one's touched a thing." They looked around. "Course there's not much to see," Derlago went on. "It's just like any of the other lumber cabins in these parts. Except for the books maybe, and those pictures of Arizona."

Krebs glanced at the black-and-white photographs that hung on the walls. "What makes you think it's Arizona?"

"He told me."

"Who?" the RCMP man asked.

"Reeve. Or whatever his name was."

The RCMP man snorted. He walked across the room and peered closely at one of the photographs. "I've been to Arizona, and that's not Arizona. It's Texas."

"So what?"

Krebs knew it wasn't Texas either. Israel, maybe. He looked at the books in the crude wooden bookcases that lined the wall opposite the fireplace. Most of the titles were in Arabic, which he had learned to speak a little, but could not read. "Is there any way these books could be packed and sent down to me?"

"Certainly," the RCMP man said. "I can radio for supplies right now." He went out.

Derlago led him through the bedrooms, one by one. In the first bedroom there was nothing but a bunk bed and a wobbly bedside table. "They didn't use this one," Derlago said.

"Is this where you slept that night?"

Derlago glanced at him warily. "Yes."

"You didn't hear anything?"

"Nope. There was one hell of a storm. Blew the whole night. Besides, the nearest road is two hundred miles from here."

That hadn't stopped them. "I wouldn't have done anything different in your place," Krebs said. Derlago rewarded him with another display of his rotting teeth.

They went into the middle bedroom. "The boy slept here," Derlago said. The bed was neatly made: An inspecting sergeant could have bounced a quarter on it. In one corner of the room stood a paddle and a pair of worn snowshoes.

"They must have frozen in the winter."

Derlago shrugged. "People get tough up here," he said. "Or they don't last."

Against one wall was an old pine chest of drawers. Krebs opened every one. He found socks, long underwear, plaid shirts, jeans, woollen gloves, leather mitts. As he turned to leave the room he saw another photograph taped to the inside of the door. It looked like the others. "Why would he say it was Arizona if it wasn't Arizona?" Derlago said.

Krebs didn't answer. It was always better than saying, "I don't know." Carefully he pulled off the tape and put the photograph in his briefcase. "What was the boy like?"

185

Derlago thought. "A boy," he said finally. "Quiet, kind of."
He thought some more. "Except," he added, pausing to choose
the right word, "he was colored." Derlago took him into the last
bedroom. "Reeve wasn't colored. He was dark, but not colored,
if you know what I mean."

It was a simple room like the boy's. A single bed, unmade. A
chest of drawers full of clothes. Snowshoes. Boots. And on the
floor under the bed, two books. One in Arabic, the other in
English. Krebs picked up the one in English. The cover was
falling off; the glue was cracking along the spine; the pages were
loose. Either it had been read many times, or it had been thrown
around a lot. *Geology and Geography of the Western Sudan,* by
F. McG. Stilton, professor of geology, Middlebury College. He
put it in his briefcase.

They went outside. The Zodiac was tied to the dock, and a
man in a full wet suit was coming up the path. "We got it," he
called to Derlago. "Some of it, anyway."

"Le's see," Derlago said. They walked down to the dock.
Krebs glanced over at the helicopter on the beach and saw the
RCMP man sitting beside the pilot, talking on the radio. They
got into the Zodiac. The man in the wet suit pulled the starter
cord of the little outboard. Two trails of mucus had hardened
on his upper lip. Derlago made a face. "Do something about your
nose," he said over the noise of the motor.

The man in the wet suit wiped his nose with his rubber sleeve
and dipped his arm over the side. "Occupational hazard," he
said, grinning at Krebs.

The little boat sped over the water. A big brown fish jumped
into the air close to the starboard side. "Like fishing?" Derlago
shouted to Krebs.

"Never done much."

"Too bad. This is great country for fishing. And hunting. We
still get moose up here."

"What?"

"Moose," Derlago bellowed.

At the southern end of the lake a seaplane had been dragged
up onto the shore. Once it had been red. Now most of the paint
was scraped off. So were the rudder, the propeller, and one of
the wings. The nose casing lay on the ground, and two men were
looking at the engine. The man in the wet suit brought the Zodiac

gently up to the beach. Krebs and Derlago stepped out and went over to the plane.

One of the men had reached deep into the engine. He felt around inside it for a long time. Then he took his hand out, looked at the other man, and shook his head. The other man turned around and punched a tree, very hard. Derlago laid his hand softly on the man's shoulder. "It was insured, wasn't it, Wes?"

"That's not the point," the other man said. He was crying. Derlago patted his shoulder.

They rode back across the lake. The sun shone, there was no wind, but the air felt very cool. Krebs fastened all the buttons of his suit jacket and turned up the collar. "Winter's coming," Derlago said, glancing up at the sky. It was the middle of August.

Krebs walked into a room full of rocks. There were rocks in glass cases, rocks on shelves, rocks in boxes on the floor, and rocks on the long table in the middle of the room. A sinewy old man with long soft white hair stood beside the table. All he wore were khaki shorts and sandals: Years of sun had dried his skin to brown leather. He had a mound of pink rocks in front of him and he was sorting them into five piles.

"Come in," he said without looking up, "once you're in."

"Sorry. I knocked."

"Didn't hear you. It's the goddamned football practice. Every afternoon while I'm trying to get something done. They've deafened me."

Krebs listened hard and thought he heard someone shouting far away, and perhaps the thudding sound of leather being kicked. He went across the room and stood on the opposite side of the table. The old man held up a pink rock. "Eeeny meeny miny mo," he said, and dropped it into one of the piles. All the pink rocks looked the same to Krebs.

"Professor Stilton?"

"Present."

"I wonder if you could tell me anything about this." Krebs slid the photograph onto the table.

The old man glanced at it and then looked closely at Krebs.

He had eyes as blue as the sky on a perfect day. They glittered in his wrinkled brown face. "You wildcatters," he said. "You just never quit, do you?"

He picked up a magnifying glass and peered through it at the photograph. After a few seconds he frowned and set the magnifying glass aside. His eyes got ready to be less friendly. "I don't get it," he said.

"You've never seen anything like it before?"

"Oh, I know what it is, all right. It's goz. Nothing unusual about that."

"Goz?"

"Stabilized sand dune country with vegetation cover—coarse grasses, acacia, that kind of thing."

"Where is this goz?"

"That's the point. There was another fellow in here a while back full of questions about the same area. Except he knew a lot more about it than you seem to." The old man picked up the photograph and handed it to Krebs. "I told him the same thing I'm telling you. There's no oil there. Not one drop. And even if there was you couldn't get at it. They've been fighting a war there for the past two years, or haven't you heard?"

"Where?"

"Christ. The western Sudan. Kordofan. Darfur. Don't you know anything?" He reached into a pocket and pulled out a little pink rock. "Jurassic," he snapped and tossed it onto one of the piles. Krebs counted the pockets in his shorts. There were eight.

"When was this other man here?"

"About a week ago. Two weeks. Why? Your partner run out on you? That's it, isn't it? He's the field man, you're the money man. I've seen it a thousand times. I can tell by looking. There's you in your three-piece suit, twenty pounds overweight. And him strong and sunburned from spending his life outdoors. Am I right?"

"Maybe."

"Maybe? What do you mean, maybe?" The old man picked a rock out of the mound. "What the hell is that doing here?" It was pink like all the others. He threw it into a box on the other side of the room. "Students," he said. "They're idiots. Every damn one of them. I don't know why they don't expel the whole damned bunch. Then I could get something done around this place." To

188

make up for lost time he increased the tempo of his sorting, moving with the speed of an assembly line worker in a silent comedy. After a minute or two the mound was gone. Five pink piles circled the space where it had been. "Where was I?"

" 'What do you mean, maybe?' "

"Right. You're not so stupid after all." He bent down and picked up a box. It was full of rocks but he lifted it quite easily. He dumped them on the desk. They were pink. "Your partner. He's about your height, but younger looking? And dark. Jewish, maybe?"

"That's him."

"Of course that's him. I told you in the first place." He started sorting the rocks, but interrupted himself almost immediately. He brandished a rock at Krebs. "If you catch up with him tell him I want my maps back."

"Maps?"

"Sure They won't do him any good. There's no oil there. Zero. Zilch. But what's the use? You guys never believe anybody. You probably think I'm trying to gobble up every damned drop myself."

"What kind of maps do you mean?"

"Maps I made eight or nine years ago. Spent about six months over there. I didn't get to finish. They started shooting at each other and I had to get out. This was the government before last. Or maybe the one before that. They weren't so bad as governments go over there. They actually paid me for some of my work. Of course by the time I got back here and had anything ready to show, they were all dead or in jail, so they never did get any results. And it might have done them some good, the way this drought's been going on."

"I'm not sure what kind of maps you're talking about."

"Wouldn't interest you," the old man said. "Nothing to do with oil, if you can imagine such a thing. They're water maps."

"Water maps?"

"Stop echoing everything I say. Christ. Don't you think I get enough of that from freshmen?" He flung another rock across the room. "And the jerkasses will be back in a few weeks."

"I'm interested in what you mean by water maps," Krebs said.

"That's smart of you. Because it is interesting. See, I had an idea that there might be certain water-trapping Maestrichian deposits quite deep under the surface, much deeper than they normally dig their wells. I won't tell you the details. They're way over your head. So I went over there and sunk a few boreholes. And found out I was onto something. But I didn't have time to do much more than make note of a dozen or so likely spots before the shooting started. I only ended up covering a little bit of territory down in southwestern Kordofan and over into Darfur." He picked up a rock and looked at it closely. "Why do people shoot each other when they haven't even got enough water to wash their faces in the morning? Answer me that."

That was easy. Because people like shooting at each other. Krebs knew that by now. He said: "Why did you give him the maps?"

The old man put the rock down on the table in a pile all its own. "I didn't give him the maps. The bastard stole them. I'd been showing him the maps. Naturally he lost interest pretty quick. Nothing to do with oil, you see. Then he asked about some samples I had upstairs. When I came back down he was gone, and so were the maps."

"I'll send them to you if I can."

"That'd be very obliging of you. They won't do you any good. There's no oil there."

"You never know."

"You guys. You're something else." The old man threw back his head and laughed. He laughed until his sky-blue eyes grew watery and stopped glittering. "You guys."

Krebs walked across the campus. Flowers grew neatly in their beds; the grass was trim and immaculate. There were no students lying on it smoking dope, drinking beer, or writing home for money. It had a few more weeks to flourish in peace.

Down on the practice field a football flew end over end through the air, not very high, not very far. A skinny young man caught it with some difficulty and ran a few steps to his right, then back to his left, then to the right again. Other young men dove at him. After a little more of this he slipped and fell down. Others fell on top of him. A man with a beer belly and a whistle in his mouth ran across the field. "Is that what you call hitting?" he screamed at a big boy who was picking himself up from the pile, uniform soaked with sweat, chest heaving. "Is that what you call hitting? A thalidomide baby hits harder than that. I want

190

you to hit. Hit. Hit, hit, hit, hit, hit." He demonstrated with his palm against the earhole of the big boy's helmet.

But first you've got to catch them, Krebs thought. He was worried. It was supposed to have been a simple mopping up of a little mess left over from the past. Now he wasn't sure.

CHAPTER TWENTY-FOUR

Fairweather met him at the airport. He was wearing a green and white seersucker suit, a pink shirt, and a red tie. He hurried across the arrivals lounge, waving and smiling broadly, as if they were friends. Maybe he thought they were.

"How was the trip? Hook any big ones?"

"No," Krebs said, trying to remember how he had been saddled with Fairweather. He felt tired; and his eyes were sore—the stale air in the plane had dried his contact lenses.

"Too bad," Fairweather said, taking Krebs's bag and wafting the smell of sandalwood through the air. "The fishing's great. When I was a kid we had a summer place up in the Laurentians. Trout, bass, pike—you name it."

"I wasn't anywhere near there."

"No? Oh well."

Fairweather led him across the parking lot to the little electric car. "Hop in. It's open."

Fairweather got in behind the wheel. Krebs sat beside him. "Did you bring the notes I asked for?"

"In the glove compartment," Fairweather replied.

"You left them in the car?"

"Oops."

They drove toward Manhattan in morning traffic that sounded like an army of golf carts. Fairweather kept pointing out all the empty buildings. "Boy oh boy. Before you know it you'll be able to buy up the whole town for a song. That's what my old man says. He's already started."

Krebs studied the old file. There wasn't much in it, and what there was didn't help. Fairweather waited until he was finished and then said, "We looked for the woman. Nothing. Disappeared without a trace. As for the drug dealer, what's his name—"

"Cohee."

"Right. Cohee. Shot four or five years ago. Some sort of gang war apparently. There was something a little odd about it though. What was it?" Fairweather thought for a while, then shook his head. "No go. Anyway, it's not important. We did turn up Katz and his wife."

Krebs reread the brief record of his talk with Katz, long ago. Katz had known nothing. Neither had his wife.

"Still want to see them?"

"Yes."

On the way Krebs scanned what Fairweather had brought on the Sudan. "Is this all there is?"

"That's what they say. It's been like that since the embassy closed down. But it's the same old thing."

"What same old thing?"

"That's happening in all those places. Islamic brown-colored northerners fighting Christian and animist black southerners. With a few secessionist movements thrown in."

Krebs looked at the last page in the file. "We've got three people in the whole country?"

"Only one full time," Fairweather said. He leaned over and pointed to a name on the page. Gillian Wells. She was a reporter for a magazine called *L'Africaine*.

Fairweather stopped in front of an art gallery on upper Madison Avenue. L'Oeil said the sign, in slim silver letters. In the window hung a large oil painting draped in black velvet. It showed a woman bathing in a forest pool. A man was watching her from behind a tree. He had hooves instead of feet. In the bottom corner a rabbit was looking on. It had a little white tail.

Krebs opened his door and got out. Fairweather got out too. "Wait here," Krebs said. Fairweather got back in.

Krebs went inside. More nudes hung on the walls. Many of them were bathing in forest pools, some singly, some in twos and threes. At the rear of the gallery a fat man sat behind a little antique desk, reading a book. His head was bald, except at the sides where hair grew in thick curly clumps like earmuffs. As

Krebs came closer he put down the book and began writing on a pad of paper.

"Mr. Katz?"

"Yes?" the man said, lifting his pen reluctantly. Krebs read the writing on the pad, upside down: "Quentin Katz, Quentin K., Mr. Q. Katz, B.A."

"Do you remember me?"

Katz looked at him closely. "Were you the one who was interested in the Bouguereau?"

"No."

"Really? You look a lot like him. Anyway, it's sold," he added as a door opened behind him and a tall, gray-haired woman emerged carrying three sides of an ornate gilded frame.

"Quentin, where the hell —" She stopped when she saw Krebs. "I knew there'd be trouble," she said. Katz looked at her, then looked back at Krebs.

"Why is that, Mrs. Katz?"

"Ms. Finkle," she said. The muscles in her thin face bulged slightly, as though she was grinding her teeth. "I've retained my maiden name."

"She was one of the first," Katz said proudly.

"Why did you know there'd be trouble?" Krebs asked again.

"Because he brings trouble."

"Who?"

"Isaac Rehv. Why else would you be here?"

Katz opened his eyes wide and his mouth a little to show that he had recognized Krebs. "You're still investigating that restaurant business? After fifteen years?"

Krebs looked over Katz's head at his wife and said, "When was he here?"

The telephone rang. Katz answered it. "L'Oeil." He pronounced it to rhyme with oy. "Just a minute." He handed the telephone to his wife. "It's your father."

"Hello, Daddy." She listened. "Can't I sign them here?" She listened some more. The muscles in her face stopped working so hard. "Okay. I'll be there. Do you need Quentin too?" Her father said something that made her laugh, a high-pitched laugh that was somehow very aggressive. Krebs would not have wanted to be on the receiving end of that laugh; he wondered if that was why Katz had grown earmuffs. "It means 'the eye' in French,"

194

the woman who had retained her father's name was saying. "Yes, L'Oeil," she said, pronouncing it in a way that sounded French to Krebs. She listened, laughed again, and hung up.

"When was he here?" Krebs asked.

"Last week. Tuesday," Katz's wife said. "Only he wasn't here. He came to the apartment."

"What did he want?"

"Wait a minute, dear," Katz said. "I don't know if we should be so quick to answer all these questions. It was never proven to my satisfaction that Isaac had done anything wrong."

"It doesn't have to be proven to your satisfaction," Krebs said. "I want facts and I want them now."

"You have no right to talk to me like that," Katz said. "Not here, on my own property." He started to rise from his chair.

Krebs leaned across the desk and pushed him back into it, hard. "Let's not open up the question of whose property it is," he said. He saw a flush rise to the surface of the fleshless cheeks of Katz's wife. For a moment he thought it was anger. Then he looked at her eyes and saw it wasn't. "What did Rehv want?"

"Money," the woman said.

"Did you give it to him?"

"No."

"How did he react?"

The woman shrugged. Katz pushed back his chair and stood up. "We told him we couldn't very well lend him money after he had left us so abruptly. He understood. Now I wish we had lent him the money. Given it to him, goddamn it." His voice broke.

"Did he say what he wanted it for?"

"No. What difference does that make? We should have given it to him anyway. He's a good man. Anyone can see that."

"Quentin, don't be a jerk," his wife said angrily. Krebs liked having her there: She did all the work. "He stole your passport."

"We don't know that for sure."

"Then who did?"

"Passport?" Krebs said.

"We let him stay overnight," the woman replied. "He said he had nowhere else. He was gone when we got up in the morning. A few days later Quentin noticed his passport was missing from the desk."

"That doesn't prove a thing," Katz said.

Krebs ignored him. "Was the boy with him?" he asked Katz's wife.

"So there is a boy."

"What do you mean?"

"Quentin's passport wasn't the only one missing. Joshua's was gone too. He's our son."

"The boy wasn't there, then?"

"No."

"None of this proves he took the passports," Katz said. "Maybe we mislaid them. What good would they do him anyway?"

They both looked at Krebs for an answer. Anyone could glue new photographs on top of old ones, he thought. It might work. "Have you got any idea where he went?"

"No," Katz said quickly.

"Stop trying to be clever, Quentin," his wife said. To Krebs she said: "Try the Aliyah Synagogue. The rabbi there has a fund for refugees. Quentin told him about it."

"Why not? He's a human being, isn't he?"

"You're breaking my heart," she told her husband.

Krebs walked out of the gallery, past the soft pink women in their forest pools. Once he had wanted only hard women, women like Sheila Finkle. At the time they hadn't noticed him. Lately they did. But now he wanted soft pink ones—like Alice had been; and maybe still was. And they were not interested.

He got into the car. Fairweather was reading a newspaper. "It's going to mean the end of baseball. No pitcher is worth ten million a year. I don't care who he is."

Krebs did not argue that. "Was that all there was in the file?" he asked.

"I think so."

"You think so?"

"Jeez. Don't get mad. Yes. That's all they gave me."

"I thought there was more." Krebs was trying to remember the psychiatrist's report. He knew there was something in it he wanted to see.

They drove to Brooklyn. Fairweather turned the air conditioner on full. He loosened his red tie and unfastened the top button of his pink shirt. "How can anyone live here in the summer?" Somewhere above the haze the sun rose higher and higher. It was good weather for growing tropical flowers, but there were

196

no tropical flowers, only a few wilted plants in dirty apartment windows.

The Aliyah Synagogue was a small brick building that stood between two takeout restaurants, one Chinese, the other Italian, both for sale. It might have been an old factory except for the stained-glass Moses over the door, holding out two tablets like the bill of fare. Fairweather parked in front and turned to Krebs with his eyebrows raised, waiting to be asked along. He wasn't.

Inside, it was hot and dark. Krebs walked down a wide hall. At the end of it a man sat in a chair by a wooden door. His chin rested on his chest, and his eyes were closed.

"I'm looking for the rabbi," Krebs said to him.

Slowly the man raised his head and opened his eyes. He had not shaved that morning, or the morning before. He reached into a cardboard box at his feet, handed Krebs a black skullcap and a white shawl, and pointed to the door beside him. Krebs opened it and went in.

It was a long narrow room with a platform at one end. The lower part was filled with rows of wooden benches, arranged in three sections. A few people sat on the benches, most of them alone. Krebs noticed that the women sat in the side sections, the men in the center. The men wore skullcaps and shawls; the women did not. Krebs put the black cap on his head and the shawl around his shoulders. He sat at the end of one of the benches in the center section.

Three men wearing square black hats stood on the platform. Two of them held open a large scroll that was lying on a table covered with white cloth. The third read from the scroll in a singsong voice. Krebs did not know the language. On the bench in front of him an old man rocked back and forth, singing along in a low scratchy mutter. His neck was far too small for his frayed and dirty collar. It was very hot. Krebs felt the skullcap making a damp itchy circle on the top of his head.

After a while the singing stopped. The man who had led the singing stepped forward and began addressing the congregation. From time to time he made harsh sounds in the back of his throat like a man getting ready to spit, but they were only part of the language. Drops of sweat trickled down from the top of Krebs's head. His shirt stuck to his ribs. The man on the platform spoke for such a long time Krebs knew it had to be the sermon. When he stopped he returned to his place behind the scroll. The singing started again. Krebs got up and went out. He dropped the skullcap and the shawl into the cardboard box beside the sleeping man. He felt much cooler right away.

Krebs walked to the other end of the dark hall. On the wall hung a plaque listing everyone who had donated money for the building of the synagogue and how much each had given. He read all the names and the amounts. He looked at his watch. He walked back down the hall. The man in the chair was snoring. Krebs watched him for a while, estimating the value of each article of clothing he wore. Through the door he heard the singing suddenly grow louder. It stopped. The door opened. A few old people came out. A few more. Then the man who had given the sermon. He was middle-aged and round, and much shorter than Krebs would have guessed from seeing him on the platform. Gray pockets sagged under his eyes.

"Are you the rabbi?" Krebs said to him.

"I am." He spoke English with a faint accent.

"I'd like a word with you."

"One moment." The rabbi touched the sleeping man gently on the shoulder to wake him and turned to Krebs. "Come with me."

He led Krebs to a door halfway down the hall. They went into a small office, lined on all sides by shelves of books from floor to ceiling. There were no windows. It was very hot. The rabbi sat behind his desk and switched on a little fan. It pushed the hot heavy air around the room.

"Problems with the air conditioning," he said. "Please sit down." He motioned to a chair.

Krebs did not sit down. He took a small photograph from his pocket and placed it on the desk. "Have you seen this man?"

The rabbi glanced at the photograph. "On what authority do you ask me?"

Krebs showed him a New York City detective's badge. "When was he here?"

The rabbi looked at the badge, looked at the photograph, looked at Krebs. "What do you want with him?"

"We think he killed his wife. We want to talk to him about it."

The rabbi sat back in his chair, watching Krebs closely. "I can't believe it," he said.

"Why not, Rabbi?"

For a few moments the rabbi sat silently, his eyes on Krebs. Finally he said, "You don't want him for some political reason?"

"No. Why do you ask that?"

The rabbi shrugged. "He's an Israeli. Like me."

"That's no concern of mine, Rabbi. I don't know anything about politics. I just want to find out if he killed his wife."

"I think you're making a mistake. He did not seem like the type."

"There is no type, Rabbi. I've worked on enough homicides to learn that. You can't tell ahead of time who's going to get mad at his wife and start hitting her with a hammer."

"Is that what he did?"

"Someone did. And he was the last person seen with her before she was killed."

The rabbi picked up the photograph. "He came here last Wednesday," he said. "But he looked older than this."

"That's an old photograph. It's from his immigration card."

"In that case he hasn't aged very much at all. Compared to most of us." The rabbi handed Krebs the photograph. "I lent him three thousand dollars from the refugee fund."

"Why?"

"Because he is a refugee."

"I meant, what reason did he give for needing it?"

The rabbi tried to look Krebs in the eye, and couldn't. "He said he had just separated from his wife and needed to find a place to live for himself and his son."

"Now he's becoming a type," Krebs said. "Was the boy with him?"

"No."

"Have you any idea where he went?"

The rabbi took out a handkerchief and mopped his face. "He said he would call when he had a definite address."

"Has he called?"

"No."

Krebs put the photograph in his pocket. "Did you talk about anything else, Rabbi?"

"Just Israel."

"Israel?" Krebs said, standing up to leave.

"Yes. We talked about Aliyah."

Krebs wanted to keep him talking about Israel, but he did not want to seem too interested. Walking over to the bookshelves he ran his eyes over a few of the titles. "I'm afraid I don't follow you, Rabbi."

"Aliyah means going up. Going up to Israel. I told him that in my opinion, and the opinion of many others in the community these days, the only hope for we Jews is to make that journey an internal one."

Krebs took a book from one of the shelves. "An internal journey?"

"Yes. Israel is a state of mind. We should make it live inside ourselves, as we did for two thousand years."

"And what did he say to that?" Krebs asked, leafing through the pages.

"He reacted quite oddly, as a matter of fact. He became very angry, and shouted at me: 'I don't want Israel to live in me. I want to live in Israel.' I suppose I should have taken more notice of his temper at the time, but I didn't."

"How were you to know?" Krebs closed the book. "Don't worry about it."

The rabbi glanced at the book as Krebs returned it to the shelf. "Do you read Hebrew?" he asked in surprise.

"No," Krebs said, and went out the door.

Outside, Fairweather waited in the car. He must have been very bored, Krebs thought, because he was reading the file on Isaac Rehv. "Maybe he's crazy," Fairweather said as Krebs got into the car.

"That's what Armbrister used to say."

"Who's Armbrister?"

"Someone you wouldn't want to trade places with."

They drove off. Fairweather wondered when the heat was going to let up. Krebs wondered how far Isaac Rehv could go with stolen passports and borrowed money. And the boy.

CHAPTER TWENTY-FIVE

It was hotter than blood. Isaac Rehv could see that by looking out the window of the train at the thermometer tacked to a post on the station platform. It was mounted on a peeling yellow board advertising Keen's English mustard. The scale of degrees ran from thirty to one hundred. Freezing, it said near the bottom; blood heat near the top. The mercury had risen past the marking for blood heat a little while before. Now it was pressing against the top of the glass column. The sun had been up for an hour and a half.

The train was full. It was full at four A.M., two hours before it was scheduled to leave. On every one of the hard wooden benches, designed for three people, sat four and sometimes five. Others sat in the aisle. When the aisles of all the cars were filled, people began climbing onto the roof, putting their feet into the windows and pulling themselves up. Rehv and the boy watched the feet go by, some in sandals, some bare with thick hard soles that were yellow and flaking: black feet, brown feet, a few white feet, all of them dusty. When there was no more room on the roof, those left on the platform sat down to wait twenty-four hours for the next train.

"Water?" Rehv asked Paul in Arabic, offering him the plastic canteen. The boy shook his head. "You've got to drink." But he didn't want to drink. He wanted to look out the window. Rehv watched him. He wore his white jubba as though it were the only kind of clothing he had ever worn. Except for his curly hair, which Rehv saw was a little too long, he looked not at all out of place.

Rehv wore a jubba too. He hoped that people would think they were traders. Under their seats were large bundles wrapped in cloth; the sort of bundles that traders carried from town to town, filled with cheap European fabrics, jewelry made from elephant tusks or plastic that looked the same, ebony phallic gods, stone fertility goddesses. But there was none of that in their bundles—just clothing, food, and water. It did not seem to matter. No one took any notice of them.

Next to Rehv sat an old man in a tattered robe. He was sleeping with his toothless head resting on the top slat of the backrest and his feet on a lamb that lay on the floor. Its legs were bound together by a piece of rope. The man had tribal markings on his forehead—two vertical scars that intersected his wrinkles in a way that reminded Rehv of a framework for X's and O's.

Nothing moved except the sun, which rose higher and higher in the sky. The train was painted white, and most of the windows were overhung with wooden eaves, but everyone's face was soon coated with a wet shine. "What can they be waiting for?" Rehv said. He felt nervous and annoyed, as though he had just had a very poor haircut.

"The engineer," Paul said.

A beggar came slowly along the track, sticking his hand into all the windows. So much of the hand had been eaten away that giving him a coin meant placing it carefully on the palm. Paul did. "Thank you, master," the beggar said in Arabic. The definition was gone from his face. He limped away on the stubs he had for feet.

Later a white man appeared, striding briskly across the platform. He wore sunglasses and a short-sleeved white shirt, and had a folded copy of the *Daily Telegraph* in his back pocket. Soon after that the train began to move. The man beside Rehv lurched forward and vomited on the lamb. Rehv squeezed closer to Paul. The lamb made a noise and wriggled on the floor. The train stopped.

A few hours went by. A man on a small skinny horse approached the train. His heavy wife walked behind. She wore a veil. The man dismounted and boosted her onto the roof. He handed her a motor oil can filled with dried salted fish, and a baby. The train started again.

It rolled slowly south, through fields of cotton. To the east Rehv could see the Blue Nile. It was brown. Later the train ran beside the river, and Rehv saw people camped along it in tents or crude shelters made of rushes and bits of straw matting. Some of them had a few sheep or a goat or a cow. They all had children with bloated bellies and runny eyes. Once he saw a mud hut flying the flag of the United Nations. A long line of people waited outside in the sun, each holding an empty bowl. The train stopped and started. People got on and off. The man with the scarred forehead slept. Rehv slept too. They rolled through cotton.

When Paul nudged him awake it was almost dark. They were on a bridge, moving west. "The White Nile," Paul said, pointing below. In the fading light it too looked brown. There were more people camped along its banks; their fires glowed like street-lamps as far as Rehv could see.

They drank water and ate sardines and oranges. Paul reached into the long pocket inside his jubba and pulled out a few balls of newspaper filled with shelled peanuts.

"Where did you get those?" Rehv asked.

"At one of the stops. They're a piaster apiece."

"It's dangerous to eat anything you can't peel or shell yourself."

"That won't be very realistic, will it?" the boy said quietly. They ate the peanuts.

The night air was no cooler, but it grew drier and much dustier the farther west they went. The dust stung their eyes and filled their pores. Now and then Rehv wiped his face with his sleeve. It made his sleeve dirty. After a while he stopped.

"Try to get some sleep," he said.

"I'm not tired."

The passengers sitting in the aisle lay down. Those who had seats leaned forward or backward or against the people beside them. Rehv had no idea what the ones on top of the train did during the night. He tried leaning forward, backward, sideways; none of it helped his back. A man snored. A woman whispered. A baby cried. Rehv slept.

In the morning when Rehv awoke, most of the seats were

taken by soldiers, dark men in khaki uniforms. Their rifles lay in the aisle. The old man with the lamb was gone. In his place slept a soldier with sweat stains on his shirt, spreading from his armpits to his waist. Outside people were going by, some on horseback or oxen, a few on camels, most on foot. They carried their belongings in straw baskets or goatskin bags or calabashes balanced on their heads. They were all moving the other way, east, toward the river, whether because of the drought or the fighting, Rehv didn't know. "It's been like that all night," Paul said. It went on like that all day. Ribs. Of horses. Camels. Men. And babies hanging onto shriveled breasts. Sometimes the train stopped, but the people outside did not ask for food or water. They just kept walking. The soldiers were very quiet.

Somewhere behind him Rehv heard a man say in English, "How do you explain the small canines, then? Or do you dispute that Ramapithecus had small canines?" He turned and saw two white men sitting a few rows away. One of them reminded him of an anthropology professor he had known long ago. That one said: "I don't dispute it. It's irrelevant. Molecularly speaking it had to happen much later, that's all." They both had well-bred English accents. They were arguing about when man had separated from the apes. They argued about it for an hour or two. All they had to do was to look at what was going on outside to see that it had not happened yet, Rehv thought.

The train crossed Kordofan, stopping at Umm Ruwaba and Er Rahad, Gaibat and Abu Zabad, and several other places where there was no sign of any habitation. But even at these a few people got off the train and started walking across the red brown plain toward the horizon. They did not seem to notice the refugees moving slowly toward the east.

The train went by villages where the huts were round with conical roofs of straw, and villages where they were square with V-shaped roofs. It passed huts huddled in the shade of feathery flat-topped acacia trees, and unprotected huts that the sun had bleached the color of driftwood. Rehv saw dark veiled women carrying bundles of sticks on their backs, and darker bare-breasted women pounding millet with wooden pestles, while sweat dripped off their nipples into the mortars.

His back hurt. He wanted to sleep. He tried different positions. None of them worked. The boy looked out the window. "You should get some sleep," Rehv said to him.

Paul turned to him. His hair and eyebrows were covered with dust the color of paprika. The rims of his eyes were red. He didn't seem to mind. "Hang on," Paul said. "It won't be much longer."

Just before nightfall the train reached Babanusa on the frontier of Darfur, where the track branched in two. Most of the passengers got out, including the soldiers and the two Englishmen. The Englishmen climbed into a Landrover with the words University of London on the door and drove away. The soldiers prostrated themselves in the dust by the rails, prayed, and then boarded another train that soon rolled away on the track leading west.

Rehv and the boy were left alone in the empty car. They stood up. They walked around. Then people came in. They carried goats on their backs and chickens in their hands; they had bottles filled with liquid butter, and lumps of millet cooked with pepper sauce wrapped in greasy scraps of paper. Rehv and Paul went back to their seats. Soon all the places were taken. And the aisle was filled. And finally the roof. The white man with the *Daily Telegraph* in his back pocket came out of the station house and strode toward the front of the train. He had a bottle of beer in his hand. One of the passengers made a clicking sound of disapproval with his tongue, either for safety or religious reasons. With a little jerk the train moved forward.

It began to pick up speed. After a few minutes it was going as fast as it had at any time during the past two days. Rehv had assumed that was the maximum speed, but it was not. The train went faster, much faster. A hot wind blew through the car, carrying invisible clouds of dust. There was a cry from the roof and a washtub sailed by the window. Round dark forms—they might have been melons—fell out of it and bounced into the darkness. People began to vomit. There was another cry from the roof. The train sped on to the next station.

A weak yellow light bulb hung over the sign on the platform. Muglad it said in Arabic. "Muglad," Paul said. Rehv felt a tightening in his chest. No one got off the train except the man with the *Daily Telegraph* in his back pocket. On the platform he met another white man coming out of the station. They talked for a few minutes. Some of the passengers watched them. The rest slept. The man with the *Daily Telegraph* said something that made the other man laugh and say, "That's a good one." The first man went inside the station. The second man walked toward the front of the train. In a few minutes it began rolling again at its normal rate. Rehv peered out the window, trying to see the town. But the only light was the light on the platform. Muglad slid by in the darkness.

The wheels beat a complicated rhythm on the rails. It put everyone to sleep except Rehv and the boy. They stared out the window, into the night. At first they could see nothing, but later the moon rose, fat and yellow, on the horizon. It showed them a dark plain and sometimes the shadows of stunted trees. After a long time Paul suddenly stiffened and whispered, "There." Rehv saw a narrow stream of rocks, like motionless waves, flowing away to the southwest. Wadi el Ghalla. The wheels beat their rhythm into an echo chamber as the train rolled over a bridge.

Paul turned to him. "When?" he asked in a low voice.

"Soon." The train was moving slowly, but he did not want to jump, not with his back the way it was. He waited, hunched forward on the seat, listening for the easing in the rhythm that would mean the train was about to make another one of its stops in the emptiness. Several times he thought he heard it; then he did. The rhythm slowed, broke into its components: wheels rattling on steel, scraping couplings, creaking of carriages. The spaces between the sounds grew longer, like a music box at the end of its song. A few passengers stirred, muttered, went back to sleep. Everything was quiet. Rehv nodded. They picked up the bundles that lay at their feet, climbed through the window, and lowered themselves to the ground.

They walked west. The night was hot and dry and sucked the moisture out of them. Rehv felt tired and dirty. He wanted a shower and soft cool sheets. He looked at the boy, silent beside him, walking away from showers and soft cool sheets, and tried not to think about it.

The moon rose higher in the sky. Rehv searched the shadows for reflections of its light in narrow yellow eyes—vipers, hyenas, lions. They were all out there. The books said so. "It can't be much farther," he told the boy.

"Let's speak English, Dad. No one's going to hear."

"All right."

But what would he say? He felt things stirring inside him,

206

trying to push themselves out into the air. He knew if he let them it would end with turning around, going back to Muglad, back along the railway line, back. To somewhere. But after Lac du Loup, after the fingerprinting, he told himself, there was no choice. While he thought about that, the things stopped pressing inside him. That was how he fooled them. It worked for now.

So they talked about maps and water and cattle brands and drum calls until they came again to the wadi. It had become much narrower, no more than a trickle of small stones almost level with the plain. They followed it. The yellow moon followed them.

The wadi shrank and shrank and finally vanished in a little pile of pebbles. Rehv turned north. "No," Paul said. "This way." And led him south. They walked through the night. It was very quiet. Their sandals padded softly on the dust that lay over the hard clay. Sometimes their jubbas caught on a thorny bush, or they stumbled on a rock. Once they surprised a vulture. It rose heavily into the air, and circled over the bones and ragged flesh of a small cow until they had gone away. "We're getting close," Paul said.

They entered a shallow depression and began walking across it. In the center they came to a small pool of water, not much bigger than a wading pool. Paul bent down, cupped some water in his palm and tasted it. "Salty."

"How much farther do you think it is?" Rehv asked.

"We're there."

"What do you mean?"

Paul gestured around them. "On the map this is all water. The whole depression should be filled."

On the far side two baobab trees stood in the moonlight, one much bigger than the other. "You're right," Rehv said. They walked up out of the depression and stopped beneath the trees. "We're here."

"Yes."

They sat down. Rehv took out his canteen and passed it to the boy. He drank. Rehv drank. They ate some more sardines. "We'd better get some sleep," Rehv said.

The boy lay down on his back with his head resting on his bundle of clothing. Rehv lay beside him. Above, the moon rose slowly to the top of the sky. Rehv put his arm around the boy.

Then his other arm. The man in the moon looked like Peter Lorre. "He looks like Peter Lorre," Rehv said softly.

"Who's he?"

"A movie actor." Rehv remembered how his little girl had liked watching Peter Lorre in scary movies late at night. Paul hadn't had a chance to see many movies. He tried to imagine the boy at home with them in Jerusalem, watching late-night television, and couldn't. But then he thought of him sitting by the campfire singing, "My paddle's clean and bright." Paul rolled over onto his side and out of Rehv's arms.

The moon slipped down the far side of the sky. Neither of them slept. After a while the blackness began to turn navy blue in the east. "You should get going," Paul said.

"Not yet."

But it was time. After a few minutes Rehv stood up. The boy stood up too. "It's getting light," Rehv said.

"I know."

"Walk with me a little."

"No."

They looked at each other for a moment. Then Rehv embraced the boy and hugged him close. He felt the boy's arms squeezing him hard. He kissed the top of his curly head.

"Dad?"

"Yes."

"You'll be at the bridge?"

"A week from tonight. Where the tracks cross the wadi. If it doesn't work, it doesn't work. We'll go back."

"Back?"

"Somewhere."

Rehv held onto the boy. Navy blue advanced across the sky. Rehv became aware that the boy had let his hands drop to his sides. "It's time," Rehv said. The boy nodded. Rehv kissed his curly head again and let him go. Two kisses. When was the last one before those? "Until next week," Rehv said. He turned and started walking away, toward Muglad. He knew he didn't want to go to Muglad. He wanted to go to the cabin on Lac du Loup. But what about the little white house on Mount Carmel? He reached the edge of the depression.

"Dad?"

He stopped. He did not want to turn around. "What?" he called.

"What if you can't make it next week? Or if I can't?"

He faced the boy. "Then we both try the next night."

"And what if you're not there the next night?"

"I will be."

"But if you're not?"

"Then it's the next and the next and the next. And so on. But don't worry. I'll be there. The first night. Okay?" He thought the boy nodded, but he was too far away and it was still too dark to be sure. "Okay?"

"Okay."

Rehv turned and walked down into the depression. "My paddle's clean and bright, flashing like silver." The song started in his head, and it wouldn't stop. It was loud and getting louder. "My paddle's clean and bright, flashing like silver." He tried to think of something else, or another song, but no other song came. And somewhere behind the music he heard the screaming start. He kept walking.

Paul went to the edge of the depression and watched his father moving away, past the shallow pool and up the other side. He disappeared in the gold fringe that had begun to shine on the eastern edge of the navy blue.

Paul walked back to the baobab trees and lay down. He felt like crying. He let himself cry. Later he slept.

When he awoke, it was the middle of the day and very hot. He was thirsty. He drank from the canteen. He ate a couple of oranges. Then he took off his sandals, his jubba, and his underwear and went down to the shallow pool. He sat in the warm water and washed the dust from his body. He walked back toward the trees. The sun dried him before he got there.

He put on a clean white jubba and sat in the shade and waited.

Soon he saw a dust cloud in the west. It was red brown and hung low in the air. He sat beneath the big baobab tree and watched it coming closer. After a while he could distinguish little figures beneath the cloud, two-legged ones and four-legged ones. They came closer. Men and women. Children. Oxen. A few horses. Cows. Hundreds of them. Paul stood up.

They moved slowly toward him across the plain. Tired, gaunt animals and tired, gaunt men. No one saw Paul. They were interested only in water. They came to the depression. The cows went down to the shallow pool. The men who had horses dismounted. The horses went down to the pool. The women removed the gourds, straw mats, baskets, and iron pots from the backs of the oxen and let them go down too. The men and women stood on the edge of the depression. No one spoke.

After a while they noticed Paul standing by the big tree. They walked around the depression and came near him. They stopped a few yards away. He saw how thin they were, how worn, how dusty; some were dressed in rags, almost naked. But their skin was the same color as his. He looked more like them than like his father.

They watched him the way he had always known they would. He pointed to a spot on the ground between the two trees and said in Arabic: "Dig here. There is water. But you have to dig deep."

They watched him. An old man, brown and wrinkled, stepped forward and crossed the space between them. He looked Paul in the eye. Paul looked back in his. The old man fell to his knees and kissed the hem of Paul's robe.

"The Mahdi," he said.

CHAPTER TWENTY-SIX

My paddle's keen and bright
Flashing with silver
Follow the wild goose flight
Dip dip and swing.

Isaac Rehv walked all day. He sang. He talked to himself.
"Okay. Muglad. Muglad. First, buy some trading goods. Get the
trading goods. Then, then. What? Get a room. Cheap. That's
it. Trading goods. Cheap room. Railroad bridge." He counted
them off on his fingers. Once he laughed and started running.
He laughed and ran, laughed and ran, his jubba flapping around
his legs. He stopped when he felt how hard his heart was pounding. Even after he stopped, it pounded in his ears for a long
time. He sat down beside a dusty bush and drank from the
canteen. He lay down. He put his ear to the ground, like an
Indian. If the earth had a heart beating under its skin he couldn't
hear it.

He jumped up. He had done it. He had done it.

Oh, God. The boy.

But the boy wanted it.

He had made him want it.

Had he?

He stopped jumping and walked. The sun pressed down on
the top of his head like a heavy weight. At first the dusty sky was
yellow ochre. It turned to red ochre as the sun sank toward the
horizon. Miles above, a plane scratched a pink line through the

redness pointing west. To Lac du Loup. It kept pointing long after the plane had disappeared.

A week from last night. Was that six nights or seven?

The boy.

Dip dip and scream: "Muglad. Muglad."

He reached Muglad as the sun went down. It was narrow dirt streets filled with sweating people, overloaded donkeys, goats, chickens, and dung. The houses were mud. The stores were shacks; the fancy ones had tin roofs. A man with no legs swung his muscular trunk onto a board with tea-wagon-sized wheels underneath and rolled off through the dirt, pushing himself along with his hands. A woman had a baby with no arms. A man had a face with no nose. They all wanted money. Rehv hurried on.

"Muglad. Trading goods. A room." But he was tired. The trading goods could wait. He needed a room. Sleep. He would ask at the railway station.

The railway station was a small red clay building. It stood beside a red clay mosque that was even smaller. A man slept on the ground by the door. Rehv walked around him and went inside.

It was dark and empty. There were no windows, and the door that led to the platform was closed. In one corner a small office had been walled off with unfinished plywood boards. Electric light glowed around the edges of the door. Rehv crossed the room and raised his hand to knock on it. He heard people talking inside. He didn't knock: They were speaking English.

A man said: "I wouldn't know about that, love." He had an English accent.

A woman said: "What about El Fasher?" She had an American accent.

The man said: "Can't get there. Too much shooting."

The woman said: "South then?"

The man said: "Not so good. The drought's hit hard. Not so much the drought, though, as the way it's been overstocked all these years. Typical."

Another man said: "I don't care about that. Can we still get through?" He too had an American accent, but it was not that alone which made Rehv feel cold the moment he heard the man's voice.

The first man said: "Oh yes. Track's clear, all right."

212

The second man said: "Good." A chair squeaked.

Rehv backed slowly away across the dark room, his eyes on the glowing outline of the office door. He was cold, but he was sweating more than he had in the crowded train or walking all day under the sun. The voices faded. Rehv turned and ran outside.

Night was falling fast. The sleeping man was turning into a shadow. Rehv crossed the street and sat down with his back against a low mud wall. He bowed his head and pulled the cloth of his robe up over it. He was another sleeping man.

After a few minutes he saw three people come out of the railway station, two men and a woman. He could just make out their faces in the fading light. The woman was young and fair. She wore a kerchief around her head and a camera around her neck. He had never seen her before. The first man wore a short-sleeved white shirt. He was the engineer who read the *Daily Telegraph*. The second man he had seen before, long ago. He had put on weight, and lost his hair, and no longer wore glasses, but his thick dark eyebrows were still the same. He was Major Kay.

Rehv sat motionless, barely breathing. Across the street the three people stood talking in low voices. They took no more notice of him than they did of the shadow sleeping at their feet. The engineer said, "Right then" in a loud, cheerful voice, turned, and started walking down the street. Major Kay and the woman went the other way. Rehv waited until he could no longer see that their skins were white before he rose and followed them.

Major Kay and the woman walked along a narrow street that smelled of cinnamon, and into a large square. A little boy in shorts was running across the square, rolling an old bicycle tire rim that he controlled with a stick. The rim got away from him, veered toward Major Kay, wobbled, and fell at his feet. Major Kay stopped and picked it up. Rehv stepped back into the shadows of the narrow street. Major Kay rolled the rim back to the boy. The boy let it go by without making any attempt to reach for it. He stood staring at Major Kay.

"What the hell is that all about?" Rehv heard Major Kay say as he and the woman continued across the square. The woman's answer was too faint to hear.

On the far side of the square was a two-story wooden building with a covered jeep parked in front. Major Kay and the woman paused beside the jeep. Rehv heard keys tinkle. Major Kay opened the door of the jeep and took out a small dark package. Then he and the woman went inside the two-story building. The little boy picked up the bicycle rim and ran off, rolling it along with the stick.

Rehv watched the building across the square, and waited. Soon a light went on in a window on the second floor, and then another beside it. A woman entered the square from a street on the other side, a large earthenware bowl balanced on her head. As she came closer he saw that she wore a veil. She did not appear to see him at all. When she was quite near she looked around, lifted her robe, and crouched beside a small tree. Rehv could hear the sound of her urine falling on the sand. She stood up, tugged at her robe, and walked away. The bowl had stayed steady on her head; she hadn't touched it once.

The earth turned the curve of its back on the last rays of light. The square grew quiet. Rehv kept his eyes on the lights in the windows. Shades were drawn over both. From time to time he saw a single silhouette move behind one or the other. Later, the light went off behind one and two silhouettes moved in the same window.

He sat down. Inside his brain the singing had died away, and the screaming too. He thought about Major Kay, and the boy naked and tied to a chair, and pointed copper wire. He began to wish he had drowned in the sea with Sergeant Levy. He stopped himself from thinking about that because he didn't want to go where it led. He watched the window. The silhouettes moved back, forward, to the side. They raised their arms and lowered them. He sat down, resting his back against the small tree. His back hurt. A big brown bird flew down out of the darkness and circled over his head. Heavy wings beat the air. The bird landed on a branch at the top of the tree. The silhouettes moved behind the shade. Rehv fell asleep.

He dreamed of a picnic. He was a boy. He ate apples and cheese in the shade of an olive tree. Then he went swimming in a pool in the rocks. He dove into the cool water and swam down, down toward the bottom. On the bottom was a human leg. It wore a big black boot. He kicked away from it and struggled toward the surface. Then he looked up and saw how far it was. He would never get there.

Rehv awoke, lying on the ground beside the tree. The light still shone in the window of the two-story building. He knew he could wait no longer. The fat yellow moon had risen. The square was quiet and empty. He got to his feet and started walking across it.

The jeep was very new—no scratches, no dents, no rust. In the moonlight he read the words on the door: Food Relief. It was locked.

Over the door of the two-story building hung a small sign he had not been able to read from the other side of the square. Victoria Hotel it said in English. In Arabic was written Hotel of the Faithful. Rehv opened the door and went inside.

He was in a narrow hall with a small reception desk on one side, two stained couches on the other, and a flight of stairs leading up from the far end. A naked bulb shone from the ceiling. The clerk was a barefoot young man who wore a wool cap and a T-shirt with the words Hey Baby! written on the front. He was sleeping on the couch by the entrance, but opened his eyes when he heard the door close.

"Good night," he said in English, sitting up. "How to serve you?"

"A room please," Rehv said in Arabic.

"None left," the clerk said in Arabic, and lay down again.

Rehv looked at the key rack behind the desk. There were four hooks. The keys for one and two were gone, but keys hung on hooks three and four. "What about rooms three and four?" Rehv asked.

"All taken."

"But there are the keys," Rehv said, pointing. He noticed a billy club hanging on the wall by the key rack.

The clerk didn't bother looking. "All taken." He closed his eyes.

"I'll pay you one pound to sleep on the other couch."

"Three," the clerk said without opening his eyes.

He settled for two. Rehv handed him the money. He tucked it inside his T-shirt and rolled over. "I can't sleep with the light on," Rehv said.

The clerk shrugged.

"Twenty-five piasters."

"Seventy-five."

Rehv gave him fifty, switched off the light, and lay down on the couch near the stairs. He waited. The clerk's breathing soon became slow, quiet, and even. A bedspring squeaked somewhere above. The clerk muttered something and sighed; and went on breathing slowly, quietly, evenly. Rehv sat up. Enough moonlight came through the window in the front door for him to see the clerk huddled on the couch with his hands tucked between his knees, and the billy club hanging on the wall. He slipped off his sandals and stood up.

The clerk did not stir. Rehv walked softly across the hall and went behind the desk. He took the billy club off the hook, glanced at the sleeping clerk, and very slowly started up the stairs. With each stair he left the moonlight farther behind; when he reached the top he was in almost total darkness. He paused there, waiting for his pupils to expand. After a minute or two he could see a corridor leading away into blackness. Several doors opened off the corridor. Under one of them a little light leaked out and formed a pool on the floor. Crouching down on his hands and knees, he crept closer.

On the other side of the door he heard the woman say, "No, really. That's all for me."

Major Kay said: "Come on, Jill. A nightcap. There are a few things we should go over."

The woman said: "All right. But please, it's Gillian."

Major Kay said: "Whatever you say."

Glass clinked against glass. Liquid gurgled. After a pause the woman said: "What did you want to go over?"

In a voice that was suddenly low and throaty, Major Kay said: "This."

The woman said: "Don't do that."

Major Kay said: "Why not? Got a boyfriend some place?"

The woman said: "It's not that. I just don't know you very well yet."

Major Kay said: "Can you think of a better way?"

The woman said: "And also I'm not sure it's very professional."

Major Kay said: "What are you talking about? I've seen your reports. I know how you get information."

The woman began to get angry: "That's different and you know it. You're my boss—that makes it unprofessional."

Major Kay's voice turned cold. "I'll be the judge of that."

"What do you mean?"

"What I said."

"I don't understand. Are you threatening me about my career?"

"Who said anything about your career?"

"But you'll be writing a report about me when you go back."

"I write reports about a lot of people."

"You see? You are threatening me."

"You're starting to bore me, Jill. Why don't you go back to your own room?"

A floorboard creaked. Quickly Rehv moved away into the darkness. The door opened, and the woman came out. She was fully dressed in jeans and a shirt cut like a man's, but she no longer wore the kerchief around her head. She turned back toward the room, and in the light that shone from within Rehv saw her thick chestnut hair, streaked yellow in places by the sun, and her strong profile, which might not always look as angry as it did now. "It's not sex I object to, Mr. Krebs," she said. "It's you."

The woman slammed the door and entered the next room. Rehv heard a key turn in the lock. Then he heard a key turn in the lock of Major Kay's room. The pool of light vanished. He stood in the darkness and listened.

For a while the woman paced back and forth in her room. Then he heard her shoes fall to the floor. After that she was silent. From Major Kay's room he heard nothing.

He waited a long time. It was very quiet. In the shadows behind him a small animal ran across the floor. Rehv began to worry about the clerk waking up.

When he had worried enough he walked to Major Kay's door and knocked on it very lightly. He turned his ear against the door and listened; he heard nothing. He knocked again, a little louder. He heard a sound that might have been a foot brushing the floor; the key turned in the lock; he felt hot stale air touch his face as the door opened; he smelled gin. He could see nothing.

"Changed your mind?" said Major Kay in the blackness.

Rehv swung the billy club at where he thought Major Kay's head should be. It cracked something hard. A heavy body slumped against him: warm skin, slightly damp. He pushed the body into the room, laid it on the floor, and closed the door behind him. Kneeling, he rested his hand on the bare chest and felt Major Kay's beating heart, strong and regular.

Rehv stood up and ran his hands over the walls until he found the light switch. He turned it on. There was blood on Major Kay's forehead, just over his left eyebrow; and swelling beneath the blood. But his chest rose and fell as though he were in a deep tranquil sleep.

Rehv searched the room. All of Major Kay's possessions were in a small vinyl suitcase at the foot of the bed. Rehv found lightweight clothing, a black case containing powerful binoculars, a book called *Great Moments in Cartoon History,* car keys, 2,500 American dollars, most of it in hundreds, 1,463 Sudanese pounds, and a British passport in the name of George Provin with a photograph of Major Kay inside. Rehv tucked the keys and the money into the leather pouch he wore around his neck.

Stepping over the naked man, he opened the door, switched off the light, and dragged him into the hall. Then he bent his knees, set his shoulder against Major Kay's waist, and hoisted him off the floor. It hurt his back so much that he could not keep in a little cry. He stood motionless in the dark corridor with Major Kay on his shoulder, listening. No one jumped out of bed, or ran up the stairs, or opened a door, or shouted. He carried Major Kay down the corridor. He was very heavy. The floor creaked with every step. So did the stairs. He came down into the moonlight. The clerk was just the way he had been. Very slowly Rehv walked past him and out the door.

He laid Major Kay on the hood of the jeep and went back to close the door of the hotel, gently. Then he unlocked the jeep, shoved Major Kay into the passenger seat, and sat down behind the wheel. He found the ignition, turned the key. The engine caught immediately: The noise of gasoline exploding drop by drop and steel whirling and pounding filled the night. Quickly Rehv drove across the square and into a narrow street, which grew into a wider street and became the southern road out of town. For a few miles he followed it, until he saw a small track leading west across the plain. He turned onto it; and drove by the light of the moon.

At first there were villages here and there along the track: some of them no more than a few huts beside a tree, others much larger, protected by low walls of mud and straw. All of them were dark and silent, asleep under the fat yellow moon. Once a dog barked; that was all.

After a while there were no more villages. In all directions the plain stretched away, flat and unbroken except for a few clusters of trees that seemed to be moving away from him very quickly, like galaxies in an expanding universe.

Major Kay moaned. Rehv glanced at him. He had slipped off the seat and lay curled on the floor with his head resting against the base of the gear shift. Turning off the track, Rehv drove toward the nearest cluster of trees. Low brittle bushes that he had not noticed before grew on the plain. They tore at the underside of the jeep. Major Kay moaned again.

The trees stopped trying to run away, grew bigger, loomed in front of him. Rehv parked in their shadow. There wasn't a sound except a soft rumble in Major Kay's throat as he breathed. Rehv climbed out and opened the back door of the jeep. Inside he found two large cans of gasoline, a spare tire, tools, and a coil of nylon rope. He slipped the rope over his shoulder, pulled Major Kay out of the jeep, and dragged him to the foot of a small acacia tree. It had a straight narrow trunk. Major Kay moaned, and mumbled something incoherent.

He went back to the jeep and searched through the tools until he came upon a pair of wire cutters. He cut three short lengths from the coil of rope. One of these he tied around Major Kay's ankles; another around his knees. He knew nothing special about knots or how to bind a man: He just drew the ropes very tightly around Major Kay's legs and doubled all the knots. He sat Major Kay against the tree and tied his wrists together behind the trunk. After looking at him for a few moments Rehv cut two more pieces of rope. One he wrapped around Major Kay's chest and upper arms and knotted behind the tree; the other he tied around his waist. As he pulled it tight he felt it sink into the soft flesh of his stomach until it met the hard muscle underneath.

Then Rehv placed the wire cutters on the ground in front of Major Kay, and beside them a screwdriver and a tire iron. He waited.

In a little while Major Kay moaned again. He said, "Don't." He vomited. It ran down his chest. Rehv smelled souring milk.

Major Kay opened his eyes. Rehv remembered those pale brown eyes and how they had gone soft and dreamy on a night long ago. The night of the permanent damage.

The pale brown eyes were not soft and dreamy now. They were dull; then they looked up at Rehv, and for a moment were frightened; finally they were watchful. They examined the jeep, the tools on the ground, Rehv.

Rehv squatted in front of him. "These things follow a pattern," he said. "First you deny everything. Then, when the pain starts you make up a long and clever story that often resembles the truth quite closely, but never really says anything. Finally you tell the truth. Everyone does."

He waited for the frightened look to reappear in the pale brown eyes. It did not.

"Who are you? Kay? Provin? Krebs?"

"What difference does that make?" Major Kay said in a tone that sounded genuinely puzzled.

He didn't like the way Major Kay was watching him. It was detached, professional, trained: Was Major Kay slotting him somewhere among the types of interrogators? Could he do that —naked, bound, with a bloody bump on his forehead and vomit on his chest? "I asked you a question," Rehv said.

Major Kay laughed.

Rehv punched his face. Major Kay's eyes went dull. He vomited again. But Rehv did not know what to do next. Finally he asked: "How did you find me?"

Major Kay spat something out of his mouth. It landed in the dust at Rehv's feet. "Routine," he said.

Rehv thought of hitting him again, or breaking his leg with the tire iron, or jabbing the screwdriver into his eye, or slicing off his ear with the wire cutters. Or his testicles. But he knew he could do none of these things: not with Major Kay tied there to the tree. He tried remembering the night of the soft dreamy eyes, he tried thinking about Major Kay and his son, but it wasn't enough to make him do what he would have to do to discover how much Major Kay knew about the boy. And that was really all that mattered: Did he know that the boy had come with him? Did he know why?

"Who do you work for?"

"The U.S. government. You know that." Major Kay looked

up at the moon; perhaps he was trying to estimate the time. Its light glistened on the hardening blood over his eye.

"What do you want with me?" Rehv asked.

"You killed a man on U.S. soil. Abu Fahoum. Remember? We have laws against that kind of thing."

Major Kay was thousands of miles from home, Rehv thought, naked and helpless, but somehow still in authority. "I didn't kill him."

"Fine. You and I will go back to the States, you'll be acquitted and walk away a free man." Major Kay spoke sarcastically.

Rehv knew he could not interrogate Major Kay. How could he make him tell if he knew or suspected anything about the boy? He could not scare him; he could not hurt him the way he would have to hurt him. In the end he would probably untie him and let him go. He was a clumsy amateur and Major Kay knew it.

So there was nothing to do but be a clumsy amateur and go on making mistakes—the kind of mistakes that would lead Major Kay far from the boy. Rehv wrinkled his brow in thought. "I know you're lying to me," he said. "You wouldn't come here because of a murder so long ago. You don't give a damn about that." He paused; then blurted: "It's the Jeddah drop, isn't it?"

Major Kay did not answer, but for the briefest instant his eyes flickered in the moonlight.

It was enough. More talk would gain nothing. He raised his voice: "Answer me."

"I don't know what you're talking about." There was a tentative sound in Major Kay's tone that had not been there before.

Jerkily, like a man on the edge of panic, Rehv grabbed the tire iron and jumped up. "What do you know about the Jeddah drop?"

"Nothing."

"You're lying," Rehv shouted. He lifted the tire iron above his head. "I'm asking you for the last time."

"You're making a mistake," Major Kay said.

"I said that once, too." With the blunt end of the tire iron Rehv struck down at the side of Major Kay's head, firmly, but with much less than all his force. A hoarse grunt climbed partway up Major Kay's throat. His head slumped forward on his chest.

Rehv let the tire iron fall to the ground. He jumped into the jeep, turned the key, and drove away with the accelerator pressed to the floor. He felt the contents of his stomach rising inside him. He fought them down for one mile, two miles, three. But in the end there was nothing he could do about it.

He drove east. The yellow moon watched him in the rearview mirror. Lena liked Peter Lorre. Naomi would make popcorn; they would sit around the television. He tried to picture them around the television, but all he could see were shadows of bodies and faces with no features. He could not even picture his own face. Lena's face, Naomi's face: decayed, decomposed in his memory, as they were in the little grave on Mount Carmel. Peter Lorre had been dead much longer than they, yet he could see his face very clearly. Of course he had the moon to remind him of Peter Lorre. All he had to remind him of Lena and Naomi were screams.

East across the plain. Dark mountains rose in the distance. The moon sank lower in the sky, out of range of the rearview mirror. When he thought he must be beyond Muglad, Rehv turned north until he found a track leading east. He took it. At first it was rocky; then it disappeared; then it was two lanes wide and paved. He pressed on the accelerator. Eighty miles an hour. Eighty-five. The pavement stopped. The jeep bounced over some rocks, spun around, came to rest. The engine was no longer running.

"Goddamn it."

He turned the key. The motor came to life. Slowly he drove on.

He began to laugh. "The Jeddah drop." He laughed and laughed. He stopped laughing when the motor sputtered and died. He tried the ignition. It whirred, but the engine did not fire. "Goddamn it. Goddamn it. Goddamn it." He pounded the steering wheel and jerked back and forth in the seat. "Goddamn it." He shouted the words for a long time, pounding and jerking in the darkness. After a while he stopped and sat quietly, his chest heaving. He wondered if the car was out of gas, and looked at the gauge. It was. With a gasoline can from the back of the jeep he filled the tank and kept going.

He drove all night. He sang. "My paddle's keen and bright, flashing with silver." He roared the words. He heard the harshness in his voice and made it harsher. Jutting out his jaw, he roared as harshly as he could.

The moon went down. The sun came up. Suddenly he thought of Major Kay tied to the tree, thought for the first time that maybe no one would see him there. But there were villages not far away and the dirt track. And nomads. Still, what if no one saw him? The sun was up; it was already hot. Squeamish Isaac Rehv, man of scruples—who couldn't bring himself to use the wire cutters the way they should have been used, to protect himself, his plans and the boy—had left a man to die of thirst. "Going to die, going to die, going to die," he roared.

No. Someone would find Major Kay. Someone would cut him loose. He would go after the boy. And stick sharp things up his penis.

No. He wouldn't. Because of the Jeddah drop. Major Kay would follow him east. He knew nothing about the boy. So he would lead him east to the sea, and while Major Kay crossed it and went on to Jeddah he would double back and meet his boy under the railway bridge. When? Five days? Six? There was time.

But what if Major Kay went after the boy anyway? He wouldn't. He had fooled Major Kay, and saved the boy, himself, everything. He had done it. And if he hadn't, was there a choice?

The choice was to turn back, get the boy, and take him somewhere safe. Another lake, like Lac du Loup. It could be done. Anyone who had done what he had already could do that. He had been happy on Lac du Loup—if not happy at least quiet inside. Quiet enough to go on living.

"It's too late for that," he roared.

He knew it wasn't.

But he kept driving east.

He drove all day. He sang. He laughed. He roared. He screamed. He screamed about Lena and Naomi and his mother and Paulette. And the boy. He saw naked black women and tiny black babies tied to their mothers' backs with strips of cloth. He saw lean brown men holding hands. He saw schoolchildren writing their lessons in the dust. Whenever he saw people he tried not to scream. But usually he did anyway.

He came to many roadblocks, manned by soldiers with rifles slung across their backs. They all smiled and waved him through. Later he noticed that people by the road were smiling at him too. Everyone had a smiling face for him: big white teeth in black faces, brown faces, or faces almost the color of his own. It was a long time before he realized that they were smiling because of the words on the door of the jeep—Food Relief.

The sun went down. The moon came up. He drove all night. He sang. He laughed. He roared. He screamed. East. But he should be going west because he couldn't see Lena's face or Naomi's face or anybody's face except the boy's. The boy was beautiful. He was hard. But that was Rehv's work. So. Why? He could no longer remember what Israel was like. He couldn't even remember how to speak Hebrew.

But he could. He opened his mouth and in Hebrew roared: "I hate myself."

In the morning he reached Port Sudan. "What's first?" he said. "One: Leave the jeep in a prominent place. Two: Catch the train going west. Two things. Jeep. Train."

He drove to the docks and left the jeep parked by a big crane hanging out over the water. "Two," he said. "Train." But he didn't turn and start walking into the city. Instead he went out to the end of a long pier. He sat down and looked at the sea, the sea that had parted for Moses.

It was as blue as the sky. The sun broke against its surface into countless golden pieces, too bright to see. Rehv thought how dusty he was, how dirty. He pulled off his clothes, wrapped his leather neck pouch inside them, and laid the little bundle carefully on the end of the pier. On top he put his sandals so nothing would blow away if a sudden breeze came off the water. Then he dove into the sea that had parted for Moses.

It was warm and clean. He swam out. Because of his back he couldn't kick very much, but his arms felt strong and soon he was gliding quickly, very quickly, across the water. He swam out, feeling stronger the farther he went. He felt strong and happy. Then he remembered Sergeant Levy.

Sergeant Levy was down there somewhere. He put his face in the water and opened his eyes. There he was, floating just above the bottom. Why was he swimming about aimlessly while Sergeant Levy was drowning? He took a deep breath and dove. Down, down he swam, closer and closer to Sergeant Levy; but the water was much deeper than it looked, and he went up for air.

He breathed in the salty air for a minute or two, then filled his lungs and dove again. It was very deep. He pulled at the

224

water with his hands, and kicked hard with his legs. Never mind your back. Swim. Now Sergeant Levy looked up and saw him. He was alive! His lips moved, but of course he couldn't hear what Sergeant Levy was saying because of the water. A little farther, not much, there. He reached out and grabbed Sergeant Levy's arm. It was slimy; it came away in his hand. He wrapped his arms around Sergeant Levy's slimy body and struggled up toward the surface. He broke through, gasping for air. Then, clutching seaweed to his chest, he lay on his back and closed his eyes against the sun. "You're going to be all right," he said.

Oars squeaked in their locks. Hands touched his body; lifted him; set him down. "Be careful with Sergeant Levy," he said in Hebrew. "He almost drowned."

"What did he say?" a man asked in Arabic.

"I don't know," another man answered.

Why were they speaking Arabic? Or was it English? It didn't matter. "Be careful with Sergeant Levy," he repeated.

They rocked him to sleep. Later he awoke. They had stopped rocking him. Something bit his upper arm. It didn't hurt very much. He slept.

CHAPTER TWENTY-SEVEN

The boy awoke, fully and all at once, as he always did. Although it was still dark, the others were already up; he could hear them moving outside the tent. Through the opening he saw the dull glow of the dung fire, and the iron teakettle hanging above. He heard the muffled ring of sugar lumps being dropped into empty glasses. Una's slender hand reached out of the darkness and took the teakettle off the fire. Una was the third and youngest wife of Bokur, the omda, but she was the most important: She had borne Hurgas, his only son.

Metal clinked against the rim of a glass. Tea gurgled out of the spout. Hurgas spoke in a low voice: "He will cry like a baby."

"Quiet," Una said. She blew on her tea to cool it.

"He will cry like a baby," Hurgas whispered angrily. "He is soft."

There was a pause. A girl spoke: "I don't think he's soft." Neimy, Una's daughter.

"No one cares what you think," Hurgas said. "Go get my sandals."

Paul heard Neimy enter the tent. Her bare feet were almost silent on the dirt floor. He closed his eyes. She went to the rear of the tent, patted her hand over the ground, feeling, and then approached his bedstead. He felt her standing beside him and made his breathing slow and even.

Outside, Una said, "What makes you think he is soft?"

"I could tell yesterday, when we bled one of the cows. He looked away."

"Did he drink it?"

"Yes. But he didn't like it. I watched him."

"Did you tell your father?"

"No."

"Good. He believes."

"Do you?"

Una did not answer right away. After a few moments she said, "I will wait and see."

"I didn't cry," Hurgas said, raising his voice. "I didn't cry once."

"Quiet," Una said. Then, "Yes, you were very brave."

"I was."

Paul felt Neimy back away and slip out of the tent. Very softly she said, "He won't cry."

"No one asked you."

Paul opened his eyes. Dawn was piercing the worn straw over his head. It was his last night in the tent. Today was the day of his circumcision: After that he would sleep outside until he was married. He had known it would happen, but he had not expected it so soon. It was only six days since he had seen his father.

He got up and went outside. Hurgas and Una sat by the fire, drinking tea. They looked alike—tall, lean, with light brown skin and noses that were more Arab than black. Neimy was different—shorter, broader, darker: the color his mother must have been, Paul thought. With a small mallet she was pounding beef into long strips for drying. There was plenty of beef: Every day a few more cows died of starvation. She had let her robe slip off her shoulders while she worked. "Good morning," he said. He was aware of the smooth muscles in her shoulders, and her breasts still too small to sway with her movements, the way Una's did.

"Good morning," Neimy said with a smile.

"Good morning," her mother said without one.

Hurgas drank his tea and said nothing.

Paul walked past them and continued slowly toward the center of the ring formed by the circle of tents, and into a cross fire of stares. He prostrated himself on the dusty ground, in the attitude of prayer. After a few seconds of silence he heard their footsteps. More than yesterday, more than the day before, they came, no longer only the old and middle-aged, and knelt around him, and touched their foreheads to the earth. They prayed. Paul did not pray: He thought about the day ahead, and the night, and the railroad bridge.

In the middle of the morning the barber arrived from a nearby tent. The barber was old and stooped, with no teeth and yellow eyes and three wide scars on both cheeks. He was the barber because he had no cattle, no wife, and was Bokur's uncle. Over his shriveled body he had put on a clean white jubba that was much too large.

With two other boys who were to be circumcised, Paul stood by the men's tree at the edge of the camp. "Salam alaykum," the barber said to them. "Alaykum el Salam," they answered.

The barber walked stiffly over to the tree and sat down with his back against the trunk. "Run," he said.

They ran, once around the tree and then around the outside of the camp. When they returned their heads were soaked with sweat. Paul saw that most of the camp—two thousand people— had gathered near the tree, and he knew it was because of him.

The barber felt the tops of their heads. "Good," he said. He reached inside his robe and drew a long knife from the scabbard strapped to his chest. Sunshine glinted on its shiny edge. "Come here," he said to Paul. Paul stepped forward. The barber raised the knife and shaved his head. Paul felt the sharp blade slide easily over his skull: No water was wasted. His black curly hair fell in a little clump at his feet.

The barber shaved the heads of the other boys. Then he said, "Undress yourselves." They pulled their jubbas over their heads and laid them on the ground. Paul saw that the others had not yet reached puberty. He had. He felt blood flow up into his head, and heat his face. For a moment he looked down at the ground. Don't be a fool, he told himself, you were prepared for this. He raised his head. The crowd grew quiet.

"It's not going to hurt," one of the boys whispered.

"No," the other answered. "It's just a little scratch, that's all."

Paul turned to them. "It's going to hurt, and you'd better be ready." They flinched.

Three men walked forward. It was customary for each boy's

mother's brother to stand with him. Bokur came to be with Paul. He was the only person in the camp who wore western dress. Today he had a white robe over his suit, and sweat was dripping off his round heavy face. He patted Paul on the shoulder. "Don't worry. You will make us all very proud."

"In sha' Allah," Paul said.

Bokur smiled. His teeth were sharpened chunks of silver. "In sha' Allah."

The barber moved in front of the smallest boy. The boy's uncle stood behind him and held his shoulders. The crowd pressed closer. The girls began to chant, "Don't cry, don't cry, we won't sing for you if you cry. Don't cry, don't cry." The barber sat on his haunches. His knees cracked. He felt inside the pouch he wore around his neck and took out a small steel cap. He placed it over the head of the boy's penis. "Don't cry, don't cry, we won't sing for you if you cry. Don't cry, don't cry." But the little boy started trembling while the barber was pulling his foreskin up over the steel cap. The barber touched his penis with the point of the knife. The boy made a little noise in the back of his throat. He was wailing long before the cutting was over.

"Keep him still," the barber growled. Paul saw the uncle squeeze the boy's shoulders very hard, saw how steady the old man's hand was, saw the blood falling on the sand.

The barber stood up, wiped the blade on his robe, and dropped the foreskin into the pouch around his neck. "Now you are a man," he said. The crowd cheered. The boy took a step toward them. His uncle picked him up and carried him the rest of the way.

The barber crouched in front of the second boy. He ran the edge of the blade very lightly over the back of his hand, wiped it again on his robe, and put the steel cap in place. "Don't cry, don't cry." The second boy held on longer than the first. He was biting his lip so hard that blood had begun to flow from it as well. He began to cry, first in a stifled way, then uncontrollably. From this Paul knew there would be pain to go along with the fear.

Blood fell on the sand. The foreskin went into the pouch. The boy was a man. The crowd cheered. He was carried away.

The barber turned to Paul, wiping the blade on his robe and leaving a red smear. Paul felt the sweat rolling over his ribs, and

Bokur's hands gripping his shoulders. "Don't cry, don't cry, we won't sing for you if you cry. Don't cry, don't cry." The chanting was quieter than it had been for the other boys; there was more at stake. Paul looked at the crowd, saw Hurgas standing with some of the other young men, watching: Hurgas's gaze was not directed at his face, but lower; and Neimy, at the front, a few yards away. He could hear her voice: "Don't cry, don't cry, I won't sing for you if you cry. Don't cry, don't cry."

The barber squatted in front of him, but Paul was taller than the other boys and he was too low in that position. He rose to his knees and took the steel cap from his pouch. Paul felt the barber's hand lift his penis, felt the steel cap slip onto its head, felt the barber's fingernails on his foreskin, pulling it over the cap. His heart pounded in his chest, not only from fear.

"Don't cry, don't cry." Now Hurgas's eyes were on his face, eager, excited.

The barber touched his penis with the point of the knife.

"No," Paul said. The barber's head jerked up; his toothless mouth opened in astonishment. In the tightening of the grip on his shoulders Paul felt how much Bokur had at stake. "No," he said again, and he heard his voice, calm, as though it was another's: "Give it to me."

The barber did not move. Paul reached down and took the knife from his hand. Then, holding his penis firmly with one hand, he cut off his own foreskin. The pain was someone else's. He did not utter a sound.

When he had finished he handed the foreskin to the barber, dropped the knife on the ground, and walked away. No one said a word.

For the rest of the morning Paul lay on his bedstead in Una's tent. For a while he was alone; then Una came and started to rub his legs with liquid butter. Outside, Neimy hummed softly as she pounded the strips of beef. Sometimes she tried a few words: " 'No no,' he said, 'Give it to me,' so brave, so brave." In the darkness of the tent the pain was no longer someone else's, it became his own. Una's fingers, strong and gentle, probed the muscles in his calves, dug into the crevices of his knees, pressed upwards along his thighs. In his mind he followed the movements of her fingers, and the pain began to go away. Sleepiness came to take its place. But he had no time for sleep.

Bokur's heavy face loomed over him. He felt Una's hands withdraw. "Here," Bokur said. There was a thickness in his voice. He held up a long spear, and a wide-bladed knife of the kind the men wore strapped to their chests. "No one ever deserved them more than you. Not in the whole history of our people."

"Thank you, Bokur."

"You have honored me," Bokur said quietly. He added: "Mahdi."

Paul closed his eyes. He was one of them, and above them too, the way he had to be. And he had a penis like his father's. "Bokur."

"Yes?"

"I need a horse."

"Any of mine are yours."

"Today, Bokur."

"Today? You cannot ride today."

"Yes, Bokur. I want to."

Bokur nodded. The look in his eyes was close to love. "Would you like the black mare?" he asked.

"Yes."

Bokur went outside. Paul heard him say: "Hurgas. Bring the black mare."

"The black mare? Why do you want her?"

"Don't question me, boy. Run."

Early in the afternoon Paul rode away on the black mare. He rode north. Although he held the mare to a slow walk, the pain returned. A dark bloodstain spread across the coarse blanket that served as a saddle. Long before he reached the two baobabs by the shallow depression, he was forced to dismount and lead the mare by her bridle.

The sun burned down on his shaved head. He drank often from the goatskin bag he wore over his shoulder. The mare's black coat began to foam. When they came to the baobab trees Paul drew a bucket of water from the new well and filled the goatskin bag. Then he sat in their shade and let the mare go down into the depression and drink from the little pool in its center. While she drank, he tore a strip of cotton from his jubba and tied it tightly around his penis to stop the blood. He closed his eyes. Horseflies buzzed around him. He got up, walked down into the depression, drew the mare away from the water, and went on.

231

Just before the sun went down he saw the pile of pebbles marking the end of the wadi. He led the mare into the dry river-bed. He thought of everything he would tell his father, and how he would tell it. His father had explained the importance of bravery during circumcision, but what he had done had not been planned. He wanted to tell him.

Night fell. The moon rose, a half-moon that pushed back the shadows in the riverbed. After a while Paul felt too tired to walk. He pulled himself up on the mare's back, and leaned forward against her neck. For an hour or two the movements of her back hurt him with every step. Then he was numb.

"If it doesn't work, it doesn't work," his father had said. "We'll go back." But it was working, and he didn't want to go back; now that he had done what he had done. As long as they could see each other every week, and talk and plan, he would be all right.

He came to the railroad bridge. It was very dark underneath. Paul slid off the mare's back and walked slowly forward, under the bridge. "Dad?" he called softly in English. "Dad?" He raised his voice a little: "Dad?" Carefully he searched the darkness along both banks, in case his father had fallen asleep. "Dad? Dad?" He climbed up the bank and onto the bridge. He walked along the ties. "Dad?" Perhaps he had fallen asleep somewhere along the bank and rolled off, down onto the riverbed. Paul went down and crawled through the shadows. "Dad?"

He sat. The wind came up, blowing off the northern desert. It began to blow very hard. He looked to the north and saw a wall of blackness advancing through the night. At first it screened the moon like a thin cloud; then the moon disappeared. The wind tore at his clothing. Blowing sand stung his eyes. He lay down against the bank of the wadi. The mare lay beside him. He huddled close to her belly and shut his eyes. The dust storm howled over his head.

At dawn the wind began to die. The sky cleared. Paul removed his jubba and shook off the sand. The dust storm had kept his father away. He was probably nearby. He would come soon. Paul waited.

He waited all day. And all night.

And the following day. And the following night.

The next morning he mounted the black mare and started

232

riding back toward the camp. He was hungry and had nowhere else to go.

When he came to the depression he saw a few tents raised beneath the baobab trees. They were like the Baggara tents, but smaller and flatter. He asked for something to eat, and was given millet and camel milk. The people looked like Baggara, but their skins were lighter, and they had camels instead of cattle. He thanked them and rode away. As he left he heard one of their women singing softly to herself:

"No," he said, "Give it to me,"
So brave, so brave, the Mahdi.

CHAPTER TWENTY-EIGHT

There was a little hole in the sand. After two days a black beetle crawled out of it, skittered over the ground, and disappeared under an olive green bush a few feet away. A lizard with a blue body and an orange head crept out from behind the bush. It bobbed its head up and down. The sun grew hotter, and hotter still. The lizard stuck out its pointed white tongue and flicked it like a tiny whip. It bobbed up and down. The black beetle darted out from under the bush, toward the hole in the sand. The lizard stopped bobbing. For a moment it was completely still; then it sprang, and caught the beetle in its mouth. There was a sound like chewing gum cracking as the beetle's hard body was crushed between the lizard's jaws. The lizard turned its orange head, the broken beetle hanging from the sides of its mouth, and looked at Krebs.

Krebs, tied to the tree, looked back. Because of the horsefly bites his eyes were swollen almost shut, and he saw the lizard through the screen of his eyelashes. He wiggled his foot and it ran away.

He had given up struggling against the nylon ropes. It only made him bleed, and the horseflies liked that. He was thirsty. His tongue was thick and coated with a hard crust that felt rough against the roof of his mouth. He kept thinking of the soda fountain he went to after school as a boy. Every afternoon he had a big Coke. Seven cents. Then it had gone up to ten. He could see the big soda fountain glass with the ice cubes floating on the top and mist around the rim. He used to blow into the straws and shoot the wrappers around the place when no one was looking. He kept thinking about things like that: drinks he had drunk, swimming pools he had swum in; he knew he was getting lightheaded.

He didn't want Coke. He wanted water.

A horsefly buzzed around him a few times and landed on his cheek. He shook his head back and forth. It flew away. And came back. He shook his head. It didn't fly away. He shook his head harder and harder, until his cheeks were flapping against his gums. The horsefly bit. "You fucking goddamned shit," he yelled. It bit again. And again. He stopped shaking his head. It went away. Blood trickled down his face and onto his lip. He drank it greedily.

At least he was facing north. That meant that the tree shaded him from the afternoon sun. But his skin was red and blistered all the same. He could see that through his eyelashes.

The next day he couldn't. He knew it was day because the insides of his eyelids were pink. His mouth was dry and crusty as sand. His throat made swallowing motions on its own. He tried to stop it, but it wouldn't stop. Horseflies bit. Mosquitoes bit. A few times something else bit, something he couldn't identify. "You fucking goddamned shit," he yelled. All that came out was breath.

The insides of his eyelids turned black. Suddenly he felt very cold, and realized that he was no longer sweating. That must be bad. He had heard of men drinking urine to stay alive. The Black Hole of Calcutta. He had no urine to urinate; and no way of getting it to his mouth if he had. But he did need to defecate. He had been holding on for a long time, afraid of the flies. Later, during the night, he could hold on no more.

He saw pink.

Ants would finish him off. They had soldier ants here, didn't they? The ants would march up in a column and pick him to the bone. He hoped he was dead before that happened.

Clip-clop. Clip-clop.

Mr. Bennett: That was the name of the owner of the soda fountain. He had blackheads all over his nose. Some of them were as big as moles. Once he had seen Mr. Bennett put a broken cigarette back together with Scotch tape.

Bite. Go on and bite. Less for the ants.

Clip-clop. Clip-clop.

Big Cokes. With ice cubes floating on the top and mist around the rim. Seven cents. After he'd chew the ice cubes, and swirl the cold crushed pieces around in his mouth.

Clip-clop. A man said something. He was very near. He spoke again. Krebs tried as hard as he could to open his eyes. The pink became a shade lighter. "Water," he said, but he didn't make a sound. He heard a light thudding sound, and footsteps. Something touched his lips.

It was wet. He drank. Water.

The man spoke. Krebs had taken enough instruction in Arabic to know the man was speaking it, but his accent was very different from anything he had heard on the tapes in the language lab, and he could not understand a word. He drank.

Cold metal touched his wrists, the middle of his back, his waist, his knees, his ankles. The ropes fell away. He tried to stand, and failed. He could not move at all.

A wet hand gripped his arm. He felt another against his ribs. He was pulled to his feet and lifted into the air, head hanging down. The pink turned dark red, then white. White spun into nothing.

Clip-clop. He jolted along; coarse hairs scratched his stomach and chest. Sometimes his toes dragged on the ground, sometimes his fingers. The man's feet tramped beside him, close to his head. At first the man spoke to him, usually in brief sentences that sounded like questions. After a while he was silent. Once he laughed, a high-pitched laugh that was more of a giggle, and Krebs felt a wet hand resting on his buttocks.

His right eye opened slightly. He saw hairy donkey legs and chipped donkey hooves plodding along. It was all blurred and out of focus: He realized that his contact lens must have fallen out, or slipped into the corner of his eye.

The donkey stopped. The man spoke. A woman answered him. Wet hands pulled at him, lifted him off the donkey's back. A bony shoulder dug into his stomach. Across his field of vision whirled a woman, naked children, a lone tent by a tree—all upside down. He was carried out of the sunshine and into the tent, and laid on his back on hard-packed, cool earth.

The woman came. She helped him sit up, and gave him water from a tin cup and something warm and pasty to eat. It tasted like rice, but thicker and more starchy. With difficulty he was able to swallow a spoonful. The man said a few words to the woman. She went outside.

It was dark in the tent, and Krebs couldn't see very well. He tried to bring his hand to his right eye to search for his contact lens, but it would not be raised that high. The man moved in front of him.

"Muglad," Krebs said. He heard how low and hoarse his voice sounded and tried to make it louder: "I want to go to Muglad."

"Muglad?"

"That's right. Muglad. Take me to Muglad. I'll pay you. Money. Felouze. Much felouze. Just take me to Muglad."

"Muglad?"

The wet hand touched his thigh. The man turned him over on his stomach and buggered him. Krebs was too weak to do anything about it. "You fucking goddamned shit," he yelled, but the sounds he made were not very strong.

It hurt. When it was over he fell asleep. He slept for a long time.

He heard a car coming. Two cars. They came very close and stopped. Their engines died. A woman said something. She was speaking Arabic, but he thought he knew her voice. The man answered. Car doors opened and closed. People entered the tent.

"Oh, my God," Gillian said.

Two soldiers carried him outside and laid him in the back of a jeep. Gillian covered him with a blanket. "Oh, God," she said gently.

"Don't give him any money."

"I'm sorry, I can't hear you."

"Don't give him anything." Through his eyelashes, through a wet smear, he saw her open her mouth to say something. "Nothing," he repeated. She nodded.

On the way back to Muglad Gillian sat by his head. She gave him water, salt tablets, and bits of bread, and wiped his face with a damp cloth; but her voice had lost its gentleness.

"I'm sorry about the other night," he said.

Gillian sighed. "Don't worry about it," she said. "It happens all the time."

He believed her.

237

The white door swung open. Fairweather's head poked inside the room. "Hey! What's all the fuss? You look great! Great for you, that is." He strode briskly across the floor and hopped up on the foot of the hospital bed.

"I feel fine," Krebs said.

"I can see that. How about a margarita?" He flipped open a briefcase and took out a large Thermos. "Wait till you taste this. It's the real thing. Hors d'âge, as they say, although they don't say it about tequila, come to think of it. Smuggled it in from Mexico myself."

"I can't have anything alcoholic. It's dehydrating."

"Nothing alcoholic?" Fairweather said, filling two paper cups. "How do you ever expect to get out of here?" He handed one of them to Krebs. "Drink up."

"I really shouldn't."

"Drink. Otherwise I'll feel deeply insulted."

Krebs took a sip. It was horrible.

"Well? Muy bien? Right?"

"It's very good." Krebs set the cup on the bedside table.

"I knew you'd like it. Don't worry. The worm's still inside the bottle. I checked." Fairweather drank and shook his head in admiration. "Those Mexicans: They sure know how to have a good time."

Krebs let his head sink into the pillow. Through the window he could see the top of an elm tree; the edges of its leaves were beginning to turn yellow. It was a perfect fall day. The sky was silvery blue and the little white cumulus clouds were in no hurry to cross it. The sun shone, but it wasn't the kind of sun that turned skin to blisters. The air wasn't full of dust, and if you were thirsty you turned a tap and water came out.

"Did you bring the files I asked for?" Krebs said.

"Got them right here." Holding his drink carefully in one hand, Fairweather tried to manage the open briefcase with the other. Files came sliding out onto the bed. Some of them fell to the floor. "Oops," Fairweather said, and got off the bed to pick them up. He had collected a few when he suddenly stopped. "Oh. I almost forgot: They found that jeep."

"Where?"

"Port Sudan. Down at the docks. It had been there for a while, apparently—it was totally stripped, doors, tires, seats, engine, everything, even the license plates. But the serial number checked out."

"Did anyone see him?"

"Who?"

"Rehv, for Christ's sake."

Fairweather looked embarrassed. "No," he said. "Not so far."

"What about the boy?"

"Nothing about him either."

"What about the Saudis?"

"They have no record of anyone entering at Jeddah or anywhere else with a U.S. passport in the name of Quentin Katz." Krebs thought he heard a hint of challenge in Fairweather's tone.

"That doesn't mean a thing," he said. "He could have slipped across in a dhow and landed somewhere up the coast. Keep checking with the Saudis."

Fairweather gazed out the window. "Okay, but —"

"But what?"

"Don't get mad."

"But what?"

"Are you sure it was him? That's all. I mean it's been a long time since you've seen him, and you've had a lot of time to think, and maybe —"

"It was him."

"Okay, okay. Don't take it personally."

But Krebs knew it was personal, now. He hated Isaac Rehv. He lay back on the pillow. He had to decide whether Rehv had deliberately left him to die. If he had, it meant the Jeddah story was probably true. If he hadn't, it was probably false.

"Fairweather?"

Fairweather turned from the window. "Yes?"

"I want Gillian Wells to keep looking around Muglad."

"But Port Sudan's a thousand miles from there."

"Just do it, Fairweather."

"Right."

Fairweather went away, leaving the Thermos behind. Alone, Krebs began to brood about what he had said: "Are you sure it was him?" It was not like Fairweather to come up with an idea like that by himself. It was like the office. He thought about the office. Then he thought about Rehv.

Later a doctor came to examine him. Krebs gave him the

239

Thermos. The doctor tasted the drink. "This is the real thing," he said. "Thanks."

Gillian Wells reported from Muglad: "Nothing." Krebs sent her south to the Uganda border, and later west into Darfur, where the fighting was. She found no sign of Isaac Rehv.

The day Krebs left the hospital he arranged private instruction in Arabic.

CHAPTER TWENTY-NINE

The Mahdi lay quietly in the tent. He had grown too big for the bedstead, and at least partly because of that he no longer slept as deeply as he once had. His feet hung over the end and there was barely enough room for Neimy beside him. She pressed against him, her chin, her breast, her thigh. Her skin was hotter than his; wherever they touched, pores opened and joined their bodies in a sticky bond. It did not bother him. He was used to sweat by now. It was always with him, like the beating of his heart.

He listened to the sounds of the night. Nearby a woman murmured. A child began to cough in mounting wheezy spasms that finally died away for lack of breath. Farther away a donkey brayed. They were in the south, beyond the Goz, where sometimes a leopard came in the darkness. He listened hard for nervous sounds from the animals, but there were none. The child coughed and could not stop.

He turned over and tried to sleep. It was no use. He was waiting for Bokur, who should have come back the night before. Bokur and the other western omdas who were still loyal to the remains of the central government had been called to Khartoum to talk about taxes. Even some of the tribes that were not in arms against the government had stopped paying taxes. "We pay tax," Bokur had said. "Maybe it won't matter if I don't go."

The Mahdi had looked at him and seen that he was afraid. But if Bokur did not go it would mean an open break with Khartoum. He was not ready for that. "Go," he had said. Bokur had gone, taking Hurgas with him.

He stood up, lifted the tent flap, and went outside. There was a crescent moon, lying on its rounded back. It was the driest season, and the dust in the air made the moon red: a thin red smile. The child began to cough again. He followed the sound, passing several tents until he found the one with the coughing child. The coughing went on for a long time. When it was over, the child gasped for breath, then panted and finally breathed normally. The coughing came again, harsh and dry. In the tent a woman sighed. The Mahdi walked away. The hospital in Wau was still open. He would have the child taken there in the morning.

In front of his tent he lay on the ground and looked up at the red smile. A man had walked across that smile once, or had it been two men? He couldn't remember the story very well. But his father, excited, had shown him a picture to prove it: a man dressed as a machine trying to plant a metal flag on an airless rock. "It doesn't look like the moon to me," he had said. His father had put the picture away.

The Mahdi closed his eyes. When is the time, he asked himself. When will I be ready? It had never been discussed. When the time came his father would tell him, and tell him how to do what he had to do, and say what he had to say. But his father was dead. Or he had changed his mind and gone away. Or he had never intended to return to the railway bridge, and had planned all along that his son would decide when it was time. The Mahdi imagined his father waiting, back at the cabin on Lac du Loup. Of course it would not be that cabin and that lake, but somewhere like it; chosen perhaps even before they left. He would be there now, waiting. His father was prepared to wait.

But most of the time the Mahdi thought he was dead.

A leather sandal slapped against the sole of a foot. The Mahdi looked up and saw Hurgas coming out of the shadows. Hurgas too had grown tall, but not quite as tall as he, and not nearly as broad. He rose. Hurgas saw him and started.

"What are you doing?" Hurgas whispered.

The Mahdi heard the fear in his voice, and the anger. He wondered if the fear and anger seemed stronger to him than they really were. Most people hid emotions like those from him now. Hurgas was one of the few who still showed them in his presence. "Waiting for you," he replied. "Where's your father?"

"Where do you think?" Hurgas said bitterly. "Khartoum." The

Mahdi looked at him without saying anything. In his eyes Hurgas saw something that made him back away slightly. When he spoke again there was less rawness in his tone. "They won't let him leave."

"What do you mean? Have they arrested him?"

"No. It's not like that. He's at the Grand Hotel. They say they want him to stay for more talk, that's all. But there's a guard outside his room, and he can't go anywhere by himself."

"What do they want to talk to him about?"

"The same thing they talked to him about the whole time I was there." Hurgas lowered his eyelids a little and tilted back his head. The lower half of his face disappeared in the shadows cast by his high cheekbones. "You."

"And what does he tell them about me?"

Hurgas looked down. "That he believes."

The Mahdi walked slowly away, past a few tents and a tethered goat standing very still. He turned. Hurgas had been watching him; now he lowered his eyes. The Mahdi went back to him.

"They must have given you a message for me."

The corners of Hurgas's mouth rose very slightly. "They said you would know what to do."

"What do you think that is, Hurgas?" the Mahdi asked quietly. Hurgas's thin lips parted for a moment as though he would speak, but all he did was shrug; he kept his thought inside. "You're tired, Hurgas. Go to bed." Hurgas turned to go. "Aren't you forgetting something?" the Mahdi asked.

"What?" Hurgas said.

"What your father told you to say to me."

After a long pause Hurgas spoke: " 'Don't go to Khartoum.' That's what he said. The fool. The stupid old fool." Hurgas's voice rose, and broke. He walked quickly away.

"Hurgas." But he was gone.

The Mahdi went inside the tent and lay down beside Neimy. He could not sleep. He saw Bokur's eyes silently asking him to say what he should have said: "Don't go." But he had not been ready. He still was not ready. He lay awake until dawn. Everyone else in the camp slept. All except the coughing child.

In the morning Neimy and a few other women walked down to the water hole with large calabashes on their heads to fetch the water for the Mahdi's bath. Because the rains had been so poor the water holes had all shrunk in only a few months to shallow ponds. The Mahdi did not want to waste water on a daily bath, but he knew it was expected. Already as Neimy carried the calabashes into the tent and emptied them into the little galvanized tub he heard the gathering outside, soft talking and shuffling feet.

He stepped into the tub and sat down, his knees drawn up almost to his chin. The water from the pond was warmer than his body. Neimy cut a few chips from a block of yellow soap and began washing him. Her hands were slow and gentle.

"Hurgas came back," she said.

"Yes."

"But not father?"

"No."

Her hands, slippery with soap, slid down over his shoulders and down his back. She waited for him to say more, but he was listening to the shuffling feet and the murmuring voices all around him on the other side of the matted straw walls.

"Are you worried?" Neimy asked quietly. He felt her breath on the back of his neck. Her arms circled his chest; her hands ran over his stomach and began soaping his penis and testicles.

"Don't worry."

She squeezed him and rubbed slowly, the way she knew he liked. Little waves rose on the surface of the bath water and slapped softly against the sides of the tub. The Mahdi shifted his hips slightly forward and closed his eyes. In his mind he saw his semen drifting in the water like jellyfish. "Don't," he said. "Stop."

Neimy had followed his thoughts. "It's all right. No one will notice. And if they did it would make them happier." She kept rubbing.

She was probably right but to have them drinking his bath water was bad enough. He sat up and opened his eyes. "No," he said.

Without letting go of his penis, Neimy moved around the tub. Her broad face reminded him of Bokur's. Even her breasts, now full and heavy, touching the rim of the washtub, seemed like the kind of breasts Bokur would have if he were a woman. It was the same body: old and male, not quite ugly; young and female, almost beautiful. "You don't understand," Neimy said, rubbing harder. "They love you."

"Stop."

"I love you too."

"Stop."

"Don't worry. I'll catch it in my mouth."

She did.

Afterward Neimy filled the calabashes with the bath water and took them outside. The Mahdi lay alone on the bedstead. His worries had gone away. For a little while his mind was empty. Then he began to hear the low voices, the moving feet, and from time to time the trickling of water; his worries returned. He did not love Neimy. And he could not be sure exactly what she meant when she said she loved him. She loved the way the Baggara loved. He, if he loved, would love partly like that, but partly in other ways as well. Even forgetting that, did she love him as a man or as the Mahdi? It did not really matter because there was no Mahdi and he was not the man she thought he was.

But of course there was a Mahdi. He got off the bedstead and went outside. The calabashes lay on the ground in front of the tent. A crowd had gathered, perhaps four or five hundred people, maybe more. There were more every day. He saw the light brown Arab faces of camel-raising nomads from the north and the black faces of cattle herders and millet farmers from the south. He saw Fur faces and Fulani faces and even a few Berber faces; and faces of other peoples he did not know, who came from the states that had been torn apart far away in the west. One by one they stepped forward, men, women, and children, and Neimy dipped a brass ladle into the bath water and held it to their lips for a ritual sip.

When they saw him they fell silent, like a concert audience when the conductor raises his baton. The Mahdi looked over their heads and saw the tents that covered the ground in all directions, as far as he could see. There were the round tents of his own people, and pointed tents and flat-topped tents. Some were big, some were small. They were all there because of him.

Slowly he turned and walked back into the tent. Outside, the low murmuring rose again. Water trickled. He covered the entrance to the tent with a large straw mat and paced back and forth in the hot darkness. He knew he could not wait much longer. Many of the people in those tents, especially the ones from the west, were armed. They had American guns, Russian guns, French guns; it depended on which war they had been fighting, and on whose side they had fought. Soon they would need food. So would their animals. Already the herds had eaten most of the grass for miles around. The few pools that still had water were now very small. Even the deep wells were drying up. Everyone was waiting for some signal from him.

Three and a half steps forward, three and a half steps back.

But what? How could he do anything before he knew more about the world beyond Kordofan, beyond the Sudan, beyond Africa? Only his father could have told him what he had to know; Bokur could not tell him. It was no use trying to find in Bokur what he needed from his father. All that did was make Hurgas hate him more.

Three and a half steps forward, three and a half steps back.

He heard horses outside the tent. A man spoke. Neimy answered. She pushed back the straw mat and entered the tent. He stopped pacing.

"A problem?" he asked.

"Yes," she said. "At the watering hole. Dinka."

Someone brought him the black mare. He rode across the camp, following the rows of tents like streets. Everyone stopped what they were doing to watch him. He did not look at them, but rode on. He was thinking about power. He began to realize how smart his father had been. Yet from the time he was a very little boy he had always thought himself much smarter than his father. Had he been wrong? His whole life had been a dream in his father's head. How could he be smarter than the dreamer? The dreamer had given him power. Now he would have to be smart enough to use it on his own.

Or he could go away. But how? Where? Why? He wanted to be what he was becoming. Was that part of the dream too? He forced himself to stop thinking about his father.

At the edge of the camp was a shallow depression about one mile wide. Bokur had told him that years before it was always entirely filled after the rains. Now there was nothing more than a little pool of brackish water in the middle. By the pool stood men from the camp; some of them held rifles across their chest. A few yards beyond them were twenty or thirty Dinka, and about a dozen cattle, short-horned animals smaller than the Baggara cattle.

The Mahdi rode down into the depression and halted in front

of the Dinka. They were tall black people, naked except for the little scraps of hide that hung over their genitals. He looked at them and saw the bones under their dusty skin; the swollen bellies of the children; the sickly rust-colored hair of the babies. He felt the eyes of his own people on his back. It was time to begin.

"What do you want?" he asked. A gaunt old man answered in his own language. "I do not understand Dinka," the Mahdi said. "Do none of you know Arabic?"

A boy stepped forward. He had a bloated belly and a cataract that covered one eye like a white glaze. "Water," the boy said in Arabic. "We are thirsty. Our cattle are thirsty." The old man called the boy to him and said something in a sharp voice. The boy nodded and looked up at the Mahdi. "Water, master. Let us drink."

"I am not your master," the Mahdi said. "There is only one master."

"Please, master."

A rusty-haired baby began to cry. Its mother held it to her thin and wrinkled breast. It kept crying. "Are your people Muslim?" the Mahdi asked the boy.

"No."

"Are they Jews? Or Christians? Because," he raised his voice so his own people could hear him better, "the Koran says that there is a special place for Christians and Jews."

"No," the boy answered.

"Then you cannot drink here."

The boy turned to the old man and spoke to him. The old man listened and said nothing. The boy looked up at the Mahdi. "We are thirsty," he said in a low voice.

"Your people may drink on one condition," the Mahdi said. "You must accept Islam. To accept Islam you must give up all your old gods forever."

The boy said something to the old man. The old man shook his head and began to walk away. A woman spoke to him. He answered her. She began to scream at him. Others began to scream. The old man argued with them. They shouted over him. After a while the old man stopped arguing. They all became silent. Another man spoke to the boy. The boy turned to the Mahdi and said: "We will accept Islam."

247

"Then drink," the Mahdi told him. "And after, come to my tent. I will give you food and show you how to be a Muslim."

The naked people ran toward the pool of water. Their cattle followed. Only the old man stayed where he was. After a while he walked slowly away, across the depression.

The Mahdi looked at his people and saw the approval in their eyes. He knew that he had done something his father could never have done. He would be better on his own. His father had dreamed. He would act.

For a few moments he watched them drink. Then he remembered the coughing child and rode quickly back to the camp, straight to the tent he had noted during the night. He jumped off his horse and looked inside. A red-eyed woman told him the child was dead.

CHAPTER THIRTY

Slowly the Mahdi walked back toward his tent. He led the black mare by the bridle. Above him the afternoon sun made the pearly sky shimmer and writhe in the heat. He had grown used to the African sun: It was part of normal life like rusty hair and swollen bellies. Now, suddenly, he felt it very strongly—its heat, its weight, its bite. The mare nudged his back with her nose. He walked faster.

Neimy sat in the entrance to the tent, sharpening a knife on a flat stone. Her head was in the shade but her hands were not. The blade flashed little suns in his eyes as it scraped back and forth.

"A woman came looking for you," Neimy said. He heard a wariness in her tone that made him want to look closely at her face. All he saw were flashing golden suns.

"What kind of woman?"

"A Turk." The noise of the scraping grew louder.

He knew a Turk could be any foreigner, or even someone from the government. "Is she from Khartoum?"

"I don't know."

"What did she want?"

"To talk to you." A spark flew off the stone and vanished in the air.

"What about?"

"I don't know. She went with Hurgas to find you. She will come back."

He tethered the horse to a stake driven into the ground beside the tent. "When?"

"I don't know." She leaned aside to let him pass. He went into the tent and lay down. The golden suns faded from his eyes. It was dark and very still. He listened to steel scraping on stone. For a while there was nothing else to hear; then from somewhere in the distance came the noise of a motor. It grew louder. The scraping stopped. He rose and went outside.

An open jeep was approaching between the rows of tents. A woman was driving. Hurgas sat beside her. Although she drove slowly, Hurgas was very nervous. The Mahdi could see that he was leaning forward with his hands on the dashboard, peering anxiously through the windshield. The jeep rolled up in front of the tent. Hurgas fumbled for a moment with the door handle, and then climbed over the side. "That's him," he said to the woman.

The woman opened the door and got out. She was white. She had thick chestnut hair streaked yellow by the sun. She wore khaki trousers and a khaki shirt with big pockets; a camera hung around her neck.

"Are you the man they call the Mahdi?" she asked in Arabic, looking at him. Her eyes were pale blue. It had been a long time since he had seen blue eyes; he could not stop staring at them. She lowered her eyelids.

"I am," he said.

"I'd like to talk to you." She spoke Arabic very well, but with a faint trace of an accent he thought was American. "I'm a reporter." She handed him a plastic card.

He glanced at it. He saw her photograph, her name—Gillian Wells, and a list of newspapers and magazines in the United States and Europe. All the print was in English. "I don't read this language," he said, giving it back to her.

"It's my press card. It just says that I'm an accredited journalist and where my articles appear." She named the newspapers and magazines.

"I don't think I have anything to say that would interest people so far from here."

Her eyes sought his and he felt her pale blue gaze. He was accustomed to brown eyes that he could look into and read. When he looked into her eyes he could not see past their blue-

250

ness. "If you are really the Mahdi they will be interested," she said.

"He is the Mahdi," Neimy said in a clear, deliberate voice behind him. He turned and looked at her sitting in the shade by the entrance to the tent. She was watching the white woman.

"Then you'll answer a few questions?" the white woman said to him.

He thought of his father, if he was alive, opening a newspaper in some far-off place and finding her article. He did not believe his father was alive, and he had seldom seen him reading a newspaper, but he said, "Yes."

"Good. Is there somewhere we can go to talk?"

"Here," the Mahdi said, sitting down. "This is my wife and her brother. I have no secrets from them."

The woman sat on the ground opposite him. Hurgas stood by the jeep. Taking a notebook and a pencil from the pocket of her shirt, the woman said, "I understand that you have not always lived here, among these people."

He glanced quickly at Hurgas. Hurgas was gazing down at his feet. The Mahdi turned to the woman and saw that she had followed his glance. Already he regretted he had decided to talk to her. "That's true," he said. "I am an orphan. For a while I lived with other nomads in the north. But I am a Baggara. Look at me."

She looked at him. So did Hurgas and Neimy. Their stares did not bother him. He was used to people staring: He was big and well formed. And he was the Mahdi.

After a pause she said: "Apparently your coming here was foretold many years ago." The blue eyes watched him closely.

He kept himself from glancing again at Hurgas. "So they say."

"Do you believe in prophecy of that sort?"

"How can you ask a Muslim if he believes in prophecy?"

"But we're living in a scientific world. Doesn't all religion, Islam included, have to change with the times?"

"Islam does not change," he said. "It makes change."

"What about science? Surely expanding scientific knowledge changes everything?"

The Mahdi looked beyond her at the rows of tents away into the distance. The sun had dipped a little lower in the dusty sky and was starting to turn it red. "Where is this science that you talk about?"

The blue eyes flickered; and he knew that soon they might be like any other eyes he had known: windows to the thoughts inside. He found himself trying to imagine the life he would be living if he had never left North America. The woman wrote in her notebook and said nothing. He watched her face. The sun had tanned it and stretched the skin tightly across her bones. The tip of her nose had burned and peeled many times, leaving a small pink spot on which he saw one or two tiny scab-covered fissures. They made him think there was something fragile about her. Fragility was much more exotic than cameras or journalists or white skin. Here fragility died young.

Suddenly he was conscious of a half-forgotten smell in the air. He inhaled deeply through his nostrils and smelled it: her smell. It was soap and apples. He remembered a bushel basket of red apples on the kitchen floor at Lac du Loup.

Behind him the knife scraped on the stone. He forced himself to stop thinking about apples or Lac du Loup. It was harder to stop thinking about the woman—there wasn't an ocean between them. "Do you have any more questions to ask me?" he said to her.

She looked up from her notebook. "Yes. But I'd like to see something of the camp first."

"Very well. Hurgas will take you where you want to go."

"If you don't mind I was hoping you would show me the camp yourself. It will be more interesting for the readers." Her white lips curved up in a little smile. The smile told him the answer was no.

"Yes."

The woman got into the jeep. The Mahdi walked around to the passenger side and manipulated the door handle in various ways until she leaned across the seat and opened the door from the inside. She turned the key and put the car in gear. They rolled off. In the rearview mirror bolted to his door he saw Hurgas and Neimy watching them drive away. Hurgas seemed happy to have been spared another ride in the jeep. Neimy didn't seem happy at all.

They drove through the camp. Everyone watched them go by. He showed her the tents of the different tribes, and took her outside the camp to where the cattle grazed on the sparse yellow grass growing beyond the shallow depression. For a while they drove across the plain looking at bony cattle; then the woman turned the jeep in a wide circle and brought it to a stop at the edge of the depression. They watched women filling calabashes from the little pool and carrying them away on their heads.

"The water level seems low," she said. He didn't answer. She reached in front of him and opened the glove compartment. Every time she moved the apple smell was stronger. She found a map. As she closed the glove compartment he thought he saw a silver gun barrel glinting deep inside.

She studied the map. After a few moments she said, "Why aren't you camped by the Bahr el Arab? It's marked in blue."

"Drive," he said. "I'll show you the Bahr el Arab."

They turned north, beyond the last of the cattle. The yellow grass turned black. Then it disappeared. They came to a winding watercourse and parked beside it. It was about twenty feet wide and half as deep. There was nothing in it but cracked red clay and a trail of polished stones. "The Bahr el Arab."

The woman took out her notebook. "You said Islam makes change. What do you want to change?"

"The lives of my people," the Mahdi said. "I want them to be free from thirst and hunger. It is not impossible. It costs money. We have no money, but some of the other Islamic nations are very rich. I want them to share."

"What makes you think they will want to share?"

"That isn't the problem you think it is. When we are all united they will want to share."

"We?"

He smiled. "Not you. Us. The Muslim world."

He saw that the pale blue eyes were gazing at his mouth. He stopped smiling. The woman bent her head and wrote a few lines in her notebook. He tried to read them upside down, but could not.

She raised her pencil and held it poised above the page. "People have been talking for a long time about Muslim unity, and it hasn't happened yet. Why should it happen now?"

"Because of me."

Again the blue eyes flickered: down to his mouth, up to his eyes. She didn't speak. Her apple smell spoke for her. It would be for Paul, he decided. It was owed to him. She looked into his eyes. "What are you thinking?" he asked.

253

When she answered her voice was very low. "I'm thinking that you are the most beautiful man I've ever seen."

He started to lean toward her, to kiss her and put his arms around her, but before he could her hand had darted under the hem of his jubba, slipped up his leg, and found his penis, shocking him into hardness. She rubbed him. He rubbed her, through her khaki trousers.

She moaned. "Hurry." They got out of the jeep, pulling off their clothes. She lay down on the dusty bank of the Bahr el Arab and opened her legs. He looked down at her slender body—firm little breasts that had never nursed a baby, pale unscarred skin, and a vagina so unlike the vagina of Neimy or any of the other Baggara women: No midwife had cut into it with a knife and sliced away the clitoris and the outer lips. He stared at the unfamiliar flesh, glistening in the red light of the evening sun.

"Hurry," she said again.

It was owed to Paul. A taste of the life he could have had. He fell on her. His penis struck against her pelvic bone. She reached between them and took it in her hand. "Here," she said, guiding him inside her. Suddenly she laughed, a husky laugh deep in her throat. "Is this why they call you the Mahdi? The guided one?"

He laughed too, as the head of his penis touched her hot wet skin. And then he realized that she had spoken English.

His penis wilted: a soft comma in her hand. Had she heard his laugh? Had she really spoken English? He felt her pause.

"What's wrong?" she said in Arabic.

The evidence against him was in her hand. "I've never been with a foreign woman before," he said. He closed his eyes very tightly to squeeze out the memory of what had just happened. He thought only of her hand around his penis and the pink lips against its tip. He grew hard. He drove himself inside her. She cried out and pushed back at him.

They pounded their bodies together in the dust.

It was almost night when they left for the camp. The blue eyes and the yellow streaks in her hair dissolved in the darkness. Only the white lips remained distinct. "It's too late for driving," she said. "I'll have to stay the night."

"Of course. We have a tent for guests." He thought of going there while the camp slept.

She shook her head. "Thank you. I'll sleep in the car. I'm used to it, and I've got everything I need here."

Ahead the camp came into view, a shadow with one or two dull orange eyes, spread across the plain. As they drew nearer more eyes opened until there were thousands: weakly glowing fires of dung and bits of wood. She stopped the jeep by a low clump of bushes.

"Good-bye," she said. "I'll be gone as soon as it's light." He felt her move toward him and turned to receive her kiss. Instead she put her hand on his penis. "Good-bye." He got out of the jeep and walked back to camp.

Neimy sat by the fire in front of the tent. He sat down beside her. She spooned his meal from the black iron pot hanging over the fire into a calabash and handed it to him. Millet covered with strips of stringy goat meat. Quickly, hardly taking the time to chew, he swallowed it all. She gave him more. He ate that too. She watched him, her face impassive in the dim red firelight. Still hungry, he laid the calabash on the ground, not wanting to ask for more. Neimy picked it up and filled it again. As she held it out to him she said, "Where is she?"

"Who?" He wrapped his fingers around the bowl to take it, but she did not let go.

"The Turk."

"She's gone." Neimy let him have the bowl. She went inside the tent. He ate.

Afterward he stayed outside and watched the fire slowly die. He thought about Neimy. Was it the woman's whiteness that bothered her? Was it her camera or her jeep or that she knew how to read and write? Or was it because she knew the world beyond Kordofan, beyond the Sudan, beyond Africa, and was at home in it as Neimy could never be? Around him the other fires began to wane. Soon the camp was dark and still and hot.

He entered the tent, removed his clothing, and lay beside Neimy on the bedstead. He felt the heat of her skin. He closed his eyes. The first image that came into his mind was the woman touching him through the cloth of his jubba and saying good-bye. It was enough to make him hard. He reached for Neimy. She turned away.

For some time he lay there remembering how it had been by the Bahr el Arab. Then, very quietly, he stood up.

255

"Where are you going?" Neimy said.

"I can't sleep."

He put on his clothes and left the tent. For a few moments he gazed at the dull embers of the fire and breathed slowly and evenly, trying to make himself relax. But in his chest his heart was beating faster, spreading excitement through his body. He started walking through the camp; at first at a normal pace, later with strides that grew longer and more hurried until he was almost running. He reached the edge of the camp and peered through the darkness beyond, looking for some sign of the low bushes and the jeep parked beside them. He saw a faint yellow light shining, not far away, and realized it was the dashboard of the jeep. Instantly he thought of her husky laugh and the joke she had made in English.

And his laugh.

Slowly and very softly he walked toward the faint yellow light. His heart was still pounding inside him, but the breathless sexual urgency had gone.

As he came closer to the jeep he heard her talking in a low voice. She was alone. He could see her face in the glow of the dashboard light. He also noticed a silvery gleam in the air above the jeep. When he drew nearer he saw that it was a tall aerial, mounted on the hood.

Taking his weight on the balls of his feet, he crept silently to the side of the jeep and stopped just behind her, a few feet away. She was sitting in the driver's seat, talking into a small black box plugged into the hole for the cigarette lighter.

"Wasn't there an immigration card?" she was asking in English. Her words were rushed, and spoken in a voice not much above a whisper. "But I don't think there's much more time. The whole of the western Sudan is gathering around him, and he won't be able to stay here much longer. I'm going to remain in the area for a few more days, then return to Khartoum. If you have Rehv's photograph, send it there."

She pressed a button on the black box and tapped her fingers on the steering wheel, as though organizing her thoughts.

With one stride he could be on her, his hands around her neck, squeezing tight. But he didn't want to do that. He thought of the silvery glint at the back of the glove compartment, and knew how it had to be done.

256

The woman seemed to make up her mind about something. She pressed the button on the black box. He stepped forward and laid his hand on the windshield. A high-pitched cry leaped from her throat. Her head whirled around. Her eyes—he could not see their blueness now—opened wide. He did not move at all. He gave her time to see the dwindling options in his eyes. He gave her time to reach for the gun.

She reached for the gun. He let her rip open the glove compartment, grab it, and swing it toward him. Only then, very swiftly, did his hand swoop down on her wrist and turn the gun away. She fought him. She was strong, but he was far stronger. He leaned over the side of the jeep and fell on top of her, feeling the hard metal between them. She struggled to turn it against his chest. She made animal noises deep in her throat. She bit his face. He did not feel the pain. Still holding her wrist, he felt slowly up the handle of the gun with the tip of his index finger, until he found her finger curled around the trigger. He laid his finger over hers and forced the gun around. She fought him with all her strength, but there was nothing she could do. Very lightly he squeezed her finger. The gun went off.

She bit his face very hard. Then there was no strength in her bite at all. A burnt smell filled the air, overwhelming the smell of apples.

It was self-defense.

He let go of her wrist and climbed out of the jeep, leaving her slumped on the seat and holding the gun against her breast. He removed the aerial from the hood, folded it, and put it under the passenger seat. He unplugged the little black box and laid it beside the aerial. Then he searched the jeep.

He found canned food, bottled drinks, water, and gasoline. He found her camera and a leather purse containing a few hundred Sudanese pounds, a few hundred American dollars, and her notebook. Holding the notebook by the dashboard light he read what was written inside. There were straightforward notes of several interviews, including the one with him. He closed the notebook and put it back in the purse.

On the back seat was a small suitcase. Inside he found some clothing and a suede toilet kit. He opened it and saw her toothbrush, her toothpaste, soap, suntan oil, sunscreen. And a hard plastic tube with a picture of an apple on the cap and words written on the side. Walden's All-Natural Apple Deodorant it said.

Leaving everything as it was, he stepped back from the jeep and bumped into someone behind him. He wheeled around. Neimy.

"She was a spy," he said.

Neimy took his hand. They walked back to the camp.

In the morning he wrote a message on a sheet of paper and gave it to a cousin of Neimy's to take to the telegraph office in Muglad. He addressed it to the general at the head of the government in Khartoum. "Send me Bokur. The Mahdi."

CHAPTER THIRTY-ONE

He stared at his feet. They were ugly. Too long. Too narrow. Too dirty. What he needed was a pair of golf ball socks to put on so no one could see.

He got off the bed and began to search for them. He didn't have to look under the blankets or the sheets because there were no blankets or sheets: only a thin mattress, stained and worn, on an iron frame. That made the search a lot easier. He lifted the mattress off the frame. No golf ball socks. He knelt on the floor and looked under the frame. They weren't there either. It meant one of two things. Either the golf ball socks were inside the mattress or . . . Or what?

He could not remember the second thing it meant. Kneeling on the floor, he thought as hard as he could. Shadows stretched across his cubicle. Slowly darkness fell. It was no use. He couldn't remember.

Still, he might as well search the mattress. He stuck his finger into one of the little holes in the cloth and started pulling out the straw. It was slow work. After a while he stuck another finger in the hole and ripped the cloth to make the hole bigger. Not much, just enough so that it would go faster. It went faster. Soon he had run all the straw through his hands and turned the cloth inside out. No golf ball socks.

That meant it was the other thing.

What was it? What? What? What?

Someone had stolen them.

He had remembered.

He laughed a triumphant laugh. Lights flashed on all around him. He stepped out of the cubicle into the hall. It was a long wide hall, lined with cubicles. Some of them had curtains you could hide behind. Not his. At one end of the hall was a toilet. It had no cover, no seat, and there was never any water in the rusty flush tank on the wall above. You could pull the chain a hundred times, but it made no difference. The toilet wouldn't flush. He hated when he had to go there.

At the other end of the hall was a steel door. Beyond that steel door was another steel door. Beyond that he didn't know. Baby-Finger always closed one before he opened the other, and dropped the long key into his pocket. Baby-Finger sat on a chair in front of the steel door. He called him Baby-Finger because he had no baby finger on his right hand—just a little yellow stump as hard as bone. His right hand held the stick. He hated that stick even more than he hated the toilet.

At the moment Baby-Finger wasn't sitting on his chair. He was walking toward him down the hall with his rolling seaman's stride. Baby-Finger was big and dark. All he wore were dirty black shorts. He had another pair of dirty shorts he didn't wear as often. They were gray.

Baby-Finger kept coming. Now he could see his little eyes. The white part was always yellow, and when you looked very closely you could see the swollen red veins crisscrossing the surface. His teeth were yellow too, but you hardly ever saw them because Baby-Finger did not have much to say.

Baby-Finger came closer. There was a lot of straw on the floor. Baby-Finger kicked at it. Straw rose in the air, glided a little way, and settled back down.

Someone in one of the cubicles shouted, "What is it?" Everyone in the cubicles spoke Arabic. So did Baby-Finger, when he talked. They spoke a careless singsong Arabic that was very unpleasant.

"The Turk," Baby-Finger said. They called him the Turk. He didn't object. After all, he called Baby-Finger Baby-Finger. Fair was fair.

"Fair is fair," he said to Baby-Finger. The red veins in Baby-Finger's eyes were more swollen than he had seen them for a long time. "Fair is fair." He repeated it a few times, trying different languages. Up went the stick. And down.

Blackness.

It was all the fault of the woman in the sable coat. She had hidden Sergeant Levy's leg. Did she think it was going to be easy for Sergeant Levy, swimming all the way with only one leg? Or for him? Because if they were going to make it, he would have to tow Sergeant Levy. He knew it. Sergeant Levy knew it. The woman in the sable coat knew it. So she was trying to kill them. She hated them because they no longer believed in the Americans. She clung more tightly to the Americans than to life itself.

But he could not be angry at her. Even before he and Sergeant Levy stumbled into the water he had heard the steel insects singing in the air. He knew that the woman would close her ears to them, but finally she too would hear them, if they had not bitten her first. Then she would follow them into the water, and her sable coat would pull her to the bottom. So there was no sense feeling angry at the woman in the sable coat.

He lay in the bottom of the boat. One of the sailors bent over him and looked in his eyes. "Hurry up with that blanket," he called to the other sailor. "The bastard's turning blue."

"Never mind the blanket," he said to the sailor. "There isn't time. Sergeant Levy's still out there."

"I think he's trying to say something," the sailor said.

They couldn't hear him. It must be the roar of the sea, drowning his voice. But the sea had not been rough when he was swimming in it. The weather was changing. He listened, and heard the roar. He would have to speak more loudly. He took a deep breath and screamed, "Never mind the blanket."

The pain hit him then. Pain like he had never felt, in the small of his back. He cried out. It hit him again, and jerked him up off the bottom of the boat. Gasping, he clung to the gunwale. Wetness ran down his legs. Warm sticky wetness. Something had bumped him in the back. When? When he was swimming. What? Something.

It hit him once more. He cried out again. Across the black water Israel burned. The little white house on the hill was burning too. And the grave he had dug behind it: all in flames. He screamed: "No. No. No." He would not let it happen.

Lights flashed on.

"What is it?"

"The Turk."

261

He saw swollen red veins on dirty yellow eyes. Up went the stick. And down.

It was wet and very cold. That meant he was still swimming. No problem. He was a good swimmer. He loved the water. He felt Lena resting on his back, heard Naomi and his mother swimming along beside him. Sergeant Levy must be far ahead by now—he was a big, powerful man. Much stronger than Baby-Finger.

Or had something happened to Sergeant Levy's leg?

"Sergeant Levy? Still swimming? Sergeant Levy?" He could hear nothing but the sea. "Naomi? Lena? Mother?" The sea. Wet and very cold.

He opened his eyes in the darkness. Someone was muttering softly in Arabic, "Snakes are biting me, snakes are biting me." He kept saying it over and over. Each time the words grew slightly louder. After a while footsteps passed nearby. "Snakes are biting me." He heard a hollow crack. The stick. The snakes stopped biting.

Footsteps passed the other way. The cold wet sea held him tight.

In the morning he found that he was lying on his back on the iron bed frame. His whole body was wrapped in sheets. They were no longer very cold or very wet, but they were so tight he could not move at all. He lay still. There was no use struggling. He knew that. He waited for the sacrifice. It was just. Everyone sacrifices someone else. Once he had sacrificed someone. He tried to remember who. He couldn't remember. He couldn't. He couldn't.

He waited, but there was no sacrifice. Waiting was the sacrifice. When it was over, Baby-Finger came and freed him from the sheets. He stood up, light and dizzy. "What's for breakfast?" he asked Baby-Finger.

"Pigeon eggs," Baby-Finger replied. That was what he always said. They never had pigeon eggs. Breakfast was stale bread and sour milk. Lunch was pasty millet. Sometimes they poured brown water on it, sometimes they didn't. Dinner was stale bread and sour milk. Of course some of the others ate better than that— they had relatives outside to bring them food. The snake man, for example. He had lamb, beef, oranges, chocolate, tea. But the snakes got him at night.

Baby-Finger was looking at the iron bed frame. "Now you don't even have a mattress," he said.

"Can't I have another one?"

Baby-Finger laughed and went away.

Slow and not very steady, he walked along the hall to the toilet. He had to use it badly. He had held on because he had had enough of pissing and shitting in the cold wet sheets and then lying there all night. And sometimes the next day too.

As he went down the hall he looked into some of the cubicles. He saw that a few of the others had been wrapped up for sacrifice during the night. They all stared at the ceiling. One had a bloody head. "Does it hurt?" he asked him in Arabic.

The man raised his head very slightly and peered at him through the cataracts that covered his eyes. "I can fly," he said. "I was out flying last night. I must have flown into a tree."

That's not what happened, he thought. Baby-Finger hit you with the stick. But he didn't say it.

"Don't say that," the man with the bloody head shouted at him. "I told you what happened. I can fly. I hurt myself flying."

"I didn't say anything."

"Liar," the man with the bloody head shouted.

The snake man was sitting on the toilet. His eyes were closed, and he was masturbating very slowly. "Hurry up." While he waited he looked out the little barred window in the wall near the toilet. Outside he saw a small dirt yard. A few chickens pecked in the dust. A man slept against the far wall. It was a high wall with barbed wire strung along the top. Beyond the wall was the blue sea, calm and gleaming in the early morning sun. A few dhows, their sails heavy and drooping, drifted over the water.

He turned to the toilet. The snake man's eyes were still closed, and he was rubbing himself even more slowly than before. "Hurry up." The snake man showed no sign of hearing him. He began to get angry. He had to use the toilet. "That's why the snakes come after you," he said to the snake man. "Because of what you're doing right now."

The snake man's eyes opened wide in fear. His hand jerked away from his penis as though it were white hot. He got off the toilet and backed slowly away. "Snakes are biting me," he said softly.

When the snake man was gone he used the toilet, trying not

to look inside. Perhaps he had been cruel to the snake man. The snake man had erections he had to do something about. He did not have that problem.

He walked back toward his cubicle. At the far end of the hall Baby-Finger rose from his chair, took the long key from his pocket, and unlocked the steel door. He pulled it open, went to the second steel door, and knocked on it. Then he returned to the chair and sat down, shutting the door behind him but not locking it. Soon after came the squeak of the second steel door opening on its hinges. Without getting up, Baby-Finger opened the first door. The laundry cart rolled into the hall, pushed by a short wiry man who was almost hidden behind it.

The laundryman went from cubicle to cubicle collecting clothes and bedding. He watched the laundryman's cart roll across the floor. He had no more bedding to give him, and no more clothes. After the laundryman had gone, he lay down on the iron bed frame. He was very tired. The sacrifice always made him tired.

He turned onto his stomach and rested his head on his forearm. His eyes fixed on the plastic band around his wrist. On it were two words written in Arabic, but they were not words he knew. He sounded the letters. Quentin Katz was what the letters said. It meant nothing to him.

The heat of the day descended on his naked body. He slept. Later he rolled over and stared at the ceiling.

CHAPTER THIRTY-TWO

Five o'clock.

Everybody who wasn't somebody had straightened the papers on his desk, locked the drawers, drawn the plastic cover over his typewriter, and gone home. The somebodies always stayed late: fighting their way to the top, already there, afraid of slipping back down, not wanting to go home.

During his career Krebs had stayed late for all those reasons. Now it was a habit. He never left before seven; but he no longer worked during those extra hours. He sat at his desk and read the paper, or he lay on the couch gazing at the big map of the Middle East on the far wall, or he stood by the window and watched the cars far below, following each other out of the parking lot in brightly colored chains. There was no point in working. He was six weeks from retirement.

Reaching into the bottom drawer, he found the brochures, bundled together with an elastic band. Once more he riffled through them. Porpoise Sands Yacht and Country Club, Florida. Tumbleweed Estates, Arizona. The Ranch at San Sebastian, California. They all promised a happy retirement heavily patrolled by security guards, with days full of sailing, fishing, golf, tennis, and macrame. And nights drinking alone in a condominium apartment much like the one he lived in now, but more expensive. Much more expensive if he wanted to look at the sea or a mountain or the eighteenth green while he drank. He was fifty years old, too young to retire.

There was no choice. No one had told him he had to retire,

but only because he hadn't let it come to that. It was expected. He had reached an upper-middle level—assistant to the head of the Middle Eastern section. But he had reached it five years before, and gone no further. He had wanted to go much further.

Krebs snapped the elastic band around the brochures and dropped them back into the drawer. He went to the window. Outside, it was raining, a hard steady rain that the March wind blew across the sky at a cutting angle. He watched it fall on the almost empty parking lot below, and spread across the black pavement in shiny pools that took as many parking spaces as they liked. He thought about the moment when his rise had come to an end, for unlike many people who had been in his position he knew the exact moment: a night, soon after his last promotion, when he had answered a knock at the door of a dirty little hotel room in a dirty little town in the Sudan. He had opened that door and let in Tumbleweed Estates.

No one had said anything at the time, but when he had finally left the hospital and returned to the office he had sensed a change in everyone's attitude. From the director of the agency to the newest secretary, they all seemed to share an understanding. After the head of the Middle Eastern section was promoted and someone else got the job, he understood it too.

Six weeks. Then he would start living the rest of his life on a pension, unless he found another job. That was unlikely because he wasn't going to look. He didn't want another job, he wanted the one he had. So he would live on the pension: more than enough, for someone who lived alone. To the pension had been added a small disability increment, although he had not asked for it. Everyone knew that his eyesight had never been the same after the Sudan.

He turned from the window. Near the couch stood a video cassette player. He inserted a tape, sat down, and watched an old cartoon about a man who finds a singing frog. He decides to use the frog to make his fortune, but the frog will sing only for him. The audience jeers. The man lets the frog go free.

It made him think of Isaac Rehv. Isaac Rehv, the singing frog who had pushed him into a short retirement many years ago and had pushed him into a long one now. As the day drew nearer he had begun to think a lot about Isaac Renv.

Krebs opened a drawer of the file cabinet by the couch and

took out a glass and a bottle of scotch. He filled the glass, drank half of it in a gulp, and put his feet up on the couch. Porky Pig and Daffy Duck came on the screen; later Elmer Fudd and Bugs Bunny. They blew each other's heads off with shotguns, threw each other over cliffs and onto bear traps, and laughed about it. Outside the window darkness fell. Krebs did not switch on the lights. He poured himself another drink and looked at the flickering little screen.

On his desk the telephone buzzed. He ignored it. Daffy Duck gave Porky Pig a hot dog bun with a stick of dynamite inside. Porky Pig took a bite and was blown apart. He emerged from the explosion as a stuttering pile of ashes, shook himself, and became Porky Pig again. The telephone kept buzzing. Krebs stood up and answered it.

"Mr. Krebs?" a woman asked.

"Yes."

"Communications. We've got something for you that just came in off the satellite. Do you want to come down here or have it piped up there?"

"I'll come down tomorrow."

"It came in off the satellite, Mr. Krebs," the woman said, sounding hurt.

He sighed. "Where's it from?"

"Cairo."

"Okay. Pipe it up here."

He touched a button on his desk. Static whispered from the speaker on the wall. A buzz saw cut in. It grew louder, and lost itself in a hurricane. Silence. Then from Cairo came the voice of Fairweather, very clear. Fairweather had been there for a year, as liaison to Egyptian Intelligence. He was good at it: The Egyptians like him. Fairweather gave a routing code, identified himself and addressed Krebs.

"I thought this might interest you so I'm sending it along upstairs," he said. "It came last Tuesday at two-forty-one A.M. local time. No. Hold it a sec." There was a pause. Paper rustled. "Okay. Forget I said that. Two-forty-one was when the message ended. It came in a little earlier, ten or fifteen minutes. I can't seem to lay my hands on the log. Anyway, we're eight hours different from you, ahead or behind, I can never get it straight." Pause. He heard Fairweather, in a muffled voice, say, "What time is it in Virginia?" Another voice responded, but Krebs could not hear the words.

"All right," Fairweather said. "I've got it now. Two-forty-one A.M. is six-forty-one P.M. your time. Got that? Six-forty-one. Anyway, I would have sent you this earlier, but I just heard about it. I've been diving down at Sharm el Sheikh. Fabulous. Eighty-five and sunny, day after day. I bet it's raining where you are."

Krebs glanced out the window. It was. "But that's not why I called," continued Fairweather. "I thought you'd want to hear what came in over the scrambler. It's unscrambled now, so I'll rescramble and send it to you. It's from Gillian Wells. She's out in the middle of nowhere. Kordofan, I think. We've got the exact coordinates around here someplace. I'll have a look while I punch this through."

Whispers. Buzz saw. Hurricane. Silence.

Then a woman's voice. It was not as clear as Fairweather's, but Krebs recognized it immediately. He also heard the excitement in her tone, the urgency, which had not been lost on the journey into space and back.

"SU-Six to EC-One," she said. "SU-Six to EC-One. Prepare to receive." Krebs imagined reels of tape begining to spin in the cellars of the embassy in Cairo. "I'm in Kordofan, a few miles south of a wadi called the Bahr el Arab and about one hundred and twenty miles southwest of Muglad."

Krebs jumped up and crossed the room in two steps. He stood beside the speaker on the wall. "I think I've picked up the trail of Isaac Rehv," Gillian Wells said. "And if I'm right it means that Mr. Krebs has . . ." A high-pitched electronic wail smothered her voice. Krebs ran to the phone.

"The sound's no good," he shouted into the mouthpiece. "Fix it."

"One moment, Mr. Krebs," said the woman from communications. He waited. The speaker wailed. "Mr. Krebs? The technician says that the problem is with the original transmission. There is nothing we can do. According to the logs it clears up after two minutes and thirty-three seconds."

He hung up and looked at his watch. The red digits flashed away the seconds. When 127 of them had passed, the wailing faded and Gillian's voice came through, but much weaker than before. He stood by the speaker, so close that his ear touched the grille.

". . . but before you can make sense out of it you need to know something about Mahdis in general. A Mahdi is a redeemer, in a way like a Messiah, except that he is not divine, but divinely guided. There have been other self-proclaimed Mahdis in the past. The most famous one, and this is important, led an uprising right here in the Sudan against the British in the 1880s: Chinese Gordon, the fall of Khartoum, all that. There are still many Mahdists in this country who believe he will return one day. Now he has. Not only that—he's appeared among the Baggara, who rode with the previous Mahdi and think of it as their finest hour. I met the Mahdi today, and he's very impressive. He looks just like a Baggara—that is, a kind of black and Semitic mixture—but I'm practically certain he is not one of them. First, I've got an informant in the tribe. Hurgas, he's called. The son of the omda. He says that the Mahdi was not born among the Baggara. He came to them, alone, as a boy. It's not easy to fix a definite date, but from what I can piece together, it must have been around the time that Rehv appeared in Muglad. Second, the Mahdi understands English. He's very careful to hide the fact, but there is no question about it."

Krebs thought he heard her laugh, low and soft and far away. He pressed his ear against the speaker. There was a long pause, filled with static. When she spoke again her voice was much quieter. "Sorry. Thought I heard something. I'm not very far from the camp." Another pause. "False alarm," she went on, more quickly. "As for Rehv, there's no sign of him at all. If there's a photograph available it might help establish a physical resemblance. Wasn't there an immigration card? But I don't think there's much more time. The whole of the western Sudan is gathering around him, and he won't be able to stay here much longer. I'm going to remain in the area for a few more days, then return to Khartoum. If you have Rehv's photograph, send it there." Static. Krebs felt the speaker vibrate against his ear. He waited.

Whispers. Buzz saw. Hurricane. Silence.

Then Fairweather, very loud. "Well, that's it. It's funny she didn't sign off. We'll keep our ears open for her on this end." Fairweather said good-bye. Before the transmission was broken, Krebs heard Fairweather say to someone, "What's he trying to do? Hijack a whole country?" The speaker went dead.

No, Krebs thought. Isaac Rehv wanted Islam itself.

On the little screen Bugs Bunny drove a steamroller over Elmer Fudd.

Krebs sat down. At last. He pounded his fist on the desk. He had done it. They could not retire him now. Rehv was out there in the Sudan. It was his operation.

He picked up the telephone and tried Birdwell's office. Birdwell was his boss, in charge of the Middle Eastern section. No answer. He called communications. "Find Birdwell for me." He hung up and waited.

He could not sit still. He rose and began to pace back and forth across the room. As he went by the video cassette player he snapped it off. A big orange carrot faded away.

He had been right all along. Not totally: There was no indication of a conspiracy, nothing to show that Rehv was not acting alone. Of course in the beginning, when the two Arabs had been killed in New York, there were others involved. Later he had seen the old prime minister. Perhaps the idea had come from him. After that Rehv had done it alone.

It was colossal. Rehv had found the core of the enemy's strength, the unifying power of its religion, and he had made it his own. Secretly: in a hidden, fertile corner of the Muslim world where he could plant his Mahdi and let him take root and grow, out of sight.

But why? Suddenly he thought: Maybe Rehv doesn't consider the Arabs his enemy at all. Maybe we're the enemy; we let Israel go down the drain. If that was the case, the implications were grim.

He picked up the telephone. "Haven't you got him yet?"

"Still trying, Mr. Krebs."

"Christ." He slammed down the phone.

It buzzed. He grabbed it. "Hello."

"Ah, Krebs," Birdwell said. "Working late right to the end?"

"Something's come up. We've got to meet."

"No problem. I'll be in my office anytime after eight-thirty tomorrow. Just pop in."

"That's not soon enough."

Birdwell sighed in his ear. "I'm at dinner, Krebs."

"Then I'll come over. Where are you?"

"The White House."

Krebs drove through the rain. He listened to the radio. Three

270

sports writers were talking about the end of the baseball strike. "It's been five years since hickory whacked horsehide," one of them said. "What makes you think there'll still be an audience for baseball when they finally start winging the old pill in April? Mel?"

"There'll always be baseball fans," Mel said. "Baseball is as American as —"

"I'm with Mel," the third one said.

Krebs turned off the radio. The windshield wipers swept back and forth. The slick black miles rolled beneath him. He drove into Pennsylvania Avenue.

Two marines stood in front of the side gate. Except for the rain dripping from the peaks of their hats, they looked like figures in a wax museum. One of them proved he was alive by bending forward to look inside the car. Krebs pushed a button, and the window slid down.

"Yes sir?" the marine said.

"Krebs," Krebs answered. "To see Colonel Birdwell."

"Do you have some identification, sir?" Krebs showed him some identification. The marine took it into the guardhouse. He talked on a telephone, watching Krebs as he spoke. He came out. "Thank you, sir," he said, handing Krebs the plastic card. "An escort will be right with you."

Another marine stepped out of the shadows beyond the gate. "Mr. Krebs?"

"Yes."

"Please follow me."

"What about the car?"

"It will be parked for you in the visitors lot, sir."

Krebs got out of the car and followed the marine through the gate and up a paved lane to the house. The rain felt cold on his bald head. They entered a door at the back and crossed a large hall. On the other side was a long corridor. At the end of it Krebs saw a dining room. A huge chandelier glittered from the ceiling. He heard faint laughter and the sounds of silver, crystal, and violins. The president was presiding over a long shining table. An oyster hung from his lips.

"This way, sir," the marine said, and led him down a flight of stairs he had not seen, into the basement.

The basement was divided into offices. The marine opened

271

the door to one of them. It was small and bare, except for a desk, two wooden chairs, and a photograph on the wall of the president and his dog. Krebs walked in and sat on one of the chairs. "Would you tell Colonel Birdwell I'm here?" he said.

"He has been informed," the marine replied. "Thank you, sir."

"What are you thanking me for?"

"Regulations, sir." The marine closed the door and went away.

Krebs sat. After a while he moved to the other chair. Later he opened the drawers of the desk and looked inside. They were empty: not even a paper clip. From time to time he heard footsteps above his head. Doors closed. He sat.

The house grew very quiet. Krebs waited until one A.M. Then he walked out of the room. It was too important to wait any longer. He followed a dark corridor to a flight of stairs, thinking they were the stairs he had descended before. At the top was a closed door. Light glowed dimly through the crack at the bottom.

When he was halfway up he heard the president say, "You're an asshole."

Krebs stood still. A woman said, "You're the asshole." The president's wife. Krebs knew her voice from the fund-raising drive for crippled children on television. He went quietly back down the stairs.

Birdwell was waiting for him in the little office. He was sitting on one of the wooden chairs, wearing evening dress and smoking a cigar. Evening dress suited him. He was lean and tanned and looked ten years younger than Krebs, although he was the same age. "Looking for the red button, Krebs?"

"I went to the bathroom."

"Careful where you go. Our leader's had a few too many tonight and he's in a warlike mood." Birdwell blew a cone of smoke across the room and smiled at a thought that passed through his head. His mouth turned down in the way Krebs was used to seeing it. Birdwell looked at him. "Okay, Krebs. Let's have it."

Krebs let him have it. Birdwell listened. He forgot about his cigar. He looked worried. When he had heard what there was to hear he said, "It's a hell of a thing." He stuck his cigar in his mouth and sucked on it. The cigar had gone out. He threw it on the floor. "What are we going to do?"

"All we have to do is pass the word to the Sudanese government. If they can't handle it, the Palestinian government as well."

Birdwell looked at him thoughtfully. "Maybe," he said. He rose. "I'd better get him up. I wouldn't want this to be our little secret overnight."

Of course not, Krebs thought. If anything went wrong, you'd be responsible. He stood up to go with Birdwell.

Birdwell shook his head. "It will probably be better if I handle this alone," he said. "Unless you know him fairly well. Do you?"

"No."

Birdwell turned to the door. "I'll have coffee sent down."

"But I've been on this from the beginning," Krebs said. "I know every detail."

Birdwell laughed. "He wouldn't be able to cope with that. Let's hope he can get the gist of it." He left.

Krebs sat down. He wondered if they would give him the South American section. The directorship had been vacant for a few months. Maybe they would let him skip a step, and promote him even higher: a sub-Cabinet post. He would have to buy a dinner jacket and go on a diet. And start running again. There had been a time when he could do one hundred push-ups with ease. How many could he do now? Fifty? Sixty? He felt very strong. He pulled off the jacket of his suit and got down on the floor. He did eight.

He waited for coffee. It never came. Later he laid his head on the desk.

A loud metallic bang startled him. He jerked awake and went into the corridor. A black charwoman stood in a pool of soapy water, an overturned tin pail at her feet. "Shit," she said. She did not seem to notice him at all.

Krebs hurried past her along the corridor, and up the first flight of stairs he saw. He did not think they were the same stairs he had climbed earlier, but he paused when he reached the door and listened carefully. It was quiet on the other side. Was it the master bedroom? Were they asleep? He opened the door.

He was in a large kitchen. Gray early-morning light entered through a large bay window. At the table by the window sat Birdwell and the president eating pancakes. The president wore a red silk robe; Birdwell still wore evening dress.

"More flapjacks?" the president said around a mouthful of them.

"Love some," Birdwell said.

The president raised his voice. "Luis. More flapjacks." He turned his head toward a door on the opposite wall, and saw Krebs. "What the hell?" the president said in a high, frightened voice. He shoved his chair back from the table and ducked his head.

Birdwell looked up. "It's okay, Mr. President. It's just Krebs. The man I was telling you about."

The president sat up. "Oh yes," he said, pulling his chair to the table. He nodded at Krebs. "Good work, Mr. . . . ah. But don't scare me like that. How about some flapjacks?"

"I don't really . . ."

"Sure. Come on. Pull up a chair. Luis! Where is that lazy son of a bitch?"

Krebs sat between them. The president ate. Birdwell ate. Finally Krebs could keep it inside no longer. "What's been decided?"

The president looked at him, blinking. "He means about the Sudan," Birdwell explained, glaring at Krebs.

"Oh that," the president said. "Don't ask me." He poured some maple syrup on his pancakes. "Luis?" The door opened. "It's about time."

But it wasn't Luis. It was the secretary of state. He poked his head into the room and said to Birdwell: "The Mahdi business: Plan B." Without waiting for a reply, he shut the door and went away.

"The hell with it," the president said. "Flapjacks or no flapjacks, I'm not sitting here another minute. I've got a day ahead of me you wouldn't believe. First I've got to have my hair cut, then lunch with that pisspot king, veto the goddamned social security bill or whatever it is, and Christ knows what else." He stood up and glanced at Krebs. "If Luis doesn't show up, you can finish that," he said, gesturing at what was left on his plate. He went out.

"What's Plan B?" Krebs said.

Birdwell speared a pancake with his fork and sliced off a corner. "The president was very pleased with you. He even spoke of a decoration when you retire."

"What's Plan B?"

Birdwell laid down his knife and fork. "Plan B means we do nothing."

"Do nothing?"

"Don't shout, Krebs," Birdwell said calmly. He watched Krebs like a teacher waiting to see if a pupil would control himself or have to be sent into the hall. Krebs controlled himself. "Plan B means we wait and see," Birdwell continued. "Times have changed, Krebs. Oil's not so important now. We don't have to suck up to the Arabs anymore. Besides, the Jews have calmed down. There hasn't been any trouble for a long time. So we'll just sit back and watch what this Mahdi does. Why show all our cards to the Arabs?" Birdwell smiled. "And don't forget, he was born in New York. That probably makes him an American citizen. As such he has certain inalienable rights."

"What the hell are you talking about?"

"Please, Krebs." Again Birdwell waited. "You have to accept the realities. He may prove very useful to us one day. If he doesn't, if he gets out of hand, we can always blow the whistle on him. His mother was a whore and his father was a Jew. The Arabs wouldn't like that."

For a long time Krebs stared at Birdwell. At last he said, "What about Rehv?"

"What about him?"

"We can't just do nothing."

"That's exactly what we are doing. Rehv's not really important. The Mahdi is important. Anyway, it's nothing for you to worry about. You've only got a few more weeks in harness. It's time to start relaxing." He raised the fork to his lips. "By the way, he was very serious about that decoration. It's a great way to go out, Krebs." He opened his mouth and closed it on a pancake.

Slowly Krebs stood up. "Do you mean I'm still retiring?"

"Of course," Birdwell said, chewing. "You've earned it."

"I don't want to retire," Krebs shouted. He whipped his arm across the table. Cups, saucers, plates, and cutlery crashed to the floor.

"It's settled," Birdwell said.

Krebs grabbed a pancake and shoved it in Birdwell's face. Birdwell's chair tipped over. He fell on the floor. A door opened and a little brown-skinned man came in, wearing a short white jacket and carrying a tray heaped with food. "Flapjacks, señors?" he said.

Krebs drove to the office. He opened the drawers of his desk

275

and sorted the contents. What was he going to retire to? He had no real home, no kids, no wife. He had a wife once, but he lost her. Eight push-ups. He began throwing things around the room.

They could make him retire, but they couldn't make him stop looking for Isaac Rehv.

He dialed the airport and asked about flights to Khartoum. "I'm sorry, sir," the ticket agent said after a long pause. "That airport was closed early this morning."

He called Fairweather on an ordinary line. There was no need to use the scrambler: Rehv had no satellites to intercept the call.

"Hello," Fairweather said. Every call was taped at both ends. Krebs didn't care.

"I've got to go to Khartoum," he said.

"No can do. They sealed off the whole country a few hours ago."

"Then find me a plane that can go the distance and someone who can fly it."

"That's no problem. I can fly you myself." Fairweather had taken lessons in everything. After a pause Fairweather whispered: "We haven't heard anything from you-know-who."

He had forgotten Gillian Wells. Birdwell hadn't mentioned her either. "Don't worry about it."

"Right."

Krebs drove to the airport and caught the first flight to Cairo.

CHAPTER THIRTY-THREE

In the afternoon a helicopter swooped down from the yellow sky and circled low over the camp. The Mahdi came out of his tent to watch it with the others. Many of them had seen a helicopter before—a few years earlier one had flown over them in the same way and then dropped dozens of sacks filled with powdered milk. Most of the sacks had split, sending clouds of white powder drifting across the plain; they were left with scraps of cloth that said "United Nations" in six languages. But no one had worried about it. As long as they could keep the herds alive they would have milk. What they needed was rain to make the grasses grow, and no helicopter could give them that.

So they watched it circle above, waiting for sacks of powdered milk. It flew very slowly. Once around. Twice. Finally the helicopter hovered over the center of the camp, a few hundred feet in the air. There it hung, shuddering slightly and giving off invisible waves of heat that distorted the sky around it. Then it dropped one sack. The sack had arms and legs. It jerked and kicked them all the way down, but none of that could make it fly. It hit hard ground near the Mahdi's tent with a sound that was soft, like a fist striking a pillow.

He ran to it as fast as he could, although he knew what it was and knew there was no point in running. Bokur, broken on the ground. His silver teeth were scattered around him.

Without seeming to hurry, the helicopter rose in the sky and flew away to the east. To those in the helicopter, the Mahdi realized, he was an insect far below, to be squashed at will as

Bokur had been. What could he do against helicopters? His father had been dreaming a fool's dream. Instead of coming true, it had killed a trusting old nomad in Kordofan and the white woman. And it had made him what he was.

He felt people press around him. Neimy. Una. Bokur's other wives, his children and grandchildren. They fell on the body and began to wail, loud ululating cries that spread quickly through the camp.

"You did this," someone shouted. A hand dug into his shoulder and spun him around. Hurgas. His face was twisted, his teeth bared. Hurgas punched at him, but he caught his wrist in mid-air and squeezed it until the fist slowly opened. The cries died down. He sensed the eyes of everyone on him. The moment had come, just when he knew that all was hopeless.

"No, Hurgas," the Mahdi said quietly. He released Hurgas's arm. "They did it." He pointed to a speck disappearing in the eastern sky. He raised his voice. "But now I will do something. Neimy, bring me the black mare."

Kneeling over her father's body, she looked at him, her cheeks wet with tears. "Where are you going?"

"Khartoum."

Neimy wiped her eyes with the back of her hand and stood up. "I'm coming with you," she said.

Somewhere in the crowd a man said, "Jihad." He did not speak very loudly, but because he was listening for it the Mahdi heard.

"Yes," he said: "Jihad." Holy war.

They caught the word like a disease. "Jihad. Jihad." Their voices rose. "Jihad. Jihad." They fired rifles in the air. The women took up their ululating cry, no longer so much in grief as in anger. The sound made the Mahdi's skin prickle. He felt power surging around him. It was real power, dangerous power, but he did not know what it could do against helicopters.

The next morning they broke camp: the Baggara and all the others who had come from the west to be near the Mahdi. Slowly they began moving east, women and children on the backs of oxen, the herds following behind. Rich men rode horses, poor men rode donkeys. The poorest walked. In front where they could see him rode the Mahdi on the black mare.

Only Hurgas had stayed behind. Just before it was time to go,

Una had taken the Mahdi to plead with him. Hurgas sat on the ground near the newly dug grave. "Come," Una said.

"No."

"Then come for revenge. Don't you want revenge?"

Hurgas looked at her. Then he looked at the Mahdi. He said nothing.

Una turned to the Mahdi. "Say something to him. He can't stay here alone."

The Mahdi laid his hand on Hurgas's shoulder. Hurgas jerked away. The Mahdi stepped back. "It's his decision," he said coldly. "He has his own cattle. He'll survive."

Hurgas stayed behind.

They moved east across the plain. From time to time they came across other people. The other people joined them—nomads, hunters, villagers. Whole towns emptied and followed. The dust they raised filled the sky from horizon to horizon. The Mahdi sensed their force at his back. Even if he wanted to he knew he could do nothing now to stop them, to turn them around. Some were hungry, some were thirsty, some were armed. They had been waiting for him for a long time. Yet he was aware that he was not really leading them: He felt their push. The most he could hope for would be to steer a little. What would happen would happen. He smiled at that thought. He was becoming like them.

"Why are you smiling?" Neimy asked when they halted for the night.

"I'm happy."

"I've never seen you so happy."

He heard the worry in her voice and looked at her. She seemed smaller. The world he had been living in was shrinking. Soon he would be entering the world he had been prepared for. If everything worked.

Campfires burned across the plain like the lights of a great city. They ate and talked and sang and finally slept. The Mahdi lay awake most of the night. Neimy laid her head on his chest. He moved away.

"What is it?" she said.

"I can smell the river. The Nile."

"You aren't sad about my father, are you?"

"Yes. I am." He was sad about his own father too. But sadness could not compete with the smell of the river. Neimy rolled over and was quiet, leaving him to enjoy his happiness alone. All night it welled up in his chest.

At dawn the camp was awakened by a shriek that came out of the east. People rushed from their tents as a jet with sweptback wings roared overhead. Orange flames shot out from under the wings. Rockets exploded among the tents. People screamed. It rained steel. The screams grew louder. The screamers ran back and forth, trying to find safety. There was no safety. They died.

The Mahdi stood in front of his tent and watched. The jet banked in a broad circle and turned for them again. They were helpless. They would all be slaughtered on the plain. His father had been a fool, and he was a fool too. Born and bred a fool.

Two more jets dove out of the sky. People fell on the ground and prayed. The two jets fired orange flames. They struck the first jet. It vanished in a ball of fire. The two jets wheeled in the sky and flew away.

It was very quiet.

The Mahdi understood. His father had not worried about helicopters or jets. All that mattered were the minds of the pilots. The jets were his.

"Jihad." He screamed.

"Jihad. Jihad."

By the time they reached Khartoum the government had fled. The inhabitants cheered them through the streets. The Sudan was his. He wanted more than that. His father had wanted more than that. Khartoum was a step. It led to Port Sudan, the Red Sea, Mecca.

"On to Mecca," he told them.

"Jihad. Jihad."

CHAPTER THIRTY-FOUR

He gazed out the little barred window, past the dirt yard where chickens pecked and a man slept, and over the high wall at the blue sea beyond. It stretched away to the horizon where it met the cloudless sky in a white haze. What was on the other side of the sea? A high wall, a dirt yard, a little barred window?

"What's on the other side of the sea?" he called down the long wide hall to Baby-Finger. Baby-Finger tapped the stick on his knee and said nothing. What the point of asking Baby-Finger? Just because he had the stick didn't mean he knew anything. "What do you know anyway, Baby-Finger?" Tap, tap went the stick. He stopped shouting at Baby-Finger. He knew Baby-Finger didn't like it. And when Baby-Finger didn't like something, he got up from his chair, came down the hall, and used the stick. He hated the stick, so he kept his mouth shut and stared out the window at the sea.

The sea had a smooth shiny skin. Sometimes it shivered, despite the heat. Once a breeze gave it goose bumps. When it passed, the skin was instantly smooth again. He wanted to lower himself onto that skin, very gently so he would not disturb it, and sink into it a little way. He wanted badly to be there. That always happened when he looked out the window long enough. But it was no use. He had asked Baby-Finger a thousand times if he could go lie on the smooth skin, and Baby-Finger was sick of hearing it.

Once more wouldn't hurt. "Baby-Finger." Tap, tap. "Nothing." Nothing. He gazed at the sea.

"Snakes are biting me," the snake man whispered in his ear. The snake man liked to come and watch the sea with him. Without looking at the snake man, he turned and left the window. He walked from one end of the hall to the other, searching for the golf ball socks.

Boom boom. Someone was banging on the steel door. Baby-Finger took the key from his pocket and unlocked it. The door swung open. A man in a white jubba was pushed inside. He stumbled and fell and lay face down on the floor. Baby-Finger locked the door.

The man in the white jubba was bleeding from the nose and mouth. Drip drip. Slowly a small red pool formed on the floor, quivering with surface tension.

He forgot about the golf ball socks and went closer to examine the red pool. Somehow he knew it would feel sticky if he touched it with his toe. Once a red pool like that had flowed around his bare feet. He stepped in it. Wet and sticky. He lifted his foot, took it in his hands, and twisted it to look at the sole. It was stained red. What had he done? He would need something to hide it.

"Have you seen my golf ball socks?" he asked the man on the floor.

The man raised his head. His face was dark and gaunt. He smiled. "What do you want socks for? It's too hot."

He showed the gaunt man the sole of his foot. "To hide this," he whispered.

The gaunt man laughed. "Do you think that's bad? Look at my face." He did. It was bad.

"It is bad."

"I know. But don't worry about it. I'm not." He lowered his voice. "They didn't find it."

"What?"

The gaunt man laughed again.

"What?"

He kept laughing.

Tap, tap. "That's enough," Baby-Finger said. "Get up."

The gaunt man turned and saw Baby-Finger sitting on the chair behind him. He got up. Baby-Finger got up too. "This way," he said. He led the gaunt man to a cubicle, one of the cubicles that had a dirty curtain across the front. "Go in," Baby-Finger said. The gaunt man went in and disappeared behind the curtain. "Don't bother me," Baby-Finger said to the curtain. "If you do you'll be sorry." Baby-Finger walked back to his chair and sat down.

He waited until Baby-Finger's eyelids began to droop before tiptoeing across the hall and peeking around the dirty curtain. The gaunt man lay on the mattress, curled up with his knees to his chin. He went inside and looked down at him. "What didn't they find?"

The gaunt man stared past him and did not answer.

"What didn't they find? My golf ball socks? Have you got them? Have you?" He grabbed the gaunt man's shoulders and shook him. "Answer me."

"Don't," the gaunt man whined. He began to cough, a deep cough that sent vibrations through the bones in his shoulders.

"Then tell me."

"Don't." The cough was taking over the job of shaking his body.

"Tell me."

"I will. I will. Stop."

He stopped. After a minute or two the cough stopped too. The gaunt man lay on the bed panting. Then he stood up and stripped off his jubba. The gaunt man was naked. There was nothing unusual about that. So was he.

"They didn't find it," the gaunt man whispered.

"What?"

"You have to whisper."

"What?" he whispered.

The gaunt man raised his left arm. In his armpit was a very small leather pouch, held there by a safety pin stuck through his skin. "This," he whispered.

"What is it?"

"Whisper."

"What is it?" he whispered.

"I'll show you." The gaunt man's right hand reached across his concave chest and up to his armpit; his fingers felt the leather pouch, the pin. They fumbled with it for a while, but they could not make it open. The gaunt man stepped toward him. "Help me."

He didn't like the gaunt man's smell, but he leaned forward so he could see what he was doing and put his hands in the damp armpit. With one he supported the pouch; with the other he unfastened the head of the safety pin and pulled it slowly out. Two drops of blood about an inch apart appeared beneath the coarse wiry hairs on the gaunt man's skin. He lowered his arm and took the pouch.

"It's a secret," he whispered.

"I won't tell."

The gaunt man untied the string that was wound around the mouth of the pouch and turned it upside down. Something very small, no bigger than a pill, fell into his palm. He took it in the tips of his fingers and carefully began to unfold it. It was a tiny wad of paper. Newsprint. The gaunt man smoothed it flat on his palm and held it up so he could see.

He saw a photograph of a dark young man. In Arabic under the photograph was written: "The Mahdi." It was his boy.

It was his boy. He fell on the floor and wept. He wept as hard as he could weep, but it was not enough, so he banged his head against the wooden boards.

"Quiet," the gaunt man whispered urgently. "Stop it." He wept and cracked his head against the floor.

Hurriedly the gaunt man refolded the scrap of newsprint and thrust it into the pouch. "Be quiet," he hissed. It was too late. A gust of wind blew into the cubicle as the curtain was swept aside. Up went the stick. And down.

When he awoke he was bound tightly in cold wet sheets. "Guard," he shouted. "Guard." He kept shouting the word until the man he had called Baby-Finger came into the cubicle and stood at the foot of his bed. "Please unwrap me," he said. "I'm not going to bother you."

The guard shook his head. "You say that every time. And every time you bother me." The guard went away.

Lying there in the cold wet sheets, his eyes filled with tears. They ran down his cheeks, fell softly on the iron bed frame. He thought about the face in the photograph. It was a powerful face. A hard face. Very little of his boy remained. He had sacrificed the boy. He had hurt a woman named Paulette, long ago. He had thrown away his own chance to make a new life. For what? Tears fell on the iron frame.

He could have enjoyed the boy. He could have let the boy

enjoy him, and be a normal American boy with friends and games and school. Now it was too late.

But it was not too late to find him, and tell him. Tell him what? That he was sorry? How would the hard face react to that? That he loved him? It would be no better. But none of that mattered. He wanted to be near him. His tears dried up. "Guard. Guard." The guard would not come. He stopped calling.

Another man came. "Snakes are biting me," he said.

"Go away."

"But snakes are biting me."

"Go." He went.

Much later the guard appeared and began unwrapping the sheets. As they were stripped away he looked down at his body. Was it really him? He had been a strong, muscular man. Now the muscles had shriveled, and most of the flesh as well. What remained hung loosely from his bones.

He noticed the plastic band on his wrist. Quentin Katz. When the guard had gone he ripped it off. He knew who he was. Isaac Rehv.

He knew who he was. But not where. Or when. Suddenly he remembered the dirty little mirror on the wall near the toilet. He rose and slowly, afraid, walked toward it down the hall. He looked in the mirror.

An old man looked back at him. He had white hair, a white beard, and a face as gaunt as the face of the man with the pouch. The old man's deep brown eyes filled with tears and he began to cry, because he knew from the photograph of his son that he could not yet be so old.

After a long time he turned away from the old man's eyes. He saw a rectangle of blue shining through the little window. The sea. The Red Sea. He knew what was on the other side.

Isaac Rehv hurried down the hall. He had to find his son. He would need clothes. And money. But first he had to get out.

As he approached the steel door he saw the guard look up and finger the long wooden billy that lay across his lap. "Guard," he said. "I'm better now. I don't need to be here anymore. Please let me out."

The guard laughed.

"If you can't do it on your own, let me see someone who can. There must be a doctor here. Call him."

"Go back to your bed."

"Please." He laid his hand on the guard's thick shoulder. The guard jumped up and kicked back his chair. Up went the stick. Rehv ducked to the side and it glanced off his arm. The guard raised the billy again and stepped forward in a wary crouch, his yellow eyes like slits in a lantern. Rehv backed away. The guard kept coming. Rehv felt a wall behind him. The guard smiled. Rehv threw his fist at him, a weak looping punch that struck nothing and put him off-balance. The guard grabbed his arm and spun him around. Down went the stick.

Blackness.

"Is this the one?" a man said in Arabic.

"Yes," answered another man whose voice he knew. The guard.

Rehv opened his eyes. He lay on the bed frame, wrapped in cold wet sheets. Looking down at him was a tall man, not much darker than he. Beside him stood the guard; the billy dangled loosely from his maimed hand. The tall man's curly hair shone with oil; so did his neat mustache. A heavy gold chain hung around his neck, and he was carrying more gold on his fingers and wrists. He wore a white laboratory coat over a Western suit.

"Are you the doctor?" Rehv asked.

The tall man frowned. "I'll ask the questions," he said, looking coldly at Rehv. Rehv stared back.

"Then ask," he said finally.

"I won't listen to rudeness." The tall man remained calm. The guard's hand tightened around the billy. "Rudeness is a sign that you are not ready to leave." He turned to go.

"But I am ready. Let me go. Please let me go."

The tall man walked away. Over his shoulder he said, "You're not ready. You're still rude. What's more, you took off your identity band. We're not blind, you know."

Rehv strained against the cold wet sheets. They did not give at all. "But it wasn't me. I'm not Quentin Katz."

The tall man turned and came back. "Do you see?" he said, shaking his head. "You don't even know who you are. That's one problem. Another is that you're a masochist. I've seen the reports. We've never had anyone who needed to be hit as much as you. It means you enjoy it."

"I don't."

"The literature is unassailable."

"I'm not a masochist," Rehv shouted.

The guard glared at him. "Just a few hours ago I caught him beating his head against the floor."

The tall man pursed his lips. "Two more years," he said. "At least."

Rehv inhaled deeply to force his anger back inside him. "I'm not a masochist," he said quietly. "And you're not a doctor. No real doctor would have anything to do with a place like this."

The doctor's calmness dropped away like a skin that no longer fit. He spoke angrily: "I am a doctor. I trained in America."

"Then let me go," Rehv said in English. "I'm an American."

In Arabic the tall man said, "Ah. You speak English. So do I." He leaned over Rehv. "Two years," he said in English; his accent was very thick.

He turned and walked away. The guard followed him. Rehv listened to their footsteps as they went down the hall, and heard the key scrape in the lock. As the door opened he called out: "You didn't graduate, did you? You failed and they sent you home. That's why you're running this snake pit. You're a fraud."

The door banged shut. Rehv waited for the guard to come running and hit him with the billy. But the guard did not come: He heard the creaking of wooden joints as he settled in his chair. He realized that he had spoken English, and the guard had not understood. The doctor had probably not understood either.

They kept him wrapped in the sheets until dinner. He ate the soggy millet and drank the sour milk. Then he slept. The squeezing of the sheets always made him tired.

In the morning he heard the guard turn the long key in the lock and open the steel door. Then he heard the wheels of the laundry cart rolling across the floor. He got up and watched the wiry little laundryman pushing the cart from cubicle to cubicle, collecting dirty clothes and soiled bedding. Rehv had nothing to give him. The laundryman left the cart at the entrance to his cubicle and went into the next one.

Rehv glanced down the hall. The guard was sitting tilted back in his chair, looking at the ceiling. Quickly Rehv climbed into the laundry cart and hid himself under the linen.

He could see nothing. What little air there was stank in his nostrils. He felt a soft thump on his back: more linen. The cart began to roll. Almost immediately he thought how stupid his impulse had been: He had no plan, no idea what lay beyond the steel doors. And surely the laundryman would notice the added weight.

But he didn't. The cart rolled along the floor. It stopped. He felt more soft thumps on his back. The cart started. It rolled. The laundryman whistled a little tune.

The cart stopped. "All done?" he heard the guard ask.

"All done," the laundryman replied. "But the Turk is in the cart."

"Again?"

Rapid footsteps. The stick. On his back. His shoulder. His head.

When Rehv awoke, he felt the sheets around him again. It was very quiet, as quiet as night. But it could not be night because the insides of his eyelids were pink. He kept his eyes closed. He would keep them closed until the pain in his head went away. He knew that the pain in his head would go away after a while; that made it different from the pain in his back. It was quiet.

Suddenly he heard a soft whisper, almost in his ear. "Snakes are biting me." He opened his eyes. The snake man stood beside him, holding a long knife. "Snakes are biting me," he repeated. He touched Rehv's chest with the knife. Rehv could feel the point through the sheets.

"Guard," Rehv called, not loudly, because he did not want to frighten the snake man. "Guard."

"He's gone," the snake man whispered. "Everyone's gone."

"Guard." Rehv listened. There wasn't a sound.

"Gone. Everyone's gone." The snake man looked at Rehv. His lower lip trembled. "You told me I deserved it," he said. He pressed a little on the knife.

"I don't know what you're talking about." He tried to keep his voice calm. Reasonable.

"Yes you do. The biting. You said I brought it on myself."

"I didn't."

"You did." He pressed harder.

"It wasn't me. It was the guard."

The snake man shook his head. "No. It was you. You said I made it happen when I, when I . . ." His lower lip trembled. He pressed a little harder on the knife.

Rehv felt sweat rising through his pores, despite the cold wet sheets. "I never said anything like that. I'm the one who wants to help you get rid of the snakes. I can get rid of them for you."

The snake man shook his head. "No one can."

"I can. I'd like to do it. They've been biting you long enough."

The snake man's eyes grew watery. "They have." He stopped pressing on the knife.

"Let me get rid of them."

"All right."

"First you'll have to get me out of these sheets."

"All right." The snake man pressed gently on the knife and began drawing the point down Rehv's chest.

"Don't do it like that. Just unwrap me."

The snake man smiled. "This will be faster. Don't worry. I'm very good with knives, and this one is sharp." In one motion he sliced through the sheets. The point did not touch Rehv's skin.

He stood up. "Let me have the knife. I'll only need it for a minute or two." The snake man handed him the knife. Rehv stepped out of his cubicle, into the hall. It was empty. The guard's chair was empty. The steel door was open, and so was the steel door on the other side.

Rehv walked down the hall to the snake man's cubicle. The snake man followed him. On the way Rehv glanced out the little barred window. The sea was full of ships.

He went into the snake man's cubicle. "Stand back," he said. The snake man waited at the entrance. Rehv walked to the bed and began stabbing the knife into the mattress. "Die, snakes," he shouted. He stabbed the mattress a dozen times. Then he dropped the knife into the straw and backed away. "There," he said. "All dead."

"Dead? Are they really dead?" The snake man moved toward the bed. Gently Rehv took his arm and led him away.

"It's not a pretty sight," he said.

"Are they really dead?"

"Yes."

The snake man began to cry. He cried so hard that he couldn't walk. He sat on the floor and cried, holding his face in his hands. Rehv went down the hall and through the steel doors.

CHAPTER THIRTY-FIVE

Fairweather, dressed like a touring golf professional in white cotton trousers and a short-sleeved cherry red jersey, reached forward and twisted a few dials on the instrument panel. Brassy marching music of the kind soldiers play on parade filled the cockpit. "You see?" Fairweather said. "Radio Khartoum. That's all they've been playing. No news, no bulletins, nothing. What does it mean?"

"I don't know," Krebs answered. He looked out the window at the yellow emptiness of the Western Desert, far below. Somewhere to the east, he knew, it ended at the Nile; to the west it stretched across Africa to the Atlantic. He slumped in the soft leather copilot's seat. He was tired: eleven hours in the big plane to Cairo and two hours in the little plane that Fairweather had borrowed from the embassy; hours more to go.

Fairweather switched off the radio. "And still no word from Gillian Wells." He turned to Krebs as though expecting a reply. When there was none he tried raising his eyebrows. That made two shallow wrinkles appear on his smooth, tanned forehead, but it didn't make Krebs say anything. Fairweather turned away, studied the instrument panel for a moment, and pulled gently on the stick. The twin jets pushed the plane a little higher in the air. "What a beauty," he said, giving the stick a little pat.

Krebs leaned his head against the window and closed his eyes. Under his jacket the long-nosed .45 caliber revolver dug into his ribs. It kept him awake.

After a while Fairweather said, "They must be related, don't you think?"

"What?"

"Not hearing from Gillian Wells and all this closing of the border stuff."

"Why should they be related?"

Fairweather squinted into blue space. "There are no coincidences in this business," he said.

"Who told you that?"

"It's common knowledge. Freddy was saying it just the other day, at lunch."

"Who's Freddy?"

Fairweather looked at him in surprise. "The ambassador."

"Jesus."

"What's that for?"

"Nothing. I'm tired."

They flew over the yellow ocean. They saw no cities, no towns, no roads, no sign of life. It reminded Krebs of the space probe pictures of Mars.

"Did you know there used to be elephants down there?" Fairweather asked. "Lions, buffalo, antelopes—the whole bit. Someone was telling me all about it. Makes you think."

They thought.

Soon after Fairweather glanced at his watch and said, "I figure we're there by now."

"Where?"

"The Sudan." Below them nothing had changed. An invisible boundary divided nowhere in half. Fairweather cleared his throat. "Maybe you should fill me in a bit. I'm not really sure what the plan is."

"Just get me to the spot where Gillian's transmission came from."

"Sure. No problem. I've got the coordinates. But what I meant was, I don't know what we're supposed to do when we get there."

"Find her."

Fairweather nodded. Twice he opened his mouth and closed it. The third time he said, "Aren't we being a bit obvious about it? What if she's just lying low? We might upset everything. I thought the procedure was to wait for the next scheduled contact."

"This is a special case."

"Right."

The yellow ocean turned brown. Here and there green dots floated on it like islands. Fairweather guided the plane down a few thousand feet. Winding brown wadis appeared beneath them, showing how water would flow if there was water; and soon there were villages, little circles of mud.

"You awake?" Fairweather asked.

"Yes."

"Good. We're almost there." He bit his lip. "I'd feel better if we had some kind of cover, at least."

"Stop worrying. We're not flying over Siberia."

"You're right," Fairweather said, but he did not stop biting his lip.

"Okay," Krebs said. "We'll be anthropologists, if that will make you happier."

"Oh no."

"What's wrong?"

"I flunked the only anthropology course I ever took. You'll have to do all the talking."

"I plan to," Krebs said. "Go down to a thousand feet."

The plane dipped toward the ground. They saw a few gray green trees, patches of yellow green grass, and red brown earth. "What are we looking for?" Fairweather asked.

"A big camp. It shouldn't be hard to spot."

It was a long time before they saw anything, and when they did it was not a camp. "What's that?" Fairweather said, pointing.

"I don't see anything."

Fairweather pushed the stick forward and let the plane descend to a few hundred feet before leveling out. "It looks liks a jeep," he said with excitement in his voice. "Can you see it?"

"Of course I can see it," Krebs said. "Find somewhere to land."

Fairweather banked the plane in a wide sweeping circle and landed smoothly by a clump of bushes not far from the jeep. He turned off the engines; except for the ticking sound the metal parts made as they began to cool, it was silent. They opened the doors. The heat rushed in and struck them like a sudden fever. "My God," Fairweather said softly. Krebs said nothing. He remembered the heat.

They climbed down from the plane and started walking toward

292

the jeep. There seemed to be a person sitting behind the wheel, a big dark brown person. He was quivering. When they were halfway to the jeep Fairweather went pale; he bent double and heaved up what was in his stomach. Krebs ran forward. He had to be much closer before his eyes could make out the dark brown vultures, and what was left of Gillian Wells.

Krebs turned away; he saw Fairweather, in his golf clothes, on hands and knees, and beyond him the clump of bushes—where a lean dark man stood holding a spear. He thought of reaching for the revolver under his jacket. Instead he called out, "Salam alaykum."

At the sound of his voice the vultures rose into the air. Krebs heard the beating of their heavy wings behind him, but he didn't look around.

"What did you say?" Fairweather asked weakly, sitting back on his heels.

"Salam alaykum," Krebs called over Fairweather's head, more loudly than before.

The dark man raised his spear. "Alaykum el Salam."

Fairweather twisted around violently. "Where did he come from?"

Ignoring Fairweather, Krebs walked slowly toward the man with the spear, smiling in a friendly way. "We are friends," he said in Arabic. He knew his Arabic was poor. "Friends," he repeated, trying to pronounce it properly.

The dark man stood perfectly still as he approached. He had a thin face, high cheekbones, and the fierce nose of a bird of prey. Krebs reached him and held out his hand. The dark man kept his hand wrapped around the shaft of the spear. His eyes were cold. They flickered toward Fairweather, then back to him.

"Are you hungry?" Krebs asked. "Do you want food?"

The man opened his mouth and spoke rapidly. He paused, pointing with his spear toward the east, and went on speaking. Krebs did not catch one word.

"Did you get any of that?" he said over his shoulder to Fairweather.

"Sorry. What language is he speaking?"

"Arabic, for Christ's sake."

"Really? That's not the way they talk at Berlitz."

He stopped himself from rounding on Fairweather. "Is there any food on the plane?"

"How can you even think of food?"

"Answer me."

"Yes. A few candy bars."

"Get them." Fairweather started for the plane. "He is going for food," Krebs said to the dark man. "For you."

The man's head tilted back; his fine face wrinkled in puzzlement. Then he spoke again, more rapidly and intensely than before. He pointed to the east, and ended on a questioning note.

Krebs smiled. "I'm sorry. I speak very little Arabic. Please speak slowly."

As he listened, the man's face wrinkled again. He cocked his ear toward Krebs. Understanding dawned. "You are not from Khartoum?" he said, slowly and carefully.

"No. We are Americans." The dark man looked beyond him at the jeep. "What is your name?" Krebs asked.

"Hurgas."

Krebs felt his heart beat a little faster. "What happened to the white woman, Hurgas?"

Hurgas stepped back and leaned the point of the spear very slightly toward Krebs. "I didn't touch her."

"Of course not."

Hurgas said something too quickly for him to understand.

"Speak slowly."

"He did it," Hurgas said, drawing out the words. "He said she killed herself, but he killed her."

"Who?"

"The Mahdi," Hurgas said bitterly. "He killed my father too." He added something rapid and angry about his father that Krebs did not understand.

"Do you think he is the Mahdi?"

Hurgas looked at him warily. "Everyone says so."

"But what do you think?"

Hurgas gazed into the distance, or into nothing at all. His eyes grew sad. "I don't know," he answered at last. "My father believed it."

"Listen to me." Krebs gripped his shoulder: muscle and bone, and surprisingly cool to his touch. "He is not the Mahdi. There is no doubt. I know his father."

"His father?"

"Did he ever say anything about his father?"

"No. He said he was an orphan."

"He lied. He has a father. His father is a Jew." The cool muscle hardened under his hand. "And his mother was . . ." He couldn't think of the word for whore. "His mother sold herself."

"You know this?"

"Yes."

"Then I must kill him," Hurgas said quietly.

Krebs nodded. "Where is he?"

With the tip of his spear Hurgas pointed to the east. "Khartoum. They have all gone to Khartoum."

"Then we'll go there too." He turned Hurgas toward the plane.

Hurgas pulled back. "No. That's how he killed my father."

Krebs tugged at him. "There's no danger."

"No. I won't go in there."

Fairweather was coming toward them with candy bars in his hands. "Can we get going soon?"

"Yes," Krebs called to him. Trying desperately to think of a way to say "dishonor your father's memory," he turned to Hurgas. He did what he could with words he knew: "Are you coming? Or do you want to hurt your father, even after he is dead?"

In one motion Hurgas jerked free of his hand and swept the point of the spear under his jaw. Hurgas's body shook; Krebs felt the iron tip of the spear quiver on his neck. For a moment he thought that Hurgas would kill him. Then Hurgas spun around and walked toward the plane.

"Hey. What's going on?" Fairweather said.

"Nothing. He's coming with us."

"To Cairo?"

"We're not going to Cairo. Not right away. We're going to Khartoum."

"Have you forgotten? The airport's closed."

"We'll see," Krebs said, moving toward the plane.

Fairweather ran after him. "But why? You said our job was to find Gillian Wells." Fairweather glanced at the jeep and looked quickly away. "We found her," he said quietly. "What else can we do?"

"Find the man who killed her. The one everybody thinks is the Mahdi. Everybody but him." He gestured at the dark man waiting by the plane.

Fairweather looked at the dark man. Then he looked at Krebs. "You're crazy. You're going to get us killed too."

Krebs laughed. "Don't be so dramatic. We're not going to do

anything. We're just going to find him, that's all. Then we'll go back to Cairo and report. Besides, don't we need to refuel?"

"But the airport's closed."

"Stop saying that."

"And we don't really need fuel. We have enough to get back to Aswân."

"Let's not argue, Fairweather. We're going to Khartoum."

They flew to Khartoum. Hurgas sat in the cabin, clinging to the arms of his seat and not once looking out the window. He would not wear the seat belt. The smell of his stale sweat, which Krebs had not noticed before, filled the plane. The air conditioning made the cabin too cold for him; his skin took on a grayish tinge. He was out of place: Krebs knew he would be no trouble from then on.

When they were near Khartoum, Fairweather called the airport tower for permission to land. There was no response. As they flew over the airport they saw several big passenger planes parked by the terminal, but no one was getting in or out. There were no other planes in the sky, and no people on the ground. "I don't like this," Fairweather said.

"Land."

Fairweather brought the plane down on the main runway and taxied to the terminal. "Stay here," Krebs said. He opened the door, climbed down to the tarmac, and went into the terminal.

It was empty. No soldiers at customs or immigration, no porters, no ticket sellers, no passengers. The flies had taken over. He walked past the ticket counters to the front of the terminal and looked out. A few taxis sat in the sun, but no one was in them. He listened for sounds of traffic and heard none.

He walked back. As he passed the duty-free shop something caught his eye. He peered through the glass and saw an old black man inside, wearing sandals made from rubber tires, torn khaki shorts, and three cameras around his neck. Under one arm he held two large radios; with his free hand he was trying to pull a portable television out of a packing case. Krebs tried the door. It was open.

The old man turned. "I'm very sorry," he said in English. "We're closed."

"You speak English."

"Of course I speak English. I'm a Christian." With a grunt he wrenched the television free and staggered toward the door.

"Wait a minute," Krebs said. "Where is everybody?"

"All gone."

"Where?"

The old man looked surprised. "Why, to Port Sudan. They've all gone to Port Sudan with the Mahdi."

"Why?"

The old man stopped. "If you don't mind me saying so, you're not keeping a very close eye on current affairs, are you?"

"I'm a stranger here."

"Ah, I see. Welcome." The old man smiled. "They've gone to Port Sudan because Mecca is on the other side. The Mahdi is going to Mecca." The old man moved past him and out the door.

"Why aren't you with him?"

"I'm a Christian," the old man said without looking back. "I told you that already." He shook his head. "I told him that already," he muttered as he struggled along the empty hall.

Krebs went outside. He found a fuel truck. They filled the tanks and took off. They flew northeast; the sun was directly behind. Ahead of them the shadow of the little plane ran along the ground.

Fairweather glanced at him. "I guess I wasn't very professional back there."

"I understand."

"It was Gillian."

"I know."

"It must have been even worse for you," Fairweather said. "After all, you knew her. I'd never seen her before."

Krebs said nothing. He looked behind him. Gray and anxious, Hurgas sat clutching the armrests of his seat. His spear lay in the aisle. Krebs leaned back. "I think I'll catch a little sleep."

"Fine," Fairweather said. "Don't worry about me. This is getting kind of exciting. History is happening and we're right here."

"Our job is to keep it from happening."

"Surely the Saudis will take care of that," Fairweather said. "There's no way he can cross the Red Sea with all those people. All they have to do to stop him is send their fleet out."

"If they do that they're finished. The crews will mutiny, every one of them."

After a pause Fairweather said, "Rehv was smart, wasn't he?"

"Why do you say 'was'?"

"Because there's been no sign of him for years. Not since you saw him."

"That doesn't mean anything," Krebs said. "He's down there all right." He closed his eyes.

The crackle of the radio woke him. He looked up. The sea shone in the distance. Fairweather flicked a switch on the instrument panel.

"Cairo Base to ATG-Eleven," said a voice on the radio. The words were almost lost in the crackling. "Cairo Base to ATG-Eleven."

Fairweather reached for the microphone. "ATG-Eleven to Cairo Base. Is that you, Freddy?"

"Yes. Is Krebs still with you?"

"Yes," Fairweather said, sounding puzzled. "Do you want to talk to him?"

"No. Now listen carefully. You are to return immediately. Got that? Return immediately."

"We're just on our way to Port Sudan right now, Freddy. Do you mean return after that or before?"

The voice grew louder; so did the crackling. "Immediately."

Fairweather turned to Krebs. "It looks like we're going back to Cairo."

"No we're not. Don't change course."

Something in his tone made Fairweather shrink back. He held the microphone close to his mouth, watching Krebs out of the corner of his eye. "Freddy? I think you'd better talk to Mr. Krebs. He's in charge here."

Crackles answered. Then came a voice that Krebs knew well. "Fairweather, this is Colonel Birdwell. Get this straight. Krebs is no longer working for us. He is disobeying orders. He is a renegade. An outlaw. Fly that plane back here now. Is that clear?"

"Yes, sir." Fairweather looked at Krebs. "I guess we should do what they say."

Krebs drew the gun from under his jacket. "If you do, I'll shoot you."

Fairweather stared at the gun. "Is it true, what he said?"

"Shut off the radio."

"He's got a gun," Fairweather said quickly into the microphone. "He says he'll shoot me."

"Don't be an idiot, Fairweather." Birdwell's voice rose to a shout. "He needs you to fly the plane."

"I didn't say I'd kill you," Krebs said. "Just shoot you." He pointed the gun at Fairweather's knee. "Right here."

Fairweather brought the microphone to his mouth. Krebs grabbed it. The plane veered in a sudden sharp circle. Krebs heard a noise in the cabin. He glanced around and saw Hurgas staggering up the aisle, his spear in his hands. Only for a moment did he take his eyes off Fairweather, but Fairweather was very fast. A moment was all he needed to tear the fire extinguisher off the wall and spray it in Krebs's face.

Krebs pulled the trigger.

The nose of the plane dipped. Krebs and Fairweather were held in place by ther seat belts, but the fire extinguisher was not. Through a stinging blur Krebs saw it fly across the cockpit and crash out the windscreen. Hurgas yelled. Then he shot by after it, flailing his arms and legs for something to grip. There was nothing.

The plane dove toward the earth. Cold wind shrieked through the cockpit. Fairweather fought with the controls. The plane turned nose over tail, again and again, spinning like a Roman candle. "Oh, God," Fairweather said softly. Suddenly it stopped spinning, shuddered, and leveled out. Krebs looked down and saw a chicken running across a dirt yard.

Fairweather was very pale. "Are you okay?" Krebs said. Fairweather did not answer. Krebs looked at his knee. It was fine. He knew the bullet had missed: He had fired wildly, and Fairweather had not cried out.

Then he saw the other leg.

There was a big hole in the inside of Fairweather's thigh. Quickly Krebs ripped off his belt and wrapped it tightly above the wound. He pulled back the shredded white cloth and examined it more closely. He saw that it looked uglier than it was. The flesh was badly torn and slightly burned from the discharge, but there wasn't much blood, not around the wound, or on Fairweather's white pants or on the seat. That was lucky: He knew there was a big artery somewhere in the thigh.

"It's not too bad. You'll be okay."

Fairweather shook his head. "We're losing altitude," he said very softly. "I can't hold her up."

Krebs peered down and saw a flat empty plain that bordered on the sea. "Just put her down here. You can do it. You're a hell of a pilot, Fairweather."

Fairweather's hands were as white as bone on the wheel. He banked over the sea and came in low. The plane touched the ground, bounced into the air, touched the ground again, and rolled gradually to a stop. "You're a hell of a pilot, Fairweather," Krebs said.

Fairweather did not answer. Krebs put his hand lightly on Fairweather's shoulder. "I wasn't really going to shoot you, you know. The gun went off by accident."

Fairweather ignored him. Krebs bent forward and examined the wound again. It had almost stopped bleeding. "We're very close to town," Krebs said. "I'll go get help." He unbuckled his seat belt and stood up. As he turned to the door he saw that the cabin was red. The shrieking wind had blown Fairweather's blood through the cockpit and into the cabin. It was splashed all over the walls.

Fairweather slumped forward. The seat belt caught him and held him tight.

CHAPTER THIRTY-SIX

The setting sun burned a fiery path across the sea. It was the path that everyone wanted to follow. Down the narrow streets of Port Sudan they pressed, squeezing forward in dense heaving throngs to the waterfront. There, shouting and shoving, they fought for places in anything that floated: dhows, lateen-rigged sloops, ferries, yachts, and tenders that would take them out to the big ships waiting in deep water. They filled the boats and ships; empty ones came in their place. They too were filled. Still the streets were packed with relentless multitudes ramming down to the sea.

From the roof of a warehouse near the harbor Krebs could see everything. For hours he had watched the crowds, the ships, the convoys stretching across the water. He saw the warships too: destroyers, cruisers, aircraft carriers. There were far too many for the Saudi fleet alone; other Muslim countries had sent their fleets, he realized. Had they been ordered not to interfere, or had the crews mutinied? It didn't matter. None of them fired a shot. Instead they sent their tenders in to shore and joined the convoys. Everywhere he looked were ships: black hyphens on the glare of the sea.

As the sun went down he walked across the roof and peered over the edge. People surged through the street below. Some of them wore the white robes of pilgrims, some wore Western clothing; some held babies in their arms, some held rifles. No one looked up at him. He climbed down the steel ladder that was bolted to the side of the building and waited just above their heads for an opening. None came. At last he let go of the ladder and dropped among them. Someone shouted. A shoulder dug into his back. Then he was swept away, hugging the long-nosed gun against his ribs.

The mob bore him down to the waterfront and pushed him toward the end of a long pier. Around him he heard cries and splashes as people fell in the water. A small car ferry was casting off. As it began to drift away Krebs elbowed someone aside, leaped across a few feet of water, and landed in human flesh. A fist struck him. He struck back. He rolled onto his hands and knees and crawled along the deck until he found a small space by a rusty winch in the stern.

With his back against the winch, Krebs watched the western sky. Very quickly it went from navy blue to purple to black. He knew he must be tired, but he did not feel it. He closed his eyes. They would not stay closed. Stars came out. He looked at them. He remembered the names of a few constellations, but he couldn't make the stars fit the patterns that went with any of the names. He grew tired of the stars and gazed beyond them, into blackness.

Around him people tried to stretch out and go to sleep. Soon he too would sleep. He would sleep all he wanted. But first there was Isaac Rehv. It did not worry him that he had seen no sign yet of Rehv or his son. The Mahdi was going to speak from the Sacred Mosque in Mecca. That meant Rehv would be there too: for his moment of victory.

Isaac Rehv stood in the bow of the little fishing boat. All around him the lights of ships winked in the night. Looking over the side he saw the hull of the little fishing boat slicing through the black water, and the red phosphorescence that frothed through the cut.

A warm wind fluttered the thin cloth of the pilgrim's robe he wore. It carried the smell of spices—cloves and cinnamon. Was that the smell of Arabia? He peered at the eastern sky, looking for the dawn, but it was too soon.

Beneath his feet old engines throbbed slowly and steadily. He wanted them to work harder. He wanted the little fishing boat to fly across the water. He wanted to see his son.

To hold him in his arms, to kiss him, to be near him. That

was all he could do about the past. But now he wanted a future too. There was still time for the future they had missed: back at Lac du Loup or somewhere in America where they could forget about war and nations and death. No one would be looking for them after all these years. They could live in peace.

That was it. He wanted to live. It was time to forget about Israel. That meant forgetting Naomi, Lena, and his mother too. He would do it. He would try. He had suffered enough. The sacrifice was over.

Behind him on the deck everyone was asleep. He knew it was the same on the other boats on the sea that night. They all loved the Mahdi. Hundreds of thousands of people were doing what he had planned so long ago. Millions more were believing what he had wanted them to believe. The Red Sea had parted for him.

The dream was coming true. But it meant nothing to him. His dream belonged to death. He wanted to live. The ships, the people, the Mahdi—these he had created, and he could destroy. Then he would take his boy back somewhere safe, where he could live the life he had not had, the normal life that everyone had a right to.

The thought excited him, and made him dizzy. He was weak. Life in the cubicle had made him weak. He lay down on the deck and rested. He was weak and tired. He closed his eyes. No. Don't sleep. He opened them. It was too dark to see.

He heard a voice: "Hurry up with that blanket."

Someone answered: "I'm coming." There was a pause.

Then the first voice: "Oh, God. Look at his back."

He looked up. It was too dark to see whoever it was. "I'm all right," he said. "Just resting." He took a deep breath and felt better.

Dawn came at last, a slice of gold in the eastern sky. Rehv rose and looked over the prow of the fishing boat. He saw Arabia; it was an easy swim away. On the shore waited crowds of people. Everywhere boats were gliding in to land.

A helicopter flew by, very low. A cameraman leaned out of the open doorway and started filming. CBS it said on the side of the cabin

CHAPTER THIRTY-SEVEN

Inside the Sacred Mosque at Mecca there was no room to move. Wedged tightly between hot bodies, Krebs stood in the huge uncovered square in the center of the mosque. It was enclosed on all sides by two tiers of galleries, packed just as densely with people: men, women, children; white, yellow, brown, black. More were squeezed on the wide roofs over the galleries. Human heat rose in the air and shimmered in the morning light.

Not far in front of him he could see the Kaaba, the holy shrine of Islam: a cube as tall as a village church, draped with gold-embroidered black cloth. In one corner was sealed the Black Stone. Black-and-gold carpeted portable stairs had been rolled to one side of the Kaaba. Krebs was not as close to it as he wanted to be, but he did not try to push forward. If he attracted attention he might have to talk: in forbidden territory for a non-Muslim. He would have to do what he could from where he was. He kept his mouth shut and did what everyone else was doing: He waited and watched the small golden doors at the base of the Kaaba. It was quiet.

The sun rose higher in the sky, drawing moisture from countless pores and bathing the crowd in communal sweat. Krebs barely felt the heat. At first he had worried about how far he was from the Kaaba, and about his eyesight, which had never been as good after that night in Kordofan. But then he had suddenly realized how clearly he was seeing everything: the faded patterns etched on the black cloth, the red eye of a bird flying overhead, a mole on the edge of someone's earlobe. Not since childhood had he seen so sharply. He had stopped worrying.

Now he was calm. He watched the golden doors and waited. He was waiting for the two other non-Muslims he knew were in the mosque: the Mahdi and Isaac Rehv. He was very patient. He had waited a long time. A few more hours made no difference.

The doors opened. A tall broad man in a white robe and a white turban walked out. Krebs looked closely at his face. It was a brown face, much darker than Isaac Rehv's, but he could see something of Rehv around the mouth, the bridge of the nose, and especially in the eyes.

It was the Mahdi. He turned and started climbing the stairs to the top of the Kaaba. Three old men came through the doors and followed him up the stairs. In a glance Krebs saw that Isaac Rehv was not one of them. He recognized the king of the Saudis, the president of Egypt, and the shah of Iran. They wore simple white robes like the Mahdi's.

Rising onto the balls of his feet, Krebs stared into the shadows beyond the golden doors, straining to glimpse a fourth man. No Isaac Rehv. A man in a skullcap pulled the doors closed.

Now, for the first time, Krebs doubted. Perhaps Rehv was dead, after all. Or he had gone mad and disappeared. He had felt the madness in him that night in Kordofan. What would he do if Rehv did not appear? Go back? To what? He had nothing to go back to. And even if he had, there was no going back now, because of Fairweather.

The Mahdi reached the top of the stairs and walked slowly across the top of the Kaaba. In the center he stopped and looked about him at the crowd. His face was cold, but his eyes burned. It seemed to be what they wanted. They began to roar.

The king of the Saudis, the president of Egypt, and the shah of Iran stood behind him. They did not roar, but they tried to look happy. Krebs saw that the Mahdi ignored them completely. His burning gaze swept slowly over the roaring crowd. Everywhere liquid brown eyes adored him. Krebs felt himself being pressed forward, and saw the fear on the faces of the three old men on the Kaaba.

He knew Rehv had won.

Krebs pushed against the crowd. He was sick of its sweat, its smell, its roar. He wanted to go. The crowd pushed back. He jabbed his elbow into something soft. An elbow jabbed him. "Let me go," he shouted. They squeezed him tighter. He thought of drawing his gun and shooting the Mahdi. He was an easy target. But there would be no point without Rehv there to see. On his own the Mahdi meant nothing to him. They squeezed.

He butted his head at the roaring face behind him. A hard foot kicked the back of his knee. It buckled, and he started to slip down to the ground. They would trample him. Wildly he clawed around him for something to grip. Cloth tore. Someone yelled. He regained his balance.

As he stood up he saw a commotion at the base of the Kaaba. Near the stairs the crowd surged together like a contracting muscle; heads rippled in a little wave; a man fell forward on the stairs. He was dressed like a pilgrim. After a moment he pulled himself up and began climbing the stairs. A hand reached out and spun him around. In that instant Krebs saw the pilgrim's face. It was old and hollow and white-bearded, but it was Isaac Rehv's.

He had been right. He had been right the whole time. All the others had been wrong—Armbrister, Bunting, Birdwell. The president. From the beginning he had done it by himself. From beginning to end. He slid his hand inside his jacket and pulled out the gun.

On the stairs Isaac Rehv jerked himself free, turned, and started walking up. Krebs let him get about halfway so he could fire over the crowd. Then he pointed the gun at the back of Rehv's head. The crowd roared in his ears. He pulled the trigger.

Rehv staggered on the stairs; but he kept going. Krebs aimed again, a little higher. The back of Rehv's head was suddenly huge: He would not miss. He wanted Rehv to know. "Isaac," he shouted as loudly as he could. "I'm killing you. Me. Krebs."

Someone knocked the gun from his hand. It bounced off his foot. He bent down to find it. Hands grabbed at him. "Stop it," Krebs said. "I'm not shooting at your goddamned Mahdi. I'm shooting at Rehv." He tried to think how to tell them in Arabic. Before he could, they tore him apart.

Isaac Rehv watched the golden doors open and saw his son step out of the shadows. His heart pounded. The air tingled around him. He felt light-headed and swayed forward. Someone shoved him back, hard. The air stopped tingling.

His son was climbing the black-and-gold stairs. He was no longer the boy he had left beneath the two baobab trees. He was a man, a big man: almost as big as Sergeant Levy. As he reached the top of the Kaaba and turned, Rehv peered at his face, scanning it for some vestige of the face of the boy who had said: "Dad, what if you can't make it next week?" He did not see any.

But he was so far away. Rehv tried to push forward; he could not move at all. He pushed harder, as hard as he could. He squeezed forward a little way. He kept pushing. His breath began to wheeze in his throat. He was weak.

Across the top of the Kaaba his son walked with an easy, fluid power. He stopped and looked around him. In that look, in those burning eyes, Rehv saw that it was too late to go back, too late for a normal life. He saw the Mahdi.

But it was not too late to be near him. He pushed forward. Shoulders, elbows, knees, feet pushed him back. He pushed harder, panting with effort. Slowly he inched forward through the crowd.

For the first time he noticed the three old men standing on the Kaaba behind his son. He had never seen them before, but he knew who they were. Once he had lain on a camp cot far away and thought that there could only be an Israel if the Arabs gave it back; and gazed into red eyes, dreaming of warrior hordes. So he knew who the three old men were.

He no longer cared.

He was much closer now, close enough to see his son's face very clearly. It was cold and calm—the face of a man who loves power. The face of the wolf he had loosed on the world. The sight of it made people roar like animals.

Rehv understood then that there was no point in asking forgiveness. His son would not want to hear that: He would want to thank him instead. But still Rehv wanted to be near him. He wanted to tell him he had not abandoned him that night under the baobab trees. Even more, he wanted to tell him to stop. Now. To stop loving power, to stop living death. He did not blame his son. He blamed himself. It was his duty to tell him, to make him listen.

Rehv strained against the crowd. It resisted him. He lowered his shoulder and pushed with all his strength. The crowd swore at him. It punched him and kicked him. He pushed. "I want to be with my son," he shouted. Suddenly he fell forward, out of the crowd and onto the black-and-golden stairs that led to the top of the Kaaba.

Rehv lay panting on the stairs. The air tingled around him. He knew it was coming, the moment planned so long ago. But perhaps the cold dark man on the Kaaba would not say what his father had told him to say. Perhaps he believed he really was the Mahdi. That was more reason to stop him: not for the sake of a new Israel, but for his own sake, and the boy's.

Rehv stood and started climbing the stairs. A hand clutched him. He jerked free and mounted another step.

Something bumped him in the back. What? A bullet. He knew it instantly, from long ago.

He stumbled and almost fell. Somewhere behind him a man screamed. He kept climbing. His back began to hurt. He wanted to lie down and rest it, to curl up, just for a little while, and sleep. Keep going. Three steps. Two steps. One more.

Rehv fell hard on the flat roof of the Kaaba. The sound was lost in the roaring, but his son must have felt the vibration in his feet. He turned and looked at him. "Paul, Paul," Rehv tried to say. "Stop." The words whispered in his throat but went no farther. Without a sign of recognition his son turned away. He did not know him.

Rehv took a deep breath. "Paul. It's me. Your father." No sound came. He tried to crawl to him, but could not move. "Paul." His back hurt. The roaring filled his head. It sounded like the sea.

As his eyes began to close, he saw the Mahdi step forward and slowly raise his arms above his head. The roaring stopped at once. In the silence Isaac Rehv heard his blood dripping on the Kaaba. "Paul. Paul."

Death reached up his spine.